The
SICILIAN
SECRET

BOOKS BY ANGELA PETCH

ANGELA PETCH

The
SICILIAN
SECRET

bookouture

Published by Bookouture in 2024

An imprint of Storyfire Ltd.
Carmelite House
50 Victoria Embankment
London EC4Y 0DZ

www.bookouture.com

ISBN: 978-1-83790-664-2
eBook ISBN: 978-1-83790-663-5

To Daddy, Major Kenneth Richard Peter Sutor, who worked for the Commonwealth War Graves Commission as Deputy Regional Director in the Rome Office from 1960–1966 and who introduced his love of Italy to his young children.

'Collar the lot!'

— ATTRIBUTED TO SIR WINSTON
CHURCHILL, 1940, AND RECORDED
IN CABINET MINUTES.

'Wicked tongue breaketh bone,
Though the tongue itself hath none.'

— CENTURIES-OLD ENGLISH
PROVERB POSTED ON SECRECY
POSTERS AT BLETCHLEY PARK.

CHAPTER 1

APRIL 1973, SUFFOLK

FLORENCE

Florence hauls herself up from the sofa where she's nodded off again. The room is icy. For a while she watches shadows of swaying trees chase across whitewashed walls like restless fingers. Stirring from the cushions, she decides to lay the fire and then bung a potato in the range for supper. Outside, she fills the scuttle with coal to bulk up wood and kindling. The effort feels like a mountain climb. Winded, she stands for a few moments, gazing towards the end of the garden. Stubbly fields stretch towards the pheasants' copse. *New buds on the branches*, she thinks. *Soon, spring will be here with warmer weather.* She loves this time of year, usually filled with hope. When Paige was little, they'd gather the first blooms: primroses and violets to make pictures, gluing delicate petals to paper with flour and water paste to decorate the kitchen. At Christmas they'd replace them with garlands of cones and fir. She winces as a sharp pain makes her double up and she bites her lip in agony. It's getting worse. They'd warned her it would.

Buck up, girl. Don't give in to it. Go on a walk with Bonnie.

She straightens up and then remembers. Stupid woman! Bonnie, her beautiful black Labrador, isn't here. Lovely Bonnie, who'd somehow known whenever she was sad and would come over to flop at her feet, looking up at her with sympathetic eyes. The place feels empty without her and it's been days now since she's been out for a walk.

Florence lifts the range top to set the kettle to boil and swallows a couple of tablets. *Tea will do the trick*, she thinks. *A cup of tea made in a chipped, brown pot. Steep the leaves for a strong brew. None of these new-fangled bags that Paige likes.*

'But, Aunty, it will make your life so much easier.'

'Yes, but it tastes like dishwater, dear girl.'

'When was the last time you drank dishwater, Aunty Flo. Honestly!'

She smiles as she thinks of her favourite person, her eyes going to the photograph on the dresser. It was taken on Paige's graduation day: dressed in velvet flares and cheesecloth shirt, her long, dark, sleek hair like curtains each side of her pretty face. Paige's deep-brown eyes smile back at her. She hadn't taken after her side, that's for sure. Florence had once been told, many years earlier, that she had the face of a madonna, but she's never been able to take a compliment. She's always felt gawky, clumsy, with her size eight and a half feet and big hands. She was never a glamour girl.

Paige has promised to come and stay this weekend. Together they can do the crosswords she's cut from *The Times* and Florence has resolved to have a long overdue, honest talk. She's written a couple of pages in an old exercise book and gathered a few bits and bobs from the past, including that letter. From time to time, she'd made half-hearted attempts at deciphering the muddle of figures scrawled across the page, but it had been pointless. He'd never been great at writing and, anyway, by the time she'd received the envelope, he was dead.

Florence has sorted her finances too, including the unexpected windfall she's put in Paige's name, and deposited all necessary paperwork with the solicitors. But it will be easier and more honest to talk face to face. She doesn't want Paige discovering stuff from newspapers. A book has been published recently about what had gone on in the war and last week – in an afternoon play which she usually enjoys on the little transistor radio Paige bought her – there'd been one about the special agents in France. They'd got that all wrong. They didn't know the half of what had gone on. She'd switched off halfway through, tutting with impatience.

Leaning back against the warm range, her mind travels back to Scotland. Early spring, 1943. She'd suffered dreadfully from chilblains: probably from holding her hands so close to the stove. What was it those cast-iron things were called? Tortoises! Yes, that was it. A pity her body is lazier than her mind... The cold had seemed to never turn to summer that year. It had been bitter and they weren't permitted a hot-water bottle or bed socks in those freezing rooms.

'When you're out in the field, there will be no such namby-pamby luxuries,' the sergeant major had barked.

They'd all had to harden up. Those interminable night exercises had been the worst: faces blackened, having to drag themselves through prickly gorse on their stomachs before enduring an umpteenth ambush. Disguises – now that part had been almost light relief. She'd had to dye her blonde hair black, learn how to apply makeup and use Culloden to add pox scars to her cheeks and change her gait to walk with a limp.

'Wrong leg, woman,' he'd shouted. 'It was the right leg when you got on that train and now you're bloody staggering on the left, you daft cow.'

That exercise on the train when she'd had to shoehorn herself into someone else: be a stranger and tail the chap in the dirty gabardine. They'd arrested her as soon as she'd alighted at the allocated stop and frogmarched her down the platform for

interrogation. When they'd turned out her pockets, they'd
found the humbug she'd slipped in at the last minute on
account of her chesty cough.

'And where in the whole of sunny, buggering Italy do you
think they supply these?' the odious sergeant major had shouted
in her face, holding a pistol to her temple after he'd slapped her
around.

Enjoying himself too much, she'd thought, *this is only a practice, for God's sake.*

She'd failed, of course, and been told to report to Hut 13. At
the time, Florence hadn't realised those in the know called it the
cooler: the destination for those who didn't make it. Nevertheless, they were strung along, given the impression Hut 13 was
another stage in the training. After a week, she was told she
hadn't made the grade and she should forget about everything.
She might be needed somewhere else and would possibly be
hearing sometime about that. She'd signed a document: Official
Secrets Act. And she'd kept quiet. All this time.

Her pain ebbing and the kettle boiling, Florence pours
water into the brown pot and waits for the leaves to steep. The
vegetable rack is empty, save for a shrivelled turnip. She will
have to walk the half mile to the village shop before it shuts to
stock up her pantry. April showers have turned to heavy rain
that lashes against the windowpanes. Rivers of the stuff stream
down the glass. If it continues, she'll have to put a couple of
buckets in Paige's attic room to catch the drops that find their
evil way through the roof tiles. It's become a real effort to lug
the pails up the rickety staircase. But, first, she needs to get in
provisions. *It will do you good to be out*, she tells herself. *Stop
moping and get a move on, gal.*

She pulls on her old mac. It's a man's, bought in a charity
shop: comfier than squeezing into a woman's fitted coat or that
stiff, waxed jacket upstairs. Her shoes too are men's brogues.
'Madam has big bones,' the fitter had said. 'Perhaps you'd like to

try these in our gentlemen's range? You might be more comfortable.' Her skirt is loose and she's tied a scarf round her middle to hitch it up. After years of trying to diet, she is losing weight. *One advantage of being sick*, she thinks ruefully, as she shoehorns her feet into the comfy old leather brogues.

It's strange to be walking the winding country lane without Bonnie. She misses her Labrador stopping at tufts of grass to sniff, tail wagging in abandonment as she investigates. She misses calling her to heel after watching Bonnie spend joyous minutes leaping across dew-drenched fields chasing pheasants.

The rain is soon replaced by the sun: a sphere of bright light that flashes through spindly trees. The truck driver delivering coal to the big house beyond Florence's cottage is temporarily blinded as he rounds the bend and Florence is too slow to press back against hawthorn bushes lining this narrow stretch. He hears a thud but pays little attention, muttering under his breath that it is high time the bigwigs in the house trimmed back their ruddy hedges.

On his return journey he slows to avoid what he believes at first to be a dead fox. It is Florence's mackintosh, soaked with blood, the same colour as leaves that fall in autumn. But it is spring and when he jumps out of his cab to investigate, his eyes are round with horror at what he finds.

CHAPTER 2

MAY 1973

PAIGE

'It's very poky, isn't it?' Anthea wrinkled up her nose as she lifted a loose corner of rose-patterned wallpaper in Paige's old bedroom. 'Damp, too. How did your aunt manage to live in these conditions for so long?'

Paige wanted to slap her future sister-in-law's hand from tugging more of the paper from the wall. 'Don't, Anthea...'

'Sorry, darling. But you must admit—'

'Let's go downstairs and you can help me make refreshments.'

Paige should never have taken Anthea up on her offer to come to Aunty Flo's funeral but her fiancé, Jeremy, had insisted his sister be there to represent him. 'I can't come back all the way from Amsterdam, Paige. I'm sorry, darling, but this meeting is too important.'

It didn't matter. Not really. Paige always had the feeling her aunt hadn't approved of Jeremy anyway, so in her mind it didn't seem appropriate for him to attend the funeral. The first two occasions when they'd come as a couple to visit, Aunty Flo had made it apparent in little ways, like making up the sofa bed for him downstairs. It was plain there was to be no sleeping together under her roof. And she'd disappeared for long walks with Bonnie, rather than spending time in the cottage together. But Paige regretted Anthea coming along today. Anthea with her long suede boots and purple corduroy miniskirt skimming her bottom. She clashed with Aunty Flo's old-fashioned cottage. She should have told Anthea not to bother coming.

But, if she was going to be her sister-in-law, she had to make an effort to get to know her better.

'Do you have a large plate for these sausage rolls, Paige?' Anthea asked.

'Try the bottom cupboard in the dresser.'

Anthea bent down, revealing more than she should and screamed as she dropped an oval willow pattern platter onto the quarry stones. The plate that had come out each Christmas for the turkey was now in pieces on the kitchen floor.

'Jeepers creepers – this place is freaking me out! A mouse. An actual mouse. In there,' Anthea said, pointing accusingly at the dresser.

'If Bonnie was here, she'd have caught that.'

'Who is Bonnie?'

'My aunt's dog. She used to love eating mice.'

'*Eugh!* I need a fag. Honestly, Paige. This dump is not fit for habitation.'

She slammed the kitchen door shut so hard that a Cornishware jug fell from the dresser and joined the bits of broken platter. Paige gritted her teeth. 'This dump', as Anthea had called Aunty Flo's cottage, had been Paige's home for most of her life. Aunty might not have had much interior design flair, but, growing up, Paige had been cosy and happy living here in the countryside in Squirrels Cottage. How many children could say they'd once shared a kitchen with a litter of rescued fox cubs in a basket by the range? And Paige had been allowed to stay up late in the holidays to sit with Aunty Flo in the forest until the early hours, sharing flasks of hot chocolate and home-made shortbread biscuits as they observed a pair of badgers and their cubs in the woods. She'd shown her how to skin rabbits for stews and pluck pheasants when money was tight. 'We had to make do and mend in the war,' she'd tell her as they bottled blackberries and plums for the winter months.

Yes, there'd been times when Paige had felt the odd one out at school, her clothes patched and unfashionable, usually purchased at jumble sales, but she'd had an enchanted upbringing and Anthea's scorn today was getting up her nose. As soon as the funeral was over, she'd send Anthea back to London, back to the Chelsea Mews flat that her fiancé Jeremy's parents had bought for their spoiled daughter. Then Paige would batten down the hatches, as her aunt used to say, and use the compassionate leave from her work as a teacher at a primary school to stay down here alone for a few days.

The church was three-quarters empty for the funeral. Aunty Flo had kept herself very much to herself, the vicar told the meagre congregation. 'But she was generous with her donations,' he said in his very short homily. 'To tell the truth, I know little about Florence Caister's background. Her niece, Paige, has arranged a couple of photographs of her on the table at the back and she'd also like to invite you to Squirrels for refreshments afterwards. Please do take up her kind offer.'

Paige switched off from his words, trying not to concentrate on the pinewood coffin resting on the stand before the altar steps. It was ridiculous, she knew, but she hoped her aunt was comfortable in the confined space. She was a tall woman, needing outdoor space. The cottage ceilings were beamed and Paige couldn't count the times she'd seen her aunt bang her head. She'd pinned ribbons to warn herself on the doorway leading up the winding stairs and one Christmas, Paige had given her a brass sign inscribed with *Duck or Grouse*.

Earlier, Paige had picked flowers from the cottage garden and hastily arranged them in a bunch. Haphazard, natural, how she knew her aunt preferred them. An early bee buzzed around the daffodils, and rose petals were already dropping from the coffin lid onto the nave tiles. They were scented roses from around the porch – 'Félicité Perpétue' – their tangled stems all that was propping up the flimsy entrance to Squirrels Cottage. She could hear her aunt saying, 'Can't prune them too hard; the cottage will fall down.' This, followed by her wheezy laugh. Florence had tried on and off to give up her smoking habit of twenty Player's tipped a day, on average. 'Everybody smoked in my day, Paige. Really difficult to stop now.'

In truth, Paige had expected her aunt to die in the end from lung cancer and not beneath the wheels of a coal lorry.

A couple of parishioners came back after the service to share the bought sausage rolls and corned beef sandwiches made with sliced bread. Conversation was awkward, the refreshments unexciting and to Paige's immense relief, she had the cottage to herself by five o'clock, Anthea having gratefully accepted a lift to the station from the vicar, who 'had to be somewhere else'. Paige wondered where he had to be and if he was lying. Did vicars tell lies easily? She had only been to church for Christmas midnight services with her aunt, purely because they had enjoyed the atmospheric flickering candlelight and carols.

Paige still hadn't cried: not when she'd had the news, not during the funeral, not now she was alone in the house. She'd loved Aunty Flo more than she could ever express. She'd brought her up from when she was a baby after the death of her parents in a tragic accident. Their house had burnt down. Everything had been lost, except for baby Paige, because her father had thrown her from the top window into a fireman's arms, her aunt had told her. There were no photographs or mementoes of her mother and father. Everything had been swallowed by flames.

Aunty Flo had loved her in her own way. She wasn't sloppy or prone to showing affection in the way Paige had seen mothers do at the school gates. She'd never been one to pull Paige into a hug on the settee or tickle her and smother her with kisses. But she'd always been there. And now she wasn't. And there was a hole in Paige's sore heart.

Later, nursing a glass of Aunty Flo's malt whisky by the fire, she realised she wasn't missing Jeremy. He hadn't called either. The mournful hooting of a tawny owl did little for her mood and she fetched a stone hot-water bottle to take to bed.

She still hadn't shed tears for her loss and Paige lay awake for a long time, feeling cold and numb.

CHAPTER 3

The morning after Aunty Flo's funeral, the lawn was strewn with storm-blown twigs and daffodils drooped sodden heads. The grey sky waited to tip down more rain and Paige's plan to don rubber boots and walk to the creek had to wait until later. The pantry was bare, save for half a stone jar of oats and an assortment of bottled fruit. She would need a grocery shop at some stage. Breakfast was a bowl of slightly stale porridge and a pot of tea. She had to admit to herself the tea tasted good. Maybe she would revert to leaves in future rather than bags, in honour of Aunty Flo.

She used the mug hanging especially for her on the dresser, bearing the cheeky face of Paul McCartney, and climbed the stairs to her aunt's bedroom. The springs of the mattress pinged as she sat down and a feather escaped from the green paisley eiderdown. She smiled. 'As old as the hills,' another of Aunty Flo's expressions, rang in her ears. But there were no hills in Suffolk: simply expanses of fields and sky, and clouds that leant down to nudge the horizon. Paige didn't mind 'old': it lent a permanence to life.

But some of her aunt's possessions would have to go. Even-

tually. Not yet. If she didn't have Aunty Flo to come back to –
because come back she definitely would – then Paige needed
one or two of her things dotted around for comfort. She couldn't
imagine not returning to Suffolk, escaping from busy London
from time to time, even if Jeremy wasn't keen. No, there absolutely was no need to sell the dusty-pink-painted thatched
cottage. They could easily afford its upkeep.

She sighed as she thought of the wedding arrangements
listed by her mother-in-law for the end of May: final dress
fitting, decisions about flowers, checking the long list of guests
(half of whom she didn't know). If she had her own way, they
would have a simple ceremony, with a celebration supper after
in a pub. But Jeremy's mother was a force to be reckoned with
and Jeremy advised it was better to 'let her get on with it'. They
would have their own flat in Richmond once they were married,
he'd told her, and then they could do as they liked. Jeremy
worked in the family supermarket chain and his philosophy was
not to ruffle his parents' feathers. 'I owe them a lot, darling,' was
his explanation. 'I wouldn't be where I am without their help.
Let her sort the wedding. It's easier this way.' *It is easier*, Paige
thought, *but not entirely satisfactory.*

Carrying her mug of tea up the narrow staircase, Paige went
over to the wardrobe in her aunt's bedroom and opened the
doors, wrinkling her nose at the smell of mothballs. She ran her
hands over the strange assortment of jackets and coats. The
mink coat could go to the charity shop. No way could she wear
that, and she'd never seen Aunty Flo wear it either, come to
think.

A tweed jacket, nipped in at the waist, with shoulder pads
and large buttons was very cool. This too she had never seen on
her aunt. She looked for a label but there was none. It must have
been tailor-made. She slipped it on and turned this way and that
in front of the mirror. It was too big but she liked it and so she
started a separate pile of clothes to keep. The old blue waxed

jacket she pulled out next made her catch her breath. It was stiff and a couple of buttons were missing. She fingered the lining of the hood, patched with what Paige remembered was part of an old linen tea towel. The lining was blue check, the tea towel red check. Paige distinctly remembered her aunt's satisfaction when she'd mended it. 'Not too bad, eh, Paige? This will do. You never know, I might start a new fashion.'

The two of them had been sitting in the kitchen as usual, next to the Rayburn range because it was the only warm place in the cottage in winter. They were on one of their 'economy drives', as her aunt had described them. 'Can't order more oil until next week when I get my cheque. Until then we'll make do.' She was always straightforward with Paige. Sometimes Paige had just wanted to a child and not be included in these adult problems and explanations. But mostly she'd loved that her aunt treated her as an equal.

If she was honest, the wax jacket was hideous and far gone. Not even a charity shop would want it. But Paige didn't want to part with it. She held the stiff material to her nose and that was the moment when tears finally began to stream.

For a full five minutes Paige sobbed and sobbed, until her eyes fell on a photograph of her aunt looking stern, herself as a baby seated on her lap. *Brace up, girl*, she told herself, using another of her aunt's expressions. She pulled a man's cotton hanky from her aunt's chest of drawers to dry her eyes. *Make yourself useful*. Aunty Flo would have sent her to fetch eggs from the hen coop, or to take whatever dog they had at the time for a long walk. *And come back when you've pulled yourself together*. 'Being emotional' – she heard Aunty Flo's description of moods and disappointments in her head – 'will get you nowhere fast, my girl.'

Downstairs, dressed in the old wax jacket, she washed her face at the sink, having decided it was best to leave sorting her aunt's wardrobe to some future date. It wasn't that crucial to sort everything in record time if the cottage wasn't going on the market. She could live with a little old tat and reminders for a while. A break to gather herself together was called for. A walk to the creek, fresh air on her cheeks to set her to rights, even with no Bonnie to keep her company. The dear old Lab had so obviously been in pain with her arthritic hind legs last time Paige had walked her. She was out of pain now. For a moment, Paige wondered if Bonnie and Aunty Flo were together somewhere in a doggie heaven and then she shook her head. *You're being really emotional now. And ridiculous. You'll be talking out loud to yourself next.*

The footpath to the creek ran behind the cottage, alongside a narrow stream. It was shallow enough for wading and splashing and she passed the point where years earlier her aunt had dug a small pool, when Paige had been at primary school. Together they'd built up a mud bank to contain the flow and during the heatwave of last summer, she'd brought Jeremy here for a picnic and he'd scoffed. 'One day, we'll have an indoor, chlorinated pool, darling. With no mud or newts to compete with.'

A streak of iridescent blue flew across her memories and she stopped still for precious seconds to observe a kingfisher landing on a willow branch that trailed grey-green leaves in the stream. *There'd be no wild birds visiting an indoor pool filled with chlorine*, she thought wistfully, as the tiny bird banged its silvery catch against a rock. Aunty Flo had taught her to use binoculars even before she went to the village primary school and how to recognise birds in the reed beds further down towards the estuary. She'd taught her to be patient and listen, to identify the different songs of reed and sedge warblers. They'd seen bitterns and, once, a family of otters. She'd pointed out where they'd slid down the bank to the water on their tummies, leaving muddy trails behind them. As Paige walked towards the estuary, the wind whipping her hair to stick to her cheeks, her aunt seemed to walk beside her and she understood how much she'd learned from the woman she would miss so dreadfully. London stifled her, she realised for the first time.

Refreshed, she let herself back into Squirrels. The contents of the wardrobe could wait. She made up a fire in the lounge and, armed with a fresh mug of tea, she opened the lid on the writing desk in the alcove. It was surprisingly tidy, empty of the usual leaflets and cuttings her aunt liked to save from newspapers, apart from two piles of bills, marked PAID and TO PAY. She flicked through the latter: one from the grocery shop in the village, another from the coal merchant and a couple from the local garage for work done on Bertha, Aunty Flo's battered Morris Traveller. That too would come to her. It was rusty and rattly and she didn't really need it for Jeremy's Richmond flat, where parking was a nightmare, but she would think up some excuse to keep it.

An oblong box under a shelf at the very back of the desk caught her eye and she pulled it out. It was an old Milk Tray chocolate box with a fading purple bow on the lid. She lifted it off. Inside were an exercise book and something wrapped in tissue paper, to her surprise labelled: *For Paige*.

With trembling hands, she undid the yellowing tissue to find a rather ugly necklace, the links of its metal chain tarnished in places and a strange pendant attached, shaped as a man's face, half-human, half-mythical, with weeds and fish resembling long hair. The face had no body but three muscular legs extended from the head in a clockwise direction. Paige frowned. It was a peculiar piece of jewellery. She had never seen it before and couldn't imagine her aunt wearing it. Although hideous, she decided to hang on to it. If her aunt had wanted her to keep it, then she would.

She picked up the school exercise book with *Nature Notes*

written on the dark-green cover, and a name: *Joy Harrison*, with
the date: *1926*. Paige took this with her mug of tea to the occasional table next to the settee. After adding a log and a scoop of
coal to the fire, she settled down to examine it.

The first pages showed hand-drawn, coloured illustrations
of plants, their roots and petals neatly labelled. Aunty Flo had
probably picked it up on one of her charity shop jaunts.
Although the notebook was charming, she couldn't understand
why it should have been in the box addressed to Paige herself,
alongside the necklace. But, after ten pages or so, the nature
notes stopped and she came across Aunty Flo's beautiful italic,
ink script. She'd hated using ballpoint pens. In her usual, practical way of not wanting to waste anything, her aunt had likely
used the blank pages of the nature notebook to write her own
messages. Paige read on.

Where to start, dear Paige?

*I haven't been honest and I shall try to fill you in more
when we see each other so that you can ask me questions. That
is, if you will still want to talk to me.*

*I need you to understand that everything I have done was
because of love. For you.*

*The papers you are going to need are in the back of my
wardrobe beneath the paper lining.*

*I haven't been well for a while. Prognosis: ovarian cancer,
little time. That's why it's time to tell you everything. Once
I've explained fully face to face, I hope you will understand,
my dear, precious girl. There – I'm turning all soppy.*

It all happened because of a beautiful Sicilian...

More tomorrow. Writing in the evening makes me morose.

*Tomorrow is another day. I've told you that often enough,
haven't I? I'm like a broken record, I know, but these little
sayings have helped me along the way. Brace up, Paige.*

And that was it. The writing ended there. For Florence, there had been no tomorrow. Paige knew she hadn't been in the best of health recently but she was used to her aunt 'grinning and bearing it' – another 'auntism', as Paige openly described these little gems of wisdom. Paige had often teased her, telling her she should compile a book of wise old sayings. But, ovarian cancer. The silent killer, they called it. Paige had never guessed it was that bad.

'Everything I have done'... 'tell you everything'... 'a beautiful Sicilian'... What was she talking about? What had Aunty Flo wanted to tell her?

'Oh, Aunty Flo,' she said out loud, chucking the notebook onto the empty seat beside her, the dent in the shabby velvet cushions still revealing the place where her aunt liked to sit. Then, still baffled, she picked up the notebook to read the words again, stopping at the paragraph about the papers. *The back of my wardrobe beneath the paper lining.*

The notebook dropped from Paige's hands as she dashed upstairs.

In her aunt's bedroom, she yanked the remaining garments from the Edwardian wardrobe and dumped them on the worn rug. The lining paper was in fact the remnants of the same rose-patterned wallpaper in Paige's room, Sellotape attached it to the back, brittle with age, and she ripped it off, eager to see what lay behind. Towards the bottom right side, taped to the wooden panel, she found a brown A4 envelope, once again bearing her aunt's handwritten: *For Paige*. The ink was faded and Paige wondered how long the envelope had been concealed there.

Her fingers trembling, she extracted a sheet of paper. It was an official document: cream-coloured, the writing in red. Certified copy of an entry of birth, she read, at Somersby Hall Hospital, Bury St Edmunds, within the district of Suffolk. The date of registration was February 13th, 1944, and the name of the baby was Paige Rose. Born to Lady Joy Harrison. There was a blank space beneath the name of the father.

Paige sat back on her heels, winded. What was going on? *Aunty Flo... what are you trying to tell me? Paige Rose. That's my name. And that is my birth date too. But it states on the certificate that the mother was a Joy Harrison. A lady at that.*

None of it made sense. None at all. And what about her father? Hadn't Aunty Flo told her that her father had thrown her from a window to the waiting firemen? Was her mother not married to her father? Or was it all a fabrication, this story of the fire? *I haven't been honest*, the line at the start of the letter screamed at her. It was not making any sense at all. What had her aunt been keeping from her and why?

The phone rang downstairs and Paige dawdled down, her mind consumed by what she had discovered. She stepped over the notebook, noticing from the corner of her eye a flimsy envelope poking from the back cover.

'Holwood, 6841,' she said distractedly down the receiver, one eye on the notebook and the envelope.

'Paige, you took your time. How are you? When are you coming back to London?' Jeremy asked.

In the background she could hear the clatter of crockery and cutlery, the sounds of laughter and people talking. Busy sounds. He was probably at one of his networking dos.

'Not sure, Jer. I'm...' She didn't feel like explaining her discoveries when she didn't understand them herself.

'Shall I come down and fetch you back? I'd like to give the new Aston Martin a spin.'

'Er... not feeling brilliant at the moment. Aunty Flo's death... it's taken it out of me. I'm staying down here for a bit. There's lots to sort.'

She really did not want to see him at the moment, she realised. But she couldn't tell her future husband that. 'I'll be back as soon as I can.'

'Mater is getting anxious, you know. She wants to sort out hairstyles for the bridesmaids, or something or other.'

No consolation, no mention of condolences in Jeremy's call. No 'Is there anything I can do to help?' Paige cut the conversation short, inventing a lie to get rid of him. 'There's someone at the door, Jeremy.' She put the phone down, thinking how down here in Suffolk, life was the flip side of a coin from her London existence.

The envelope was half stuck to the inside back cover of the notebook by its flap. The paper was flimsy and the address written in untidy block letters:

MISS JOY HARRISSON,
c/o SUMERSBEY HALL
SUFFOLK

The postage stamp was Italian and she could just make out letters on a circular stamp in the top centre: SIR. The rest were blurred but she made out a date: *September 10, 1943.*

'Curiouser and curiouser.' She mouthed the lines from her well-thumbed copy of *Alice's Adventures in Wonderland* that Aunty Flo used to read at bedtimes.

The airmail paper inside was even more intriguing.

I am in paradise.
VIII, 15
I, 55, 4
I, 88, 5
XXV, 110, 8-L
VIII, 38, 4, 5
i vivi vivono con i morti
I can't plan in a muddled place, 9 Last n=a.

It was signed with a single name, *Dante.*

It meant absolutely nothing to Paige. In fact, none of Aunty Flo's enigmatic messages were making any sense at all.

What the hell had she planned to tell her? Who was the woman on Paige's birth certificate – and the Sicilian she mentioned?

Aunty Flo had spoken about dishonesty. Had she spun lies to her? What a tangle and where on earth to begin?

CHAPTER 4

1927, ENGLAND

SAVIO

Savio's knuckles smarted. The fight today at school had been tougher than usual: Smithy and his gang of three had cornered him behind the bike shed where he'd been puffing away on half a Player's his mamma had left in the kitchen. Papà didn't approve. He raised his hand to her if he discovered her smoking – always threatening but never slapping – and he'd swear in his Sicilian dialect that England had turned her into a bad woman. Poor Mamma, who always tried her very best. *She doesn't know how to smoke properly anyway*, Savio thought, as he blew smoke rings in the air like in the movie, *The Silent Hero*, he'd watched last Saturday.

'Oi, spaghetti basher,' Smithy had shouted as he sauntered round the bike shed at morning break. There was nowhere to escape. To scale the fence behind him, Savio would have to take a running jump, but there wasn't enough room. Or time. Fred and Stinker grabbed him and held his arms back while Smithy spoke, his face so near that Savio could see the gap in Smithy's front teeth dislodged in one of their scraps last term.

'I saw the way you was looking at Belinda in class before break. What was you doing with your hands down your shorts, dirty boy?' He delivered a punch to Savio's stomach. 'She's mine. You better remember. Anyways, she don't like dumbos like you. Nobody does. You should go back to dirty Tally where you come from, you greasy wop.'

No matter how many times he'd heard this, how many times he'd tell everybody he'd been born in London and was English, he still heard comments like Smithy's. His parents spoke little English, that was true, but both he and his brother, Federico, spoke English better than Italian. Nobody understood what it was like for them.

A curtain of red descended and, with it, the fury that made him an unstoppable force. Savio might only be thirteen years old, but he was strong and wiry. Smithy's thug-friends weren't restraining his legs – sturdy legs that had earned him position of centre half in the school football squad. He kicked Smithy hard in the balls and wrenched free of Fred and Stinker, delivering an uppercut to Fred before stamping hard on Smithy's prone figure and tailing it from the schoolyard.

Liam, seated on the allotment bench he'd cobbled together from spare timbers picked up here and there, was puffing on his pipe. The middle-aged war veteran took one look at Savio and patted the space beside him. The pair sat for a while without exchanging words. Savio inhaled the aroma of Liam's tobacco, the thumping of his heart slowing down as a robin chirped above them in the drifting blossom of a pear tree.

'Want to help me dig?' Liam asked, packing more tobacco into the bowl of his pipe. 'Got to get me seed potatoes in before Good Friday. My stump is playing up this morning. I could do with a labourer.'

Savio worked up a sweat, venting his anger on the ground,

double digging as Liam had shown him in the past, working to the depth of two spades. He'd helped him on and off for the past three years, his allotment being two rows down from his parents', where Papà planted his 'strange Italian thingummies', as Liam called courgettes, aubergines and garlic. Savio liked Liam, a man of few words. He wasn't judgemental and offered wisdom in tiny doses that worked for Savio. He'd lost his right leg at the knee in the Great War. 'Trench foot,' he'd said, leaving it at that. 'Got to get on with it, otherwise life will get you.'

His calm was the antithesis of Papà's anger, who ranted on: 'Why you not settle down, study hard like your brother? Why you think we come all this way to England? Not for you to bring trouble in our lives.'

As Savio worked the earth, weeding out couch grass and docks, his mind was besieged with angry thoughts about what life continued to deal him. It wasn't fair. His parents were illiterate but hard-working. When they were young back on the island of Sicily, school had come second to helping their parents work. It wasn't their fault they were unable to help Savio with the schoolwork that caused him so much grief. His classmates called him thicko, amongst other names. At primary school they'd scribbled on his exercise books, stolen his pencil case and written obscenities that Federico had read out to him. Mamma and Papà hadn't come to England to help him with schoolwork; they were in England to make money and a better life, they constantly told him.

'Trace your fingers over the letters. Start again. Slowly,' his brother said. Fede had tried to help with homework but when Savio told him the letters jiggled about and didn't make sense, Fede had eventually given up.

Savio's resigned shrug of his shoulders and his response were defence mechanisms: 'What do I need letters for anyway? I'll be leaving school as soon as I can and I'll end up working in Pa's hairdresser's. I don't need to know letters to cut hair.'

Fede had shrugged. 'I suppose you're right. But stop getting into fights. Try to fit in like I do, Savio.'

But it wasn't easy to emulate his golden-boy brother, two years older and top of his class in most subjects. The only lesson Savio enjoyed was art. Blonde Miss Nuttridge was pretty and patient. 'You've got a talent there, Savio,' she had told him, looking over his shoulder at his pen and ink sketch of their Victorian school building. 'You can come and draw up in the art room in lunch hours if you like.'

He had done so for a while, but then the taunts started: 'Who's got the hots for Nutty then?' 'Does she ask you to pose naked so she can draw you?' They'd left a saucy Valentine's card on her desk and signed it with Savio's name and despite him insisting it was not from him, she was cooler with her praise from then on. There were to be no more lunch hours spent in the art room, escaping from bullies in the playground.

Savio fetched barrows of horse muck from the corner of Liam's allotment and raked it into the rich soil, while the old soldier looked on, smiling in approval.

'Good job, lad.'

He handed Savio an old metal army flask covered in khaki cloth. The water was refreshing and welcome. Savio downed half of it and wiped drops from his mouth with the back of his hand.

'Can't wait to leave that blinking school. Only one more year,' Savio said, slumping down on the bench next to Liam.

'Still giving you stick, are they?'

Savio smiled sheepishly. 'More like me dishing it out.' He rubbed his bruised knuckles.

'Don't let the buggers get you down. There are plenty of bullies and idiots in this world and you have to learn how to cope. Take some of them army officers, for example. They had no idea of what we went through out there while they were safely tucked up in their bunkers. No going over the top for them. But, Savvy me boy, live up to your name. Pick your fights carefully. You can't go round knocking the daylights out of all and sundry. In the end, it won't get you far. You got to work out an easier way.'

Savio liked the nickname he'd earned: Savvy – it gave him a feeling of having knowledge. As Savio listened to Liam, he kicked at a tuft of grass by the bench.

'I often wonder what life would have been like if my people hadn't come to England,' Savio said. 'If they'd stayed in Sicily, I'd have been a proper Italian. Here, I'm neither one thing nor the other.'

Liam paused before replying, as if considering what to say.

'It was the same for me. When I came over, there were signs in the windows of lodging houses: *No Irish. No dogs. No blacks.* You have to ride above everything, Savvy. Life must have been hard on the island to cause your folks to leave. At least you have a job to go to after school.'

'A job sweeping up hair from the floor.' Savio pulled a face.

'It's a trade. And you have a bed to sleep in and your mother's good food on the table. I've seen the underneath of many a hedge in my time, my belly grumbling with hunger.'

'When I've saved up enough, I'm going to Sicily.'

'Have you ever been?'

'A few times.' Savio sank back against the bench as he remembered. 'It's different from this dump. My family are from a place outside Syracuse, near the sea. Swimming in it's like having a warm bath. We picked peaches and ate them there and then. So juicy and sweet, I ate so many I got the trots... and my cousin Carmelo took me fishing in his boat with his friends and we cooked what we caught on the beach. There's a volcano too 'and at night, you can see fire pouring out the top... I'd like to meet up with my cousin and his pals again. Great lads, they are. Nobody messes with *them*.'

'Sounds like a great holiday. But holiday it was. Remember, your folks left that place for a reason.'

'Why did you leave Ireland?'

'Same as them, most like. Poverty. It was either die of starvation or emigrate after the potato famine. My people died. My cousins went to America, but I decided to try my luck here. And all in all, it's not been too bad.'

Liam stood, easing his legs and back in a long stretch. 'There's no place like home, they do say. But you have to make your home first.' He pulled a sixpenny bit from his pocket. 'Treat yourself, lad. I'm finished for today.'

Savio's eyes were round with glee as he took the shiny silver coin. It would buy him a box of Rowntree's Fruit Gums and – Liam's words had made him think about his parents' sacrifices – he would get a slab of Cadbury's chocolate for Mamma too. He could do with one of her hugs. Some of his woes soothed, he thanked Liam and hurried to the corner shop.

CHAPTER 5

JUNE 1940

SAVIO

Savio's responsibilities in his parents' business had painfully and slowly progressed from sweeping hair from the floorboards, cleaning the windows of steam and fetching tea for the ladies under the dryers. Mamma was more generous in letting him be hands-on and he preferred helping style women's hair. Customers liked his cheeky banter and compliments and there were plenty of ladies who asked for him when they booked their perms and cuts. Papà was more protective of his side and Savio resented he didn't have the same easy relationship with his father as Fede.

Wednesday was half day and his parents had left him to shut up shop while they hurried off to work on their allotment. 'It's our little corner of Italia,' Papà would say. He'd built a greenhouse using old timber and window frames, where they grew tomatoes and peppers and they'd shelter in there on colder days. Sometimes they'd roast vegetables or one of their free-range hens for supper over a brazier created from an old oil drum. 'There is no view of the sea and mountains here, but we can pretend,' Mamma said, tucking her hands into the pockets of her pinafore. In summer, a row of sunflowers and roses provided a barrier against the rest of the world and Savio had painted the back of the greenhouse door with an image of Mount Etna erupting at night to remind them of Sicily.

At call-up, at the beginning of September 1939, Savio had quickly acquired an additional part-time job helping at the local Italian bakery to exempt him from conscription. He'd been in two minds what to do for the best. Maybe he would join up if this phoney war worsened, but so far there hadn't been much doing and he couldn't see the point. Fede, on the other hand, had enrolled in the RAF and had been immediately accepted for training.

As he swept the floor, there was a knock on the door and he ignored it. The sign clearly said closed. Another hard rap and he sighed as he leant the brush against the wall. Unbolting the door, he was about to give whoever it was an earful, but when he saw the telegraph boy standing there, his heart missed a beat. Telegraphs invariably meant bad news. The nickname for those who delivered them was 'angels of death'. With shaking hands, he asked the boy to read it out for him.

'I lost my glasses this week,' Savio lied, employing one of his excuses to avoid stumbling over reading.

It didn't take the angel of death long to deliver the two-liner.

'The Air Ministry regrets to inform you of the death of your son, Federico Rizzo. Letter to follow,' the boy read, his voice trailing off at the end. 'No reply, sir?' His young face was pale and Savio felt sorry for the messenger.

'No, sonny. No reply.'

'I'm very sorry, sir.'

Savio nodded and bolted the door again. He sank into the barber's chair. *Stupid, stupid Fede. Why did you fucking go and get yourself killed? How am I going to tell Mamma and Papà?*

He rubbed tears from his eyes. He and Fede were as

different as mashed potato and pasta, but they were brothers and his brother had always looked out for him. From the very start of Savio's schooldays, his big brother would walk roadside along the pavement to prevent little Savio from stepping into traffic. He'd stash his little brother's mittens into his own satchel as soon as they got to their pegs, so that Savio didn't lose them and get a clip round the ear from Papà. Fede always tried to steer him along the straight and narrow, despite the scrapes Savio managed to get into.

Damn it. Damn life. Fuck this phoney war. Not so phoney, after all, if it had got Fede. For Christ's sake, he'd only been training, hadn't he? As ground crew. What a fucking waste of a good chap. How on earth had he died whilst training?

Savio blew his nose on a towel and scrutinised the telegraph again, willing the words to be different. What about this letter they'd said would follow? Maybe he'd wait until that arrived. It might say there'd been a mistake: *The Air Ministry apologises for its error*, or something like that. But he knew that was clutching at straws. He couldn't not tell his poor parents.

Delivering the news had been the worst thing he'd ever had to do. From one moment to the next, he'd shattered the tranquil scene of his parents seated outside their little greenhouse, faces lifted to the sun's lukewarm rays, brazier lit for their supper. The contrast of Mamma wailing like a wild animal, his father trying to calm her while she beat him off with her fists was something he'd never forget. And her howling, 'No, no, no,' pierced Savio's ears and heart. She'd thrown herself prostrate on the newly dug soil. 'I want to die, I want to die...' she'd howled over and over. 'Why not me? Why my precious boy?'

Liam had come running over from his patch and the three of them had tried to lift her from the ground but she'd clawed at them, leaving a scratch down Savio's right cheek. 'Leave me be.

Get off!' Eventually, when she had no more energy, they'd somehow got her home. She'd taken to her bed for almost two weeks after hanging a large black bow on the door of the hairdresser's. Savio had laboured over the sign: **CLOASED UNTIL FURHTER NOTISS**. Maria Angela from the bakery had helped him write out another sign and he'd told her he'd written it in haste; because of the shock the words had come out wrong.

Every day, dishes of baked pasta, precious roast chicken, stews and bottles of wine were left by the Italian Soho community on their doorstep. Maria Angela knocked on the back door and delivered a basket of ciabatta, biscotti and a couple of white loaves, telling them that the Bianchis at the restaurant had also sent a message. 'They asked me to say you're all welcome to come and eat at their place every day if you want. For free. How is your mother? Can I go up and see her?'

He watched as she climbed the stairs to the living quarters above the shop. She was a sweet girl, dumpy and dark haired, with a slight squint to her left eye. Both sets of parents had hinted that an arranged marriage would do wonders for their families. 'I'm too young,' Savio continued to insist.

'I married Mamma when she was sixteen,' his father, Alfonso, retorted.

'Times are different now. And I don't love her, Papà. She's like a sister. That's the sum of it. Let her marry somebody else.'

'Love will come later,' Mamma had added. 'Like it did with us. Your father seemed like an old man to me at first: me sixteen, him nearly twice my age.'

It might have been the Sicilian way but it was not what Savio wanted for himself. And anyway, he was not the marrying kind. He didn't see the point. He'd joined the *Fascio di Londra* group, not because he was particularly political, but because they put on the best dances. It was a way of meeting pretty girls and keeping in with local businesspeople at the same time. You never knew who or what might come in useful in the future. Wasn't Papà always saying so?

The thought of a wife and babies was like having a ball and chain tethered to his ankles. He had no intention of imprisoning himself in an institution for the sake of satisfying the economic ambitions of two families. When this stupid war was over in a few months or so, he planned to travel back to Sicily and start a new life. He might even paint on the island and become a famous artist. The Camisas had commissioned him to paint a mural for their delicatessen and that had led to a couple of requests for the dining area in Quo Vadis. It was a start. *Fingers in pies, Savio,* he told himself. *Fingers in pies.*

He tried his best in the following weeks to help his parents and ran the shop while his parents grieved. The war was turning into more of a reality now and life in Soho didn't have the same happy-go-lucky atmosphere that the Italian and other foreign shopkeepers and restaurateurs had enjoyed in the past. One of Papà's customers, a German professor who had escaped Berlin to find refuge in England, discussed an article he'd read in the *Daily Express.*

'I fear things are going to become difficult for us, young signor Rizzo,' he said. 'All this talk about Fifth Columnists after Germany invaded the Netherlands. They say Germans dropped women parachutists as decoys. They think we are *all* spies. Even though we have escaped from the Nazis and disagree with Hitler, they are branding us all enemies of the state. Look here,' he said, banging his hand on the page and peering at the words as he read aloud: '"No matter how superficially charming and devoted they appear, every German or Austrian in Britain is a real and grave menace." This journalist, this Mr Bland, sounds like Herr Hitler himself. Mark my words, young man, all foreigners will be treated badly before too long. Not just we Germans. You Italians will be next. I did not expect this of England.'

Savio didn't take much notice, thinking Italians were different from Germans. And anyway, he'd been born in London; he might look Italian, but he was British.

On the afternoon that his father decided it was time to open again after Fede's death, Savio offered to cut his hair and shave off his ten-day stubble. 'Papà, you're not a good example to customers looking like that. Let me help you prepare for tomorrow.'

His father agreed. 'You are right. Thank you. I have let myself go, son. *Grazie, figlio.*'

Savio applied the cream with the thick brush to make a lather, his father urging him to use plenty. 'I don't want you to cut me, Savio.'

'Papà, leave it to me. I've watched you often enough.'

He began to pass the sharp single blade over the wrinkles of his father's skin, using the thumb and fingers of his left hand to stretch out the grooves. One side completed, he was applying a warm cloth to his father's face when an almighty crashing of glass caused him to jump. He watched in dismay as a line of blood seeped through the foam.

'*Ahi!* I knew it,' his father cried out, pulling the razor from his son. 'Useless and clumsy. And what has your mother dropped now? *Mannaggia!*' He tugged the wet towel from his face and held it to his jaw to stop the bleeding. 'You should stick to working at the bakery. You're not ready for this job—'

His words were interrupted by more shattering of glass as a brick was hurled through the shop window, smashing the pane into pieces that showered over them.

His mother's screams added to the mayhem and Savio dashed to the door, the bell pinging as he wrenched it open.

He was confronted by half a dozen youths yelling abuse from the pavement. One of them held up a newspaper with the headline:

Mussolini Declares War

'Dirty wops! Traitors! You oughta be locked up. Bleeding Nazi lovers.'

Directly in the line of fire now, Savio was struck on the head by another stone hurled from the mob. He recognised the young man who had thrown it from schooldays. Blood trickled from his hairline and he cursed, his familiar red rage descending.

'What the bloody hell are you fucking on about?' he shouted. 'I'm as cockney as the rest of you.' He threw himself in their midst, his fists delivering punches left, right and centre. He felled a couple of lads and delivered a blow to the ring-leader's ugly mug before a piercing whistle caused the rest of the rabble to scatter as a couple of policemen ran across the street, truncheons at the ready. A man in a raincoat followed them from a Black Maria parked nearby.

Savio's father emerged. 'Thank you, thank you, Inspector Sutor, for coming to our rescue,' he said, his voice full of gratitude. 'Those hooligans... twenty years I've worked on this business and look at it now—'

'Best we deal with this inside, Mr Rizzo,' the detective inspector interrupted. The two policemen steered Savio and his father back into the salon.

'Very sorry this happened, Mr Rizzo,' the inspector said, after asking his men to wait outside. 'But it's only going to get worse. Your Mussolini has caused you trouble by joining up with Hitler. I suggest you board up your windows for the time being. And let me know if there are any more attacks like this.'

He shook Savio's father's hand and turned to Savio. 'And you watch your back and keep those fists in your pockets.'

. . .

A few weeks later, the police returned. This time, it was they who barged into the salon. The same police inspector who had regularly had his whiskers trimmed by Savio's father ordered them to lock the door, adding, 'Pull down the blinds, young Mr Rizzo.'

Savio nodded at the inspector. The man's face was sombre as he spoke. 'You need to pack a bag quickly and come with us to the station.'

One of the policemen started to open cupboards, dragging the contents to the floor, bottles of shampoo shattering as they fell.

'Hey, what are you doing?' Savio yelled. 'There's no need for that. What's going on?' He moved over to his bewildered parents.

'We have orders to arrest all aliens between the ages of sixteen and sixty and to search your premises for arms.'

'Are you mad? This is a bloody barber's, not an army barracks. And what are you on about aliens for? We're British, we are,' Savio shouted.

'Leave it, Jenks. I'm sure we'll find nothing here.' The inspector, who had come in every Saturday morning for the last five years for a wet shave and trim, pulled his man back.

'It's orders, sir.'

'And my orders are to stop.'

'My son was in the RAF, training for war,' Alfonso said. 'He died learning how to defend this country. And you are treating us as enemies? We have lived here since 1914. There must be some mistake, sir.'

'Nevertheless, our orders from up high are to arrest *all* Italians between the ages of sixteen and sixty. I'm afraid we're at war now, sir.'

The use of 'sir' grated on Savio. It was absurd they were being arrested like criminals while the inspector was addressing his father as 'sir'. It didn't make sense. 'This is bloody stupid.'

He struggled as the younger constable grabbed his arms to handcuff him.

The inspector intervened. 'No need for that, Jenks. I know these people.' He removed the cuffs from Savio's wrists. 'It's best you come quietly, sonny. Hopefully this will all blow over soon and you'll be home before you know it. If you ask me, this business has been cobbled together in too much haste. Now, I'll give you ten minutes to gather your belongings together and then you must come with me. Don't forget your gas masks.' He turned to Savio's mother. 'Mrs Rizzo, there is no need for you to accompany us, madam. Just the gentlemen.'

She pulled herself up as tall as she could make herself, all of her five-foot-one inches, bristling as she pronounced, 'Where they go, *I* go.'

Savio helped his mother pull down the big suitcase from the top of the wardrobe and place it on the bed. She told him to fetch food from the kitchen while she organised Papà, who had gone to pieces, slumped in a chair, his head in his hands. 'There must be some mistake; we've done nothing wrong. Twenty years of hard work gone in one night...' he kept repeating.

Downstairs, Savio grabbed a prosciutto hanging in the pantry and a large round of cheese, wrapping them in a towel. Bounding back up to his room, he pulled his sketchbook and pencils, a warm sweater from the chest of drawers and then went back to his mother. The suitcase bulged with clothing and he had to sit on it to do up the clasps.

Ten minutes later, suitcase on his shoulder, Savio accompanied his parents into the back of the black Daimler waiting outside. A crowd of onlookers jeered and one thumped on the window as they were driven away at speed. An egg was hurled at the windscreen and his mother tutted, 'What a waste,' as the car drove down the dark streets, southwards away from the centre of London.

Savio could not bear to see his father in this state, a defeated expression on his face.

'It will be all right, Papà,' he said, squeezing his father's arm. 'We'll soon be back home.'

He hoped to God he was right.

CHAPTER 6

SAVIO

Arriving at Kempton Park Racecourse where they were to be processed, Savio and his parents were comforted at first to recognise some Italian friends from Soho queuing, clutching possessions as they waited. Cooks, waiters, shopkeepers and even a couple of customers from their hairdresser's were packed into what appeared to be one stable block of many, the distinctive stench of horse manure strong in their nostrils, hay scattered about the dirt floor. Savio was separated from his parents, who were led away with a group of older people. He watched as his mother put her arm firmly though his father's to lead him on as they were bundled out of the building. Papà was still in shock and Savio marvelled at the way Mamma was taking control of her bewildered husband. She turned to raise a hand to her son and he caught the last of her words, spoken in Italian: 'We'll see you soon, son. There's been some mistake for sure. Do as they tell you and we'll be together soon.'

'Where are they going?' Savio asked, stepping forwards to

ask one of the soldiers keeping him and others cordoned in a corner. 'My father's not a well man.'

The guard pushed him back and raised his rifle.

'Hey – don't you dare do that to me,' Savio said, raising his fists, red mist filling his head.

The guard called for help. Three soldiers dashed over and Savio was promptly restrained in handcuffs, wriggling and protesting all the while. 'Get your filthy hands off me. Who do you think you are? Let me go.'

An older man, chevrons on his upper sleeve showing he held the rank of sergeant major, stood up slowly from behind a desk at the end of the room from where he had been directing proceedings and, glaring at Savio, he marched over.

'I see we have a Fifth Columnist amongst our undesirable aliens,' he said. 'Take him next door, men.'

'I've done nothing wrong,' Savio shouted as the soldiers dragged him into a small side room, bare save for a table and chair. A smeared, barred window set high in the wall leaked in grey light. Savio was ordered to stand to attention behind the table, two soldiers flanking him while the sergeant sat down.

'Remove your clothes,' he barked, drumming his fingers on the table.

'How can I if I'm handcuffed? And why should I take off my clothes?' Savio's tone was belligerent.

'This whole matter will be a whole lot easier, young man, if you cooperate.' The sergeant major nodded his head at the two guards, one of whom released the cuffs. Savio rubbed his wrists.

'Strip!' the officer ordered.

'Why?'

'We need to check there is no weapon concealed about your person.'

'This is utterly barmy. I'm a hairdresser from Soho, not a spy with a gun up my arse. I was born in London; my brother was in the RAF. Why should I be treated like this?'

'You either strip off – as all other detained aliens will be ordered to – or you spend time in Pentonville. And there's no guarantee when you'll be let out from there.'

The soldiers tipped the contents of the family suitcase onto the table. Savio already felt degraded: naked and shivering in front of the three men. But he turned furious as he watched his family's belongings being sifted through: his mother's petticoat held up to the light, his father's thick cotton pyjamas examined, while the second soldier thumbed through his wallet. He removed the pound notes and placed them on the desk in front of the officer, next to his mother's gold bracelet and her string of pearls.

'What are you going to do with those things?' Savio asked. 'My parents will need their clothes and money. Where have they been taken?'

'You'll see your parents in due course, but these items are confiscated for now,' the sergeant major said, nodding at the soldier who was holding a knife that Savio had packed for cutting the ham. The ham and cheese were added to the pile on the table.

'We shall give you a receipt for most of these things, but the knife you will certainly not be getting back. Or the razor blades. They are weapons!' the officer said.

'And who do you think I was going to kill with the ham?' Savio spat. He watched in disgust as his sketchpad and drawing pencils were also removed from the case and put to one side.

'And I suppose you think I shall be using my pens and paper to write down everything to pass to the enemy. This is bloody ludicrous. You're as bad as the Nazis, you are. Where are my rights? My father needs his pyjamas. Why take those?'

It did him no good. He was hit in the ribs with the butt of a rifle and pushed from the room to join a queue of other naked men. After a cold shower he was ordered to dress again, his clothes damp and reeking of disinfectant. Afterwards, he and other 'enemy aliens', as the soldiers continued to describe their charges, filed into another large stable block.

Savio lay awake that first night, shivering on the straw spread thinly over the cold stone floor. Whispered conversations bounced back and forth between the men. The fellow bedded down next to him was a young German Jew and he was hopping mad too.

'I escaped from this kind of thing in Berlin two years ago,' he told Savio. 'Qualified by the seat of my pants for the first *Kindertransport* train that left for England. Thank God I was still only sixteen. But eventually the police caught up with me here simply because I am German... If you're a German, then people automatically think you must be a Nazi or a spy.'

Savio shook his head. 'Maybe they'll let us go free tomorrow after they've checked properly.'

'I doubt it. Haven't you been reading the recent reports in newspapers, my friend? All that talk about Fifth Columnists and the danger of allowing foreigners to live freely in Britain? The politicians have cooked up a story saying they are saving us from danger and retaliations from the public? Pah! That's simply an excuse for locking us all up. It's less trouble for them than having to sort us all out.'

Savio ignored the reference to reading newspapers. His way of learning about the news was by listening to conversations between customers in the salon or news bulletins on the radio.

'I'm Pieter Fleischold, by the way,' the young man said, holding out his hand.

'Savio. Savio Rizzo.' Pieter's grip was firm, despite his lean, hungry look. 'Your English is very good.'

'My father was insistent that education is important. He made me study hard.'

'Are they with you?'

The young man shook his head. 'I don't know where they are. I left them in Germany.'

'I'm sorry. My parents are holed up in here somewhere too. They won't like sleeping on a hard floor. I can't find out where they are from these bloody guards.'

'My parents disappeared in one of the round-ups. Despite my hoping they will turn up some day... I am told I'm an orphan.'

Pieter turned quiet after that and Savio didn't trespass on his silence.

The next morning, after a tin mug of watery tea and a slice of bread and marg, Savio found Pieter hunched in the back of a stall, sketching on a small pad balanced on his knees. He sat down next to his new friend.

'What are you up to?'

'My morning exercises. Others like physical exercises; I limber up by drawing.' He held up the page to show a pencil sketch of half a dozen horses tangled together. 'I can't get it right somehow.'

'It's good.' Savio whistled. 'Very good.' The impression was one of chaos: an angry composition. He pointed at the nearest horse. 'Perhaps work more on that one in front, then the other images will blend better.'

Pieter looked at him. 'You like art?'

'I like painting. Yes!' Savio nodded. 'But I only dabble. Your work looks professional.'

'I wanted to go to art school. That dream was shattered. But I did some work here, up in Manchester before I was captured, that helped a lot.'

'What were you doing?'

'The business specialised in colouring in old photographs of soldiers of the Great War. The owners were pleased with me. It's kept my dream alive of becoming an artist.'

'They took my pencils and paper away from me, the bastards,' Savio said.

At that, Pieter tore half a dozen pages from his own book

and handed Savio a pencil. 'I always carry my tools in a hidden pocket in the lining of my jacket,' he said, patting his chest. 'We got used to all kinds of subterfuge back in Germany. My mother sewed her jewellery into the seams of her skirts...' He paused. 'But I never expected we'd be treated this way in England.' He sighed before continuing to sketch.

'Thanks, pal,' Savio said. He pushed the gifts into his vest and hauled himself up from the ground. He wasn't in the mood for drawing right now, angry with the way Pieter had been treated and frustrated at the whole situation. His own parents were very much on his mind and he needed to find them, but despite searching every corner of the building and asking the soldiers on duty where they might be, he was unsuccessful. Savio slept fitfully, waking in a sweat, reliving the nightmare he'd had: his parents had been lined up by Nazi soldiers against the mirrors in the salon and shot, glass shattering everywhere and his mother's screams were loud in his ears. It was as vivid as reality. He wiped the sweat from his face, his hands shaking. Where were his parents? How could he find out?

On the third morning all the arrested were ordered to vacate the stables and line up with their belongings. Many of them carried gas masks but Savio hadn't managed to pick his up in time. The family suitcase was handed back to him but it felt far lighter. By now he understood it was pointless to kick up a fuss – what good would he be to his parents if he was banged up in Pentonville? Playing meek on the outside, but seething on the inside, he took his place in the shuffling queue. Everybody was loaded onto the backs of army trucks and escorted to Euston station. One of the soldiers told them they were bound for the Liverpool docks, but he had no idea where they were going afterwards.

As the crowd of men and women of all ages filed from the

trucks to the waiting train, he spied his parents ahead of him and he shouted, but his cries were drowned by jeers and hysterical abuse from onlookers at the railway station. Savio's fists curled into tight balls as they were taunted with cries of 'Dirty scum, spies, traitors. Go back to Dirty Tally.'

He hoped his parents could not understand the degrading and undeserved comments. He wanted to shout back at them to tell them he was English; it was written on his birth certificate back home. But what good would it serve to reason with an ignorant, howling mob? He resigned himself to keeping his head down and staying calm. If he did so maybe he would be reunited with his parents. Soon.

CHAPTER 7

JUNE 1940, ISLE OF MAN

SAVIO

The sea was choppy, the salty air tangy and sour with vomit as a light drizzle fell on Savio and Pieter sleeping on the deck of *The Rushen Castle*. In happier times, this packet steamer had been used for transporting holidaymakers to the Isle of Man. But now this cargo of passengers was bound for the hastily erected internment camps on the island. As the boat ploughed through choppy waters, Savio worried constantly about his parents. They were in the dry, below deck, this much he knew. He had waved to them from a distance as they'd been led towards the stairs. But he feared for them. Conditions below would be worse without fresh air. His parents were most likely feeling seasick. He hoped to God this crossing would not last the seventy-one hours that one of the crew had told him had happened back in January in terrible gales.

It was disgraceful, Savio thought as he chatted to others on the boat. Everyone was confused, nonplussed at why the country they considered home was treating them like this. One man had told him he'd walked from Italy seven years earlier over the Alps to make a new life in England. He'd worked hard on building up his ice cream business and he couldn't believe what was happening. 'They've rounded us up like a lot of damn sheep, good and bad. My cart got smashed up by thugs calling me a fascist. Bloody rubbish. I left Italy because I hate the bloody fascists. But nobody wants to listen.'

When they landed at the port of Douglas and were escorted from the boat, islanders watched their arrival with suspicion, wary of the hundreds of foreigners carrying gas masks, which hadn't yet been issued on the Isle of Man. But there was no jeering from bystanders like there had been at Euston station and the Liverpool docks. Instead, there was a quiet curiosity. Landladies, whose establishments had been requisitioned and transformed for the arrival of this human cargo, watched with not a little satisfaction, pleased to receive income at last because of these new internees.

A grey-haired British officer welcomed the lines of new arrivals. He spoke politely, explaining they would have to pass through Manx police first to check their details. There was no 'quick march', or 'get a move on', as at Kempton Park and on the steamer. This older man was kindly, explaining about curfews, how detainees would be housed chiefly according to nationality. Women would stay in hotels and boarding houses further down the coast. He concluded his talk with: 'Now, please get going.' The 'please' sounded like a good sign to Savio.

It took over two hours to be processed. When it came to his turn, Savio pushed a terrified-looking young lad forward. 'He's only a kid,' he explained.

The policeman took one look at the teenage boy's round face and shook his head in dismay. 'Not another one. What do they think they're doing on the mainland?' He raised his eyebrows and shrugged at Savio, then directed the lad to a group of men and women, amongst them a few elderly, children and a handful of heavily pregnant women. 'You'll be going right back to Liverpool with that lot when they're ready to leave. Wait over there, lad. If you're lucky, you'll get a cuppa.'

Savio felt heartened by the authorities on this island. They were much more human. Maybe he would be able to convince them that he and his parents were also eligible to return. At least here they seemed to have some common sense. His spirits lifted.

It didn't happen.

'I know I look Italian,' he told the policeman when it was his turn. 'But I was born in London. I'm English, sir. Can't you tell from the way I talk?'

The policeman shrugged again. 'You might get a chance to put your case forward in a couple of days but, in the meantime, you'll be staying in Palace Camp along with other Italians.'

He could feel rage filling his head but he managed to control his temper. For the sake of his parents.

'Can I at least speak to my folks? They were detained along with me: Mr Alfonso Rizzo and Mrs Rosalia Rizzo. But Mother might have given her maiden name, Lentini. That's the Italian way,' Savio added.

The policeman looked down his list. 'They're already on the list to be sent away on account of their age.'

A wave of relief rushed over him. At least they would be safe. But would they manage back in London? Savio thought of the ruined shop, the mob, the hatred in their faces.

'What about me? Savio Rizzo. I work in a bakery, you know. Important work. Why aren't I on the list with my folks?'

'Look, son. You'll get a chance to argue your case later but for now be grateful your parents are not staying here. They can go.'

'They need looking after. The night we were arrested, our place was ransacked. They won't be able to manage on their own.'

The man looked at him sympathetically, but he could only

shrug again with resignation. 'Be patient,' he said. Then indicating for one of the guards to come over, he beckoned him nearer. 'Let Mr Rizzo say goodbye to his parents.'

His mother clung to him and wept as she kissed her remaining son goodbye. 'Just be good, Savio, *tesoro*. Curb that temper of yours. We'll be fine, *figlio mio*.' She pushed a small roll of pound notes into his hands and pulled her Sicilian pendant from around her neck. 'Keep this for me, son. It will bring you *fortuna*. See if you can send word to us, Savio. Be good.' She smoothed back his hair and kissed him, pulling him to her as if she never wanted to let go. It broke his heart to see his mother weep. The sharp edges of the pendant dug into his palm as he held it tight.

His father looked stronger than when he'd been in Kempton Park but he needed a shave. It made him look old, Savio thought. He needed looking after.

'We'll soon get the business started up again, son,' his father said. 'And when they realise they've made a mistake, you'll be back helping me too. It's time you took over the shop anyhow. I'm getting past it.'

Savio gave his parents back their half-empty suitcase, urging them to put in a complaint and demand the missing items be returned, but his mother shook her head. 'You take the case, Savio dearest. We have everything we need. Best not kick up a fuss. I just want to get home.'

The policeman intervened. 'Time's up. Join the queue again.' He pulled Savio away.

'I'll see you soon, Mamma *e* Papà,' he called as he was moved away. 'I'll get word to you as soon as I can.'

He opened his palm to stare down at his mother's necklace with the strange three-legged symbol of Sicily he remembered hanging from his parents' bedpost. His eyes misted over. They had come to England for a better future. It would have been better if they had stayed on their beautiful island.

. . .

A row of Victorian houses on Douglas seafront had been converted into makeshift camps, wire fencing extending to the edge of the promenade to segregate the internees from island inhabitants and, Savio thought ruefully, to prevent them from escaping. His new friend, Pieter, had been ordered to join a group of German speakers bound for Hutchinson Camp, whilst Savio and a large group of other 'Italians' were marched by armed guards with fixed bayonets to the far end of the central square to Palace Camp. The location overlooked a stretch of sandy beach and had it not been for the barbed wire, the scene before Savio would have looked more like a postcard view of the Riviera than an internment camp. The sun was shining on a blue sea of white-tipped waves. If he had to spend a couple of days holed up in this place, he would try to relax and treat it as a holiday.

A couple of days, however, stretched to a couple of weeks and Savio began to grow restless. He had to share a double bed with a middle-aged man. Paolo played the harmonica, badly, and spent all his free time sleeping. But he snored almost as soon as his head touched the pillow and nothing seemed to wake him. At night, Savio slept with his head under his own hard pillow, the desire to throttle his bedmate strong. There were no blackout curtains; the windows had been painted with dark-blue paint and the lightbulbs orange, in case of light escaping during air raids. One day, not being able to bear the depressing light any longer, Savio scratched some of the paint off the window and left patches in the shape of women. If he was to be marooned here for a while, at least he would have something to remind him of female company.

Reveille sounded at seven each morning, when the couple of thousand internees had to line up within the perimeter fence for roll call. Afterwards, and before breakfast, everybody joined in physical exercises. Savio worked doubly hard at this. He was determined to keep fit, unlike his bedfellow, and keep his nose out of trouble. He needed to be out of here. Each day at five p.m. names were announced for release. And each day, thousands of internees were left disappointed when their names were not called.

Savio avoided the bickering between the fascists and anti-fascists in Palace. They usually broke out on a Friday evening, frustrations rising to the fore. Although the camp commander had tried to segregate these two groups, putting them into different houses as far apart as possible, it was not totally successful and there were always plenty of arguments. The hardcore political types looked set to stay on the island as the releasing process continued and Savio kept out of arguments. He was anxious to stay uninvolved, keep his slate clean and show he could behave, to get back to Soho and his parents.

On an early evening in July, he was sitting near the fence perimeter, sketching the distant hills and open countryside. The tide was out, a couple of people walked along the wet sand and he was drawing their outlines when one of the guards came over and tapped him on the shoulder.

'You're wanted by the captain. In his office. Now.'

Savio's heart skipped a beat. He was going to be told he could leave the island – that after careful consideration, the authorities had concluded they'd made a huge mistake and he was free to join his parents again in London.

He snapped closed his sketchpad and followed the soldier. He wanted to whistle and skip like a child. One of the men, who slept in the next room, waved as he passed, calling out, 'Lucky bugger. You got a smile as wide as the ocean on your ugly mug. Does that mean we're going to be saying *arrivederci*? Got any smokes to dish out before you leave?'

'Of course. Come and see me later when I'll be packing. I might have spare fags for you.'

The soldier stood outside the camp leader's office while Savio knocked on the door.

'In!'

'Good evening, sir. Lovely one, sir,' Savio said, beaming with expectation.

The camp commander's face was grim as he spoke.

'Won't you sit down? Please. I regret to have to tell you, Mr Rizzo, that I have bad news.'

'I'm all right standing, sir. What's up? Is it my father? Is he ill? He's taken all this enemy alien stuff badly—'

'The ship your parents were sailing on was lost at sea last Tuesday.'

Savio sank down on the chair but when the commander gave him further details, he went berserk. In an explosion of fury, he went for the officer, leaping over the desk, anger consuming him like an erupting volcano. The last thing Savio knew was the door bursting open, soldiers bundling in and then after a heavy blow administered to his head, he was knocked out and knew no more.

CHAPTER 8

MAY 1973, SUFFOLK

PAIGE

'You're miles away. Oh, *Pa-ige...*'

Jeremy waved the menu in front of Paige's face and she tore her gaze and thoughts away from the view over the river. But she wasn't really taking in the scenery. All her thoughts were of the letter, the strange pendant, and the birth certificate. Her name, her date of birth... and some lady's name she had never heard before. It all seemed much more interesting to Paige than sitting opposite her fiancé this evening. Nothing felt right anymore.

'Sorry! What were you saying?' she asked, dragging her gaze from the river.

He topped up her wine. 'I was talking about my speech. How I haven't written it yet. And how Mother's been on at me to *pin* you down about your final dress fitting. No pun intended.' He chortled at his own joke, the way he did, finishing with a snort.

She sighed. He wasn't funny. *Mind you,* she thought, *nothing would sound amusing at the moment.* 'Couldn't we...

postpone the wedding?' she said. Even the question in her voice was half-hearted: as if she knew what his answer would be. His reaction told her she wasn't wrong.

'You what? We've spent so much on this wedding. The guests have all been invited, the venue's been paid its final instalment. We can't, Paige. You're joking, of course.' He paused, a forkful of crayfish halfway to his mouth and repeated his question nervously.

She pushed away her plate of samphire and crab risotto, the signature dish of this famous waterside inn. 'I can't concentrate on the wedding at the moment. Not since Aunty Flo's death. It's been a huge shock, Jeremy. You must see that. My head is full of questions, wondering what it is she wanted to tell me. She's left me in a mess...' She looked up at him, willing him to understand. 'Can't we just elope? It's our day, after all, but it's turning into your mother's.'

His answer was not what she'd wanted to hear. 'It's out of the question,' he said, his fork clattering onto his plate.

She stared at him, wondering how she had got to this point. She stood, crumpling her damask serviette onto the table next to her full plate. She knew in that moment she didn't want to be tied to him anymore. 'I can't do this tonight, Jeremy. I don't feel well.'

'You're overwrought, that's all. Upset. Your aunt's death has unbalanced you,' he said. 'The wedding will make you concentrate on something else... like me.' He beamed. 'Sit down, Paige, and I'll take you home when I've settled up.'

'I want to walk.'

Without waiting for him to protest, she picked up her jacket and stepped away, turning to say, 'I'll phone you, Jeremy. I'm sorry.'

She left him sitting there, mouth agape, pleased he didn't run after her. Or was she simply relieved? In a film or a book, wouldn't the boyfriend chase her? Tell his girlfriend they would walk together and talk everything through?

How had it come to this? In the early days, when they'd first got together, Jeremy had been all over her: sweet, solicitous, kind, bringing her gifts of flowers and chocolates. He'd swept her into a fairy-tale romance and she'd enjoyed it. 'I like bringing you out of yourself,' he'd said more than once. He had made her less introverted and introduced her to things she'd never dreamt would happen – Paris for two nights in a hotel overlooking the Seine, gold necklaces from Hatton Garden to layer as bracelets up her arms, a Mary Quant hairstyle (that didn't really suit her and was now growing out). But now that he had brought her out of herself, she didn't feel she was Paige Caister anymore. She wanted to climb back inside her old self and she wanted her aunt to still be alive.

The moon was heavy and full. She took off her sparkly slingbacks and walked along the riverbank, the grass and mud squelchy between her toes. Aunty Flo had encouraged her to walk barefoot as often as possible. 'It will ground you to the world,' she'd say. 'Better than squashing your feet into horrid shoes.' Aunty Flo had been like a forerunner of the hippies with some of her far-out ideas. She missed her so much. Knowing that she wouldn't be at Squirrels to ask her about her evening; not be there with her strong tea and listening skills; simply not be there, full stop. It was unbearable. 'You've left me feeling discombobulated, Aunty,' Paige said out loud, remembering a tricky crossword answer that had turned out to be an anagram. Disturbed by her voice, a coot skittered into the shallows as the tide turned and began to flow slowly upriver again.

For a while, she sat on a bench, listening to night sounds: the occasional squawk of waterfowl, a shriek of laughter from revellers outside the pub, the clink of rigging over by the yacht club. Now that she'd reached a conclusion about Jeremy, she felt more honest. She'd been kidding herself for some time now, really. Alarm bells had started to tinkle when Jeremy had begun to control what she should wear to his business functions. When he'd taken her away on a convention to New York, he'd wanted to check her suitcase first. He'd pulled out a tie-dye dress she'd put in, as well as a pair of flared jeans and held them up. 'You can't wear these, Paige,' he'd said with a grimace. 'We're not going to a music festival. We've got to dress to impress, darling. It's all part of marketing. We'll pop into Harvey Nichols tomorrow on the way to the airport. They'll kit you out.'

She hadn't protested at the time. If Jeremy wanted to treat her to expensive designer clothes, that was fine. But when she wore the fuchsia-pink, maxi cape-effect dress to dinner on the first evening at The Biltmore, she hadn't recognised herself.

There'd been other occasions too, like when he'd tried to choose her circle of friends: wives of men on the board. Aunty Flo had wrinkled up her nose when she'd talked about the ladies she lunched with and asked, 'But what do they actually *do*, Paige?' She'd answered that they picked up their children from school. Before she could finish, Aunty Flo had interrupted. 'Yes, and I suppose the little darlings get packed off to holiday clubs so they don't have to entertain them at home and interrupt lunch gatherings.'

She'd been right to wrinkle that nose. Paige had quickly grown bored of the women's conversations about where the best place was to get your legs waxed, or boobs enhanced. And she'd begun to invent excuses not to join them. She'd embarked instead on a post-graduate teacher training course and, although Jeremy couldn't see the point – 'You don't need to work, darling' – it had been wonderful and like a small victory when she passed with distinction.

Why had she fallen into the relationship in the first place? She had to admit the glamour had appealed but she'd swum along with it long after it had begun to pall and once the wedding preparations had begun in earnest, it had seemed too complicated to extricate herself.

It had taken losing Aunty Flo to wake her up. It was as if she was haunting her and wouldn't give up until Paige came to her senses. She felt very alone and the only person she could think to talk openly with at the moment was her old friend Charlie, from uni days. It was too late to call him now, but she would phone first thing tomorrow and see if he fancied a couple of days away from the Old Smoke. Shivering in her spangled minidress, she picked up her pace along the footpath back to Squirrels. Back at the cottage, she half expected Jeremy's Aston Martin to be parked outside on the gravel, but she was grateful it wasn't.

Paige had fallen asleep with the strange cryptic letter by her bedside. Her first call next morning, after a night when she couldn't stop thinking about Aunty Flo, was one of duty. She dialled Jeremy's number with a mixture of dread and relief.

Her fiancé wasn't giving up without a fight, insisting Paige was overreacting to her aunt's death. 'It's been a shock for you,' he said. 'Wait a bit and have a think before you ruin our future.'

'But I *have* thought about it, Jeremy,' she said, pulling the receiver further from her ear. When he was angry, his voice was always slower, but raised by at least two more decibels.

'As I said last night, Paige. You're overwrought. You're not talking sense at the moment. Let's see how you are by Friday. Got to go. Meeting's starting.'

He put the phone down and Paige listened for a couple of moments to the *whir* at the other end, confused again, thinking that maybe he was right. Perhaps she was overreacting. She breathed a deep sigh and dialled Charlie's number in London. But it went straight to his zany answerphone message, telling her he was tied up at the moment: '... But not by a dishy highwayman, more's the pity. Call me later when I'm unfettered.'

She grinned. He changed his messages according to his mood or the time of year. He'd been 'in rubber gloves, up to his eyes in soap suds', even, 'swinging from his standard lamp', amongst others.

'One day, Charlie, you'll be called by somebody offering you an important contract and your messages will put them off,' she'd told him.

She'd imagined him shrugging at the other end of the line. 'They can take me as I am or leave me, Paige dearest. You know by now I'm very much my own person.'

And he was. Free spirited and true to himself. They'd been good mates since Freshers' Week at university: the time when everybody was finding their feet, getting to know each other, letting their hair down in the first heady days of freedom. Paige had been shy and envied the cool, trendy girls who fitted in better than she did, and she hated the chatting-up bits and boys looking for an easy lay. The disco evenings when she danced for hours were when she lowered her inhibitions, swept up in the music, not having to make small talk.

Charlie had been hard to ignore in his red-striped fitted shirt and trilby. The colour clashed with his ginger hair and trendy Beatles style. But with a body like his, he looked good in anything. They had gravitated towards each other, moving together to The Rolling Stones belting out 'Come on', Charlie jigging his Jagger hips. She wasn't looking to get hooked up with anybody and it was just as well. He was gay. He'd told her more or less straightaway, and they became a regular couple at the disco evenings, dancing until they dropped.

Now, Charlie no longer sported his sixties Mod look, and his hair hung to his shoulders. He no longer had snake hips and blamed it on his writing muse and being chained to his type-writer for hours. He still wore his waffle-knit cardigan, however.

'To keep me warm in my attic.' His 'attic' was a smart top-floor apartment in a converted warehouse along the River Thames, purchased with the royalties of his sexy blockbusters. Paige always knew when he was between boyfriends, because that was when she was invited to stay.

She was upstairs in Aunty Flo's bedroom, reading the note in the exercise book for the umpteenth time when the phone rang downstairs.

'What's up, sweetie?' Charlie asked.

'Is it that obvious?'

'You're miserable because of losing Florence, is that it? You've got to be patient. My mum died three years ago and it still hits me at unexpected moments. I started blubbing in the supermarket queue the other day. I might start to do it more often, actually. The guy in front reached out to me and asked if I wanted a coffee. But he turned out to be as straight as my father... unfortunately.'

Paige giggled. 'It's more complicated than that, Charlie.' She couldn't continue, her words choked by a huge lump in her throat as tears began to fall.

'Oh, Paige. Honeypie. Right. I'm coming to you now.'

'But your writing... and you're in London.' She blew her nose.

'That's the beauty of my job. Have notebook, have pen and a deadline that's not looming, for a change. My new editor *loves* me. I'll be there in two hours, traffic permitting. Hang on in there, baby doll.'

It didn't escape Paige that it was Charlie and not Jeremy who was rushing to console her. But the two men had very different jobs: Charlie a freelance writer, Jeremy the finance director of his parents' flourishing supermarket chain, who found it harder to drop everything to come running... even if he was her fiancé. She washed her face and combed back her hair into an untidy topknot. She'd make Charlie a cake and rustle up lunch. He had a huge appetite and didn't function properly without regular meals. She'd found that out to her cost on their first holiday together when they'd hitched round Italy after they'd both graduated in mathematics. When his blood sugar was low, it was the only time he got ratty.

Charlie had stopped off at a service station to buy flowers and a couple of bottles of Blue Nun, her favourite tipple of the moment, and they'd polished off the first over macaroni cheese and salad. Patting his stomach, his long legs spread under Aunty Flo's pine table, he thanked Paige.

'That's better. Now tell Uncle Charlie all about it, honeypie.'

She fetched the old chocolate box and handed him the contents. 'Take a look at this stuff while I make coffee. It looks like my birth certificate, but that woman's name... that's not my mother. My parents died in a fire when I was a baby and my mother certainly wasn't a "lady". Aunty Flo was obviously going to tell me something, something about my parents maybe... And it's killing me not knowing what it was.'

Coffee poured, she watched Charlie scribbling figures in his notebook after picking up the envelope and letter to examine.

'What are you up to?' she asked, her hands cradled round her Paul McCartney mug.

'This letter is obviously in code,' he said. 'But it's beyond me at the moment.' He held it up and read out some of the figures: 'VIII, XXV – some numbers are Roman numerals, like headings, I imagine. Whilst others are ordinary, cardinal: thirty-eight, four and five.'

'Like in a poem or a play?' Paige said. 'Or the Bible, maybe. Like, Chapter Two, verses one to six.'

'Maybe,' Charlie replied, chewing the end of his Biro. 'We

need more time to decipher it all. Do you have a Bible in the cottage?'

'Don't think so,' Paige said. 'We were never really into religion.'

'Let's leave the numbers for a while until inspiration hits.'

'If it ever does,' Paige said. 'Perhaps we should get help.'

Charlie picked up the pendant. 'However, I *do* know something about this,' he said, swinging it back and forth hypnotically. 'I believe it's Sicilian. Ma had a hideous jug on her mantelpiece with a similar image. Dad bought it for her on their one and only holiday abroad, before they knew that meat and two veg were the only meals they liked.' He rolled his eyes. 'What a waste. All that delicious pasta.'

'Of *course*, Charlie...' She grabbed the notebook and, skimming through the lines, she read out: '"It all happened because of a beautiful Sicilian..." With all the other cryptic stuff, I'd sort of glossed over that sentence.'

'And the letter, of course, posted from Sicily,' he said, picking up the envelope to show her the postmark. 'Don't you have *any* idea what Florence was going to tell you?' He took the notebook to read the lines again and then held up the birth certificate. 'Perhaps she was going to tell you more about your mother,' he said. 'Because this' – he traced his finger over the columns – 'this Lady Joy Harrison, she's got to be your mother, wouldn't you say?'

There was a pause before Paige replied.

'I'd already thought that, but, oh, Charlie... it's so weird and... such a shock and a muddle.' She flopped back in the chair, looking about the kitchen where she'd eaten so many homely suppers, thinking of evenings she and Aunty Flo had sat together by the fire in the lounge reading or playing board games. There had been plenty of time for her aunt to tell her about her real mother. Why had she kept it secret for so long?

Charlie performed a mock bow, grinning as he said, 'What

does that make you then, Paige? What title does the daughter of a lady hold? Are you an honourable, or something?'

She shook her head. 'I have no idea, Charlie. That's the trouble. All of a sudden, I have no idea who I am.'

'Jeremy will be cock-a-hoop to find out he's marrying an aristo.'

She fell silent.

'That's another thing,' she said. 'Jeremy...' Her voice trailed into a silence that spoke a thousand words. 'I'm not sure about Jeremy either.'

CHAPTER 9

Charlie opened the second bottle for their 'council of war', as he described it. But he held up his fingers in a peace sign at the same time. 'As I see it, this is an emergency. We need to sort you out, Paige, and pretty damn quick.'

They moved from the kitchen to Aunty Flo's sitting room, chilly on this early summer day, and while Paige busied herself with lighting the fire, Charlie found paper and pens in the desk drawer.

'I'm going to quick-fire questions at you and you answer the first thing that comes into your head. No thinking, just belt out your answer.' He raised his glass and they clinked.

'Are you trialling a plot idea?' Paige asked.

'No. I'm asking you the type of questions I put to my characters when I need to get inside their heads.'

Paige took a large swig of her wine, already feeling more relaxed. It may have been because they were on the second bottle, but it was also because Charlie's company was always a breath of fresh air.

'Question one. What is the first thing you think of when you wake up?'

'Tea. Definitely tea,' Paige answered, without hesitation.

'Favourite colour?'

'Green.'

'Who do you miss the most when you're not with them?'

'Aunty Flo,' Paige said, after a slight pause, a frown creasing her brow.

'Favourite book?'

'*William the Outlaw* by Richmal Crompton.'

Charlie snorted and looked at her, bemused. '*Really?*'

'I thought these were quick-fire questions,' Paige said. 'Get on with it.'

'It's your last supper. You can invite one guest. Who would that be?'

'You,' she replied. 'Only if you cooked your scrummy salmon en croute with spinach.'

He smiled before throwing out another question. 'Favourite memory?'

Paige sipped at her wine, looking over the rim of her glass at him: his ginger hair glinting gold in the firelight, his matted Aran sweater with the leather patches on the elbows making him look cosy and huggable. This was a trickier question, however, and she thought for a moment before answering. 'A midnight sail down the creek to a spot where otters made their couch. With Aunty Flo, of course.' She sighed. 'She taught me so much and I took it all for granted. We watched otter cubs play at the edge of the water. I had to keep very still and I remember the moon and stars shining that night. It was perfect.'

'Fab! Final question. Biggest problem on your mind right now.'

'My glass is empty,' she said.

'Be serious!'

Now, she was definitely squiffy. 'Who am I? Did my parents really die in a fire?' Her voice trailed away and she put the glass down on the table and covered her emotions by turning away to chuck another log on the fire.

Charlie looked at his scribbled answers and she waited, listening to the fire crackling comfortingly in the grate.

'You do realise, don't you,' he eventually said, 'that in not a single answer do you mention Jeremy?'

She shrugged. 'You asked me to tell you the first thing that came into my head.'

'Exactly.' He looked at his notes. 'First thing you think of in the morning is tea. Not your future husband. The person you miss most is your aunt. Maybe that's understandable at the moment, but the thing I miss most, for example, is Luke in bed next to me. I miss him every day since the bastard dumped me.'

'You said "thing". Jeremy's not a thing.'

'It would seem not.'

She slumped back against her aunt's saggy feather cushions. 'Have you spoken to Jeremy?'

'I tried to talk to him the other day...'

'And?'

'Not sure if he took it in.'

'You can't go through with this, Paige.'

'I know. I know. Just... everything's happening at once, Charlie. Don't go on. I know what I've got to do.'

'Put the poor bloke out of his misery, then. Put yourself out of your misery too. This is something you can easily solve. What your aunt wanted to tell you is more complicated. Cross Jeremy off your list.'

He pulled her up from the settee. 'Phone him. Phone him *now*.'

She shook her head. 'I'll phone him tomorrow, when you're not here. When you're not listening to what I say. I promise.' She swayed a little as the room spun. 'I'm going to make us a strong coffee and then, let's go for a walk to the creek, Charlie.' She hugged him. 'But thank you for listening to my tangles.'

It was nippy as they made their way down the footpath to the creek, the air carrying the remnants of winter. The path was barely wide enough for them to walk side by side. Willows trailed silver-green stems in the stream that travelled to the wide estuary and they stopped to watch a kingfisher perch on a low branch over the water.

'He's often here. Another treasure that Aunty Flo made me aware of,' Paige said, sad that her aunt was now only to exist in the past tense and memories. The bird flew off and they continued their walk. Charlie interrupted her reveries.

'Jeremy is only the first item you need to tackle on your list, Paige. What about the letter? And the birth certificate?'

'I know, I know. I'll start by trying to track down this Lady Joy Harrison. Perhaps I'll go to the library and see if they've got one of those Debrett books, with lists of poshos.'

'Good plan. And don't forget I'm always at the end of the phone.'

'I do know that. But I need to rediscover my old independence.'

'That's the spirit. Now, let me fill my lungs with luscious Suffolk air before I head back to the smog tomorrow.'

Charlie squeezed her goodbye next morning, telling her he would be checking on her in the next few days to see how she was getting on. She waved as he bumped down the track in his bright green VW. Squirrels felt even emptier without him but she busied herself, stripping the spare bed, procrastinating over the moment she would speak to Jeremy.

She was pegging out the sheets with Aunty Flo's wooden dolly pegs when she heard a car approach, a door slam and then, Jeremy's distinct voice call, 'Where are you, Paige?'

It wasn't like him to be spontaneous and turn up without warning. He had dismissed her on the phone but at least now she could be firm, face to face, and tell him there wasn't going to be a wedding. She pegged out the last pillowcase and went to the front of the cottage, steeling herself for what was to come. Dressed in his city suit, he didn't fit in with the country scene. He didn't fit in with her life at all.

CHAPTER 10

Aunty Flo had never approved of Jeremy and she hadn't liked Paige's giddy new lifestyle, she had sensed that. But she'd never actually said anything much about it to Paige's face. Maybe because Paige was no longer a child. Although, at twenty-nine, she supposed she should know better.

Their noses bumped as Jeremy pulled her to him, and Paige turned her face away. She didn't want him to kiss her. She hadn't had a chance to call him and now here he was, turning up out of the blue, giving her little time to prepare what she wanted to say. How to explain this wasn't just a reaction to Aunty Flo dying, but a bigger realisation. How to explain she'd let herself be swept along with him and his set, without stopping to think? She felt ashamed she'd allowed herself to be seduced by unimportant things.

Her poky flat in Brixton didn't compare with Jeremy's house in Marylebone and his treating her to dinners in Little Venice and Mayfair, as opposed to her simple meals of tinned soup and beans cooked on a tiny tabletop hob. She'd enjoyed the buzz, driving around London in his Aston Martin, rather than using the double decker or Underground. She hadn't been out with many men. So, when Jeremy had produced the box with the ring, it had been like being in a romantic film and she'd said yes.

'Mother will be so pleased,' he'd said, getting up from his knee. He'd proposed formally in a restaurant when the waiter had come along with the Black Forest gateau, with *Marry Me* scrolled on the top with whipped cream. She'd clasped her hands together at his originality. Later, at a Christmas party for the family company, his secretary had told her it had been her idea. 'He's such a clumsy, awkward chap, isn't he? This is the first time he's talked about a girlfriend.'

So, in effect, they'd both been inexperienced in romance. Two shy people bumbling along, helping each other out.

Jeremy's mother had looked her up and down before pecking her cheek when Jeremy had taken her down to Winchester for the first time. 'Thank God! I was beginning to think there would be no little Radleys to carry on the line,' she'd said and Paige had felt as if she was being scrutinised like a farmer assesses a foal or calf at cattle market for breeding potential.

'Jeremy's never brought a girl home before. About time. He's almost forty-five, for goodness' sake. You must be special,' Mrs Radley had said. But Paige often wondered if she was ever going to be special enough for Mrs Radley from Dudley Hall, with its stone lions from the garden centre guarding the bright-red front door.

Weekends at Squirrels had been difficult to fit in as Jeremy had preferred to travel to Dudley Hall whenever they were free, but whenever she could, Paige made sure to visit her aunt.

'New dress? Different hairstyle?' Aunty Flo would greet her with. 'I've planned a roast for tonight and I've made lemon meringue pie.' They'd been her favourites once upon a time but Paige had grown more used to more sophisticated meals: fondues, or pineapple chicken and Chinese food, eaten with chopsticks. Aunty

Flo's meals were rather run-of-the-mill in comparison, except when she prepared lasagne that she'd learned from an Italian 'years ago'. Aunty Flo never complained about the infrequency of her visits. Maybe if she had done, Paige thought, it would have been better and she wouldn't be in this mess right now. But there she went again: putting the blame on everybody else, except herself.

'I'll put the kettle on, Jeremy,' Paige said as they walked down the path.

'Goodo!' Jeremy put his arm around her shoulder and it felt like a dead weight to Paige.

'What you said the other day when you rang... I'm sorry I put the phone down on you, my lovely. Work has been full-on. Two new supermarkets in the counties and I had to sort a new deal this week. Maybe you could come along to Spain with me. Site visit. Oranges. Andalucia.' He talked in his usual fast, staccato way, as if words had to be used sparingly. In case they wasted precious business time.

When they were sitting opposite each other at the scrubbed table in the kitchen, she told herself it was now or never but as she opened her mouth to deliver her badly rehearsed speech, he opened his mouth at the same time.

'I really am sorry, Paige, old thing, I...'

She put her hand out to cover his. 'No. It's me that should be saying sorry. I should have been more straightforward with you the other day on the phone.' Taking a deep breath, she blurted out, 'But I really can't go ahead with the wedding, Jeremy. I'm sorry.'

The look on his face: the hurt in his eyes, the way his mouth gaped open and shut like a fish on land, was awful. He kept shaking his head in disbelief.

'Say something, Jeremy.'

And then the hurt changed to anger and he stood up, his chair crashing to the kitchen quarry tiles. 'What do you want me to say, Paige? I cannot believe this. We're supposed to be marrying in a fortnight. You can't do this. Mother will be furious...'

'But it's not about your mother, is it? It's about *us*.'

'What have I done to deserve this? What can I do? I'll be a laughing stock.'

He wasn't worried about her feelings at all, she realised. He wasn't asking her why she couldn't go through with it. It was as apparent to her now, as night follows day, that she was doing the right thing. A life lived with a man who was more concerned about how his mother and friends reacted was not the man for her. Why hadn't she understood this before?

'We wouldn't have been happy together, Jeremy.'

'Haven't we been happy? *I* have been.'

'We've had fun, yes. But... I don't love you. I mean, I love you, but as a friend—'

'Oh, spare me all that gush. What were you expecting? Love is not like it is in slushy films. Love grows as you go on.'

'What if you realise it's not enough to start with?'

He shrugged his shoulders. 'The death of your aunt has sent you loopy. Give yourself time.'

She shook her head. 'More time will make no difference. I'm sorry, Jeremy.'

'For Christ's sake. Stop saying you're sorry. You're not sorry at all. If you *were* sorry, you'd not be ruining everything. I really don't understand women. Well, Paige. YOU can tell Mother. I'm not going to.'

Hearing that was the final nail in the coffin for Paige. But she would have no qualms about informing Jeremy's overbearing mother that she would not be the girl to become her daughter-in-law or provide her with grandchildren. And somehow, Paige reckoned, Mrs Radley would not be too disappointed either.

Jeremy didn't say goodbye as he slammed the door behind him.

After he'd gone, she sat for a while and then she made up a flask of strong coffee and a sandwich with a slightly out-of-date tin of corned beef she found at the back of Aunty Flo's pantry. Packing her picnic lunch into an old rucksack hanging in the hall, she went for a long walk around the creek.

There was a point along the pebbly shore where reeds grew tall behind a line of trees that had fallen from the eroded shoreline. The branches were like arms of giants fallen asleep and since she'd been a little girl, it had been a place where she and her aunt had come to picnic and get away from jobs. 'Housework can wait,' Aunty would say and scoop up Paige to play in the fresh air. 'But time for having fun will fly by.'

Paige hadn't enjoyed a picnic so much in a long time. She felt a lightness in her head, a weightlessness, her tangle of anxieties dispelled. After she'd eaten, she climbed a trunk and leant back, her face tilted to soak the sun's rays. The beach was hers and, with a smile, she realised her life was hers again. She was free and she jumped down onto the sand. A couple of wobbly cartwheels sealed this recognition and she laughed out loud but then, without warning, she collapsed to the pebbly sand, her head on her knees as tears soaked her jeans. She was free but she was desperately sad. The woman who had been Aunty Flo was gone forever and Paige suddenly felt angry with her for dumping so many unresolved questions. She was free but too free – untethered and utterly lost. Paige stayed crouched on the sand for a long while, her occasional sniffs mingling with the lonely cries of sand plovers and the lapping of the estuary waters until eventually she pulled a tissue from her pocket. *Buck up, old girl*, the wind seemed to whisper. *Life goes on.*

She'd phone Charlie and tell him the deed had been done.

And tomorrow she would start on her hunt to track down this aristocrat who must be her mother. The sun began to slide down behind the sea's edge, dragging with it streaks of crimson. Red sky at night... Tomorrow *must* be a good day, a new beginning. She hoisted the rucksack on her back and almost called out for Bonnie to come, before she remembered she had gone to doggie heaven. She imagined Bonnie and Aunty Flo cushioned together on puffy clouds.

With each stride along the footpath back to Squirrels, questions jumped into Paige's mind: *Why did you want me to have that birth certificate, Aunty Flo? Who is Lady Joy Harrison? Why the big mystery? Why didn't you tell me about her before?*

It was dark when she let herself into the cottage. For a while she sat in Aunty Flo's sagging armchair, feeling confused and lost again. And then she told herself to snap out of it, to light a fire and move on. As she went outside to fetch dry kindling, wind stirred the trees at the end of the garden, their branches swaying like skinny, admonishing fingers. She could almost hear Aunty Flo's raised voice telling her not to let her moods swing up and down like yo-yos and she hurried back indoors to start a cheerful fire.

CHAPTER 11

1943, SUFFOLK

JOY

'It's really too bad of Peggy, leaving us like this,' Lady Celia Harrison said, scraping charcoal edges from her burnt breakfast toast. Blackened crumbs fell onto the freshly laundered white damask tablecloth. 'She's gone and enrolled at that local Land Army headquarters, apparently, to help with the pigs. She could have stayed here to work on our own vegetable garden: Lord knows we need help here too.'

Joy bit her lip. Her mother's mouth was pursed into little corrugations. If she knew how ugly it made her, she would think twice. But more importantly, if she understood how wrong she sounded when she started on these selfish rants, she would keep her thoughts to herself. In fact, this was the practice Joy herself adopted: keeping schtum, grinning and bearing. She knew it was pointless arguing with her mother; it got her nowhere. But it was increasingly hard to stifle her feelings.

'First the gardener and now Peggy.' Her mother's voice was rising to that familiar, petulant whine. 'Somersby Hall is falling apart at the seams. *You'll* have to learn how to cook, Joy, and make yourself useful now she's gone.'

'We could cook together?' Joy suggested. 'I can't manage every day, not now I'm teaching the little ones at the village school. But it might be fun to try our hands in the kitchen. Apparently, you can make no end of delicious cakes from beetroot and parsnips.'

The withering look she received at this suggestion told her what Mother thought of the idea and Joy avoided confrontation by going to the sideboard for more bread.

'Are you sure you want another slice, Joy? You won't fit into that new frock we altered. There's not much leeway on the seams, you know.'

Lady Harrison slit open a letter from the top of the pile by the side of her plate and gasped. 'Impossible! We simply can't.' Her hand went to the pearls at her neck and she thrust the paper at her daughter.

Joy skimmed through the official requisition letter. Somersby Hall was under consideration for use as a convalescent home for army officers. An inspection was planned within the next fortnight.

'But that's wonderful, Mother,' Joy said. 'We can at last contribute something. The two of us are rattling around here since Daddy died...' She racked her brains for ideas to convince her mother. 'There'll no doubt be a cook and gardener provided, so that will solve our domestic problems.'

'We cannot *possibly* be expected to share our home with all and sundry. What would your father have said?'

'I think Father would have been ready to help with the war effort. And, in any case, when it comes to it, we won't have any say. If the government want Somersby Hall, then it will happen.'

'It's too bad. But what about the paintings? The furniture

and carpets. And all the family silver and chinaware?' Her face now quite pink, Lady Harrison looked around the grand dining room where oil paintings of her deceased husband's aristocratic ancestors stared down, their eyes seeming to follow as they listened in on the discussion. 'They'll break everything. We shall have to pack anything precious away and hide it in the attic. And I've no doubt our treasures will be looted.'

'Oh, *Mother*. You're... impossible. In fact, I cannot believe how selfish and thoughtless and... difficult you always are...'

Joy couldn't suffer her mother any longer. She slammed her porcelain cup down on its saucer and rushed from the room. Three Labradors, who had been dozing in a patch of sunshine streaming through the French windows, leapt up to follow Joy as she escaped. It wasn't their usual walkies time and their tails wagged ecstatically at the extra treat.

She strode to the stables and tacked up Dream, stroking his sturdy flanks before pulling her riding hat from a hook in the stall and mounting her favourite horse. Within a couple of minutes, the Irish Hunter, girl and dogs were racing down the track leading from Somersby Hall. They skirted the edges of the ornamental lake where ducks, startled by the rumpus, squawked indignantly and flapped across the water. The group took the track that encircled the woods and made for the edge of the grounds left to grow wild now that staff were hard to obtain, the able-bodied men of Somersby Village having enlisted for war.

There hadn't been time to don jodhpurs in the flight from her mother and Joy's skirt crept up her thighs as she rode across the grounds. She urged Dream on, squeezing his broad flanks with her strong calves, putting as much distance as she could between herself and her unbearable mother.

Conscious of the dogs tiring, she slowed to a trot as girl and animals made their way into the periphery of the woods and a clearing where an old beech tree, its towering branches supported by a thick trunk, had stood for over one hundred years. She slid off the horse, tied the reins to a branch and climbed her way to a treehouse her father had built for her when she was only six years old. She could have climbed with her eyes shut, so often had she come to this place of refuge. Father had always found her there when she'd disappeared to be free of Mother, who never ventured this far. She leant back against the trunk as she thought of how utterly futile her life had become. What was she doing, aged twenty-seven, wasting her life in a country house in Suffolk, looking after a cantankerous old woman she didn't love and who patently didn't love her? All because she'd promised her father on his deathbed that she would look after Mother.

Right now, she should be helping more towards the war effort. Doing her bit. Work at the village school, although important, seemed trivial. Since December 1941, there had been compulsory conscription of women, unless involved in essential work and, deep down, Joy felt teaching and Mother were not essential work. Rows of posters hanging outside the village hall – *Dig for Victory, Become a Nurse, Your Country Needs You!* – filled her with guilt every time she passed. The latest – a picture of the countryside that could easily have been surrounding the walls of Somersby Hall, a soldier pointing to the observer, the question: *Isn't this worth fighting for? Enlist Now* – always rubbed salt in her guilty wounds. Of course the Suffolk countryside was beautiful, but there was more to the fight than preserving the nation's hallowed turf.

Frustrated, curtains of beech leaves hiding her from the world, she decided her mother could jolly well fend for herself. If the house was requisitioned, there would be other people around to tend to Mother. The job she was doing at the village school, helping the little ones read, could easily be filled by someone else. Joy wanted to experience life in the raw. And that wasn't going to happen if she stayed at Somersby Hall.

That evening, Joy stood before the cheval mirror in her bedroom and pulled a face. Mother's hand-me-down Edwardian frock, the pale-pink lace material doing nothing for her blonde colouring and straining at her hips, was hideous. She found her nail scissors and snipped off the white bow sewn to the front of the waist, making her look like a five-foot-nine wrapped-up Easter egg, and flung it to the floor. She had inherited her father's large bone structure rather than Mother's petite figure. It was easier to pull on slacks or jodhpurs than a frock and she had always been a tomboy, preferring outdoor life to being stifled indoors.

Her eyes strayed to her favourite photograph by her bedside, taken arm in arm with her father on the terrace of the family villa in Sicily on a last visit before the war. Mother hadn't wanted to come along and father and daughter had enjoyed rare, precious days exploring the coastline in a hired sailing boat, anchoring in isolated coves, diving into clear, aquamarine waters to look for wrecks. She remembered how the years had seemed to drop from her father, how they had laughed over nothing at times, spending evenings hunting out simple trattorias visited by locals. He had never divulged how ill he had been, how little time they would have together. His death had left a gaping hole in her life. She had to stop herself poring over her photo album every night: reliving visits they'd made to the Greek temples of Agrigento and Selinunte, the theatre at Taormina – places Mother had never wanted to visit. At times, she felt angry he had left her alone. 'If only I'd known, Daddy.' She spoke out loud to his photograph, tracing her fingers over his image, biting back tears which would only ruin the makeup she so hated to wear. She tore her gaze back to the mirror.

'I suppose your face isn't too horrific and your hair will do,' she said aloud to her reflection. Long, thick and golden blonde, it looked better loose than tied up in the bun she scraped back for horse riding or outside activities. As a last-minute concession to femininity, she pulled a deep red rose from the vase on her dressing table and stuck it in her hair before sighing and trudging down the stairs, reciting in her head lines from Father's favourite poem: *Forward, the Light Brigade...*

When she'd been a young child and sent off to bed on the evenings of her mother's dinner parties, she'd sneak from her bedroom onto the landing after Nanny had tucked her in, and peer through the fluted banisters at the guests as they arrived. Now, as she descended the carpeted stairs, careful not to trip on the hem of her floaty dress, she glanced down at the group of usual victims congregated in the hall, sipping small glasses of last year's home-made apple cider made by Peggy. It was a substitute for the dry sherry Lady Harrison could no longer get her hands on. This evening she spied a couple she had never seen before: slightly younger than the usual vintage of Mother's county circle. She wondered who they were. The man leant on a walking stick and the woman with him was tall and elegant, wearing a simply cut blue velvet dress that Joy would have preferred to Mother's discard.

She found herself seated between the couple. Lieutenant Colonel Harry Ponting introduced himself and his wife, Lydia. He reminded her of Father in his easy manners, and in fact, early on in chit-chat over soup, he'd confided that the two of them had both been up at Oxford.

'You were at Oxford too, I believe,' he said, his comment more of a statement than question.

'Yes, back in thirty-seven,' she said. 'Although it seems a life-time ago now. I honestly think I got in because of Daddy. We women were still made to feel as if we were honoured guests rather than undergraduates. Still, I have my degree in Italian and French and that is what I wanted.' She fiddled with the bread roll on her side plate, crumbling it up as she spoke. 'Not that I've used it much. Except for when Daddy and I popped over to our place in Sicily before the war.'

He nodded and his beautiful wife asked, 'So, what are you doing at the moment?'

Joy hesitated, not wanting to sound bitter. 'I... it's been hard for Mother since Father died. I came back from London to look after her and I've been helping out at the local school. But...' She didn't finish her sentence. She still hadn't talked to her mother about wanting to leave Somersby and it didn't feel right to tell two complete strangers first.

'I hear a big "but" in your voice,' Mrs Ponting continued.

Joy glanced towards the head of the table, checking Mother couldn't hear. Her head was bent close to the vicar's wife, no doubt exchanging news of some minor village scandal. It was safe to talk.

'I want to do more, you see. I feel guilty stuck here when everybody else is making such an effort. We received notice this morning of possible requisitioning of the Hall for a convalescent hospital, so I'm hoping if Mother moves into the east wing, she won't be alone and I can apply to move away to do something worthwhile.'

The lieutenant colonel didn't say anything, his wife doing all the talking at this stage.

'It must be lonely for you being marooned in this place. No young people. Are you engaged, Joy?'

'No, no. There's nobody on the horizon and, actually, I'm not too bad in my own company. But I do hate feeling so useless.'

'Well. You must come and see us up in London as soon as

possible, take in a show or something. Don't hide yourself away, Joy.'

A few days later, with her mother issuing orders left, right and centre to the nursing staff and VAD volunteers recently arrived to rearrange the rooms in Somersby Hall into hospital wards, the post girl arrived with a letter for Joy.

> *Dear Joy,*
>
> *It was so interesting meeting you at Somersby.*
>
> *Harry and I have not stopped talking about you. Can you come up to London to the Victoria Hotel next Monday? We can run through some ideas I've had.*
>
> *Call me on Kensington 4432 to confirm arrangements.*
>
> *Yours,*
>
> *Lydia Ponting*

Mother was fine now, Joy concluded. There were plenty of people to help her move into the other wing, from where she would doubtless continue to pontificate. The new arrivals had the measure of her, however, and Joy had smothered a grin the previous afternoon when Mother had begun to fuss over the sight of dozens of beds being erected in the dining room, complaining how the casters would ruin the carpet. Matron, as formidable a female as Mother, had turned to her and suggested she might like to help her girls, as she called the squad of young VADs and nurses, to roll up the carpet and push it to one side of the room. 'It's not sanitary for our purposes,' Matron had said. 'Very moth-eaten, a magnet for dog hairs. Goodness knows how many germs it's been harbouring over the years.'

Mother's eyes had rounded and her mouth gaped. Needless to say, she hadn't got down on her hands and knees to help move the Royal Aubusson carpet. She'd turned on her heels with an indignant, 'Well, really!' as she left the room.

Joy looked forward to her London visit. Not least because it would give her a break from Mother.

CHAPTER 12

1940, ISLE OF MAN

SAVIO

In his dream, Savio is playing on the beach with his brother whilst their parents collect driftwood at the sea's edge, beckoning them to help, otherwise there will be no picnic. The sun bakes his limbs and he's looking forward to tucking into Sicilian *cannoli* filled with fresh ricotta and pistachio.

Once again he woke to reality and the odour of horse droppings, the fouler stench of human excrement somewhere near his nose. He was confined in a three-foot wide by six-foot long wooden partitioned stall, a small ventilation grating set high in the far stone wall letting in measly light. The cobbled floor was damp, a metal bucket stood in the corner for his business and a manger filled with straw was his bed.

Holding on to the side of the manger, he struggled to his feet. His head smarted and he touched his fingers to his tender temple, flinching at the pain. 'Oi!' he shouted at the top of his voice. 'What the hell am I doing in this place? Let me out.'

A heavily accented male voice answered from the other side of the partition. 'Do not waste your energy, my friend. The guards are busy with their English cups of tea.' His tone was sarcastic. 'Do not dare to disturb them during this *important* time.'

'What is this place?' Savio asked, going to the door and finding it locked. 'Let me out,' he shouted again, kicking at the wood.

'You are wasting your time. This is the camp prison. Best not to make the guards angry. They've kept me in here another two weeks for my protests.'

Savio slumped down on the uncomfortable manger. It was not right he was locked up like this. Yes, he had reacted aggressively against the soldiers when the terrible news of his parents' drowning had been delivered, but who would not have done so, after learning they were now alone in the world, their family totally gone? And the thing was, he had done *nothing* wrong. It was a bloody nightmare. His parents had been forced from their home, despite living in England for twenty-six years, despite having two children born in England, one of whom had died in training to defend their country. They were being treated like scum, without recourse to trial or jury. He was still ignorant of the exact details of his parents' deaths, other than they'd been lost at sea. Again, through the fault of the English. His heart filled with hatred for the country he'd considered his homeland.

'Why are you in here?' he asked the man in the neighbouring cell.

'I tried to escape. In a sailing boat.'

'So, it's possible to get out of this camp?'

'The guards are lazy. They are not good at taking roll calls. They don't always check.'

This was an encouraging piece of information. Though, Savio didn't fancy the idea of crossing to the mainland in a flimsy boat. He'd never learned to swim.

'What is your story?' the man asked.

'I hit an officer. Maybe another guard too. It's all a bit hazy.

They told me my parents were dead. Drowned. Bastards... we've done nothing wrong. I shouldn't be cooped up like this. It's madness. Simply because my mother and father came from Italy, we're considered the enemy. I was angry. I lashed out. And I'd do it again.'

'Well, we are allies now, my friend. I am German. If you are Italian, then we are in this fight together.'

'I was born in England. I'm no ally of yours.'

Resentment and confusion washed over him again. The situation was ridiculous.

The two men fell silent and about ten minutes later, Savio heard heavy footsteps entering the stable complex. The door to his makeshift cell was unlocked by a burly middle-aged man who stepped in with a metal dish and beaker.

'So, you've decided to wake up at last. Here's your tea.'

'I want to talk to whoever's in charge,' Savio said. 'I shouldn't be in here.'

'The way I see it, you shouldn't have given my mate a black eye either, not to say tried to throttle the living daylights out of the guvnor.'

'How long am I going to be in here?'

The guard shrugged. 'Guv does his rounds in the mornings. I suggest you calm down in the meanwhile and eat this. There's nothing else until breakfast.'

Savio glared at him but decided to take his advice. Yet again, his quick temper hadn't helped and he remembered his old neighbour Liam's words about choosing his fights. This definitely had not been a good choice.

On the following morning, Savio was ordered to 'make himself lively' and was escorted by an armed guard from the prison who marched him to a different camp compound in Hutchinson Square, formed from another row of Edwardian houses. While he waited, he made out the letters on the door – *Captain Daniels*.

'Come!' a firm voice answered at the guard's knock.

A uniformed man in his late forties, whom Savio had never seen before, stood to shake hands with Savio. 'Captain Daniels,' he announced.

'I'd say it's a pleasure, sir, but...' Savio replied, surprised at the officer's courteous greeting.

'Sit down, Mr Rizzo.' The officer gestured to the chair opposite his desk. 'And, Corporal, you can wait outside.'

When they were alone, Captain Daniels looked down at a typed report on his blotter and then, clasping his hands on the desk said, 'I've read what happened, Mr Rizzo. And I'm very sorry for your loss.'

This floored Savio for a moment and he felt his shoulders relax on sensing he might be finally about to receive a fair hearing. 'I was upset, sir. I'd like to know what exactly happened to my folks.'

'Yes, indeed.' Daniels paused. 'I'm afraid your parents were put on a ship bound for Canada...'

'*What?*'

'Along with other internees who were accepted for immigration. There were more than seven hundred Italians on board the *Arandora Star*, many of your parents' age. I regret to say it was torpedoed less than twenty-four hours after leaving port by a German submarine.' He paused. 'Apparently most of the elderly were below deck and...' He stopped again, embarrassed. 'There were insufficient lifeboats and... as a result, great loss of life.'

Savio bent his head, willing the red mist to dissipate. 'Why would my parents want to leave for Canada when they had a home and a business in London? When their only remaining son was here – confined on an island off England? Why were they on that ship in the first place?' He shook his head, his fists clenched at his sides, and looked up helplessly at the senior officer.

'I don't know the answers to your questions, I'm afraid, son, but I do know there have been hasty decisions made by our government, and the *Arandora Star*, regretfully, had no escort. The decision-makers say they were trying to protect your people from xenophobic attacks – from the hysteria in our nation concerning foreigners and spies—'

'The thing is, we *aren't* foreigners, are we?' Savio interrupted. 'How many times?' He clenched his fists tighter, and then with great self-control repeated in a calmer voice, although seething inside. 'How many times do I have to say that I – am – not – Italian. I might look it, but I was born in London. I'm British.'

The camp commandant shrugged his shoulders. 'Regretfully, you are not the only one in this position, Mr Rizzo. We've already sent hundreds of internees back to Liverpool.'

'Well, send me back too.' Savio leant back in his chair, staring hopefully at the man opposite him, who seemed to be on his side.

'I'm afraid I can't do that. Not until you prove to us that you aren't going to be a troublemaker. It doesn't do to punch a senior officer, you know. If I may give you one valuable piece of advice: keep those volatile fists in your pockets next time you have cause to flare up.'

He read down his notes again. 'There's a space here in Hutchinson, or "P" Camp as we prefer to call it. And I'm prepared to do the very best I can for you, Rizzo, in view of the tragic circumstances.' He glanced at his notes again. 'Savio, isn't it? I think you'll find Hutchinson not such a bad place.'

In Hutchinson, Savio met up again with Pieter, his artistic friend from the boat. He came to find Savio on the second day, carrying the suitcase that Savio had thought he would never see again.

'I kept this safe for you, Savio,' Pieter said as they shook hands.

'Thank you, my friend.' Savio took the case and opened it, a huge sadness filling his heart as the loss of his parents flooded back. It was far emptier than before, containing one or two poignant reminders of his parents: a cotton pinafore of his mother's, his father's shaving brush and cream, as well as the chain his mother had pushed into his pocket, the very last time they had seen each other. He pulled it out and rubbed his fingers over the strange pendant. The metal on the three legs extending from a man's face, like parts of a wheel, was tarnished in places: a gaudy souvenir of Sicily but precious to his mother. He remembered again how it used to hang above his parents' bed, next to a sprig of dried olive twig from Palm Sunday stuck down the back of a picture of the Madonna and Child. The pendant was a simple reminder of their home island where his parents had planned to return one day. 'You can take a man's body away from his island but you can never take away his heart,' his father would say when he was feeling maudlin after too many glasses of wine. Remarkably controlled, that only happened at Christmas or Easter when his mother and her Italian friends would prepare special feasts to share with the Soho community: platters of home-made *busiati* macaroni with a sauce of garlic, almonds, basil and tomatoes, fried fish and sweet dishes of *cannoli* stuffed with ricotta, expensive as it was difficult to make in England.

He remembered his father telling him of a peasant who had travelled over the seas to England with them who'd confided that in his suitcase he had packed a small sack of Sicilian earth. 'So, when I grow my vegetables, they will think they are in *bella* Sicilia,' he'd said. This story and similar anecdotes were repeated frequently, as if, by repeating them, they would cement the ambitions to one day return to their homeland.

Savio's eyes filled with tears as he caressed the pendant and held it tight to his heart. He knew he had been a disappointment to his parents at times, but he vowed he would do his best to return to their birthplace one day. A black-and-white photograph of their stone house on the handkerchief of land in the countryside outside Syracuse had hung in the salon and his father would show it proudly to new customers when they asked him where he was from. He'd point at it with his scissors and say, 'That's my estate. It might not be Buckingham Palace, but it's my little piece of *paradiso*. One day, me and the signora, we're going back. To harvest grapes in the sunshine.'

Savio intended to do it on their behalf.

The months moved slowly for Savio and he settled into a routine of sorts. On a cold but sunny October morning, he was working hard on a farm near Port Erin, on the opposite side of the island about fifteen miles west of Douglas. Each morning a party of agricultural workers was taken in trucks from Douglas to help on the land. With most of the young male Manx having enlisted, the island needed a workforce to help plant and dig potatoes and tend to cattle, so the internees were put to good use. Savio had volunteered, because it was a way of getting out of the camp confines, and he took advantage of the drive along the bumpy tracks to sit at the back and observe the scenery and commit to memory the lie of the land.

The island was not short of food and everyone ate well. As the truck drove along the high street, Savio took in the butcher's shop where great hams and sides of beef and lamb hung in the window. The guards were always telling them how lucky they were to be living on an island of plenty, how the newspapers were full of complaints from mainlanders about strict rationing, whilst shops in Douglas had everything on their shelves. But Savio didn't care about food. All he craved was freedom. At night he lay plotting how he would make his escape, using everything he had mentally collected about the island's geography. One day he would get away. He had no doubt. It was the one thing that kept him going.

A day earlier, one of the guards on duty, a newly conscripted young civilian called Arthur, had fainted whilst watching over Savio's small group as they prepared a new field for cabbage planting. Savio had gone to his rescue. The guard was armed with a rifle and Savio had thought afterwards that it would have been the easiest thing in the world to have stolen the rifle to use for an escape. But Arthur, a civilian who chatted amiably with Savio, was a decent chap and he was obviously in great pain. And Savio, when he escaped, intended it to be peaceful. There was no point in making more trouble for himself if he was caught with a gun.

He'd lifted the lad on his back, fireman-style, and carried him to the farmhouse from where the farmer's wife telephoned the cottage hospital. Savio had saved Arthur's life – he turned out to have acute appendicitis. He had earned three days free of work and a commendation for services rendered from Captain Daniels. When Savio had asked if this meant he could now be liberated from the island, the officer had said, 'You're going in the right direction, Savio. Keep it up and we'll see. There might be the possibility of volunteering for the Pioneer Corps.'

'Come again, sir?'

'Helping behind enemy lines. Churchill is all for this new scheme. He believes his aliens could be helpful after all...'

Curbing his impatience all this time had been hard, but he was slowly learning to control his temper and he took Captain

Daniels' information on board. Everybody liked Daniels and they'd taken to referring to him as the camp father.

Savio and Pieter spent their free time together. The German lad was perfectly content to stay put in Hutchinson. His friend was the only person with whom he'd shared his secret desire to escape but Savio knew Pieter was discreet and, moreover, had no intention of escaping himself. 'I am happy to lap up what I can while I'm here,' he'd said. 'With all that is on offer here, it is like the university I could not attend back in Germany.'

Savio did not tell him that study was the last thing on his mind, that he struggled with reading. He still felt ashamed about his near illiteracy.

Artists, musicians who formed their own orchestra, and Nobel Prize winners offered lectures in the gardens within the square in front of the Edwardian houses and Savio had reluctantly at first joined Pieter in a watercolour class.

He found it relaxing and he wasn't bad at it. When he was approached by a middle-aged Italian and asked to paint an artistic likeness from a dog-eared photo of his family, he'd accepted. 'Makes me feel warm when I look at it,' the man had said. 'I miss them too much.' More requests followed and it became yet another of Savio's sidelines. Slowly and steadily, he was putting earnings aside for his escape.

'You should learn a new language while you're here. There's even a teacher offering Chinese,' Pieter said.

'Why would I want to learn Chinese? And, anyway, I'm not good on grammar and stuff,' Savio admitted.

'You could teach me Italian and I could teach you German. You wouldn't need to write anything down.' Pieter had understood Savio struggled with reading and writing. He'd picked up on it quite early, when Savio had found difficulty reading information posted on the noticeboard. 'We could simply speak with

each other and not write anything down, Savvy. It's always good
to have another language up your sleeve.'

'Whenever am I going to find German useful?'

Pieter had shrugged. 'You never know.'

So, while they painted and sketched together, they shared
conversations in their mother tongues and Savio turned out to
be an excellent mimic. Pieter asked for explanations about
tenses or idioms, but Savio could only tell him he didn't know
why. 'It's just what we say. I can't explain.'

Soon Savio was able to conduct an everyday conversation in
basic German.

'Your accent is not bad. Most British sound British when
they speak German,' Pieter said.

'Maybe it's because I grew up listening to another
language?'

'Yes, you definitely have an ear for it. *Das ist sehr gut, mein
Freund.* Well done, pal.'

Savio's roommate in this camp was Eugenio: an excellent
swimmer and a quiet, unassuming man. Born of Italian
parents like Savio, he was also indignant about being
interned. He wore his jumper with Great Britain sewn along
the front in protest every day. He had represented Britain in
the 1936 Olympics and Captain Daniels allowed him to
train. Every morning he was escorted by two guards to the
beach.

'I don't know how to swim,' Savio confessed to Eugenio on
the evening of his second free day from work awarded by
Captain Daniels as they were settling down for the night.
Eugenio was doing his nightly press-ups and Savio watched in
admiration. 'I never had the chance. When I went to Sicily I
stayed in the shallows, watching my cousins. They swam like
fish. Is it difficult?'

'Obviously, swimming's not like walking. And if you're
afraid of water, then it's hard. But I believe everybody should

know how to swim. Tell you what, why don't you come with me next week?'

'But how? Won't it be obvious for the guards?'

'They're lazy. They usually disappear for their cooked breakfast at the café as soon as we're down at the beach. They know I'm not about to swim across to Liverpool. I'll give you a lesson once I've put in my own training. It will make a change for me to have somebody to help. And the guards like me.'

It was all very well attending art sessions in Hutchinson, but no way was Savio going to rot away on this island forever. Three free days from work were all very well, but it was obvious by now he was not going to be released from the island. For all Captain Daniels' promises, nothing changed.

It was a brisk October morning when Savio accompanied Eugenio to the beach, but it didn't seem to affect Eugenio. Savio watched him slice through the water in an effortless crawl and swim back to shore in a peculiar stroke that Eugenio told him was butterfly, his speciality. 'I didn't win any medals back in 1936, but I was proud to take part.'

'Doesn't it anger you that even though you were asked to represent Great Britain you've been banged up on this island?'

'I'm resentful, yes. But call me a coward, I'd far prefer to be here than fighting. It's not such a bad life. I'm not married, got no family left to worry about me. I'm happy to bide my time here on this island of plenty until the war ends.'

Savio started near the shore but even so he swallowed a fair amount of water the first time, spluttering and coughing it up from his lungs until he wanted to be sick, but by the time the guards dawdled back from their morning tea, he could at least stay afloat.

'Best get out and do press-ups,' said Eugenio. 'I've told them you're a professional swimmer too. No need to give them reason to doubt it. We'll do this little by little. When can you come again?'

Savio sniggered. 'Well, they won't think I'm a professional swimmer if they watch. Tell you what: I work on the fields above Port Erin. There's a beach below that I can sneak to for practice and maybe I can join you on Sundays?'

Eugenio shook his head. 'The guards are different at weekends.' He thought for a while. 'We'll do strengthening exercises in the evenings.' He pinched Savio's shoulders. 'You need to bulk up for more power. Sea swimming against the waves and tides is not as easy as swimming in a pool.'

'Why are you helping me?' Savio asked.

'Why not? There's nothing else to do. You can give me free haircuts in exchange.'

Cutting hair was another of Savio's sidelines. In exchange for camp-issued currency that could only be exchanged in Hutchinson, he offered cuts and wet shaves, using his father's brush from the suitcase and a pair of scissors he'd bought from a fellow who had been a tailor on the mainland. Arthur, the guard with appendicitis, had given him a razor when he'd asked Savio if there was anything he would like by way of thanks.

'Leave it with me. We get them issued with our kit. I'll tell them I lost mine. They might dock my wages, but if that's what you want, I'll do my best,' Arthur had said.

The camp-issued currency system had worked at the outset but now Savio was earning real currency, which he was hiding away for when the time came to leave. There was a loose floorboard under his side of the double bed where he kept his earnings in an old Erinmore Mixture tobacco tin.

When Savio was not working at Port Erin or going on his occasional trips to the beach, he built up his strength by jogging around the perimeter fence of the communal gardens on a fitness regime Eugenio had drawn up for him. If he was to row across the Irish Sea to Liverpool, he needed to be strong. The sea was the most likely route for his escape.

CHAPTER 13

SPRING 1942 ONWARDS

Two years had dragged by for Savio. The field where he was planting young leeks was on the edge of a gentle slope that looked over the lighthouse in Erin Bay. It was the first warm spring day and he was not the only one eager to plunge into the sea.

He looked up from where he was kneeling on the ploughed earth to the sounds of shrieks and laughter wafting from the beach. Half a dozen women were splashing each other and he smiled at their happiness. One of them climbed from the shallows to execute a shallow dive and he saw she was naked. He let out a low whistle and stood up to watch. Yes, he had drawn naked women in his art sessions with Pieter; he'd had fun trying to emulate Matisse's Fauvism figures, but it had been too long since he'd seen an undressed female in real life. He held up a hand to shield his eyes from the bright sunlight and the woman caught a glimpse of him and shrieked again, shaking her fist. She shouted in German and he understood the gist: she was warning the others, who ducked down to conceal their breasts below the seawater. Then, she yelled at him in broken English. 'Turn your back. We want get out. Water freezing.'

He obliged. Maybe he shouldn't have been snooping. But he wondered if they would come again. He had heard that almost the whole of Port Erin, both the residential and holiday villages, had been taken over, along with its smaller neighbour, Port Saint Mary, to house women and children, but he'd never seen them before. Somebody had said they weren't restricted behind barbed wire, as in the male camps, and he wondered how he could wangle a visit to the beach.

Two weeks later, he decided to take a chance. He told Arthur – the same young man whom he had saved from his appendicitis attack – that he was going down to the beach to rescue a sheep escaped from the field and that he would probably only be a quarter of an hour. He slithered down the hill. The women weren't there but it was a warm day, he'd worked hard under the sun and the sea called. He stripped before plunging into the salty water and swam a brisk twenty crawl strokes. He was growing stronger with Eugenio's training and enjoyed the sensation of water around his naked limbs. For a while he floated on his back, squinting his eyes against the sun breaking through cotton-wool clouds, before returning reluctantly to shore.

It was then he saw the young woman who had shouted at him before. She was seated on a rock like a mermaid watching him, naked save for a thin towel wrapped around her hips, long blonde plaits falling below full breasts. He felt himself harden and bent to retrieve his trousers, to cover himself.

The woman laughed softly: a seductive sound that reeled him in like a fish on a hook. 'No need, my friend. I think your need is like mine,' she said, with a wink. He didn't stop to think twice. Where the cliff sloped to the sand a hollow had been formed by incoming tides, hidden from view by a rock fall, and she spread her thin towel on the ground and lay back, smiling with anticipation as she waited. She was like a cat, Savio thought, and he would make her purr with pleasure.

Her skin was soft, her body strong as she pulled him up to ·sit so that she could coil her strong legs about him. It had been too long since he'd made love and he was greedy for her. He ran his hands over her body and she moaned, rubbing herself against him and at the same time, murmuring to him to slow down, 'Langsam, langsam.'

They smoked afterwards, lying on their backs as they shared a cigarette, passing it to each other to inhale. Savio was drowsy. The woman had been demanding and he had been only too willing to satisfy her lust.

'What's your name?' he asked, using the German he had learned from Pieter.

'You don't need to know,' she said, taking the cigarette from his mouth to share. Her reply was in English, more fluent than his patchy German.

'Will you be here again?'

'On which days do you work in the fields?' she asked.

'All of next week and the following. There are three fields to sow.'

She shrugged. 'Then, take your chances.'

'It's not easy. There are guards.'

'If I'm here, I'll leave my towel at the sea's edge.'

A shrill whistle pierced the air and he scrambled to his feet. 'Bloody hellfire. I have to go.' In his haste, as he pulled on his trousers, he caught his foot on the material and stumbled to the gritty sand.

She laughed. 'You have to practise more, my friend, if you want to be fit for the job.'

He ran across the sand and reached the point where he had slithered down an hour earlier. When he turned to glance back, she was still there and she lifted a hand in a languid wave.

Arthur was waiting for him at the top. 'And the sheep?' he asked.

'It must have fallen. Lost at sea...'

'One of those, eh?' Arthur said, a grin lighting up his face. 'Wagging its tail behind him? Did you see Little Bo Peep too while you were down there?'

Savio looked at the young guard. 'I have some money saved. How much for you to keep your trap shut?'

He shook his head. 'Nah. You're all right, mate. You saved my life back when I was sick. But don't make a habit of it. I can't cover for you again. I need this job and I don't need trouble. My girl's on the island and I want to stay here too.'

Savio nodded. 'Understood.'

He managed to see the woman once more. They were down to one guard the following week. Arthur had reported in sick and Savio took advantage, making sure to work again at the far corner of the field near the edge of the hill, telling the guard he had to clear brambles. He put his back into it, removing his shirt as he worked up a sweat. The men had nicknamed the guard on duty today Porkie. He was obese and lazy, easily buttered up with bribes of biscuits and breads baked by Hutchinson's talented Austrian pastry chef. This morning Porkie had fallen asleep, seated against a tree trunk, his rifle on the grass beside him, and the other internees had slowed down with their work too.

The towel was there, held down by stones, the fringes of the thin material flapping in the sea breeze like beckoning fingers. He scrambled down the grassy slope and raced towards the hollow in the cliff. They were ready for each other, her feline fingernails digging into his back as he drove into her. This time she spoke more, asking if he was Italian, which camp he was in, what he did in peacetime. He told her his story, not omitting his resentment at being cooped up and his frustration at still being on the island.

'And you?' he asked.

'Married to a Scotsman who accused me of being a spy. His way of getting rid of me and my son,' she said, spitting into the sand. 'He had a thing going on with another woman. Unfortunately, he's in the police and they prefer to listen to his side of the story. She's welcome to the bastard. He's useless. And boring in bed; she'll soon find that out.'

'No trial and jury for you either, then? What's your name?' he asked.

'You can call me Lili.' She laughed. 'Not my real name. But it's good to pretend.'

She began to sing a snatch of the popular German song, her voice low, seductive and slightly out of tune. '... *Darling, I remember the way you used to wait, time would come for roll call, Time for us to part.* The words are different in German, you know,' she said, breaking into song in her own language and then stopping abruptly. 'Have you a cigarette?'

'Not today. But I'll get some for next time.'

'Who says there'll be a next time?'

He pulled on his trousers; there was no time to play these games. 'I have to get back,' he said, doing up his buttons.

'There's a boat moored further down the bay. Nobody ever uses it,' she said. 'When you talked about escaping, I thought you might take me with you.'

'I'll think about it.'

'Well, don't think about it for too long, Savio.' His name sounded strange from her lips – the way she pronounced the 's'. Hard. Guttural. Foreign.

A few weeks later, he found another excuse to put to Arthur. 'Shall I fetch driftwood for the brew-up?' he asked, pushing a full packet of smokes into the guard's hands. 'We're running low and... well, workers and guards alike need a strong cuppa in their billycans if they're to work efficiently.'

Arthur gave him a long look. 'I'm giving you thirty minutes maximum to fetch wood from the beach. Thirty minutes,' he repeated, tapping the face of his watch. 'Any longer and I'll send out a search party.'

How and from where Arthur would summon a search party would be a wonder, Savio thought. Nevertheless, he took the young man's warning on board. It served no purpose to rub him up the wrong way or indeed to get him into trouble. Savio knew when he was on to a good thing.

Lili wasn't there and he left half a dozen cigarettes for her on the ledge where her towel was folded up, before wandering further down the beach to have a nosy at the boat she had mentioned. To cover himself, in case he was apprehended, he gathered driftwood as he went, aware that time was ticking by fast. The tide was in and he waded over to the anchored boat. It wasn't very big: fourteen feet long at most. The sail wrapped around the mast was torn in places, and paint was peeling from the sides of the boat, but there was no water slopping around in the bottom, so it wasn't about to sink. He hastened up the cliff path with his meagre bundle of sticks.

'Not much luck today?' Arthur said, one eyebrow raised.

'The tide had only brought in these. But there's enough to burn for a brew,' Savio said, throwing the bundle down.

'We're finishing off in these fields today. So, it's time to bid farewell to Erin Bay for the time being.' He offered Savio a cigarette, lowering his voice as he bent nearer to light it. 'Thanks for these, Mr Savvy.'

In one sense, Savio minded. Gone was the chance of more snatched moments with the delicious Lili. On the other hand, it meant he would keep his nose clean. Plus, he had found a boat. He had to get away from the Isle of Man. Before he went crazy.

· · ·

Savio was alone in the front garden, caged in by the wire fencing like a frustrated cockerel. Pieter was sick, so Savio was painting on his own. A bleak illustration of dark mountains and broody skies was the result of his mood that morning, although in fact the day was crisp and the sun glinted on a calm sea. What the hell was he still doing here? He'd been so controlled with his emotions but being with Lili, making love to her on the beach, feeling free for those few wanton minutes, had served to scratch an itch. But even if he escaped, what would he do? Where would he go? Being in the camp, living with Germans and people from other countries had shown him that not all Germans were his enemy. The British authorities were, though. They were the cause of him being cooped up here like a bloody cockerel unable to strut his stuff. So even if he escaped, he didn't have the urge to fight for England. England had stamped out any nationalistic pride he'd had by wrongly imprisoning him and sending his parents and brother to their deaths. He dipped a thick brush into the black paint, scrawled it over the paper in zigzags and added a splash of brown, paint splattering over the page in a crazy pattern. He ripped the page from his sketchbook and screwed it up, the paint smearing his fingers, and threw it to the far end of the fencing where it rolled in the sea breeze and escaped through the bars. His paper could escape but he couldn't. A guard called out, 'Hey, Rizzo! Pick up your litter.'

He lay awake for hours at nights, thinking over his plans and eventually, several weeks later, as his roommate slept, Savio crept from his bed and down the stairs, avoiding the creaky tenth step from the bottom. He'd made mental notes over the last months of as many details as possible for his escape.

'Mind if I stretch my legs outside?' he asked the sleepy guard. 'I've got cramps. Too much digging today in those ruddy fields, I reckon. Can't seem to settle tonight.'

'Five minutes.'

Savio rushed to a section of fence he had earmarked along-side a grassy walkway in a gap between the next terrace of houses.

The search lights on the tall standards were not on because of the danger of air raids and no windows looked over this alley-way. He knelt down to feel the wire fencing and then pulled out the old saw he'd dug up when working in the stony fields. At the time, he'd concealed it by shoving it down the side of his boot and taping it to his calf with a piece of twine, thinking it would come in useful some time. And he'd been right.

Savio had left his canvas knapsack hidden earlier in the day beneath a dense bush. Inside was spare clothing, provisions for the first days: a couple of apples, a tin of sardines, a lump of bacon and a bottle for water. He also had a World War One compass in a leather pouch won in a poker game in Hutchinson. He'd paid a handsome amount for a forged passport, no ques-tions asked, from a German Jew whose past job had been in a bank, compiling documents. He had barely any cash left as a result of these preparations, but once back on the mainland, he reckoned he could wing it back to the salon by hitching rides, or even walking by night if necessary.

If Savio's heart hadn't been in his mouth, he'd have relished the freedom: noticed how the sickle moon cast a moody shimmer of veiled light over the sea in the bay, smelled the scent of roses rambling over the walls of houses, their perfume enhanced by evening dew. He might have felt the world belonged to him again. Everybody else was asleep in their beds and they didn't own the night as he did. But Savio's blood was hammering in his ears and he felt his heart might burst through his ribcage. Every single night sound was a threat to his freedom as he half-jogged, half-strode the route to Port Erin. At one stage, outside

Newtown, he flung himself prostrate into a ditch as the drunken song of two revellers broke the still air. Two men were approaching: two happy souls swilled with grog, talking and singing gibberish. One of them stopped near where Savio lay and he heard a trickle and a splashing, followed by a deep sigh of satisfaction. The second man belched, muttering, 'Better out than in, my pal,' as he also relieved himself rather too close for comfort to Savio. He lay there, thanking the stars they hadn't drenched him with their piss.

The pair moved off, the sound of their heavy boots clinking against stones as they staggered away, both continuing their backslapping and out-of-tune caterwauling.

Now he had to really hurry and he broke into a run. He had to be on the beach before daylight.

The night sky was lightening and mist rose from puddles on the shore as gulls started up their dawn calls when Savio arrived in the bay. He swore aloud. In all of his planning, he hadn't taken the tides into consideration. The boat was marooned on the mud, the sea far out, beyond rock pools.

Damnation! You are an out and out prize fucking idiot, Savio Rizzo! He pulled off his knapsack and retreated to the hollow beneath the cliff to wait for high tide. This was the spot where he had whiled away two pleasant interludes with Lili. Those two meetings had been a highlight of his stay on this island, as well as his friendship with young Pieter, of course. All in all the island had not been such a bad place really. Ideal for a holiday. A *chosen* holiday, however, he grumbled. *Not* a place to be marooned against his will. He had no regrets about taking his leave.

Drizzle quickly turned to heavy rain. A blessing, he thought. Nobody would venture onto the sands in this weather. Lili had told him how some women from Rushen Camp occasionally came to collect seaweed and shells from the shore. The weed was used to make shampoo and it was mainly Italian women who collected crustacea. For their sauces, she'd told him.

'One day I'll go back to my island and eat spaghetti with delicious morsels of swordfish,' he'd said and she'd replied, 'It's good to have dreams to cling on to, Savio. Never stop dreaming.'

He nodded off. He'd had no sleep, anxious to stay awake for his dash to freedom. His dreams were of *caponata* and *arancini* prepared by his aunt and mother under the Sicilian sun. His parents' moods had been quite different on those couple of holidays, he remembered fondly. The sun had melted them from the frosty, hard-working couple he knew in England. They'd belonged on that southern island. And that was where he belonged too. There was nothing left for him in this country anymore: this heartless country that had abandoned his family.

He woke with a start. Something was tickling his nose. He opened his eyes, scrabbling to grab a rock from the sand. A young boy of about six or seven years of age grinned at him.

'Did you think I was a mouse? My mother hates mice. They make her scream.'

He inched himself up to lean against the cliff wall at the back of the hollow. 'Where is your mother?'

'Still asleep. She sleeps all the time and doesn't take much notice of me. She's got a baby growing in her tum. I think she swallowed it. She said Daddy gave it to her. You haven't come to steal my fossils, have you, mister? Because this is my secret hiding place, you know.'

'No, sonny, I haven't. I promise.'

'My name's not Sonny. It's Davey. Well, David, really. But Mum only calls me that when she's cross. What's your name?'

'I'm not allowed to tell you.'

'Why not? Are you a spy?'

'Well, you're a clever one. You've got it in one.'

'Are you waiting for the Germans to come? The lady who lives in our house with us is German and she says she can't wait for the Germans to arrive and take her away. I wish they would too. She's not very nice. I saw her strangling Dad on her bed and I had to rush in to save him. He was very cross with me. Can I wait with you?'

'Sorry, but it's all very hush-hush, Davey. But you can help me if you really want.'

'How?'

'By keeping me a secret. Not telling anybody. You can be part of my spy ring. What would you like to have as your under-cover name?'

'George,' the little boy answered immediately. 'Because Mum says I'm like him 'cos I'm always poking my nose in, like in *Curious George.*'

'Well, Sergeant George,' Savio said. 'Your very first mission is to go home and not say a single word about what I've told you. And if you hear about anything suspicious, you have to let me know...' He faltered. 'Do you know what that word means?'

'Course. Like when the butcher gives Mrs Tring extra sausages on a Friday night. Mum always says that's suspicious and it's because she gives him favours. I overheard her say that to the lady next door. What are favours? Do they taste nice?'

Savio swallowed back a chuckle. 'Probably,' he said. 'Any-way, Sergeant George. Off you pop.'

The little boy was hampering his escape; he hoped he would scarper and not come back too soon, with suspicious information. The tide was in now and it had stopped raining. He wanted to sail away before they came looking for him.

Davey stood up tall, all three foot six of him, and saluted. Savio copied him, before saying, 'Stand down, Sergeant George. Dismiss!' He watched the little boy run off, his wellington boots slapping against his bare legs, and lifted his finger to his mouth as Davey turned to wave.

When the child disappeared from view, Savio waded through the water and clambered into the boat that rocked gently on the incoming waves. His heart hammering, freedom within his grasp, he loosened the sail and it barely flapped when he freed it. *Bloody hell, not much wind.* There was only one oar in the bottom of the boat. *Damnation!* It would have to do; he'd use the oar as a paddle and hope the boat didn't go round in circles. He pushed the oar down to the seabed to drive the vessel from shore and swore some more as the oar, riddled with woodworm, snapped in two places. There was nothing for it now but to hope the wind picked up so he could make some progress with the damaged sail. Time was ticking by; people would be stirring from their beds and at the moment he was sitting like a duck on a fairground firing range in the middle of the bloody bay for everyone to see.

He hadn't reckoned on the fishermen of Port Erin setting off for their morning's catch. It wasn't long before a boat came alongside and a gnarly, wizened old mariner shouted, 'Hey, you, what do you think you're doing in Jeff's boat?'

A little over one hour later, Savio found himself locked up again. But this time he was taken to the police station in Douglas. Wryly he thought that at least the odour of horse droppings was not as strong as almost two years earlier when he'd first graced the converted stables with his presence. He wondered how long he would be banged up for this time and cursed his lack of proper preparation. What was the saying about not being able to organise a piss-up in a brewery? Well, he couldn't organise a prison escape from the Isle of Man. Not so far, anyhow. But you couldn't knock a good man down either. He would try again. He had to.

CHAPTER 14

1973, SUFFOLK

PAIGE

Returning to Squirrels Cottage, Paige caught a whiff of Jeremy's expensive aftershave still lingering and she opened the tiny kitchen casement windows wide to let in fresh afternoon spring air. She'd taken a walk along the estuary shore, which had renewed her energy and determination to get to the bottom of what Aunty Flo had been going to tell her and she decided to read over her aunt's notes again.

Mug of coffee at her side, she sat at the kitchen table and pulled out the contents of the old chocolate box again, re-reading the flimsy letter paper. Paige needed a key to unlock this mess of numbers.

VIII, 15
I, 55, 4
I, 88, 5
XXV, 110, 8-L
VIII, 38, 4, 5

What did they refer to? The idea of referring to the Bible was a good one, but she had no copy in the cottage. So, she used the supposition that each number represented a letter, like in a codeword puzzle. She was good with numbers. From way back before she'd started school, her aunt had made up number games with her: little mental arithmetic quizzes, games to make maths interesting. When Paige had started school in the village, she'd been way ahead of her classmates. So, why couldn't she work this puzzle out?

When she and Aunty had done codewords in the Sunday supplements together, they'd worked on the fact that 'e' was the most common letter in the English alphabet and so now, she looked for the symbols that appeared most frequently. That didn't help. She tried different tactics: writing the alphabet backwards; starting from the middle and working backwards and then forwards again. Soon her notepad was a muddle of scribbled figures. She threw down her Biro in exasperation. *Oh, Aunty Flo. What have you done to me? It would have been better if you'd never written anything in your blessed book.*

She made herself a pot of tea, and moved upstairs to see if inspiration might come in a different location. Aunty Flo's bedroom smelled musty and Paige opened the window and sat on the old wingback with its worn arm covers near the little Victorian fireplace. Filled with pine cones, it hadn't been used since storage heaters had been installed a while back. After a good tidy up, she would move into here. The walls needed whitewashing again, the nicotine stains were particularly yellow above the bed where her aunt had smoked, but it was roomier than her own single room set in the eaves that leaked in stormy weather. Paige looked about the space. She'd replace the sunlight-faded floral curtains with something plainer and splash out on new bedding. The bookshelves needed sorting, as well as dozens of porcelain animals and an array of decorative tins piled on the mantelpiece. She steeled herself to make a start, sensing it would be an emotional task. And it wasn't long before memories of her happy childhood returned.

It was hard, but if Paige was to make some sort of start on the next phase of her life, some of Flo's clutter would need to go. She worked late into the night, sorting items that could be donated to charity. Most of the clothes were too patched and worn to give away. Bundles of magazines kept for recipes were added to piles by the back door. She sifted through the books in the alcove of the living room, keeping only a small box for herself, including a couple of old *The Girl's Own Annual* that they'd found in a charity shop and which Paige had loved, and a couple of leather-bound volumes in a case, the lettering in Italian on the spine: *La Divina Commedia* by Dante Alighieri in gold. There was a gap where one volume was missing. *They might interest a dealer but they would also look classy on a bookshelf*, she thought, adding them to the KEEP pile. Many of the paperbacks were damp, their pages stuck together. These, together with scruffy old shoes too big for Paige that she could never imagine anybody wanting, saggy underwear, bobbly jumpers, cardigans and an old sun hat were taken downstairs and added to the growing assortment of rubbish. She thought for a moment about making a scarecrow with some of the clothing for the vegetable garden she might create one day. But then she banished that idea. To see an effigy of Florence standing with arms outstretched on moonlit nights would be too spooky for words.

She wasn't sleepy at all so she fetched a wheelbarrow and made several trips to the brazier at the bottom of the garden, where she and her aunt had sometimes placed potatoes wrapped in silver foil, poking them into the remnants of a gardening-day fire. Wrapped up warm, they'd devoured scalding hot potatoes dripping with butter, the skins toasted to a crisp. Paige was allowed to stay up later on these evenings, listening to the sounds of the night. 'The sounds we ignore by being too busy,' Florence would say. 'We need to make time for these moments, my darling,' she had told Paige. How long had it been since she'd done anything like that? Paige wondered.

The pile of unwanted belongings went up in a whoosh and as Paige fed the bonfire, it was sad to see parts of Aunty Flo's life reduced to what was basically rubbish. As she added each item, she made herself think something positive, thanking her aunt for everything she had done throughout her simple but idyllic childhood. 'You made it magical for me,' she whispered, gazing up at the sparks rising into the black sky. 'It's time to make my own magic now.'

It was far too late to call Charlie to update him on her progress. It was chilly indoors and she filled the stone bottle before climbing the stairs to bed, pleased with the progress made. There was still a lot to do to sort the cottage, but top of the list was to solve these puzzles that Florence had left her. The last thing she did before falling into a deep sleep was to apologise for getting rid of so much of her clutter. 'Less is more, Aunty,' she whispered, 'but how I wish you were here to answer the questions you've left behind.'

CHAPTER 15

The next day, Paige rose early, intent on continuing her quest, and drove to Ipswich Library, a cavernous Victorian building in the centre of town. She made her way immediately to the reference section.

Her finger stopped at the tenth Harrison she found in Debrett's directory and she let out a little squeal of triumph:

Lady Joy Harrison, born on April 4th 1916, to the honourable Lady Celia Harrison, née Hatherway, and the honourable Lord Rupert Harrison of Somersby Hall, Bury St Edmunds, Suffolk.

'Eureka!' she said aloud and the librarian looked over his horn-rimmed spectacles and frowned, tutting and putting his finger to his mouth. She was the only other person in the reading room. She shrugged her shoulders in apology, her face beaming. Finally, she was getting somewhere. She'd found the woman who was probably her mother.

She wrote the information carefully in her notebook, feeling strangely detached from what she had discovered, and glanced at her watch. Twelve thirty. Time to buy a map, grab a sandwich and plan a route to the outskirts of Bury St Edmunds. She had to hope Lady Joy was at home. Or should that be 'at her residence'? Goodness, it was another world. Maybe that was why it all felt so unreal. Shouldn't the possibility of meeting your birth mother make you terribly emotional? Was there something wrong with her that she felt so unmoved?

It was a pleasant drive along Suffolk country lanes lined with frothy cow parsley. In parts there was hardly passing space for two vehicles and she had to stop a couple of times – once for a tractor, the driver flashing a cheery wave, and the other a sleek, silver Jaguar. The bearded man at the wheel stopped his car and stared her out until she reversed to find the nearest passing place. The fact there had been one nearer him than her was annoying and she stuck her middle finger up as he zoomed past, revving his engine like a racing driver.

She was still fuming when she drove past the entrance to Somersby Hall, its forest-green sign half-concealed by ivy, the faded gold lettering patchy. She reversed and drove gingerly towards the entrance. One of the wrought-iron gates was hanging askew and she slowed down further to avoid scratching Bertha's sides on thorny bushes straying onto the rutted drive. The land to either side of her could, once upon a time, have been landscaped lawns but the grass was overgrown: poppies, dog daisies and corncockle poking their heads to the light. She spotted the top of a stone folly in the distance, strangled by brambles.

Seen better days, Paige thought. As she followed the curve of the drive, a Gothic Victorian pile came into view, its two imposing towers topped with pointed, tiled roofs soaring like sentinels to the clouds. A huge oak door, flanked by stone hunting dogs, one with a chipped muzzle, their paws crossed, guarded the old property.

Paige parked next to a flowerbed full of leggy rose bushes

choked with bindweed and checked her appearance in the mirror: flushed cheeks, hair tousled by the wind that had blown through her open car window... but she'd have to do. She rubbed her scuffed ankle boots against the back of her jeans, took a deep breath to calm her racing heart and stepped from the car.

A metal bell-pull hung beside the blistered door and after she'd tugged on it, she heard chimes resound deep within the building.

After an age, and mere seconds before she was about to pull on it again, footsteps made her pause, her heart pounding in expectation and anxiety. The door opened a crack at a second attempt, the base dragging against the tiled floor.

The woman who peeped round the half-opened door was petite, her sleek black hair scraped back in an immaculate bun.

'House not for sale no more,' she said, in an East Asian accent.

'No, no, I haven't come to view the property. I...' Paige stepped nearer, wishing the woman would open the door wider so they could speak more easily. 'I've come to talk to Lady Harrison, if she's in.'

Her heart was hammering against her chest now, the strong possibility that Lady Harrison was her birth mother finally hitting home.

'Lady Harrison not want visitors. Too many these past days. She tired.'

Paige persisted. 'But I've come a long way to see her. I want to ask her something very, very important.'

The woman sighed. 'I go ask...'

She withdrew into the house and Paige heard the voice of an elderly woman ask, 'Who is it now, Maganda? Didn't you tell whoever it is that the Hall is sold?'

Paige seized the opportunity and raised her voice. 'Lady Joy Harrison?' she called.

'Who's that?' The sound of tapping – from a walking stick maybe – before the door was opened wider by a liver-spotted hand. A very old woman, thin wispy hair framing a shrivelled face that might once have been handsome, stood in the doorway, leaning on her stick. She stared up at Paige with milky eyes. 'Who are you and what do you want?' she snapped.

'Lady Joy Harrison?' Paige asked, her heart sinking at the idea that this scrawny, angry old woman might be her mother. Surely, she was too old to have given birth to her? She must be at least eighty years old. Could she have possibly given birth at fifty? It had been known. *Please don't let her be my mother*, Paige prayed.

'Who is asking? And who are you?'

'May I come in to talk for a moment, Lady Harrison?'

'You're not one of those tiresome witness people, are you? Trying to convert me? Because I've no time for cold-callers and nosy parkers, like the hordes who have traipsed around my home and besieged me these past months. And as for converting me, it's far too late for that.'

'I'm not trying to sell you anything, Lady Joy—'

'I am NOT Lady Joy, for heaven's sake. That was my daughter. I am Lady Celia Harrison and I haven't seen or heard from Joy for more than thirty years. And as far as I am concerned, out of sight, out of mind. I've nothing to say to you. Good day.' She turned and called out, 'Maganda! See this young woman off the premises.'

'But won't you explain to me? You see, I believe Lady Joy might be my mother,' Paige blurted, frantic not to miss the chance to talk, having come this far.

But the old woman had gone, the sound of her walking stick tapping away on the stone floor swallowed within the cavernous house. Paige doubted the old lady had heard her comment about Lady Joy being her mother and if this horrible old woman was indeed her grandmother, she dreaded to think what Lady Joy was like. Her hopes dashed, she turned to leave.

Maganda stepped forward to touch her arm. 'She is very difficult. Very old. I've been housekeeper for a long time. You ask Mrs Peggy in village. At the tea shop. She knows many things.'

She turned to go and before she shut the door, she shook her head, her eyes sad. 'I sorry, madam.'

The door was firmly shut on Paige and she stood there for a minute trying to compose herself, listening to crows cawing from the lopsided monkey puzzle tree at the front of the house, one of its branches hanging like a broken limb. She shivered. Whoever had bought this place was welcome to it.

The village, a five-minute drive away down the road, was picturesque and consisted of a line of colour-washed cottages, interspersed with imposing Georgian villas that straggled up the hill. Paige parked at the top in a compact square where a bank, telephone kiosk, grocery-cum-post office and a Norman church were arranged around a cobbled area. As she wandered towards the shops, she spotted a sign painted like a hand, pointing to The Copper Kettle Café. Mentally crossing her fingers, she followed the cobbled alleyway, past a ladies' dress shop, a charity shop and finally, at the end, a café, tables and chairs arranged cleverly in a compact space. Milk churns and decorated pots brimming with colourful flowers created an attractive welcome. The door pinged as she entered and a comely, late middle-aged woman looked up. She was talking to the only customer in the café and he turned to look at the newcomer. Paige was embarrassed to recognise the obnoxious bearded driver of the flashy car.

'I'll be with you in a moment, my dear,' the woman said as

she opened her cash register to give change to the man. 'Take a seat and I'll come and fetch your order.'

'Road hog' nodded at Paige with a smile as he left and she was relieved he hadn't recognised her.

Paige scrutinised the menu. She wasn't hungry, her stomach churned up by her visit to the Hall, and she ordered a pot of Earl Grey.

'Erm, are you Mrs Peggy? Only, if you're not too busy, the housekeeper at Somersby Hall told me you might be able to help me,' she said after the woman had taken her order.

The woman laughed. 'I'm Mrs Peggy Ambrose, yes. Maganda always calls me Mrs Peggy, bless her. She pops in here on her day off. Lovely woman.'

'Could I pick your brains? Would you mind?'

'About the house? It's sold. In fact, that gentleman who just left, he's bought it. Wants to knock it down and build an executive estate.' She sniffed. 'Crying shame. We need more homes for local people, not for Londoners' second homes. That house used to be so handsome in its time... were you interested in buying it then?'

'Oh no... I...' Now it came to it, talking to a complete stranger was leaving her tongue-tied. It sounded crazy to announce she was looking for Lady Joy Harrison, who might be her mother. On the other hand, this might be her only chance of finding out more.

'I'm trying to find Lady Joy Harrison. But Lady Celia at the Hall, she told me she hasn't seen her for over thirty years and her housekeeper told me you might know something.'

The woman looked shocked. 'Maganda has the patience of a saint. Lady Celia is a trial and a half. I should know: way back I used to work for the harridan doing all sorts. Poor Joy. She was such a lovely person.'

'*Was?*' Paige's heart stopped a beat. 'Has she passed away?'

The woman shrugged her shoulders. 'She might have, for all

I know. Cut herself off completely. Mind you, who could blame her? Lady Celia was awful when it happened. Banished her, set up some kind of allowance and after that she left. Nobody's seen or heard from her since.'

'What happened?' Paige's voice was a whisper.

The door pinged and the woman rose, lowering her voice. 'Look, come back at five o'clock after I've shut the café and we'll have more time to talk.'

Paige settled up for her pot of tea and wandered back into the village. She had over an hour to kill. The crimplene dresses in muddy shades displayed in the haberdasher's shop window were frumpy: a pink twinset and polyester pedal pushers adorning a mannequin were more suited to the older woman, so she didn't bother entering. The charity shop was closed, so she made her way to the church. She wasn't religious but it was quiet inside and she sat for a few moments, her eyes drawn to a shaft of light dancing through the stained glass, dust motes swirling in its beam. A plaque high on the wall commemorated the death of Lieutenant William Harrison, son of Lord and Lady Henry Harrison, their youngest son, struck down at the Battle of Alma, 1854. His death was recorded but was there anything to commemorate Lady Joy? Was she even still alive? Where was she?

Paige felt an urge to light a candle to place next to the other two flickering on the sill beneath a stained-glass window and she mouthed a kind of prayer as she lit it. *This is for you, Joy. Wherever you are, I hope you're happy and being looked after. If you're my mum, then rest assured I've had a fantastic life.* And then, as tears came unaccountably to her eyes, she left the church. She had another fifteen minutes to kill. The sun was strong for the time of year and she was uncomfortably warm in her jeans. A bench in the shade over in the far corner of the graveyard beckoned. She wiped twigs from the seat and sat down, willing herself to be calm while she waited to speak to the café owner.

Leaning against the back wall of the graveyard were two tiny gravestones. The writing was hard to decipher but the surname Harrison was unmistakable and the two dates showed they had not lived long. She made out what she could of the poignant inscriptions: *Cordelia Harrison: August 14th–August 23rd, 1750. In the Good Lord's arms.* The second brought tears to Paige's eyes: *Suffer the little children...* The remaining words were worn away but she knew them well enough. They were for a baby who might have been stillborn or only lasted a few hours: *James Harrison, July 17th 1752.*

She thought about what Mrs Ambrose had said. The Hall had been sold, most likely to be knocked down. Modern houses would replace years of history. The Harrison family had obviously been established in Somersby for a long time. *Everything passes with time*, Paige thought. *And stories are cancelled over the years – lives forgotten, secrets and memories lost forever.* It made her more determined than ever to find out what she could about Lady Joy.

Paige hurried to the red telephone kiosk in the square. A teenaged girl, her leather skirt skimming her bum, was occupying the booth. Paige listened to her muffled giggles, hoping she was not going to be too long. After an age, the girl emerged. 'All right?' she said to Paige and Paige nodded, eager to call Charlie. She pushed in the coppers and dialled his number. The kiosk smelled of stale smoke and what she thought might be urine. She wrinkled her nose and then tutted as Charlie's posh answerphone started up. 'Sorry, darlings. Not in at the moment. Writing my next bonkbuster in my nearest...' She replaced the receiver and pressed for the change.

Maybe it was better to speak to Charlie later anyway: she might have more to tell him by then. Checking her watch, she saw it was time to return to The Copper Kettle.

CHAPTER 16

APRIL 1943, LONDON

JOY

It was good to climb onto the train at Diss. The last time Joy had been up to London was for a debutantes' ball that Mother insisted she attend. It was ghastly and she'd always hated dancing, her feet wanting to lead all the time. She had invariably taken the part of the man at ballroom-dancing lessons at finishing school on account of her height and it was automatic to take over. On one of these ghastly occasions, she remembered being saved by finding a corner table and chatting to another girl called Vanessa – 'Essa to you' – who'd confessed she felt awkward too and had come to the high society do under sufferance. The kindred spirits had moved to another table behind a pillar near the buffet table and grown steadily squiffy as they'd swapped life stories. 'Not that my life has taken off yet,' Joy had said, knocking back another glass of orange juice, heavily laced from the bottle of whisky Essa had taken from her father's drinks cabinet and transferred to a hip flask stuffed into the top of her stocking. Towards the end of the evening, Essa had made a pass at Joy.

'Sorry, I'm not... a girls' girl... if you see what I mean,' Joy had told her.

'Pity! I won't hold it against you,' Vanessa had replied, before both of them, sozzled, had disintegrated into fits of laughter at the unintended pun, attracting the attention of a couple of young men who'd wanted them to share their joke.

She thought about Vanessa as she looked out of the grubby train window at the suburban houses lining the tracks and wondered what she was doing, certain she was the type of woman who'd have rolled up her sleeves and got stuck in straightaway with volunteering for the war effort. The nearer the train steamed its way towards the outskirts of London, she was shocked to see gaps in the rows of terraced houses where bombs had destroyed homes. Somersby Hall had avoided this devastation and, once again, she felt a fraud for putting off doing her bit for so long.

The sights of Liverpool Street station and surrounding streets were mainly of sandbags, barbed wire and an absence of signs. Joy asked for the quickest way to the Victoria Hotel from a warden and it didn't take long before she was climbing steps to a dingy entrance. She was early but as it was drizzling, she decided to wait inside now she had found the building. When she entered, the hotel was not what she'd expected at all. There was no smart reception area. In fact, the place looked bare and institutional.

A uniformed Wren manning a switchboard at the front desk instructed her to climb the stairs to the waiting room on the top floor. 'You can't miss it, Lady Harrison,' she said. 'There's a sign on the door.'

Joy was surprised the receptionist knew her name as she hadn't fully introduced herself.

Alone in the gloomy room, she looked about. A bare bulb

hung from the ceiling and despite the poor light, the polished floor shone and an overpowering whiff of cleaning fluid and nicotine made her move to open a window. But it was shut fast. Four chairs were placed on the left-hand side of the wall like a doctor's waiting room, and in the centre, an armchair, worn at the arms. A low table, its surface scratched and covered with rings left by teacups or glasses, finished off the institutional furnishing. She wondered where she was supposed to sit. Was the comfortable chair for her or for Lydia Ponting, who had invited her? She had expected their meeting place to be more comfortable. Joy shivered. There were no pictures hanging on the sludgy-green utility-emulsion walls. Below the dado rails, the walls were painted dull brown. She willed herself to relax and closed her eyes for a second. It was worse than being in a doctor's waiting room.

Joy continued to wait, occasionally glancing at her watch. It was now twenty minutes to midday and Lydia had arranged to meet at eleven. Maybe she'd made a mistake and gone to the wrong building? But no, the receptionist downstairs knew her name, had known she was expected. From somewhere in the building she heard the clatter of typewriters, carriage return bells and ringing phones. Any moment now, she would get up to leave; it was too bad to be kept waiting like this. Resentment began to seep in as she considered the wasted journey up to London. It had cost her dearly in travel coupons. Maybe she would try and catch a show or film while she was up here to make the trip worthwhile. She hadn't seen *Gone with the Wind* yet. She leant down to pick up her battered crocodile handbag just as the door opened and Colonel Ponting entered.

'So sorry, my dear,' the colonel said, extending his hand. 'I do apologise but we had something of an emergency to sort. Sit down. I'll explain briefly why we have brought you all the way to town. I'm afraid I had to get Lydia in on the plan, otherwise you might not have come.'

'This sounds very mysterious, Colonel. Please explain.'

'You made it plain when we met at Somersby Hall you wanted to do something more with your life, Joy. And I've understood by that that you mean with the war effort. I'm correct, aren't I?'

Joy nodded, a slight frown displaying her need to understand better what the colonel was getting at.

'There are some people who want to chat to you today. I'll leave you for the time being but don't worry, my dear. I'll be back to rescue you. I'm not going to do you out of that promised lunch.'

A couple of minutes later, wondering what on earth she had let herself in for, there was a light tap at the door and the receptionist popped her head round. 'Lady Harrison, they're ready for you. Follow me, please.'

Feeling like Alice in Wonderland following the white rabbit down a hole, she walked behind her messenger, observing that the lines on the backs of her legs were on real nylons, and not drawn. Perks were obviously more easily available in London. At the end of a corridor on the floor below, the young woman stopped. 'This is the one.' She knocked and opened the door for Joy. 'Good luck, madam,' she said as she closed it.

A haze of cigarette smoke enveloped Joy as she moved further into the room. Lydia was nowhere to be seen. Three men – one in uniform, another wearing a kilt, an untidy beard matching his thatch of ginger hair, and the third, a civilian, in his late fifties she guessed – appraised her as she sat down. She could have done with a cigarette herself to calm her nerves, but none was offered. There was a moment of silence as the bearded man raised his eyebrows at the uniformed officer. *A major general*, Joy assessed. *A bigwig. What is going on?*

The civilian was the first to speak. 'Thank you for coming up to town, Miss Harrison. Was your journey straightforward?'

'Yes, thank you, sir.' *It's* Lady *Harrison, actually, but we'll let that go*, she thought. It was always easier to merge into ordinary life without the title.

He continued. 'I see you have connections with Italy?'

Bloody hell. How does he know that?

'Mostly Sicily, sir. My father bought a villa in Syracuse and we spent whole summers there.'

He looked at her over the rim of his glasses, the steel frames ugly but doubtless doing the job. 'Quite so.'

His next question was in Italian. He asked her if she knew the island at all.

Dreadful accent, Joy assessed. *Correct grammar, but a little old-fashioned. Like Prof Merry at university. Most likely an academic himself.*

Her reply was mixed with Sicilian dialect. Well, he'd asked her about Sicily, hadn't he? So, she told him she'd loved exploring the island, even as a young child. There was a small swimming pool at her parents' villa, but she'd opted for the sea beneath the terrace instead, and her parents had let her do her own thing, preferring to read their books and stay sitting in the shade. So, she knew Syracuse like the insides of her pockets, as it happened, and she'd cycled everywhere in the area. When she noticed a slight frown on his face at some of her Sicilian words, she'd corrected them to Italian so that he could understand, and he'd nodded.

'Gingerbeard' fired a question midway through a sentence she'd started about the catacombs of San Giovanni where she and her Italian friends used to play hide and seek.

'Can you shoot?' he asked in a broad accent. Glaswegian, she guessed.

'Of course. I started beating for Father's shoots as a nipper and he let me join in culling pheasants and rabbits when I was ten.'

'So, you didn't mind shooting the little bunnies?'

She bristled at his sarcastic tone. *He doesn't like women... But don't let it get to you, Joy. Keep calm.*

Her nails dug into her palms as she answered, trying to appear unruffled.

'Well, put it like this, I'm a dab hand at skinning bunnies, as you call them, and they make the most delicious pies.' She stared at him and he was the first to look away, but then he fired another question and she faltered when he asked, 'How fast can you run?'

'Erm... as in a race?'

He shrugged and, again, she was annoyed at his standoffish attitude. 'You tell me.'

'I can run fast when I have to, but I'm no Olympian.'

He looked her up and down, his eyes as cold as a wintry Suffolk sea. 'I meant if you had to run for your life.'

'I imagine I would run like the wind. Wouldn't anybody?'

'Sleeping rough. Would you cope?'

'I was brought up in the countryside. Camping and cooking over a bonfire suit me fine. I'm not afraid of the dark or creepy crawlies, if that's what you're worried about.'

Maybe she should be addressing this semi-uniformed fellow as 'sir' too. But he didn't conjure that kind of respect. His appearance was of somebody who slept rough most of the time, with his uncombed hair curling over his grubby fisherman's roll-neck sweater. And she detected a whiff of whisky on his breath.

'Death,' he shot back. 'I'm talking about fear of death and being hunted down, danger round every corner. Would you be a liability and expect to be looked after?'

She narrowed her eyes. She didn't like this man, wanted to tell him he was an insufferable prig, but she wanted action too. Of course he was testing her for a reaction, goading her to see if she would lose it, so she kept her voice calm, despite the urge to punch him on the nose.

'I could be killed by a bomb any night of the week,' she said, looking 'Gingerbeard' straight in the eyes. She was not going to let him bully her. 'But I'd prefer to die doing something useful, rather than in my bed.' She added 'sir', even though it went against the grain.

'That will be all for now,' the major general said, bringing the strange interview to a sudden close. 'Can you make yourself scarce for half an hour and then come back here, Lady Harrison?'

'Of course, sir.'

She picked up her handbag from the side of the chair and stood to leave. Should she shake their hands? Salute? No hands were extended, just three sets of eyes glued on her as she straightened up, squared her shoulders, hoping her height would show she was no wimp.

'Thank you,' she said, before turning to open the door. She had no idea for what she was thanking them, none the wiser after the grilling. She'd done her best and she hoped that was enough to get her doing something useful in this awful war. She'd stood her corner against the bearded monster. Maybe that would be enough, but as she made her way out of the building and into the park, she had her doubts. All she'd proved was that she could shoot rabbits and cook over a campfire.

Half an hour was not long and she checked her watch. Twenty-five minutes to walk a little, smoke a cigarette and calm herself. She barely noticed the blossom on the ornamental cherry trees or the huge vegetable beds that had replaced the greenswards in the park. She put one foot in front of the other and crossed her fingers as the minutes ticked agonisingly by.

. . .

'You were a bit harsh on her, Hamish,' Major General Colcott said, lighting up a cigar.

'My job. We don't need liabilities. I'm not a nursemaid,' Major Hamish Moyes replied, tipping back so far in his chair that it rested on the two back legs. 'I'm not sure about her. And how the hell will she fit in? She's a typical English country girl... tall, blonde. She'll stick out like a sore thumb in Sicily. No way can we send her there. What's the point?'

'She's damn good at the language,' offered Professor Brian Whitlaw, a senior lecturer in Italian studies. 'Far better than my academic Italian. I'm sure she'd be useful. She knows that part of the coastline too. Shame to let her go. What's she doing at the moment?'

Colcott looked at his notes. 'Teaching in a village school. Ponting says she's a strong possibility. Mentions she's eager to join the ATS. She'll end up driving a truck or compiling weather reports or some such. Waste, I say.'

'Let her do that,' Moyes said. 'I can't see her being fit enough. There'll be no hanging around on this mission.' He tipped the chair forwards again and stood. 'As far as I'm concerned, it's a no from me. Will that be all?'

Major General Colcott was stern as he answered, 'No, Hamish. I haven't dismissed you yet. You don't call the tune on my patch. You're not doing your own thing in the North African desert now.'

A grimace from Moyes and a muttered, 'More's the pity.'

'She's definitely worth a punt,' the major general declared. 'We'll send her to Glenaig and see how she fares. I'll get Ponting in here to do the business and explain things to her. That will be all, gentlemen. More interviews here tomorrow. Same time. There's a chap I've got my eyes on who's been stirring it up on the Isle of Man. Dead cert you'll like *him*, Hamish. He's a troublemaker. But you'll have to go and interview him there. Speaks

Italian and a fair bit of German too. He's in prison at the moment.'

There was an almost imperceptible raising of Moyes' ginger eyebrows when he heard this.

When Joy returned from her nervous stroll around the park, the same room she'd been ushered into was empty of her three inquisitors, the windows were wide open and Colonel Ponting greeted her with a smile.

'Smelled like a Soho dive in here. Come in, come in. You did very well, apparently.'

'Can you please tell me what is going on, Colonel? Today has made me feel like Alice in Wonderland.'

He grinned. 'Yes, well, we're a bunch of Mad Hatters here. But... for good reason.'

'Put me out of my misery.'

For the first time, she noticed a revolver on the table. The colonel's tone turned serious as he leant forwards in his chair.

'You're an intelligent girl... an intelligent young woman,' he corrected himself. 'And it's patently obvious you want to help your country. That was plain when we first met. Combined with your excellent knowledge of Italian, you'll be of great use. But what we're looking for is a woman with absolute discretion and loyalty, prepared to undertake vital work. You'd need to be trained up but I think you would catch on very quickly.'

'I'm still none the wiser. This is all so vague.' Why had Lydia and Captain Ponting brought her here?

He sat back as he explained.

'We have a place in Bucks where intelligence is gathered and decoded. But I rather think we'll see about training you up first in Scotland. To assess whether you're suited more to the field, or ops back here. All vital to the war effort. Are you willing to embark?

It's no picnic, I have to warn you. But if you're as patriotic as I think you are,' he said, a grin starting at the corner of his mouth, 'and really want to get away from your mother, as much as I think you do...' He gave her a look and she returned hers, a twinkle in her eye. 'Then we'll have you like a shot. Unfortunate turn of phrase,' he said, lifting the gun from the table. 'You'll have to sign the Official Secrets Act first, of course, and... if you breathe a word of this to anybody...' He paused. 'And I mean *anybody*... you'll be hanged or... shot. This is a deadly serious business, Joy.'

Joy's eyes widened but her reply was instant. 'My answer is yes, sir. Yes, to everything.'

He nodded his appreciation at her acceptance and extended his hand, grasping hers firmly. 'Splendid!'

He pushed over a document, *War Office* typed at the bottom of the first page. She read the heading: *King's Regulations relating to disclosure of military information.*

Colonel Ponting gave her a moment to finish reading and then ran through the basics. 'Joy, you must not talk about your work or pass on information, unless authorised. You must not keep any drawings or documents unless it's your job to do so. You must take care not to lose any documents. Above all, keep mum. And remember walls have ears. You know the score. You've seen notices posted everywhere.' He pointed to where she should leave her signature and with slightly trembling fingers, she signed her name and dated it: *April 9th 1943.*

Placing the signed document in a leather briefcase and doing up the buckles, he said, 'Now, I hope you're hungry. The rations aren't too bad at the Four Hundred Club. We'll go there now and meet Lydia. After that we'll sort out the rest of the arrangements. You'll be given a week's notice about where you have to report. Plenty of time to prepare your mother. Tell her you've been called up for secretarial duties. And don't forget to pick up a travel warrant at the desk downstairs to pay for your train fare today.'

Her spirits lifted as he ushered her through the door. Nevertheless, she couldn't quite believe what was happening. This opportunity to spread her wings and, at last, to hopefully be of some use to her country was like a dream. She so wanted to tell somebody about it, but she'd been warned in no uncertain terms about absolute discretion. And anyway, apart from Father, there was nobody else she could think of to share her news. Somehow, she felt her father knew anyway.

CHAPTER 17

1942 TO APRIL 1943, ISLE OF MAN

SAVIO

It was damp in Savio's cell in Douglas Prison, the rations far worse than in Hutchinson and his bed hard as mountain rock. The Manx police had no jurisdiction inside the camps, but dealt with serious matters, including felony, violent assault and breaking free of camps onto Manx territory. Every morning, no matter the weather conditions, Savio was made to run around the exercise yard on his own, and he was banged up in solitary confinement for three nights for swearing at one of the police guards. From a nearby cell, he could hear a prisoner singing the same chorus in a language he didn't recognise. The man was out of tune and he began to wonder if it was a cleverly devised form of punishment: maybe a gramophone recording played over and over to send him round the bend. Each morning he scratched a day off on the wall in a space between signatures and crude drawings of penises and naked women. After fourteen nights, he was given the job of working in the kitchen in the police headquarters. 'Where we can keep an eye on you,' the over-weight police sergeant told him.

He deliberately burnt food, left peel on the potatoes, made the gravy lumpy. 'Hey, what's all this? I thought Eyeties were good cooks...' the chef reprimanded after Savio produced a tray of unappetising shepherd's pie, the grey potato topping half-cooked and the meat full of gristle.

One morning after dishing up fried eggs and bread for breakfast, he deliberately left the pan of fat on the cooker whilst he washed a teetering pile of dirty plates. The sink was positioned near the door, left ajar to let cool air into the kitchen. Savio kept glancing at the pan, checking for the moment when it would burst into flames. He threw a dishcloth over it, which caught alight immediately and he waited until the flames spread across the work counter, before shouting at the top of his voice: 'Fire, fire!' The canteen was evacuated and the prisoners left to stand in the exercise courtyard until the fire was extinguished. It gave Savio a moment or two of satisfaction. The fire wasn't blamed on him, despite the cook's suspicions. The prisoners were grateful for extra time out of their cells and Savio notched up a small victory against the British who had detained him on this godforsaken island in the first place.

Captain Peters, his camp commandant, leaning heavily on his walking stick, came to see him one afternoon. Savio was sitting on an upturned log outside the kitchen, enjoying a smoke from a scavenged cigarette stub in his break and nursing a stewed cup of tea, sweetened with condensed milk.

'What are we going to do with you, Mr Rizzo?'

'Hopefully let me out of here, sir?' He stood up when the captain approached and saluted. He had respect for this middle-aged man.

'I believe you're coming back to Hutchinson soon enough. Try to keep your powder dry until then. If you avoid trouble, then I may have interesting news for you.'

'What news, sir? Am I to be released?' His spirits lifted. It seemed like an eternity that he'd been in prison. Weeks turning into months.

'We'll talk more in good time. It's not bad news but let's see if you are capable of toeing the line and... exercising restraint.' He handed Savio a packet of Camel cigarettes and Savio took them gratefully. He had been down to his last smoke and the police station was not a place where he could make deals. There was no bartering to be done if nobody had anything to exchange in the first place and the few locked-up prisoners were always kept apart from each other.

The police guards were a different kettle of fish from the camp guards and Savio had learned that camp officers, like Captain Peters, were usually either military veterans or men with war wounds who had been granted light duties while still on active service. They were generally a relaxed bunch, nearing the end of their careers and not disappointed to be away from action. Their wives came occasionally to visit them and went back to the mainland with suitcases stuffed with provisions easily available on the island: dairy products, vegetables – especially potatoes, which were not rationed. There was plenty for everybody, including the prisoners.

It was a long couple of months for Savio, during which time he'd been on his best behaviour, eager to return to Hutchinson after the tedium of prison, and at ten o'clock on a spring morning in 1943 when Savio was escorted back to his old camp by two policemen.

'We don't want to see your nasty face back in our cells again, son,' the older of the pair said as they waited for the guard to unlock the gate to the camp close to the Broadway. 'There won't be no special treatment if that happens.'

Savio couldn't think what he meant by that remark. Special

treatment? Solitary confinement for swearing? Skivvy work in the kitchens? What were they talking about? They were all potty.

Savio had the reluctant feeling of coming home as soon as he made his way into the gateway of Hutchinson. The garden was beginning to flourish with a mixture of neat rows of vegetable seedlings and spring flowers that provided colour to the surroundings. An Italian, raking between rows of herbs, raised his hand in greeting as Savio walked by. 'Welcome back, *ragazzo*. The place hasn't been the same without you. *Ben tornato!*'

Pieter wandered over from where he had been sketching. 'See you later, friend. I'll save a place for you in the dining room. Good to see you back at long last.' He pumped Savio's hand up and down.

Yes, Savio had to admit, it wasn't too bad to be back. For a while, at least, until he could think up another plan.

'You're wanted in the commandant's office,' a young lad said, running up to Savio, lowering his voice to add, 'You've been missed. People still talk about how you tried to escape.'

He knocked on Captain Peters' door and on hearing, 'Come!' turned the handle and stepped in. He immediately spotted an eccentric figure sporting a beard the colour of fire, wearing uniform of a kind: a khaki shirt unbuttoned at the neck and a beige beret worn aslant his head. The strange clothing was finished off by a kilt, thick socks reaching the young man's knees. He was stocky, the muscles on his arms like great hams. This man was certainly not one you would want to pick a fight with. Savio tore his eyes away before saluting Captain Peters.

'Sit down, Mr Rizzo,' Peters said, indicating the chair in front of the desk. 'Major Moyes has come specially to the island to meet you.'

The officer called Moyes came to perch on the desk near

Savio and he couldn't help thinking how peculiar it was to see a man wearing a skirt.

'I hear you've been in a spot of bother?' he said to Savio, picking up a paperknife from the captain's desk and running his thick index finger along its blade.

'I'm not supposed to be here,' Savio replied. 'That's the chief bother to me, sir. In fact, there are many of us who shouldn't be here. I want out,' Savio replied. 'Have done since the beginning.' There was little point in stating otherwise.

'Your escape plan last year wasn't thought through properly, though, was it? A dash for freedom carried out on a whim.'

Savio remained silent. To be fair, he was right.

'Do you think you'll try again? If you're so desperate to get away?' Moyes replaced the paperknife on the desk. 'They tell me you're Sicilian.'

Again, Savio remained silent about the question of escape. But he corrected Moyes on his nationality. 'I'm British. Born in London. My parents were born in Sicily, but they lived and worked in Soho and came over before the last war. They managed to escape from the injustice of imprisonment, but in the wrong way...' Savio's eyes blazed with anger and he clenched his fists tight, forcing himself to appear calm.

'I heard about that and I'm sorry. But I'm interested in your connections with Sicily. How well do you know the island?'

Savio shrugged. 'Not as well as I'd like. The surrounding area of Syracuse I know very well. Where my folks came from: a district they call Capo Murro di Porco. It's where we holidayed and I spent my days with my Italian cousins.'

'That's on the south-west coast, right?'

'South-east.'

Captain Daniels intervened. 'Rizzo. I've been as fair with you as I could. I believe you're not a Nazi sympathiser.'

'Well, you took your time, sir.'

The captain held up his hand. 'Let me finish, Rizzo.' He

pulled a document from a folder on his desk. 'I think you should enlist in the Pioneer Corps. It's a way of proving you're anti-Nazi and getting you away from here.'

Moyes took up the discussion. 'Once you're off the island, you'll be going to Scotland for a while and afterwards to where I train my team. You need to be fitter.'

'Team?' Savio asked, hardly daring to believe he might be leaving the island. Even if he had to pretend to join up, it was worth a punt. And there would be ways of disappearing once he was on the mainland.

'No details yet and what you hear in this room is to remain a secret. All you need to know is you've been heard to talk about Sicily a lot. If you decide to help us, you'd leave here tomorrow and we'll decide after that whether you're what we need. In the meantime, one of my men will stay by your side the whole time. There is to be no divulging to a soul about what we've discussed.'

'And if I decide I don't want to?'

'Then, you'll be removed back to the police prison cell and kept in solitary confinement until such time as I deem necessary. Most likely when this war is over.'

'I don't seem to have much choice.'

Moyes stood up from his perch on the desk and, looking at him, Savio thought he had never met such an intimidating man. Apart from his sheer bulk, there was something about him he couldn't put his finger on.

'To my way of thinking, Rizzo, it's a no-brainer. You'd be a fool not to accept. I'll give you the rest of today to come to a decision.'

Turning to Captain Peters, Moyes saluted and said, 'Don't let him out of your sight. Two guards with him every single minute. Even when he takes a leak.'

CHAPTER 18

APRIL 1943, GLENAIG, SCOTLAND

JOY

Joy had thought she was fit, a horse rider and tough country girl to boot, but she'd never had to turf herself out of a warm bed at three o'clock in the morning in the driving rain and crawl on her belly through peat bogs. To top it all, she had come on last night with a very heavy period and she knew her trousers were soaked through, and not only from the muddy puddles. Her irregular periods were the bane of her life and she was often caught out. This morning, she was working in a team of three and one of them happened to be the perpetually shouting trainer, worst luck, screaming at her and the other woman in the trio to get a bloody move on. Maria was a pretty, slight brunette and Joy's roommate.

The final hurdle in their cross-country endurance test was a seemingly unscalable vertical rock wall and Joy wanted to burrow herself in the sodden leaves at its base and pretend she wasn't there.

'Get a fucking move on, Harrison!' the instructor yelled from where she was sitting astride the top, staring down at her slow teammate. 'You'd be dead by now or worse if Jerry was really chasing us. MOVE that FAT arse!'

It was a good thing the Sten gun strapped to her back wasn't firing live ammo, Joy thought, otherwise the trainer would be a goner by now.

Later, back in the canteen, every sinew in her body screaming, the windows fuggy with steam from wet garments, Joy almost fell asleep in her bowl of porridge. How she longed for a hot bath and scented bubbles, filled well above the five-inch regulation line, preferably followed by at least two days of deep sleep.

'Eat, Joy!' Maria urged. 'Get your strength up. You don't know what they're going to spring on us next.'

Joy downed her cup of stewed tea and ate as much as her churned-up stomach would allow. The first two days of her periods were usually accompanied with diarrhoea and nausea. She wondered how she would ever cope in the field.

A siren began to wail and the trainer, for Joy fast becoming the most hated woman in Christendom, or at the very least in this desolate corner of Inverness-shire, stood on a chair, yelling instructions at the exhausted recruits.

'Everybody out. Quick march to the loch. Enemy approaching. Evacuate the premises.'

Down at Loch Glenaig, they were shoved into new teams, this time with a mix of men and women. The only consolation was the absence of the female instructor. *In bed, wrapped up in her feather eiderdown*, Joy thought enviously.

'Find a way to get across the water,' a male instructor commanded. 'Last group in will forfeit sleep and be put on kitchen duties for a week. I'm reliably informed there's been a new delivery of spuds to peel.'

'We should build a raft,' a young man with a strong cockney accent suggested. She'd never seen him before. He was dark-haired, lean and barely taller than Joy.

The third member of this new team was as fair as the cockney was dark and spoke with a cut-glass accent. 'Jolly good,' he said. 'We need timber. How about we use our combat knives to prune branches?'

'How about we use the canoe I saw the other day?' Joy suggested. The two men looked at her in surprise. 'I went for a walk the other evening,' she continued. 'There's a well-equipped boathouse over there.' She pointed down a narrow path almost hidden by brambles.

She occasionally escaped the grand house, in need of space to think on her own, enjoying the tranquillity as shadows crept across the lake, mist rising from the dark waters, the still air broken by the occasional calls of waterfowl.

'Best be prepared for the cunning bastards having some surprise up their sleeves though,' the dark-haired fellow muttered. 'Nothing's ever straightforward. They've always some trick or test to prolong the agony. They've no doubt spies about, to spring another surprise. Let's be wary.' He scooped up a handful of mud from the edge of the lake and started to smear some on Joy's face. 'Best darken ourselves up. Your skin's as light as the moon.' His fingers on her skin were firm but gentle.

'I can do it myself,' she said, pushing his hand away. 'Concentrate on yourself.'

They approached the boathouse stealthily, keeping low behind the dark-haired chap, who had fallen into the role of leader. A glow of light from the stub of a cigarette showed where a guard stood smoking, and their leader held up his hand and indicated for them to separate, pulling down the skin under one eye: the signal for them to be observant. They advanced, Joy to the left in the shrubs and the other chap to the right. Joy crouched low, the cramps in her stomach so painful now that she had to bite down hard on her lip to distract herself, telling herself this was a sniff compared to the sufferings of others in occupied Europe. She had to forge through to help others.

There was a sudden movement as their leader jumped the guard, one hand clamped over his mouth, as he kneed him to the ground. 'He's alone,' he hissed to his team. The guard struggled and tried to talk and the leader punched him in the face.

'Steady on, old chap. That's Brown – one of ours. Playing a part, no doubt,' the posh member of the team said and the leader removed his hand from the groaning guard.

'For fuck's sake,' Brown said, rubbing his jaw. 'There's no need to throttle me, Dante. And you can put away that knife. Christ, this is only a practice.'

'Or is it?' Dante clamped the man's mouth again. 'How do we know you're not a double agent?' Keeping his voice low, he ordered Joy and the other fellow to check there was nobody else on guard. 'You're coming with us, Brown. I'm not peeling fucking spuds for a week.'

Inside the wooden hut, Joy found a coil of rope and she tossed it to Dante. 'Bind his arms and use this to keep him quiet,' she said, pulling an old scarf from her pocket that she'd stuffed in earlier to use as an emergency sanitary pad. 'All clear,' she said. 'Help me get the canoe in the water.'

'Paddles?' Dante asked.

'Yep! They're both here.'

Thankfully they didn't come last in the exercise and were sent to their beds with assurances they would not be ordered out again that night.

On the following morning, before debriefing, a cooked breakfast was served, with real eggs, instead of the powdered variety. What just about passed as sausages, although more bread than meat, were demolished by the recruits.

Seated in the hall afterwards, Joy's team were singled out for initiative by the commanding officer who added, with a tinge

of humour, that Brown expected a couple of rounds of drinks
that evening on account of his badly bruised jaw.

Afterwards, over cups of ersatz coffee, Dante approached
Joy. 'You did well yesterday. Saved us lots of messing about in
building that raft by remembering the canoe. Thanks.' He held
out his hand. 'I'm Savio. And you are?'

'I thought you were Dante? I'm Joy.'

'My name for the night. An alias that's turning into a
nickname.'

'Are you Italian? Or is Savio another invention?'

He smiled. 'My parents are...' He corrected himself. '*Were*
Sicilian. I lost them on the *Arandora Star*.'

'*Mi dispiace tanto*. I'm so very sorry. That's very tough luck.'

'Hey! You speak Italian.'

She nodded. 'And I know Sicily well. Been visiting since I
was a child. My parents have a house in Siracusa, near the
harbour.'

'Well, we're practically neighbours then. My folks were
from Isola, across the bay.'

He smiled and she thought how good-looking he was, like
most of the Italian boys she remembered from her Sicilian holidays: blessed with thick dark hair and brown eyes that laughed
and promised fun. Always friendly, their families hospitable
and generous, inviting her to share in meals: cousins, aunts,
grandparents and neighbours seated at long tables while her
own parents sat in deckchairs on their terrace overlooking the
yachts, sipping martinis and keeping themselves to themselves.
But Joy had always wanted to explore and play with Sicilian
'street children', as her mother disparagingly called them. She'd
be off after breakfast, dressed in shorts and an Aertex shirt,
brown sandals and a straw hat 'to stop the freckles', as Mother
ordered. She'd lost countless straw hats, blown off her head into
the sea from whatever fishing boat she'd found herself on that
day. She'd picked up Italian like a sponge, diving with her

young friends from the harbour walls to harvest sea urchins from the rocks, learned to cartwheel into the water with the boys near the Fonte Aretusa, their skin gleaming mahogany-brown from endless days of sunshine.

The language was so different to what she'd studied when she'd later gone up to Oxford. The Italian in her university text-books had been classical, complicated. Sicilian dialect was like learning a totally new language. The subjunctive had never been necessary in her Sicilian sentences peppered with dialect and idioms. *'Bedda Matri'* for 'wow', *'troppu bedda'* for 'very nice'. None of the professors had understood the words she'd uttered in conversation tutorials and she'd had to unlearn them, but in the ensuing days at Glenaig, she rekindled her interest in the Sicilian dialect, remembering the passion of her childhood holidays.

Whenever possible she sat with Savio and he always seemed pleased to see her and chat for a while in his parents' language. Sometimes Maria joined them but she laughed and said she didn't understand what they were saying. The Italian side of her family was from northern Italy, near the Austrian border. She was trilingual, speaking English as well as German and Italian. Knowledge of foreign languages was common to all of them, Joy realised – most likely why they'd all been recruited. She presumed they were being trained to be special operators, to be dropped behind enemy lines, but nothing had yet been spelled out. Secrecy was the byword, posters hanging up in the common room and corridors cautioning them about careless talk costing lives, a horrific image of a young soldier collapsing with a bullet to his neck bringing home the importance of 'keep your trap shut'.

She'd hated it when Italy had allied herself to the Axis and made themselves the enemy. But meeting Savio, knowing that he was a British citizen, albeit of Italian parents, gave her a legit-imate reason for fraternising with him.

. . .

Yet again, she failed to come up to muster with the arduous field exercises over the following days and Savio found her one afternoon nursing a mug of strong tea in the canteen, her face as miserable as the damp, 'dreich' Scottish weather. She was seated on her own, feeling utterly exhausted and dejected.

'Mind if I join you, Joy?' he asked, sitting down next to her anyway. 'You're not living up to your name this afternoon, are you?'

She pulled a face. 'I don't think I'll ever manage to please that... woman,' she said. It had been on the tip of her tongue to say 'that bitch', but you never knew who was listening in on conversations. Everything they did seemed like a test. Even the kitchen staff might be planted to spy on them, she suspected.

'Be always on your guard. Learn not to trust. You will have to have your wits about you at all times once you are out of here and in the field,' was advice constantly repeated throughout every lecture.

It had crossed Joy's mind that Savio could very well be a plant too, reporting back to the 'bitch' or some other commanding officer. She was starting to be paranoid, forever on edge.

'Come running with me. I'm on a fitness drive too, you know,' he said, biting into a powdered-egg sandwich. 'And there's nothing much else to do in this place. I follow a route round the loch before a morning swim. Before breakfast most days.'

Each weekday morning from then onwards, Joy rolled out of her warm bed to join Savio in what she declared to him was madness but, secretly, she enjoyed. He was easy going, didn't try anything on, despite him flicking an admiring gaze at her the first time she revealed herself in her one-piece costume. The idea of plunging in the water was not so frightful after their run around the lake. Savio sometimes brought a flask of coffee for after their swim and they'd taken to chatting in the boathouse, before reveille.

'I only learned to swim quite recently,' he told her, as he lit up. He'd offered her a cigarette and lit hers from his.

'Really? You'd never believe it. I've been swimming since I was tiny, but you're stronger in the water than me.'

'I needed to learn quickly.' He paused, as if considering whether to explain and then shrugged, before pulling on his cigarette. 'I had a good teacher.'

She sensed he didn't want to explain and left it at that. Glenaig was a place of secrets where people rarely opened up; she'd quickly understood that. Even spending time together like this would be frowned on.

The early morning sessions were invigorating and over the next weeks, she found the assault courses less arduous, even overtaking Maria and a couple of other girls. The instructor was grudging in her praise. 'Well, this is a turn-up for the books, Harrison. Well, well, well! Didn't think you had it in you. Let's see if you can keep it up.'

Joy said nothing in reply and the instructor stopped picking on her and found another victim to taunt.

The sessions were varied in topic but all designed to train them for survival in the wild, once they were dropped behind enemy lines and had to survive alone. A local gamekeeper was called in to give them a talk. As he explained what to do with a snared rabbit, Joy watched rather than listened as he demonstrated how to skin it like peeling off a glove. His local accent was as impenetrable as a foreign language. They had a session on how to disguise themselves, which they all found quite entertaining: how to apply makeup and create authentic scars, how to dye hair, how to blend in by wearing the local style of dress.

Tobermory was the nearest large town, with a cinema and

dance hall, but Glenaig was effectively shut off and anywhere beyond the grounds was out of bounds.

One morning, as coffee steamed in the flask cup that they shared back and forth, Savio spoke of trying to escape for a drink. 'I'd like to feel normal for a few hours,' he said.

'If we're caught, it's curtains for us both,' Joy said. She was reluctant to jeopardise her chance of completing the course. She had never felt so alive. Somersby Hall seemed a continent away and she'd not once thought about Mother. Her horse, yes. She missed cantering through the woods on Dream and walking the dogs. But here, Joy felt she was working towards a purpose and meeting Savio was a breath of fresh air. He was totally unlike any of the suitable but dreadfully boring young men her mother had kept pulling out of the social woodwork. From the few comments Savio had related about his work as a hairdresser in Soho and his modest home above the shop, she wondered what he would think of Somersby Hall if she were to ever invite him.

They were worlds apart but Glenaig was a kind of neutral zone: a place where an assortment of individuals was pooled together, each with something different to offer. She hoped she would prove to be useful. But, sometimes, in the canteen, when she cast her eyes over the tables – the geeky table, as she dubbed it in her mind, where the academics congregated, or the sports-men's table, where muscly men and women chatted loudly and excelled at all the physical exercises – she wondered if she was up to the mark. Would she make it? Was her knowledge of Italian sufficient for her to pass? Maria, on her linguists' table, rattled off Italian as perfectly as German.

She'd voiced her insecurities to Savio over a flask of coffee and he'd told her to stop comparing herself to others. 'You're you, not them. That's what I keep telling myself when I'm talking to some toff. The people who run this outfit wouldn't have asked us here if they weren't interested in what we have to offer. Don't put yourself down.'

It was good to have these pep talks.

He told her he'd hated school, found lessons difficult, but she admired his outlook on life and his unscholarly intelligence that made absolute sense to her.

'I've got a week off soon,' she found herself telling him. 'If our leave coincides, we could have that drink then. That's if you really want to.'

'I wouldn't have suggested it otherwise, Joy,' he told her, re-screwing the cup on the vacuum flask. 'I DO want to.'

In the end, their leaves didn't coincide. Joy was disappointed but told herself it was for the best. She didn't need to be involved with a man at the moment.

CHAPTER 19

'You need to learn how to breathe properly,' Savio said, turning round to see Joy practically collapsed on another early morning run together. They'd arranged to meet before breakfast for a 'spot of light training', Savio had said. 'You've improved loads, but we need to get you up to speed with the top bitches.'

Joy had stopped after the first mile and a half of sprinting, her lungs fit to burst as she bent over, hands on knees, gulping in the misty Scottish air that rose in a theatrical haze above the loch. She was on her monthlies again, but she didn't feel like explaining the reason for her slow pace this morning. They'd chatted about many things but the problem of menstruation wasn't a topic she wanted to share.

He pulled out his army water bottle and handed it to her.

She brushed it away, panting as she told him in gasps. 'Will puke up... if... drink now.'

'Take little sips. You need to rehydrate. Believe me.'

Afterwards, when she felt a little better, he showed her how to take in air, how to use her stomach muscles and her nose, rather than gulping in air with her mouth open. 'You need to use those muscles more when you run too. Engage your core.'

He moved over and put his hands on her abdomen to show her. 'Imagine you have a belt there.'

'Over my fat, you mean?' Joy said.

'You're not fat, woman. Don't do yourself down. You're... womanly. And you have a core to keep you strong inside there.' He patted his own hard stomach this time.

She grinned at him. 'Good to hear you think I'm a woman. Trouble is, my exercise was always done on the back of Dream, my horse. I do miss him so.'

Although she was bantering with him, inside she was pleased. He'd given her a kind of compliment, hadn't he? Telling her she was womanly? She liked that: nobody had ever described her in this way. She was the 'girl who was game for a laugh'; good at French cricket at weekend house parties; the one who didn't mind getting her hair mussed up or mascara running down her face. Joy had always been a tomboy. But that didn't mean she disliked kisses when she'd played Sardines, hiding in wardrobes or understairs cupboards. She liked men. So far, she hadn't met the right one.

Savio was not the lad she'd first judged him to be: a Latin womaniser. He had always been the perfect gentleman. Maybe he would try it on some time. To a good-looking chap like him it must be second nature but she wasn't going to encourage him. There might be a war on and, yes, lots of young people didn't think twice about jumping into bed after their first date. 'Here today, gone tomorrow' was the justification. If you weren't sure how long your luck was going to last, then why not grab fun while you could? But that was not her way. And anyway, she knew what a lot of Italian lads were like. Hadn't she spent most of her summers in the company of Syracusans with their handsome looks and flirtatious ways encouraged at Mamma's knee?

She wondered if Savio was happy to spend time with her simply because she knew the island where his parents came from. He'd told her one day he planned to return.

'My parents, God bless them, they held on to that dream too. It was what got them through smoggy London winters. They were determined to return to their little farmhouse when they'd saved enough.

'"When you and Federico are settled, we'll leave you in London", they'd say to us,' he'd told her one foggy morning by the lake. '"Then, you can keep the salon going and come to stay with us in your holidays and fill yourselves with sunshine to fight the English winter."'

Increasingly he told Joy more about himself and, over their coffee breaks, she listened as he haltingly related the loss of his parents and brother and being locked up on the Isle of Man. Every now and again, he'd swallowed back his emotions and she'd waited patiently, sensing he needed to talk about the tragedy, but also understanding it was hard for him.

'I'm so sorry for your loss,' she said, when he had finished. 'That's absolutely appalling. And that you should have been locked up in the first place. It's shameful, Savvy.'

He'd bitten his lip and lowered his head. She'd covered his hand with hers and he'd smiled a watery smile. She'd wanted to hug him, but she'd held back, not sure if he'd want her to.

'I can do what I want now,' he'd said, standing up and picking up a pebble to skim over the loch. 'And I reckon I can make a go of it over there when all this is over. Got to have dreams, Joy. You got any?'

She really didn't. Apart from knowing she would never marry purely to suit her mother's will. As long as she had her horse to ride each day, dogs to walk, food to eat and a comfortable bed to sleep in, she had no great ambitions for the future. She'd not imagined being married with children. Who would want her?

'Oh, I'll just plod along,' she'd told Savio. 'I don't have big dreams, really. Let's get this hellish war over and then I'll have a think again. But for now, I'm concentrating on what I can do to help fight ruddy Hitler.'

And it was true. She hadn't said that to impress him. For too long she'd wasted time looking after her mother, who really didn't need looking after at all. For now, she wanted some independence and to do her best in her training so she could concentrate on helping end this war.

On the first day of parachute training, Joy broke her ankle. She was aggrieved she'd not even managed to jump from the tower and had missed her footing, tumbling from the ladder leading to the jumping platform. Her early morning runs with Savio came to a halt, as well as group physical exercise. In one sense she was relieved, as she recognised this aspect of training was definitely not her strong point. She'd struggled particularly in the assault courses, her frame larger than most of the other women. Wriggling under barbed wire, or squeezing herself through a gulley whilst carrying a weapon and a heavy rucksack, was tough. She excelled on the firing range, however, beating most of the men. Years of joining in with her father's shoots had honed that ability.

Whilst recuperating from her ankle injury, she was ordered to concentrate on perfecting the Morse code. She was quick on the uptake and soon she found herself tapping out sentences that came into her head on any hard surface. She was pulled up for this by her instructor one day in the canteen, when her fingers drummed on the table at the end of the meal.

'You want to watch that, Harrison,' the instructor said. 'Imagine if you were sitting on a train out in the field somewhere, working undercover, and you started on that. You'd be sussed immediately as an operator.'

She was right, of course. Joy knew that. Nevertheless, with the intense drills she was practising in the classroom, it was hard to switch off. Sometimes before falling asleep, she'd find herself tapping messages on the pillow. Dots and dashes filled her head and she guessed that was the aim of the course: total immersion so it became second nature. She cursed herself for being so clumsy at parachute training and was sure this would lead to her not being sent overseas. She'd far prefer to be used as an undercover agent in the field than stuck indoors tapping out and receiving messages.

A couple of weeks later, Joy and Savio revealed to each other they'd both been ordered to attend twice-weekly Italian lessons in one of the huts dotted around the grounds of Glenaig. In total, there were half a dozen students in the class, run by the same middle-aged professor Joy remembered from her interview. His accent sounded very Anglo-Saxon and his conversational skills had obviously been learned from old textbooks.

'Wouldn't last five minutes, if that, if he was dropped behind enemy lines,' Savio whispered to Joy when the professor had turned his back to write on the board.

Halfway through the course, Savio and Joy were asked if they could lead a session on Sicilian dialect for the following week and so they were thrown together in the preparation for this. They were in fits of laughter as they planned, both of them well-versed in the filthiest of swear words.

'I reckon it's more important to know how to come out with a few meaningful sayings, rather than understand the subjunctive and all that rigmarole,' Savio said, using some ripe expressions, peppered with references to the 'sit-upon', as Joy demurely put it. But the terms she knew in Sicilian were coarse: *pannàru, cacchero*. Somehow the local words for 'arse' sounded less filthy in dialect. They giggled like schoolchildren as they debated whether to teach these words.

'I think we should, Savvy,' she told him. 'It could make all the difference between blending in as a local or sticking out as a foreigner. But you can teach the pronunciation.'

'Happy to oblige, you old *buttana*. Whore.'

She thumped him.

It was during these classes that Joy twigged Savio's difficulty with reading and writing. He'd mentioned before he hadn't enjoyed his time at school and she understood why now. He seemed to find ways of avoiding exercises: his pen was empty of ink; he had a sore throat and couldn't read aloud; or he'd forgotten his glasses and he'd ask Joy to read for him. Her time helping at the village school had helped her identify a couple of little ones who'd struggled with words. She'd drawn up ideas of her own for them to manage.

But helping an adult was a different matter.

'Want to stay behind to practise more Sicilian swearing?' she asked him after everybody else had left the hut and she and Savio were collecting papers together.

He grinned. 'That sounds interesting, Joy. What do you mean?'

She took the bull by the horns. 'You... you can't read very well, can you, Savvy?'

He frowned as she shut the door.

'Your secret's safe with me, but I'd like to try and help. I told you I was teaching in the village school before coming here. I recognise your problem from nippers I worked with. Will you let me have a go?'

She sensed a barrier go up: his shoulders hunched, a bite of the lip she had begun to recognise when he was stressed. 'Give me half an hour. It might make all the difference to... everything. You never know when you might need it once you're dropped behind enemy lines.'

She sat down and he took the chair next to her. She'd cut out a card from stiff paper for him and she showed him how to move it along the page to reveal one word at a time. How to help Savio without offending his pride was her main concern. He stumbled over some of the letters and swore.

'I feel stupid,' he said, shoving the card away.

'Don't give up. What did you say to me when you were helping me exercise? "You can do this, Joy." You convinced me I could and look at the progress I made.' She retrieved the card and placed it on top of the page again. 'You can do this, Savvy.'

'Running is easier than reading,' he said. 'You put one foot in front of the other and you breathe.'

'Let's try and tackle one word, even one letter at a time.'

'Nobody else has been able to help me, Joy. I'm a lost cause.'

'Let me try, Savio. It will come in useful, I promise you. And I have a few tricks to help you unscramble the words.'

'My friends at school used to call me Savvy – you could count my friends on one hand back then. Everybody else called me thicko. Not the teachers, obviously, but nobody really understood my difficulties and I was left to get on with it. Only trouble is, I didn't get on with anything much at school – except my drawing. My exercise books were full of pictures. And words that made no sense to anybody.'

'Do the letters dance about?'

He looked up at her with surprise. 'Yep! My brother tried to help me read but he gave up. My folks didn't have much schooling to speak of, so they didn't know how to help either.'

'Shall we have another go now? Skip lunch? Are you hungry?'

His face lit up. 'If you're willing to give me a go, then do your stuff. Bet you'll find I'm a lost cause.'

'One good turn deserves another.'

She carefully printed some letters on a piece of paper.

'Can you read those out to me?'

He confused many and she recognised the difficulties she'd come across before.

'So, you confused the b and the d.'

'I told you I'm a thicko when it comes to this.'

'And I bet you've always managed to bluff your way through? Compensate in different ways?'

'Correct.'

'One thing is absolutely certain, Savio, you are *not* thick. Not at all.'

'Because I'm savvy.'

She smiled, all too aware, however, of his embarrassment. She pressed on, making him put his left hand at the top of a line of writing, advising him to look across and then down to the next line, sitting beside him, guiding his hand at times. He smelled good: a mixture of outdoors and a splash of aftershave she rather liked.

'It's helping,' he said after a few minutes, looking at her with a huge smile. 'But not everybody is patient like you.'

'Find strategies,' she said. 'Stall for time. So, for example, you could get hold of glasses with ordinary lenses. Make a thing of cleaning them to calm yourself down and then try the reading again. By which time, the person will either have read it for you or you will have had time to work it out. But in the meantime, I'm determined to do my best to help with these annoying letters so that you don't have to pretend. We might have to start from scratch, mind.'

She taught him tricks to help distinguish his b and d. 'A b has a great backside,' she said, pointing to the part of the letter looping behind the straight line. 'Whilst d is in the dumps because her boobs have drooped.'

'So, you teach schoolkids that sort of thing?' he chuckled, scribbling two cartoon characters from the letters. 'I wish my teachers had been like you.'

'I made it up to suit you,' she said, returning his smile. 'Those sketches are wonderful. I think you like the ladies.'

'You think right,' he said, rising from the chair. '*Mille grazie, bedda.* I've enjoyed our lesson. Are you free tonight for a drink? I've found me a bike and a track that leads out of this prison.

Let's escape for one evening. Hang the consequences. Just the once.'

'Honestly, you don't have to buy me a drink to say thank you, Savio.' She changed his name to Savvy and he grinned that grin again: the one that made his dark eyes shine and his face light up.

CHAPTER 20

He'd 'borrowed' a BSA motorbike for the night, he told her, and concealed it in the bracken next to a path not far from the boathouse. The owner was on compassionate leave and he would never know. 'Stupid chump left the keys in his bedside cabinet. He owes me a favour anyhow.'

She'd taken him at his word to dress warm and brought along her coarse uniform jacket, plus something to change into. She'd told Maria what she was up to and her roommate had promised to cover for her. 'I'm a dab hand at making pillows look like a body asleep in a bed,' she'd told Joy. 'Don't you worry. I'll say you're not feeling too good and have gone to bed early.'

'Wouldn't be the first time, eh?' Joy had replied. Every month she took to her bed early if she could, her pillow clutched to her stomach to soothe her cramps. Maria had managed to smuggle a hot-water bottle into Glenaig and she loaned this to Joy when the pains were bad.

Maria had lent her a pale-blue cashmere sweater to wear with the tweed skirt she'd arrived in at Glenaig. It was tighter than she liked, leaving little to the imagination, but Maria had reassured her she looked fine. 'You have a lovely figure, Joy. If I had a bust like yours, I'd flaunt it. Unfortunately, I inherited two mosquito bites from my mother,' she'd said, laughing self-deprecatingly.

'We're never happy, are we?' Joy had said. 'I'd trade your height in for mine, any time. I always feel so galumphing.'

'You are priceless – don't be silly! All the models are tall, like you. You don't realise how attractive you are.'

It was well known that Joy liked her evening constitutionals, so nobody batted an eyelid as she walked briskly along the path that led to the loch. She carried a small rucksack on her back containing her mufti and she'd planned to say she was carrying a book if she was questioned. 'I need some quiet to finish off the day,' she'd say. 'It's so noisy in the women's block.'

To her relief, nobody stopped her and nobody else was walking along the path. Even so, she turned to check before she pushed through the overgrown rhododendrons that almost concealed the track Savio had described. She walked about a quarter of a mile and then saw him, sitting astride a motorbike, smoking. He threw the stub to the forest floor and ground it out before waving and dismounting.

'Well done! You made it.' He pushed the motorbike off its stand. 'I'll manhandle the brute first so we get well out of hearing range when I start up. Can't be too careful. I'll turn my back while you change out of your uniform. Promise!' he said, with a wink.

Joy changed behind a tree, while Savio lit up again.

He pushed the heavy bike along the overgrown, brambly path and she helped by snapping off twigs overhanging the track as she walked ahead, wearing his leather gloves to avoid her hands being scratched as she pulled at thorny briars. Eventually they reached the boundary fence where there was a wide gap in the flimsy fencing.

'Helpful deer probably did this. I'm surprised it hasn't been patched up.'

He started the engine and she climbed onto the back of the bike, donning the helmet and goggles he'd handed her. He was already wearing his, and she thought they both looked like toads. She smothered her nervous giggles while she tightened the strap on her helmet.

'Hold on tight,' he said as they roared off and she clasped her hands around his leather jacket. She was conscious of her breasts resting against his back as she clung on for dear life, her skirt riding up her thighs as the bike roared down the country lane, the verges frothy soft with spring foliage.

Half an hour later they were sitting in the garden at the back of the pub, nursing beers at a table by the stream. They were alone, other customers sitting snug inside near a peat fire. Despite it being spring, it was nippy. The water gurgled over stepping stones that led to an island where ducks nested and for a while they gazed on the scene, pleased to be away from institutional surroundings.

'If my ma were here, she'd devise ways of sneaking one of those ducks away and wringing its neck for the pot,' Savio said, breaking the silence. 'Although we lived in London, she was a country woman at heart. She worked hard in our hairdressing salon, but she was always happier on the allotment with her green fingers. Green thumbs, she'd say. That's the way Italians say it.'

'I know. *Pollici verdi.*'

'Of course. It's still strange to me that you speak fluent Italian. You look so... English.'

'And I'm tall. Italian women are petite and... beautiful.' She spread her fingers in a fan, thinking they looked as large as a man's.

'You're a fine-looking woman, Joy. Your face... my parents had a painting, a kind of holy picture, above their bed: a madonna holding a fat baby Jesus. Your face reminds me of hers.'

She'd been swallowing a mouthful of beer as he said this. She spluttered and it sprayed over his shirt. 'Sorry, Savvy, but I've never been described as a madonna before,' she said with an embarrassed laugh, pulling a cotton handkerchief from her pocket to dab ineffectually at his shirt.

He grinned. 'Not saying you're the holy sort, like the real Ave Maria and that. But you do have a very pretty face.'

She was pleased that the light was fading because she felt a blush start above her breasts and rise up her neck to flood her cheeks. She covered her confusion by dropping the handkerchief to the grass at her feet and bent to retrieve it from under the table.

'Did you work full-time in your parents' salon?' she asked, changing the subject.

'I worked at a bakery as well as the salon, mostly with my mother on the ladies' side. The male side was Dad's kingdom. I'm not bad at cutting hair, you know.' He looked at her and then picked up a lock of her blonde hair. 'If you ever wanted me to style yours, I could. Just find me a pair of scissors.'

Her insides did a strange flip at his touch and for a couple of seconds she was nonplussed. 'Do you think it needs restyling?' she asked. 'What's the point? I have to wear it tied back when I'm in uniform.'

'You're not always in uniform, are you? What about evenings out? When you get dolled up for dances and that.'

'The only time I "doll up", as you put it, is for awful debs' balls my mother made me attend. Before the war.'

'What in hell's name are debs' balls? It sounds dead rude,' he snorted.

She gave him a sideways glance. Of course, he wouldn't know what she was talking about. She didn't imagine he read society magazines. And he wasn't from the social set her parents belonged to either. How different they were. What fun it would be, though, to take him along to one of those events. Much more entertaining than being on the arm of someone from the boring young county crowd. What a hoot it would be.

'It's a party mostly for wealthy aristocrats,' she explained. 'To see if they can hitch up with suitable husbands or wives.' Describing it in so many words reinforced how much she detested the gatherings.

He whistled. 'Like a cattle market. Not so very different from what goes on with the Italian community in London with their parties in Little Italy. My parents always told Federico and me that it would be easier to marry a girl from our way of life who understood our ways. Stick to our own...' He took another swig of beer. 'In fact, in Syracuse, Sunday evenings are when young people get a chance to formally meet each other. Walking round and round Piazza Duomo for the *passeggiata*. Always with parents and grandparents looking on, acting as chaperones. Everybody kitted out in their finest clothes, the girls done up to attract the boys, like peahens attracting peacocks. It's nature. The birds and bees do it too.'

He drained his glass and asked if she wanted a top-up. 'A drop of brandy or something else?' he asked. 'I'm feeling flush tonight. Won at poker this week.' He pulled a roll of banknotes from his blazer pocket and once again Joy thought how different he was. Nobody she knew would flash their cash like that. It was common. But she liked the honesty of Savio.

They had to speed to get back to the house before curfew ended.

'Cut it a bit fine this time,' he said, as he covered the bike up with bracken. 'I'll have to think of a way to get this back to where it was parked. Or I could leave it here for next time?'

Joy hoped there would be a next time. She couldn't remember enjoying an evening so much.

They hurried back along the path and when they reached

the women's block, he pecked her on the cheek in a brotherly way. 'Don't forget to find me those scissors,' he said.

'And don't forget to practise those letters,' she whispered back before he left for his bed.

She listened to him whistling as he disappeared towards the men's block: happy-go-lucky, a survivor. Many others, faced with the difficulties that life had thrown him, might have given up. But he was a fighter. She liked that.

That night it took her a while to fall asleep. She'd taken longer to brush her teeth, gazing at her reflection in the small mirror over the washbasin. Was she really as pretty as a madonna in a painting? Even if he'd been born in London, Savio was Italian at heart, wasn't he? She shook her head. Words like his were easy to toss out. But, all in all, it had been a good evening. It was probably the risk they'd taken that had made it seem so thrilling, she thought, as she pulled on her pyjamas and slipped between the sheets.

'Good evening, was it?' Maria asked in a sleepy voice.

'Oh, you know. So-so,' Joy answered, wanting to hug the evening to herself, go over it in her mind before sleep eventually claimed her thoughts and turned them into dreams.

Over in the men's wing, in the room shared with five other men, Savio removed his shoes and tiptoed across the wooden floor-boards to his bed. As he sat down, the metal springs squeaked and the chap in the bed next to him turned and grunted, whispering to Savio, 'Sarge was on the warpath, looking for you this evening. I had to invent something about you going for one of your mad swims in the loch. Have your story ready, chum.'

Savio pulled the towel from the end of his bed and made his way to the door. In the gloom, he tripped over a pair of boots. He tried to break his fall by grabbing a chair and that clattered to the floor, waking up a couple of roommates.

'Fuck's sake, can't a man get a kip?'

'What the devil's going on?'

Savio apologised. 'Gippy stomach. Sorry, lads.'

As he made his way to the washroom, towel in hand to soak as proof of a night swim in case the sarge came to find him early, he hoped his noisy fall hadn't woken anybody else. Next time he'd use a torch to make his way about, using a handkerchief to smother the glare. He berated himself for yet again not organising himself better. Moyes had pointed that out about his escape efforts.

Back between the cold sheets, he couldn't sleep, his head full of Joy's face and her gorgeous figure. She was a good kid: shy, a refreshing change from the girls he'd bedded. The kind of girl a chap respected. He was grateful for the patient way she'd coaxed him to read; he was no longer nervous about having a go and he even took time now to read the noticeboard or pick up a paper in the common room to glance at headlines. The tips she'd given him were good and he looked forward to more reading sessions together. She'd given him a copy of Dante's *Paradiso* to dip into for practice. 'It's the only Italian book I have with me,' she'd told him, 'but I love it. See what you think.'

Yes, she was a special woman. Nevertheless, he couldn't stop his mind from wandering to what she would be like to make love to. He could tell she hadn't much experience. There'd been plenty of opportunity this evening for her to welcome a move and he'd had to divert his thoughts when she was behind him on the bike, her body warm and soft against his. Savio tossed and turned before giving up. He needed a smoke and he made his way – carefully this time – to the window.

He opened it gently and lit up, leaning out for the smoke to disperse in the night air. There was a rustling and he looked down to see a fox nosing at something on the ground. The women's house was not visible from where he stood but he wondered if Joy too was thinking over the evening they'd shared. Probably not, he thought, as he flung the fag end through the gap in the window and pulled it to. Why would a chap like him even feature on her radar? What could she possibly see in a working-class boy from London? She'd talked about horses, dogs and a big country house. Sumersbey Hall, or something. Posh! *Nah, Savvy, me old fellow, forget about it*, he told himself. *Don't delude yourself. Stick to your own kind, like Mamma and Papà advised.* Nevertheless, the last thing his mind envisioned, before he snatched the one hour of remaining sleep, was Joy's smile and the way she tipped back her head when she laughed, her untidy blonde hair, that needed a good styling, fluffing out in a haze of gold around her pretty head.

He woke to the snarling voice of Sergeant Scott as he boomed, 'Out of bed, you horrible lazy lot. Close combat drills on the football pitch in five minutes. Shake a bloody leg and make sure you bring your FS fighting knives...'

CHAPTER 21

JOY

We sneak away from Glenaig again towards the end of May. One whole night is ours. We're living dangerously but the world is a dangerous place and why should we be denied one night of happiness? Maria is an angel: she promised to cover for me and Savio bribed his pals to do the same. They can hardly shoot us for treason, can they? Is love a crime? Is love a contravention of the Official Secrets Act?

We dance first and he moves well. Our bodies as one on the crowded dance floor, his strong thighs against mine, his heart beating against mine. I know he wants me as much as I want him. In his arms I'm not clumsy. I'm desired. And I see the desire in other women's eyes as they watch with envy. Can they hear the things he murmurs: that I am beautiful with my face of a madonna? On this bewitching evening I believe everything he says.

The guest house is shabby and the elderly owners think we are married and they ply us with shortbread by their fireside and something called black bun. All I want is to hurry upstairs and love him. He wants the same, I know. His gaze burns into mine as we sit opposite each other by the hearth. The parlour bristles with embroidered cushions and knick-knacks and a motheaten stag's head with glass eyes glares down at me. Who cares if the animal knows Savio and I are unmarried? The beastie knows full well what will happen upstairs in the poky bedroom with its faded wallpaper and darned eiderdown.

Alone at last, the moment the door closes behind us we tear at each other's clothes, stifling murmurs as we move to the bed. The springs are old and the wooden headboard clatters against the wall even though Savio is gentle. He grabs a towel from the rail and whispers to me to raise my hips as he slips it underneath. 'I know you've not been with a man before, my darling Joy. You might bleed the first time.'

He tells me how lovely I am, how he adores my every curve as he traces his lips over my breasts, down to my hips and then to my most secret part. He wants to spend the rest of his life with me, he says: I am special and he will never let me go. And I want to believe him but still I test him to hear his words.

'But we hardly know each other.'

'But you feel it too, don't you, Joy?' he replies. 'What we've found in each other.'

Our conversation is furtive. The walls are thin and the elderly folk sleep next door.

'What do I feel, Savio?' I stare into his eyes, searching for the truth. The moon, framed in the tiny window, lights his face with an unearthly glow. And the whole night is unreal, out of this world. How can he feel this way about me?

Before he enters me, his eyes search mine. 'Are you sure, my darling? Are you sure?'

He does not need to ask.

It hurts at first and his eyes are closed now, his face

changing as he moves inside me, slowly, his expression abandoned, moving inside me as if he has no control and then he
withdraws, rubbing himself over my tummy and I feel his liquid
spread over my skin like a lotion gluing us together.

'Shit!' he says, falling away. 'I didn't use anything. Are you
all right? Did I hurt you, Joy?' He leans up on his elbow, tracing
a finger round my face, brushing back my hair and kissing me
deeply. 'You are so very beautiful, you know.'

Afterwards, when he is asleep, I tiptoe to the bathroom
down the narrow corridor to rinse streaks of blood from the
towel, embarrassed at what the old lady might think. For the
remainder of the night I lie awake on my side, watching his
chest rise and fall as he sleeps, listening to his steady breathing,
full of wonder that he wants me. I wish the morning will never
come.

But in the morning, we make love again. He shows me how
to help him roll on the johnnie, as he calls it, and this time I feel
what he must have felt last night because when he comes inside
me, I am falling, falling, falling to a place I've never been before.
He stills my cry with his hand, laughing afterwards as we catch
our breath.

'Next time, we'll make love in the boathouse and it won't
matter about the noise we make.'

When I return from washing myself in the poky bathroom, flannelling away the smell of sex, soaping between
my legs where it stings, he is sitting on the bed waiting.
He falls on one knee and tells me to close my eyes and put
out my hand. I open my palm to see a chain with a charm:
a strange trinket made from metal – a man's head coiled
with snakes and leaves, with three legs protruding like
sunrays. I've seen this kind of emblem everywhere in
Sicily.

'It was my mother's,' he says. 'I can't give you a ring yet, but
take this as a token of how I feel. It was one of her lucky belong-

ings. Please say you'll be mine, Joy. I love you. Next time we make love, it will be better for you. I promise.'

I fall into his arms and nod, hardly able to believe that this wonderful man loves me He traces away my tears and we slowly dress and tread downstairs to smoked kippers, eggs and knowing looks from the elderly couple.

'We know what young love is like, don't we, Ian,' the silver-haired woman says. 'We were only sixteen when we first met. It's been more than fifty years we've been together. We wish you as much happiness as we've been blessed with. Now, eat up. The hens have been busy. And you must be starving, my dears.'

I am not hungry at all. I am too full of Savio.

On the train back, we hold hands. I don't want to ever let him go.

'Do you have a photograph you can give me?' I ask. 'To put under my pillow?'

He smiles and pulls out his wallet. 'Only if you give me one of yours.'

'I'm awful in photos. And I've only a hideous one of me in uniform.'

He shrugs. 'You can have mine if you give me yours.'

We are acting like children and I love this carefree feeling that wraps itself around me. We swap our snaps and I snuggle into him, wanting the train to never arrive.

He kisses me before we reach Glenaig and we move to different carriages. When I alight at the station I make sure to keep my distance, as if I'm a different person, trailing him like a spy, my training kicking in, but I cannot tear my eyes from his body as he strides towards the gates. How long will it be before we're together again? My fingers touch the pendant in my pocket and I think I am the luckiest woman alive.

.   .   .

But there was to be no next time, because the day after they returned to Glenaig, Joy was summoned to the main office. At first, she thought they'd been discovered – that she was going to be expelled immediately.

She was told she was being sent away somewhere else, that her time at Glenaig was over. She had failed her physical test and the parachute episode had been the final downfall. Her ankle was shot and she would not be required overseas but they had a vital job for her further south in England which was equally as important. They wanted to use her Italian skills and everything would be explained in due course. In the meantime, she should go home. When she searched for Savio to say good-bye, it seemed he'd disappeared from the face of the earth. Nobody knew where he was.

In her heart she prayed he would send word to her some-how. On the train south, she gazed at the countryside wakening to summer: blossom on fruit trees in orchards, a drooping scare-crow standing in the middle of crops, a creek that reminded her of Suffolk, a flock of gulls clouding over a tractor as it ploughed, like dozens of fluttering handkerchiefs. Such sights usually entertained her but as she fingered the pendant in her pocket, her mind was full of Savio. Surely, he'd meant every word he had whispered to her that night. Surely? He wanted to be with her forever, his promise sealed with a pendant. She couldn't believe they'd been words simply to seduce her. Maybe Savio had been sent away somewhere too, somewhere dangerous.

She pulled the pendant from her pocket and kissed it before putting it away again. The woman sitting opposite her smiled at her sympathetically and Joy sat up ramrod straight, telling herself to get a grip as the train steamed onwards.

CHAPTER 22

1943, PALESTINE

SAVIO

It was harsh, it was brutal, it was the worst of times, it was the best of times. Savio had never worked so hard in all his twenty-nine years and it left little time to dwell on Joy. There were times, last thing at night, as he stared at the stars in the inky desert sky, that he'd wondered about her. But there was precious little time during the day to dwell on her loveliness or send word whilst Moyes put his men through the mangle: training them until they dropped each night into their sleeping bags or rudimentary hammocks slung up in the ruins.

Major Moyes would spring exercises on them in the middle of the day when the sun beat down mercilessly, sweat blinding their eyes as they marched with heavy backpacks. Despite the assorted bandanas or cotton shemaghs worn around the bottom of their faces, the men still swallowed gritty sand. Some favoured caps as worn by the French Foreign Legion to keep the unforgiving rays from the backs of their necks. In fact, Moyes had enrolled a couple of these hardened warriors in his motley group for the special mission he promised them would be the beginning of the end of this war.

He woke up groups of troops in the middle of the night at varied stages, devising different exercises to harden them. Savio was in the first lot. Moyes entered the tent where he and five others slept and shook each man awake.

The desert was 'as cold as a nun's fanny', he warned, and ordered them to quietly and quickly assemble outside on the cold sand, line up and be ready for the off. Then he drove them in his Jeep to a destination known only to himself and shouted at them to jump out. He left them there, his wheels skidding in the sand as he roared off. Those men who had jumped last from the back received the full benefit of the Palestinian desert with Moyes' hasty departure, and they rubbed their gritty eyes, brandishing their fists in the direction of his battered Jeep. His laughter followed as he sped away like a madman. 'See you in the morning for breakfast, chaps,' he shouted. 'Navigate by the stars. Remember the night I pointed them out to you. And, if you've been listening to me, your kit bags should at all times contain full canteens of water. If not, then sort yourselves out. Remember not to drink your piss if you're thirsty. It tastes like the worst beer from the worst brothels...'

They made it back to camp long after breakfast had been cooked up. All of them. They'd stayed in a group and it had been Savio who had encouraged them onwards. He and the others had taken turns to fireman-carry the youngest member of the team: one of the Frenchies, who was suffering from dehydration as a result of a stomach upset the day before the crazy exercise.

'Gawd, he's a ton weight,' one of the men had complained as he took his turn. 'Why don't we leave him here and fetch him once we get back? Use the bastard Moyes' Jeep? There are enough of us to stage a rebellion against his crazy shindigs.'

'We can't leave the Frog here on his own and the chances of

finding him again before some other desert creature does are slim. We stick together,' Savio had ordered. 'If it had been you, would you appreciate being abandoned? Anyway, never under-estimate Moyes. He'll have something else up his sleeve, sure as a Palestinian viper lays eggs. Wouldn't be surprised if he was spying on us all at this very moment. Disguised as a camel herder or something else madcap. And he'll shoot anybody who goes against his orders. He's not known as the desert wolf for nothing. Now, bloody get a move on before I shoot you myself.'

Yes, it was tough and Savio surprised even himself at how hardened he had become. But it was infinitely better than being holed up on the Isle of Man. He had discovered a strength he hadn't known existed. Joy's beautiful smile sneaked often into his head and he wondered how she was doing. But she was a world away and survival meant bottling his feelings. If he allowed himself the luxury of heartbreak, he'd fail. But it was difficult to blot her out and there was no way of contacting her at the moment, anyhow.

'So, Rizzo, what can you tell us about this place?' After the latest exercise in the desert, Moyes unrolled a reconnaissance map across the old door used as a makeshift table in a corner of the ruined fort they were using as a base.·

He and Moyes were alone in what was known as Moyes' Lair – an area benefitting from the only section of intact roof amongst the ruins. It was a strategic point too, having gaps in the stone walls which afforded Moyes all-round views of his temporary desert kingdom.

Savio bent to examine the map, immediately recognising the distinctive shape of the south-eastern corner of Sicily, known variously as Maddalena Island, the peninsula, or the pig's snout: Capo Murro di Porco. To the north, the city of Syra-cuse extended like a pointing finger into the water.

'I can tell you quite a lot,' Savio replied. 'It's where my parents were from.' He pointed with a grubby finger to a light-house. 'As nippers we were always getting chased away by the military from here.'

Moyes nodded and then indicated a track running parallel with the coastline. He stopped and tapped his fingers on a shorter track leading off this to the sea. 'And what about this point? Is it possible to gain access from the sea here, do you think? The photos don't show the height.'

'It's easy enough to jump into the sea from the rocks, but you have to be careful climbing back on land. The stones there, they're razor-sharp and there's plenty of holes to fall down and sprain your ankle. Your feet would be torn to shreds without thick boots.' He looked up at Moyes. 'Is this what we've been preparing for? All those exercises you've set us? The climbing of the bluffs? Getting us up in the night?'

Moyes ignored his questions and Savio continued. 'Yep, I know the area well, sir. It's where I hung out with my cousins when we went in summer. You could say it's...' He paused, wondering what his commanding officer would make of what to him was the truth. 'It's... my territory.'

Moyes nodded his head. 'As I thought, Rizzo. When was the last time you were there?'

Savio thought before answering. 'Seven years ago, maybe more.'

He bent to examine the map again, pinpointing the large farmhouse his cousins had shared with extended family. His parents owned a simpler dwelling on the edge of the land. He recognised the orange and lemon groves that surrounded the old building and the vast plantation of almond trees, the main source of income for his uncles. He'd helped harvest them one July and they'd tried to smuggle back a huge sack to England, as well as half a dozen bottles of his father's favourite Sicilian tipple: Amaro Averna.

Each time they'd visited their little Sicilian house, it had grown shabbier. His father spent most of his holiday patching it up, a hat folded from newspaper protecting his head, dressed in shorts and a grubby vest.

Savio shook his head free of these memories because Major Moyes was talking to him again.

'What do you know about this area?' he asked, pointing northwards on the promontory.

'The cliffs are really high at that point and undercut by hollows carved by waves. The spray funnels up through the rocks. It's quite a spectacle.'

Savio recalled how he and his cousins would dare each other to stand over the holes where the seawater pushed up.

'Hard to land craft there, then?' Moyes asked him.

'I'd say so. The sea's always rough. There's a line of rocks that form a natural jetty – apparently the Greeks used the stone to build in—'

'I'm not asking for a history lesson, Rizzo.'

'No, sir. Sorry, sir. I'd say it's better to land here.' He prodded a finger south, near to the lighthouse.

'The drop in the rocks lower?' Moyes asked.

'Definitely.'

There was a pause in the discussion while the unkempt officer combed his tanned fingers through his beard, as matted as a nest. His father would have sorted that in no time with his sharp razor. Savio batted away more sentimental thoughts. His father was gone. No use dwelling on it.

'Thanks, Rizzo. I'll be sending these details back to HQ. You're to be my scout and interpreter for this mission. You'll need to pick a code name.'

'Dante' was Rizzo's immediate reply, fleetingly remembering his reading sessions with Joy and stamping down the memory immediately. It would help nobody if he wallowed in heartache.

'So, we *are* bound for Sicily, sir?'

It was half question, half statement but Moyes put a finger to his mouth, almost concealed by his beard. This was quickly followed by drawing a line across his throat.

'This discussion is to remain between you and me for now. Churchill has described your island as the soft underbelly of Europe. The way in. And we shall be the first men in. So, I need to know exactly what the terrain is like and go through everything with you again – any detail, however small, is useful. *Anything.*'

For the next hour, aided by swigs of excellent malt whisky shared from Moyes' hip flask, Savio helped fill in the map, detailing buildings he could remember: the local school, church, various farmhouses and ruins, olive plantations, the fountain used by women for washing and a couple of wells. He told Moyes where to be wary of dense thickets of prickly pears, where the rock outcrops were with caves used as storerooms or for housing animals, sometimes even as poor folks' dwellings. He sketched out locations of all buildings he remembered.

'My uncle told me this part of the island has always been fortified, but I don't recognise those new buildings on your map. It's seven years or so since I was there, sir, remember. I can't tell you about changes since then.'

'Of course, man. But what you've told me is really useful, especially concerning the terrain.'

They called it a night and Moyes warned him there would be another exercise early but not to tell the others. 'Surprise is key.' And then he lowered his voice. 'After that we say goodbye to this place.'

That night, Savio hugged to himself the thought he might be drawing nearer to his beloved Sicily. Perhaps one perfect day, Joy would come to him there. She loved the island too, an island carved into his being, unlike the Isle of Man, that also

boasted the three-legged symbol on its flag. He found that an
ironic coincidence.

At five next morning, Moyes summoned them rudely from their
makeshift beds and ordered them to remove their footwear.
'Even your socks, you soft lot,' he shouted. He himself stood
barefoot and he ordered them to run three times round the
boundary of the fort, over rocks and hot sand. He led the way,
his long legs making it look easy. 'You need to toughen up, you
lily bastards. Make those feet do their job. *Faster*,' he urged
them, ordering a fourth lap because he was unhappy with their
sluggish performances. Savio knew why he'd ordered this exercise but many in the troop swore it was the last straw, that the
major had gone barking mad. It was time to teach the bastard a
lesson and give him a taste of his own medicine.

That had never happened so far. Moyes had a way of
coming down to his men's level. They all knew of the drunken
episode that had landed him up in the military police cells for a
couple of nights. He was one of them but at the same time, he
was a canny leader.

On their last night in the Palestinian desert, Moyes played
on the old honky-tonk piano he and some of the men had 'requisitioned' from a bar in Hadera. He started off with Chopin's
'Nocturnes' until his men whistled their disapproval: 'Come on,
sir. Play something better.'

The evening ended with their leader sitting on top of the
piano holding the stray mongrel he had been feeding all the
time they were at the fort. 'I need four tins of bully beef at least
for my friend for a farewell feast. And then I'll play you buggers
something more suited to your uneducated ears.'

It didn't take long for a pile of tins to lie at his feet. He
opened a couple with the end of his bayonet and set the dog
down to eat the food. The sound he managed to coax from the

untuned keys, his jazzy rendition of the 'The White Cliffs of Dover', followed by his own version of 'Moonlight Serenade', went down better than Chopin. Even the dog howled his appreciation.

Moyes climbed on top of the piano when he'd finished, lit his pipe and then ordered Savio to break up the piano. 'Pick a couple of the strongest men and destroy this poor, out-of-tune piece of crap. It's done its job. We move out tomorrow, men,' he said, jumping down. 'Drink up and then grab some kip.'

With the piano reduced to a pile of sticks, he trickled the remainder of his whisky onto the broken keys and piano frame and then threw a match at it. The bonfire went up in a whoosh, illuminating the expressions on the men's faces: some suddenly sober, some too drunk to care.

Savio watched Major Moyes crouch down beside the dog and then pull his revolver out to place it at the dog's head. A shot rang out across the desert sands and the dog slumped in the dirt at Moyes' feet. Catching Savio's horrified look, he shrugged his shoulders. 'It was for the best, Rizzo. Who would have treated him half as well? He had a good end.'

Savio was shocked. Dispatching the dog was unnecessarily harsh and he resolved never to tell Joy about the incident. She'd spoken so fondly of her beloved Labradors and the horse she'd left behind. He was happy enough to be Moyes' scout once they landed on the shores of Sicily, but he could never imagine him becoming a friend.

That night, Savio took a long time to fall asleep as he relived Joy and their first night together. He wished she were next to him here now on the desert sands, the stars haloing their lovemaking. It was hard to compartmentalise his feelings, as Moyes had urged his troops to do on many occasions. *Bugger the man*, he thought, as he gave himself up to the luxury of dreaming of a future with the most kind-hearted, beautiful girl he'd ever met.

CHAPTER 23

EARLY JULY 1943, BLETCHLEY PARK

JOY

'So, are you one of Dilly's fillies?'

The young woman in the small bedroom of the house where Joy had been billeted looked up from her book as Joy dumped her kit bag on top of a paisley-patterned eiderdown on the second bed.

'Come again?' Joy responded, not knowing what on earth the drop-dead gorgeous brunette was talking about.

'Codebreaker? In the cottage?' the brunette said, as if this was all the explanation Joy could ever need.

Joy had no idea what she was talking about and even if she did, hadn't she just been yet again put through the mangle about utter secrecy, reliability and trustworthiness? When her interviewer had asked her to sign the Official Secrets Act again, she'd dared to ask him what it was she had to do and why. He'd practically barked at her. 'You do NOT ask questions. You get on with the job.'

She wasn't about to fail at the first test and fall into another hidden interview with this woman. She had in all likelihood been planted to see if Joy was reliable and all the rest of it.

'Look, I'm whacked,' Joy said. 'You don't mind if I catch some shut-eye?'

This much was true. She felt bone-tired and miserable. After their blissful night, Savio had failed to contact her, despite his promises which to her had amounted to a kind of betrothal. She'd asked after him but there'd been little time to search for him at Glenaig as she'd been told to leave at very short notice. Staying with Mother over the past weeks had been as awful as ever and she was thankful when word came for her to make her way west to a station in Buckinghamshire.

Here today, gone tomorrow the train seemed to rattle along the tracks. Should she believe the lovely things he had whispered to her or had she been fed empty promises? The railway tracks outside Bedford had been bombed in a recent raid and so she'd had to traipse to the next station in the mizzle, along with all the other passengers. Her lace-ups were caked with mud, her precious stockings laddered and her uniform crumpled and creased. She peeled her wet clothes off down to her underwear and left them in a soggy mess on the threadbare carpet.

'Any chance of a hot bath?' she asked.

The brunette snorted. 'This is definitely not The Ritz, worst luck. Mrs Perkins allows us a hot bath once a week in five inches of water. She's drawn a black line and woe betide if you go an eighth of an inch over.'

She jumped from her bed and extended a warm hand. 'I'm Rosanna; Rosie for short. I'll see what I can do. Perks usually goes to her whist drive at the village hall this evening. Can you wrap yourself in your eiderdown for a bit and then I'll go and boil the kettle on the range as soon as she's out?'

'Lord! What a palaver,' Joy said, pulling the eiderdown around her and wondering what she had let herself in for. At least back in Glenaig there had been plenty of hot water and the tea urn was always available for a drink in the canteen. She sat shivering.

'You poor thing. You do look all in,' Rose said, bending to pick up Joy's sodden clothing and hanging them over the back of the only chair in the room. 'What name do you go by, then?'

'Joy. Joy Harrison. Sorry – you don't have to do my dirty work for me. I'm just whacked at the minute. A little snooze and I'll get going again.'

'It's absolutely no problem. I had a quiet shift today. *Very* quiet, actually. Makes a change, but in actual fact I prefer to be kept busy; it makes time pass faster.'

The front door slammed and Rosie moved over to the wardrobe. Joy watched as she proceeded to push it to one side. 'She's so stingy – she thought she'd hidden it, but... ta-da!' Rosie held out her hand to show the gas fire previously hidden behind the furniture.

'Got a match? We'll soon feel cosy and have your clothes dry before the old bat returns. Let's hope she wins something at her whist drive and we get a decent breakfast.'

Joy flopped back against the hard pillow and shut her eyes. Quite honestly, she could have slept on the floor she was so exhausted. At least her roommate seemed a good egg. The last thing she was conscious of as she drifted off was mumbling a thank you to Rosie for covering her with her own eiderdown.

Half an hour later, Joy woke to somebody gently shaking her.

'Sorry, old thing. You were dead to the world but if you want that wash before Perks returns, then you'd better be quick about it. Will be more of a cat lick than a proper bath, to be honest, but beggars can't be choosers. And I'll make us some toast and Oxo for after.'

'You're so kind. What a brick.'

Joy followed Rosie down the stairs, through a poky kitchen and into the lean-to bathroom, stuck onto the back of the two-up two-down terraced house. The lino flooring was cold to her bare feet and mould spotted the back wall. Rosie poured water from the enamel kettle into two cups and told Joy to pour the rest of the scalding hot water into the bath tub. It barely covered the base.

'Add some cold and I'll leave you to freshen up,' Rosie said, reappearing with a plate of toast. 'Enjoy! I'll be in the kitchen, acting guard. Be quick, mind.'

It did the trick and Joy made sure afterwards to leave the bathroom as she'd found it. Afterwards, sharing cups of warm-enough Oxo with Rosie, she began to feel human.

'I've been here at BP a year already,' Rosie told her. 'Can't tell you exactly what I do. It's all frightfully hush-hush. But I'm used for my language skills.'

'Really? German?'

'Italian.'

Joy's eyes widened. But she was not going to fall into the trap of revealing this was why she'd been sent here. However, she was prepared to listen to anything her roommate could tell her.

It would have been so easy to share at this point that she too spoke Italian. At the interview, after she'd been told she'd failed the physical test for the SOE, they had tested her again. An officer on the panel had asked her what she knew about the inside of a submarine and to describe it in Italian.

Feeling bolshy, but wanting also to prove she could be of use to the service, she'd replied truthfully. 'I know nothing about submarines but I can explain to you in Italian how to sail a fishing boat off the Sicilian coast.'

In for a penny, in for a pound, she'd thought. 'I bet you couldn't tell me in Italian how to fish for a sea urchin or gut a swordfish, sir, or even swear authentically in Sicilian dialect.'

She was peeved they hadn't wanted her for the SOE. *Never mind, it is too late for that now,* she'd thought. *Water under the bridge.* It was their loss if they didn't want her but she may as well make a go of whatever else was on offer.

The officer had actually laughed at her. 'Well, you've won your bet, Miss Harrison. I cannot swear in Sicilian. And I feel sure your technical Italian can be improved with time. Of which we do not have an awful lot, as a matter of fact. However, you have passed your interview.'

He'd left the room, but she was still none the wiser as to what precisely she was wanted for. A sergeant had come in afterwards to tell her that she would be earning £150 a year and that on arrival at X, as he'd put it, details of her shifts, leave and cost of accommodation would be explained. He'd handed her a rail warrant and a pass. And then when she was at Mother's, she'd received word that her destination was Bletchley station, but he gave nothing else away. He'd warned her not to lose it, and that was that. It was all so mysterious, like playing a part in a Hitchcock film.

She pulled herself back to Rosie in the room they were sharing, steam rising from her clothes as they dried by the gas fire.

'I lived in Rome, you see. That's where I learned Italian,' Rosie was saying. 'My father worked at the Embassy. I *adore* Italy.' She paused and her expression turned melancholy and Joy watched as she made a huge effort to compose herself.

Here was the moment when Joy could have shared her same passion for the country, but she was reminded of that updated Official Secrets Act, the officer leaning over her to make sure she turned each and every yellow page of the bulky document. He'd spoken of the awful consequences of breaking confidences and warned her even her parents should not know what she was doing. So, she merely listened to Rosie.

'We met Mussolini, you know. He had a villa at the seaside next to our place. Funny little man... he liked the girls, that's for sure. But life in Rome took a turn for the worse. Undercurrents... fear in the air. Hard to explain. Awful, uncouth young men in black shirts. I was badly shaken up when I saw a man beaten up in the Villa Borghese Gardens – where Daddy used to play cricket against the Australian Embassy team. These three fascist thugs were kicking him where he lay on the ground. I felt helpless to intervene. You know: three against one and everything. I felt awful. They bundled the poor man into a truck and I'll never forget their horrible, snarling leader: his expression of pure hatred as he turned to me. *"Signorina,"* he said, *"lei deve dimenticare..."* I should forget what I had seen.' She shuddered. 'Evil men!' She picked up a hairbrush from the chest of drawers and pulled it through her thick black curls. 'I vowed that day to do whatever I could to prevent Mussolini and his *fascisti* winning this war. It's got to change; we *have* to win...' She looked at Joy. 'The thought of never being able to return to my beloved Italy – it's simply too beastly for words.' She set the brush down again. 'Have you ever been? It's a heavenly country.'

'A while ago,' Joy replied, leaving it at that.

Rosie opened the window to let out the telltale aromas of toast and Oxo and stuck her nose in her book again. When Mrs Perkins returned she was in a good mood, having won a tin of rock cakes in the whist drive raffle. She shared a couple with her young lodgers and made them a cup of weak tea before they all retired for the night. She wasn't as bad as Rosie had made out, Joy thought, and her landlady's arrival back at the terrace house had at least saved Joy from further talk about Italy. But, goodness, wasn't it hard to keep schtum about something you loved so much? What must it be like for operators in the field? Had Savio been dropped from a plane over occupied land? Is that why he hadn't contacted her? The reality drummed into them all in training – that it was best not to know, best not to reveal – was hard to accept when your heart yearned to know. If she was finding it hard to stop revealing about her past here in her billet in southern England, how on earth did operatives cope? She longed to find out what her job was going to be in this place called X. Rosie had also referred to it as BP. But she had no time to dwell on any of her questions because as soon as her head touched the pillow again, she was away to the land of Nod.

CHAPTER 24

1943, SICILY

SAVIO

Early in the morning of July 10th, well before dawn, the landing crafts hanging from the davits of the *Ulster Monarch* launched successfully into the Mediterranean and travelled towards the Maddalena Peninsula of south-eastern Sicily. The first night of Operation Husky was windy, the sea choppy. Savio put his head up to breathe in the salty air, remembering the times he'd been out night fishing along this coastline with his uncle and cousins. But tonight was different; his nerves were taut as wires at the thought that death might come knocking any minute. Would it matter anyway? His mother, father and brother were all gone. Who would care? A vision of Joy suddenly filled his head, her languorous smile as she'd stared adoringly at him after making love.

She was a lovely woman – a keeper. The times they'd made love had stirred something deep within him. She'd given him her virginity and cried afterwards. The other women he'd known in his life were forgettable in comparison. No matter how many times he'd told Joy she was beautiful, he sensed she'd doubted his words. If he got through this Sicilian mission, he vowed to prove his feelings were true.

As the craft bounced over the water towards battle, he knew he truly wanted her to be at his side forever. He'd told her so but he was sure she hadn't believed his words. Funny how in desperate moments truth shone though like a shining beacon. He should have declared his feelings better on that last time they'd had together. But how was he to know he was about to be whisked away to another secret location? That was the way it was in war. You lived from moment to moment and tried to spin gold from sorrow. And, anyway, he couldn't have told her where he was bound. He'd had to sign papers to swear secrecy and there'd been no time for anything else than hastily packing his kit bag and clambering onto the truck and then the train that had taken them to board the *Ulster Monarch*.

He hadn't been able to write. Each day since then had been a matter of life and death. He wondered what she was up to at this minute. Where was she? Tucked under a warm eiderdown, safe somewhere? Had the SOE taken her on? Or had she been unsuccessful? Her Italian was excellent but there was no way she could disguise her height and very English looks. Maybe she was working in some operations room, helping coordinate this very mission? How good it would be to know they were linked in some way until they could catch up with each other again. This thought alone would keep him going, keep him safe. He clung on to the dream of a future together.

As the craft ploughed through the waves towards shore, the sea was suddenly lit up like day by the sweeping glare of a lighthouse beacon, followed by the brighter ray of a military searchlight.

'Fucking Christ,' Moyes blasphemed. 'We're sitting ducks...'

A small miracle happened. The drone of a plane saved them and the searchlight swung abruptly to the dark sky, followed by a volley of fire from the shore directed at a

Wellington roaring low over the coastline. A commando next to Savio chose that moment to heave last night's meal over Savio's boots and it trickled off his ankles to add to the swill of vomit splashing about in the bottom of the landing craft. But all that mattered to each and every man at that moment was that one of their own planes had miraculously timed its assault on the Italian gun battery of Lamba Doria to perfection. Savio sent up a prayer of thanks. He had survived the first hurdle and was still alive.

The LCR chugged past one of the many gliders carrying troops, now being buffeted by the stormy waves. Two squaddies clung to the wings for dear life. They yelled for help, begging to be pulled aboard. There had been six gliders on the *Ulster Monarch* as part of Operation Ladbroke and Savio recognised one of the men. He was holding tight to a radio destined for signalling once onshore and Savio spotted a folding cycle too. There were dozens of fallen gliders dotted around the surface of the choppy sea and Savio also noted with dismay several bodies floating on the waves. Moyes ordered the craft onwards. 'We can't stop to pick them up. Not our mission. They'll be rescued by their own. We have to get on land ASAP and put those bloody guns out of action before they kill us all.'

Savio tried to block out the sounds of the Tommies' cries for help as they left them behind and to concentrate on the job in hand. He held tight to one of the scaling ladders destined for climbing the cliffs just west of the Capo Murro di Porco Lighthouse, hoping the men in the sea would be rescued before the enemy got to them. As it happened, they didn't need the ladders and just before scrambling ashore, they were jettisoned in the waves that crashed against the tufa rocks. These were not the soaring cliffs they had expected. Instead, the men easily navigated a gap in the rocks, carved out like a road. As he set foot on land, Savio recalled the sharpness of the tufa underfoot from childhood days and was glad of his gloves and sturdy army boots as they progressed.

According to Moyes' instructions, after cutting through coils of barbed wire, they crept low, moving at almost a crawl over the scrubby, thorny vegetation that tore at their clothing. Savio heard a rip and then felt fresh air on his behind. He swore softly but continued to follow Moyes closely, whispering to him that they were veering off course slightly and should bear right.

The Italians had not been expecting a landing on this stormy night. Moyes and his men could hear laughter and chat coming from over by the first gun. The major indicated to Savio to follow him down the steps to a bunker and pointed at his sergeant to carry out his side of the plan, which was to shoot the machine gunner nearby and any other guards.

The rat-a-tat-tat of a dozen Sten guns opening up simultaneously rent the night air, followed by screams of terrified Italians manning the machine gun. Savio followed as Moyes burst down the steps, giving the militia below no time to react as Moyes threw three hand grenades, one after the other, into the underground space. Blood spattered over the walls, together with shrapnel and Savio heard the terrified shouts: '*Non sparare*. Don't shoot. We surrender.'

But Moyes gave them no time to surrender and Savio felt sick inside. They could easily have been taken prisoner.

In no time at all, many Italians had been annihilated but it was the three heavy six-inch guns that had been the main target and they were captured without much trouble. The remaining Italian militia offered no resistance and stepped forward with their hands in the air after laying down weapons.

In fact, there were far more Italian prisoners than Tommies, and Moyes ordered Savio and a couple more of his men to tie their arms behind their backs, move them away and keep guard whilst the big guns were put out of action.

'Shoot any more you round up,' Moyes ordered Savio, his

voice low. 'There are too few of us to watch over them. It will ruin the whole operation. Be ruthless.'

Hardly daring to believe his ears, thinking this was not what he had signed up for and having witnessed Moyes' ruthless action in the bunker, Savio felt sick. He was being ordered to shoot Italians, his own people, in cold blood.

With sickening realisation, Savio knew he could not follow Moyes' orders.

He spotted a handful of civilians standing amongst the soldiers, no doubt a family who had taken refuge in the militia barracks: an old man, two women and three children cowering behind the skirts of the women. He separated them from the shabbily uniformed men, fearing Moyes might spot them first and led them to a nearby cave with a door that he remembered. It had been used as a storeroom and he'd played there as a young boy with his cousins. It was only a handful of metres away and, checking nobody was watching, he led the civilians away to secure them in the cave.

He explained in Sicilian dialect what he was about to do and the old man spat on the ground, accusing him of being an enemy of Sicily. 'What are you doing, shooting your fellow men? *Bastardo!*'

There was no time to explain and in rough words he told the man to shut up. It was simpler that way.

One of the women seemed reluctant to enter the cave. 'Don't make us go in there,' she pleaded, going down on her knees in front of Savio. 'Bad things happen in there. *Spiriti,*' she said, her voice verging on hysteria. 'The ghosts of the dead lurk in the rock walls. Anybody who spends time in that cave has a lifetime of bad luck.' Her voice rose to a wail as she started to sob and rant and rail about how her milk would turn sour if they were forced to stay inside the cave. Her goats would die, as well as all her children, she said, using the Sicilian *picciriddi*, that Savio recognised so well from his own childhood.

Savio knew Sicilians were a superstitious race, believing strongly in the *malocchio*, the evil eye. But for their own safety, he had to lock them in the cave, even if all the herds of goats, sheep and cows in Sicily died.

Just as he pushed her in, an almighty explosion rent the night as the coastal guns were blown up, illuminating everything for metres around. It was then he caught sight of a man in the corner of the cave, lying still against the wall. So, that was why the woman hadn't wanted him to enter.

He used his torch and then raised his gun before stepping into the cave. *'Mani in alto!'* he shouted in broad Sicilian. 'Hands up, and if you do anything stupid, I'll blast you all the way to the burning rims of Etna.'

'Savio?' the man whispered, raising himself up, his voice hoarse, sickly. 'Of all the men in all of the wide world. *Porca Madonna!* Bloody hell, can it really be you? Put that fucking gun down and help me, *cugino mio.*'

At that, the man flopped back, the woman rushed to his side and Savio was left with a quandary. His very own cousin was lying there before him... What the hell was he to do now?

CHAPTER 25

EARLY JULY 1943, BLETCHLEY PARK

JOY

The two young women biked the eight miles along the lane from Stony Stratford. Rosie knew several shortcuts along footpaths. At one point they had to open a gate to a field where cows grazed, watched over by a large bull.

'Keep to the edge and ride like the clappers if old Hitler starts moving towards us,' Rosie called over her shoulder.

But 'Hitler' the bull simply stared at the women, not moving an inch as they pedalled past.

'Here we are,' Rosie said, dismounting in front of imposing gates topped by barbed wire where two guards stood sentry.

One of them eyed Joy up and down. 'Pass please, miss. Not seen your face here before. Welcome to the biggest loony bin in Britain.'

Joy fumbled in her pocket and then followed Rosie along a sweeping path skirting an emerald lawn and a boating lake, to the entrance of a large, nineteenth-century building.

'Report in there. They'll tell you where to go,' Rosie told her, pointing to an oak door fronted by two stone gryphons.

With a cheery wave and a 'Toodle-oo' and 'Expect we'll see each other in the canteen,' Rosie pedalled off in the direction of a huddle of wooden buildings.

The place was teeming with men and women, young and middle-aged, some in uniform, quite a few not. A couple of buses drew up spilling out passengers and everybody looked purposeful, the opposite to how Joy felt. As she stepped through the main entrance of the old house, this busyness was repeated: people were bent over their work on trestle desks in every corner, the clatter of typewriters and phones ringing constantly in the background. To Joy, it felt as if there was adventure in the air and an atmosphere of determination permeated the place.

A young woman dressed in khaki-grey approached, carrying a clipboard.

'Lady Joy Harrison?' she asked.

'Yes, that's me.'

The woman ticked off her name. 'Mr Birch is ready for you. Welcome to Bletchley Park. Follow me.' Her smile was genuine and Joy's nerves calmed a little as she was led down a corridor to the far end of the grand mansion. Or at least it probably had been grand in its day, Joy thought, taking in more desks and tables positioned in every possible space beneath the corbelled ceilings and beside ornate fireplaces. Now it was an institution, no longer a country residence despite its graceful features – very much like Somersby Hall, with its subtly coloured stained-glass windows and plush carpets that her feet sank into. They stopped at a door. The woman with the clipboard knocked gently and left as a man's voice called out, 'Come in, come in.'

She entered a library, the walls lined with shelves holding hundreds of books. The middle-aged man perched on the edge of a tidy desk was pleasant looking, his hair combed neatly back from a chiselled face. He wore a tweed suit and she thought his gaze was kindly but piercing at the same time, as if he were assessing her.

He gestured to Joy to sit down. 'I've been asked to fill you in as far as I can. Do make yourself comfortable. I hope your lodgings are satisfactory. It's getting harder to find decent digs now the Park is filling up with more staff.'

'My digs are perfectly adequate. Thank you, sir.'

'I expect you've twigged we want you here because of your Italian and, more precisely, your knowledge of Sicily. I believe some of the vocabulary is completely different from the mainland.'

'Yes. sir. That tends to be the case all over Italy with regions, I should say. It's not only words that differ. People in the next village use their own idioms, cook different foods, have other traditions.'

'Quite so. Fascinating,' the man said, looking down at notes beside him on the desk. It was obvious to Joy from his tone that he was *not* fascinated.

'We have a good team here at Bletchley Park. We work well together. Sicily is very much in focus at the moment. There will be increased activity over the next weeks with our codebreakers concentrating on traffic concerning the island. Hence the need for expert language help with deciphering and translation.'

He rose to step towards the window, hands in his pockets. 'Of course, you are not to breathe a word of this to a soul outside Hut 3 – which is where you will be working.' He pointed to posters pinned on the wall of the library. One that immediately caught her eye showed a woman seated on a sofa: two officers were chatting her up, and words in capital letters spread over the image proclaimed: *Be like Dad – keep Mum*.

'Of course, sir. I understand. I was at Glenaig where we—'

'Yes, yes. We know.' He looked at her over the top of his spectacles. 'Indeed, no need to tell *anyone* that, not even within this place. You are here at BP now and it is even more imperative you do not say *anything* to *anybody* outside of our select group. No matter whom. I'll be asking you to sign the Official

Secrets Act again, Lady Harrison. I cannot stress too strongly
the necessity for the maintenance of security. After we've
completed the necessary formalities, I'll take you to meet the
others.' It was only after she had signed that he extended his
hand to grasp hers in a firm shake. 'Welcome to the team at
Bletchley Park and Hut 3.'

Over the following days, the comments that Joy had heard
about adventure through service and setting Europe ablaze did
not ring true at all for her in the work she was being trained to
carry out. It was boring in the main, long shifts made lighter
through having seen Rosie on the first morning, occupying a
desk in the very same hut as hers. Rosie had looked up briefly
and winked. At least Joy could now share something of her
Italian experiences with her roommate as they were working for
the same group. Indiscretion was never an option – this was
instilled into Joy at every stage of her training. One simply did
not blab.

By day they sat in Hut 3 in their khaki tunics and skirts in a
haze of cigarette smoke where some rather academic-looking
men sorted groups of letters and figures that arrived in thousands of messages via the registration room, arriving either by
motorbike dispatchers or from teleprinters. You never knew if
some might be hot information about the Italian Air Force or
naval movements. Many of the messages were deciphered from
the Hagelin machine used by the Italian navy. The team's
purpose was to detect useful information and to neatly trans-
pose data about technical and military locations, enemy sight-
ings and movements onto card indexes.

Behind Joy's desk was a notice with the word **SECRECY**
written across the top in bold black print: *Don't talk at meals. Be
careful in your hut. Do not talk by your own fireside* were some
of the headings. Joy felt a tingle of pride at being part of Bletch-

ley. Her deep longing for Savio might well be dampened a little if she concentrated on her duties here, she thought, for there was little time to think about him during her shifts.

Anything of any use that came into the hut was put onto a card and cross-referenced. Most ended up with NHR scrawled through their notes: nothing heard required. Quite often, what they had worked on was classified as ULTRA, the cover name for high-grade intelligence, and this was hurriedly taken from the hut to be communicated to special liaison units by dispatch riders.

In the self-service cafeteria, Joy and Rosie occasionally sat with their fellow hut workers but, more often, they preferred to sit together at an unoccupied table at the far end of the dining room. Joy felt safe opening up to Rosie. Nothing they were sharing was of importance to eavesdroppers or would result in a 'Target for Tonight' by the Germans, as the notices described.

'I'd joined up, expecting to experience life in the raw,' Rosie confided in Joy as she stirred her cup of stewed tea. 'But, so far, life in this place is not terribly exciting. I'm so glad you pitched up.'

'Me too,' Joy said. 'And it's wonderful that we have Italy in common. I was busting to tell you that first day but I thought you'd been set up as a snitch. Careless talk costs lives, and all that. God, how I hate that Mussolini has made enemies of our two countries.'

'Absolutely agree. Not the best. But it is what it is, I fear.' She leant closer in to Joy as she spoke and lowered her voice. 'You'll be really useful to the team with your Sicilian know-how. It's definitely hotting up there.' She changed the subject, looking about her to make sure she hadn't been overheard. 'I suppose I should be kissing you on both cheeks, Italian-style, when we greet each other... but it would look rather strange to everybody in here.' She clinked her white cup against Joy's. '*Cin cin*, instead, signorina.'

'Would be better to have some delicious strong espresso instead of what passes for coffee, don't you think?' Joy said with a rueful smile. *'Pazienza!'*

'Pazienza is what you're definitely going to need in this work. In bucket loads. You'll be spending hours and hours of your life huddled over bits of paper, hoping something useful will jump out at you.'

The atmosphere in the hut was highly charged and there was total silence and total concentration as the team pieced together fragments of information, but they were not sure what exactly that was at this stage, apart from the fact that Italy, and Sicily in particular, were of major interest.

The two young women talked mostly about their time in Italy in the evenings, keeping clear of anything to do with their hush-hush work. You never knew who might be listening. They joked about their landlady being a spy, but Joy doubted it strongly. She wasn't the most worldly-wise female on the planet. Near the start of Joy's stay, Perks, as they called her in private, had expressed curiosity about the brassiere hanging from the clothes horse next to the kitchen range.

'What be them?' the old lady had asked, pointing to the drying underwear. After Joy had explained, the old lady had said, 'Ah! They keeps 'em from a-dangling, does they? Never seen anything like 'em afore. I simply wears me vests to keep mine in control.'

The girls were in stitches later.

'I'm so tiny up there,' Rosie said, 'so she's never seen a bra before in her kitchen. I take after my nonna. She was small-framed too.' She went on to explain something of her Milanese grandmother. 'Nonna Rosanna. She's a *contessa*. They named me after her. I do long to see her, but it's not possible at the moment.'

'Your surname, Strawbridge, sounds English, though. So, do you have an Italian mother?'

'Yes.'

'You're lucky she wasn't arrested and sent to the Isle of Man,' Joy said, 'like my friend.'

'Oh, bad show. An Italian living in England? No, that didn't happen to Mamma. Daddy is rather high up in the navy, so it never happened. He pulled strings.'

Joy was quiet for a few moments as she remembered Savio, thinking of the unfairness surrounding the arrest of his family, the hurt in his eyes as he'd described his internment on the Isle of Man. Life was unfair: if he'd been born into aristocracy or known people like Rosie's father, it would never have happened. Poor Savio. He'd had so much to put up with. He was easy to love and she wanted to love him more, do what she could to take care of him. Most of the time she managed to push him to the back of her mind because she couldn't bear the heartache, but it wasn't easy. She half-listened as Rosie talked about the lakes near Milan, how she loved to hike in the mountains. She dragged herself back to the present when she realised Rosie was asking her about her own family.

'Sounds like your family is more interesting than mine,' Joy said. 'I don't know the north of Italy but down in Sicily, where my folks have a villa, I mostly ran wild in the holidays. That's how I picked up the language: playing with local children, mostly sons and daughters of fishermen. Bit different from the high life in Milan.'

'I'd say so. Literary soirées with Nonna's friends, shopping and cafés in Corso Vittorio Emanuele. I was definitely not allowed to run wild! Listen, let's go for a drink tomorrow night in the Park Hotel in Bletchley. If I spend another evening cooped up in Perks' cottage, I shall die of stagnation.'

'Sounds good to me. What's the form? Do we wear mufti or uniform? I haven't much in the way of frocks.'

'I can't lend you anything, I'm afraid, as we're different

sizes,' Rosie said. 'Doesn't matter what you wear. Skirt and blouse? I'm not on the prowl for a beau. Are you?'

Joy shook her head vigorously. She hadn't talked to a soul about Savio and, although Rosie was a wonderful roommate, she had no wish to confide in her new friend about that part of her life. It was her secret – a delicious secret that nevertheless tormented her, for she hadn't heard a word from him since the night they'd spent together. Sometimes it felt as if it had never happened.

CHAPTER 26

The pub in Bletchley was lively, full of young people from the Park and Joy and Rosie enjoyed a couple of glasses of Gin and French and a brandy bought by Rosie's friend, a freckly-faced pilot called Sandy. When time was called, the young man and women spilled onto the pavement outside the Park Hotel.

'Fancy a nightcap?' Sandy asked, pushing between the two girls, linking arms with them. 'The night is young.'

'I'm all in,' Joy said. 'And I have a long week of late shifts to look forward to. I'm ready for my bed.'

'Aw! Don't be boring,' Sandy complained. 'What about you, Rosie-Posie? You used to be such fun.'

'Thanks, Sandy, but...'

'You can't live your life like a nun.'

'Sandy. I know you're trying to be kind. But...'

He held up both hands in surrender. 'Can't blame a man for trying. I promised Bill I'd look after you.'

Rosie hugged the young man close and Joy heard her say, 'I know, I know. But I'm not up to it yet. Don't be too kind to me.'

He held her close for a few moments and then pulled away. 'Oh well, dear ladies. You don't know what you're missing. As I said, the night is still young. Go and hug your hot-water bottles instead. Maybe another time.'

He walked away, waving his white silk pilot's scarf behind him, his voice breaking into song. 'Kiss me goodnight, Sergeant Major...' and Rosie shook her head.

'He never gives up.'

They pulled their bikes from behind the hedge where they had parked them at the start of the evening.

'Don't much feel like going back to Perks yet,' Rosie said, 'but I wasn't up for partying with Sandy either. Shall we push the bikes for a bit? Are you very tired?'

Sensing that Rosie needed to get something off her chest and despite her aching fatigue, Joy replied, 'Fine by me. We have our own key. At least Perks doesn't insist on a curfew.'

They walked together without speaking, the spindles turning on the bicycle wheels and their footsteps treading the road the only sounds. A car approached in the distance and they pulled well back to avoid being hit. The headlamps were dimmed in case of air raids and there had been cases of drinkers returning home from the pub being run over, with drivers having reduced visibility.

'Shall we stop here for a bit?' Rosie asked as they reached the village pond, a half-moon fingernail reflected in the water.

Rosie leant her bike against a tree and Joy copied, before following her to sit on a bench close to the water.

'Sandy went to school with my boyfriend,' Rosie said. 'He's a kind fellow, but I can't give him what he wants.'

She turned to Joy as she wiped her cheeks.

'Don't like to go on about it,' she said. 'But you might as well know I was engaged for the briefest, most wonderful time. Bill was a midshipman. Torpedoed in the Med. He was only nineteen, Joy. A bally stupid waste. We'd known each other since we were toddlers. Both our families predicted we would marry one day. But they were wrong.'

'I'm so sorry.' Joy took hold of Rosie's hand, small in hers. 'What can one say?'

'Saying is all very well. Doing is the solution.' She blew her nose and straightened her shoulders. 'That's why I came to BP. Deadly dull as it is at times, I'm sure we're helping. I used to think I was merely fiddling while Rome burned, as they say. But Daddy assures me that all the hush-hush work we are busy with is essential. They are simply terrified that word will get out about this place – about the decoding machines and what have you and all the clever people we have here, like Turing and Birch. That's why we have to be so careful to never talk about it.'

Joy squeezed her hand. 'You know I *believe* Mum's the word, Rosie. And... about Sandy. Follow your heart. And if your heart's not ready, he's not the one for you. You can't replace true love with second best.'

'You're very wise. Do you have anybody, Joy?'

Joy paused. She didn't feel wise, as Rosie had described her. It was always easier to dish out advice than put it into practice. If she were wise, she would forget about Savio. He'd either forgotten about her or he was not in a position to get in touch. She hoped it was a case of the latter. But to keep her sanity, it was best to banish thoughts of him, if possible.

'No,' she replied. 'There's nobody.'

The two women were put on different shifts and they hardly had time to catch up with each other. They acknowledged each other at the handovers in the hut when Joy finished her night duties at eight in the morning and Rosie took over during the daytime, but that was the extent of it.

On her third consecutive night shift, Joy felt exhausted and out of sorts. It was hard to sleep during the day with Mrs Perkins thumping about as she beat carpets or sang in her tuneless voice whilst going about her housework. Everyday sounds filtered through the window, open against the summer heat, and she tossed and turned, willing sleep to come. Her night shifts from midnight to eight o'clock seemed to never end and there were times when she wanted to pillow her weary head on the desk in front of her and sleep the sleep of the dead. But she couldn't. The work they were doing was of vital importance, she reminded herself, and their team supervisor had now explained about Churchill's orders to invade Sicily to pierce the under-belly of Europe. It was more important than ever to scrutinise all information coming from Italy and, in particular, Sicily. Operation Husky was imminent.

She felt so queasy, she had to take frequent toilet breaks, putting up her hand to ask permission. She splashed her face in cold water in the basin, sticking her wrists under the tap to run over her veins, hoping the cold would seep into her blood and make her feel less drowsy. She'd grabbed a sausage roll before coming on duty, not fancying the corned beef with prunes or curried fish on offer in the canteen, and she began to wonder how long it had been sitting around as she rubbed her grumbling stomach. There were short tea breaks every two hours and usually nothing much seemed to happen during the dark hours of night, but lately there was the same flurry of activity as daytime. Speed was always of the essence to get information delivered to the most relevant services. It was her duty to keep vigilant but she felt exhausted.

Rosie had been deeply upset the previous week and when they'd managed to catch up with each other briefly, she had talked of an incident she could not get out of her mind.

'It was right at the start of my shift,' she'd told Joy. 'What I'd translated was important, I knew it. The hairs on the back of my neck literally stood on end. In about three and a half hours, Italian torpedo bombers and transport carriers were due to leave Tripoli and head across the Mediterranean towards Sicily. I passed on the information and it was radioed immediately to the RAF in North Africa.' She'd paused. 'All the aircraft were shot down because of what I'd translated.'

Rosie had burst into tears after telling Joy because she'd found out later there had been civilians, including children, on the planes. They had all died. 'They were escaping from Tripoli to come home,' she'd sobbed. 'It hit me badly, Joy. I mean, war is war, but sitting in our hut sifting through information doesn't bring home the reality of death, does it? To think I killed my own people. I feel awful.'

Joy had tried her best to console her distraught friend, but she wasn't sure her words had helped much. She hoped she had at least made the burden a little lighter by allowing her friend to share.

'But, Rosie, you did what you had to,' she'd said, her arm round her friend in the cloakroom where they had bumped into each other. 'You weren't to know there were civilians aboard. How could you? It must be the same for the pilots. They drop their bombs but they can't know if ordinary people are targeted. It's part of war.'

Now, on her long night shift, she glanced at the calendar on the wall: July 10th. Almost mid-July. A time of year she usually loved. What she would give to have Dream stabled nearby. She remembered a summer holiday on the Norfolk coast when she'd saddled Dream up and ridden down the honeysuckle-filled lanes to the sea. Dream had enjoyed the surf and there was nothing quite like clinging on to the back of her horse in the salty water, trusting each other after a canter alongside frothy waves rolling onto the sandy beach. She suddenly felt a strong wave of nausea and without asking permission, she rushed for the door. She just about made it to the ladies' cloakroom where she vomited the contents of her stomach, heaving over and over until nothing was left.

Splashing water over her face, she looked at herself in the

mirror, eyes huge, her skin clammy. *That's the last time I eat a sausage roll from the canteen*, she thought. Even the idea made her feel sick again, and she pushed open the cubicle door and vomited up bile, nothing else left in her stomach. She leant her head against the cold tiles until some of the dizziness passed. Dabbing a smear of lipstick on her mouth and squaring her shoulders, she made her way back to Hut 3. With relief she saw there was only one hour and a half left before her shift ended.

'The Admiralty sent in an odd message received from Sicily by our lot while you were away,' the professor said as she returned to the hut. 'It didn't make much sense and they wanted somebody to check over the Italian in case they were missing anything. I've had a look but I don't think it's terribly important. Do you think there are any Sicilian dialect or euphemisms involved? Take a look and see if it needs action or filing.'

She sat down wearily to read the slip of paper.

Lamba Doria and Porco secured. Sicilian gallini rounded up by Dante.

Her heart missed a beat, the name Dante jumping out at her. It had been Savio's code name at Glenaig. Could it possibly have been sent by him? Her work normally involved translating messages intercepted from the enemy. Occasionally they'd receive a query from the Admiralty to double-check something, but rarely.

She read the message over and over. *Porco* meant pig. *Galline* with an 'e' on the end meant chickens. Was it referring to cowards, maybe? But *gallini* ending in an i meant nothing to her. She reached for the Italian dictionary to make sure. But could it also be a mistake? Savio's spelling was poor, she knew that personally. She'd helped him with his reading and he'd vastly improved. But there had been a limit to what they could achieve over that short time together. She held the message tight to her chest. Was she trying to convince herself this was a coded message intended for her? From him? Telling her he was in Sicily? But... chickens? What did that mean? If he was trying to say something, it was lost on her. And anyway, how the hell would he know where she was? Unless somebody at Glenaig had told him before he'd left. There were too many impossible questions to answer.

'Are you all right, Harrison?' the professor asked her. 'You look concerned.'

Despite working in such close proximity over the past weeks, the workers in Hut 3 were formal with each other. Christian names were never used.

Joy shook her head and opened her hand. The piece of paper was crumpled up and she placed it on the desk to straighten it up.

'Fine, Professor. I... I must have eaten something that disagreed with me. The Italian they use is strange. *Porco* obviously means pig, but there's confusion about *gallini*.'

'Well, our shift ends soon. I'll take a gander at the map of Sicily to see if that sheds any light. In the meantime, check this new stack of papers for me, please. They're coming in fast and furious.' He glanced at her over the rim of his glasses. 'The invasion has started on the island. Morning shift are going to have their hands full. You might be called in to help out.'

She sat down and pulled the first piece of paper to her, willing herself not to turn the odd message into something personal. She was simply being fanciful and not thinking straight because she felt so ill. Her mind was playing tricks. The mention of Dante could mean anything. For the next hour, she worked at translating words that had been decoded. The lines spelled out a desperation from the enemy: gun positions destroyed on the outskirts of Syracuse, Porto Pantelleria destroyed, a message from Kesselring to the Italians warning of imminent invasion sent at 4.40 p.m. but only received at 8.05 p.m. – an indication that telegraph wires had possibly been destroyed. A message to General Frido von Senger from General Guzzoni, expecting imminent attack on Gela; another message sent by Guzzoni notifying of a future strike against the British and Canadian landings, warning Oberst Schmalz should head south, away from Etna. Savio was forgotten whilst Joy kept her head down. All the messages she was working on were marked ULTRA and dispatched immediately to the Admiralty.

When Rosie arrived at five minutes to eight, Joy looked up, eyes red and sore. 'You're going to be extremely busy today. Operation Husky is red hot. The invasion of Sicily has started. Good luck, Rosie.'

'You look done in, Joy. Get some rest and tell Perks to keep the noise down.'

'If only...'

If this was what death warmed up felt like, Joy thought, as she made her way out of the Park, then she wanted to remain alive for longer. Twice on the way back to her digs, she had to hop off her bike and vomit into the hedgerows. But she was heaving up nothing; her stomach was empty.

Mrs Perkins took one look at her when she opened the door and helped her up the stairs to her bed. 'They be working you too hard. Best you take the night off.'

'Can't, Mrs Perkins. We're really busy.'

'My advice is you take off that garment that keeps your bosoms tied up so tight and slip into bed, comfy. Shall I bring you a nice cup of Bovril, my dear?'

Joy shook her head, her hand over her mouth at the mention of Bovril, and pushed past Mrs Perkins, only just making it in time to the toilet to heave bile again into the bowl. Her stomach and ribs ached now. Mrs Perkins popped her head round the door.

'Dearie me. You got it bad. Best not to eat anything to calm that stummik. But you can't go into work feeling like that. I'll have a word with your friend when she gets in. I'll be downstairs if you needs me.'

Joy staggered to her bed and, without undressing, slipped between the sheets, hoping her stomach would allow her to sleep. She couldn't remember the last time she'd felt so utterly ghastly.

Her alarm went off at seven that evening. Gingerly she sat up and swung her legs round to sit on the edge of the bed. For goodness' sake, she hadn't eaten anything for hours; there was nothing to sick up, but she felt terrible. Groping her way to the door, she rushed to the bathroom, heaving again over the toilet. She needed a doctor; there was something dreadfully wrong with her.

As she pulled on her skirt over her swollen stomach, there was a knock on the door and Mrs Perkins came in. She stood with her arms folded over her pinafore-encased bosoms. 'If you be in the family way, me dear, then you'll have to leave.'

CHAPTER 27

10 JULY 1943

SAVIO

In the cave, where Savio had herded to safety the small group of civilians, he knelt beside his cousin Carmelo on the straw and felt his head. He was burning up. The children whimpered as a burst of gunfire sounded in the distance. Carmelo was going nowhere. He was no threat to anybody, least of all Moyes and the troops. Family was family. Savio was only too aware of this. Automatically, he moved to touch his mother's Sicilian charm at his neck, but of course he had given it to Joy. He would have to get through this episode with his own guile, and literally dodge the bullets.

'How long has he been like this?' he asked the young woman hovering over him.

'Ten days, signore,' she answered, fetching a bucket of water from the back of the cave and squeezing out a rag to mop Carmelo's face. 'It's malaria, but he's injured too.' She pulled up his shirt to reveal a deep gouge below his ribs. 'He was gored. Trying to get milk from the cow. For the children.'

The wound looked and smelled nasty. Gangrene might

already have set in. But, even so, Savio had to confine these people for the time being, until the mission was over. They would be safer from trigger-happy men too, he assessed, thinking ruefully of his madcap boss, Moyes.

He told the woman he would return, but in the meantime, they would have to stay locked in the cave. 'You're safer from the guns in here. Do you have enough food and water to last a while?'

The woman nodded but grasped hold of his hand. 'If you lock us in, how will we get out... what if you don't come back, signore?'

'I'll be back. I promise. And if I'm not back within a day, then you'll have to make a lot of noise and shout. Somebody will surely let you out. I'll find medicine for Carmelo.'

His cousin was out for the count but he bent down to whisper he would bring help, hoping he could hear the message. He also hoped he himself could stay alive to fulfil his promises.

Savio pulled the chain through the padlock and turned the key before pocketing it. The door was strong. Somebody would have to shoot through the lock or bash it with an axe to let the poor devils out, but he intended to be back himself.

He made his way back to the group of men he had lived with in the desert. A rum lot. But wasn't he a strange one himself? They were a band of odds and sods, misfits in the ordinary world, but Moyes had managed to bond them in his own way and train them ruthlessly. Their uniforms were scruffy and tatty and Moyes did not conform to the usual image of an officer, but this mission, to pierce the soft underbelly of Europe as Churchill himself had described it, was working well so far. And this was partly down to Moyes and the men he had selected for this initial push. Savio no longer felt proud of what he had helped come about. His mind was intent on embarking on his own mission: to disappear within Sicily and distance himself from the officer who had ordered him to shoot his own countrymen so mercilessly. It was wrong and it brought bile to his mouth at the thought.

'Orders carried out, sir,' he told Moyes as he returned. It was approaching five o'clock in the morning and daylight was seeping in after the night's activities, displaying the devastation of battle. Bodies were strewn about the scrubby terrain over and between tufa rocks. Moyes' band had all managed to survive but Savio counted dozens of dead soldiers from the airborne division that had flown in troops. He counted plenty of Italian militia too, many of them older men. War was bloody. Men were trained to fight and kill. The instinct for survival and self-preservation was foremost in the warrior's mind. And Savio intended to survive.

'Good work, Dante,' Moyes said, using Savio's code name cum nickname. 'Get the message relayed to HQ. Now, men. Our orders are to return to the *Ulster Monarch* to move on to Syracuse, our task seemingly done here.' He let off flares that showed green in the pearly sky, signifying the battery had been destroyed. 'But...' Moyes paused as he straightened his beret that sat awkwardly on his unruly ginger mane. 'There's something else on my list to complete before we advance.'

He sketched a map, using a stick in the sand. 'There are more militia holed up in this second battery inland, north-west of here,' he said, indicating behind him. As he spoke, a sudden boom caused all the men to duck and brace themselves against an incoming shell. A huge spray of water in the sea showed where it had landed short.

'That's enough justification for me,' Moyes pronounced. 'The buggers are still alive and kicking in the other battery.'

Savio perceived what was almost a look of glee on Moyes' face as he urged his men forward. At some stage, he had to put his own plan into action. Somehow, he had to extricate himself from this next bloody skirmish. He had seen enough for his own liking. It didn't sit comfortably killing his own people. It weighed heavy on his conscience, like a betrayal to his parents. Hadn't his family been damaged enough?

The commandos advanced inland, past a scattering of farmhouses dotted about squat military buildings near guns defended by snipers. Dead civilians lay along the track. The engineers who had destroyed the guns at the first battery expressed surprise at the weapons they'd found. 'British made,' one of them said, as they marched along. 'Left over from the First War, when we were allies. They're not properly equipped, poor blighters. This next battery should fall easily.' Even so, the Italians were putting up a fierce fight and the men had to take cover several times.

Savio thought how crazy war was. Moyes' callous actions at the first bunker, when he had taken no prisoners despite their plea of surrender, had upset him deeply. And the old man's comment in the cave about him shooting his own had struck a guilty chord. If his parents had not chosen to emigrate, then he too would likely have been amongst these Italian soldiers, shabby and ill-equipped, but fired up with patriotism. He might even have been involved with writing one of the slogans he'd seen printed neatly on the walls of the first bunker: **DIO, NAZIONE, FAMIGLIA**. GOD, NATION, FAMILY. But writing skills were not his forte.

He thought fondly again of Joy and resolved to write her a letter as soon as he possibly could. He patted his volume of the third part of the trilogy of Dante's *Divine Comedy* she had given to him for reading practice. It fitted perfectly into the breast pocket of his army shirt and on evenings in the Palestinian desert he'd pulled it out to read. Moyes was often to be seen engrossed in a book and Savio had been surprised when the officer had mentioned he'd read the whole three parts of Dante's *Divine Comedy* at university. It had relieved him of the boredom of his legal studies, he'd said. In truth, Savio would have preferred something lighter to read, like a thriller, but it was all Joy had at the time and he remembered his pride when he'd managed to read the first canto to her, stumbling only a few times. A pity he hadn't had such patient teachers when he'd been a nipper. Yes, she was a good 'un.

The battle lasted the rest of the blisteringly hot July day. Moyes and his men captured a dormitory building nearest the dirt road first, metres from where the militia were holding ground in another building. Savio crouched beneath a window next to one of the bunk beds. A poster of a half-naked woman, long hair not quite covering her generous breasts, hung from the same rusty nail as a wooden rosary and he wondered who usually slept there. He might even have known the fellow, played with him on the beach nearby or raced him on his cousin's bicycle, perched sideways on the crossbar.

Feeling the urge to open his bowels, he crawled across the glass-strewn floor towards the open door, as more heavy gunfire was exchanged. Behind the shelter of the building within a bamboo thicket, he relieved himself. He crawled further into the plants and flinched as his fingers touched something sticky.

Flies buzzed from the body of a Tommy. His head had been blown off, but the rest of him was intact and he still held a Sten gun in his hand, his finger on the trigger. Savio gently removed the gun. When the body started to bloat from decomposition, and the fingers swelled more, his dead hand might easily end up pulling the trigger. What irony to be killed by a dead man, Savio thought. His mind was all over the place and he told himself to shut the fuck up, to keep calm and to concentrate on the rational. *Don't blow it now, Savvy me old pal. It's now or never.* Here was his chance to escape from this mad, mad world.

Savio removed his own identification tag and draped it round the neck of the dead man. Gingerly, he picked up the fallen man's tag, spattered with blood and brains, and shoved it into his trouser pocket. He remained next to the body until darkness fell, listening to intermittent gunfire and greedy insects feasting on the remains. The nausea he felt was heightened by adrenaline coursing round his body. If Moyes found him shirking here, he'd shoot him outright as a coward for abandoning his post. And by the rules of war he'd be right to do so. But Savio felt little loyalty to England's green and pleasant land now, or to Moyes and his SAS outfit who 'carried fire and sword', as he'd frequently been reminded. England had sent his parents to their deaths and put him effectively behind bars for no good reason. Savio wanted nothing more to do with the killing of his Italian relations. Enough was enough.

As he crawled away from the body, the ominous sound of cannon fire sounded in his ears and the ground shook with mighty explosions. Savio tried to make for shelter but the last thing he thought before the ground tilted and he was showered with debris, was that Moyes would now be short of two of his men.

CHAPTER 28

1973, SUFFOLK

PAIGE

Mrs Ambrose from The Copper Kettle stood behind the café door, the sign turned to CLOSED, her arms folded across her pinafore. Gone was her welcoming smile from earlier. The expression on her face was frosty as she opened up, blocking Paige from entering.

'Who actually *are* you?' she asked. 'I've been thinking about your nosy questions. I should have found out more about you first, but my head was full of the news of the sale of Somersby Hall. What exactly are you trying to find out about Lady Joy? If you're from a magazine or newspaper, I can tell you straight-away I am not divulging anything.'

'I promise you I'm not a journalist, Mrs Ambrose. But it's complicated. Would you let me come in so we can talk?'

'You can tell me from where you're standing,' Mrs Ambrose said, opening the door a crack, her expression grim.

Paige decided to get straight to the point. 'I've been led to believe that Lady Joy is my mother. That's why I need to track her down.'

Mrs Ambrose's eyebrows almost disappeared into her hairline and her mouth fell open. 'The baby...' she stuttered. She pulled Paige into the café and bolted the door behind her. 'Let me have a good look at you.' She switched on the strip light and it flickered for a moment before settling down. 'You don't look like Lady Joy at all. You're dark; she was blonde. You're quite petite; she was a tall girl with blue eyes. As blue as Christmas hyacinths, bless her. How do I know you're not an imposter after her money?'

'I'm definitely not an imposter and I'm not even one hundred per cent certain she *is* my mother. But I need to at least check.'

Mrs Ambrose frowned. 'You're not making sense.'

'I know. It's a shock to me too,' Paige said, wondering how to explain something that was a mystery even to herself. She drew a deep breath and started from the beginning, telling Mrs Ambrose everything she'd discovered so far.

'My aunty Flo died recently, before she could tell me something she felt she needed to. She was knocked down by a lorry. But she'd left me a notebook where she'd started to write an explanation. That wasn't finished either. Actually, it was barely started, to be honest. My aunt had always told me my parents had died in a house fire but that I was rescued. Obviously,' Paige said, pausing. 'Otherwise, I wouldn't be here today.' Even as she was relating the story to this stranger, it all sounded terribly weird. But Mrs Ambrose was still listening, so she ploughed on.

'Anyway, Aunty Flo left a birth certificate with the same Christian names and birth date as mine, but a different surname: Harrison. Mine is Caister. And she left me a couple of other things: a strange letter and a piece of Sicilian jewellery. Rather hideous actually... but it's the birth certificate that led me to Somersby Hall.'

'Do you have it on you, my dear? Can I see?'

Paige pulled the envelope from her bag and Mrs Ambrose took it. She shook her head as she examined it, looking at Paige and back at the certificate a couple of times. 'I think you'd better come to my home after all. It will be easier to talk there.' She shook her head again. 'Well I never. What a turn-up. My word...'

Mrs Ambrose's home was a few yards down the road from the café, tucked into an alleyway too narrow for vehicles. She lived in a picture-postcard thatched cottage, two pheasants created from the same thatch adorning the roof. White and red hollyhocks, a mass of scented roses, sweet peas and marigolds were planted in every inch of the pretty front garden. 'Welcome to my hidey-hole,' Mrs Ambrose said, unlocking her post-box red front door, a polished knocker in shining brass shaped like a fox's head plumb in the centre. There was even honeysuckle curling round the windows like a nostalgic scene on an old-fashioned greetings card.

'It's charming,' Paige said, thinking that Aunty Flo's cottage could look like this with some care and green-fingered attention.

'Rather than stick the kettle on, I think I'll pour us both a large sherry. I make hot drinks all day long and I rather think your turning up is cause for celebration.'

'So, you know Lady Joy, do you?'

'I certainly did. A while back.' She produced a bottle of dry sherry from a sideboard and poured two schooners. Next, she pulled a photograph album from a bookcase nestled in one of the alcoves.

'This is the last photograph I took of her.'

Paige stared at a picture of an attractive woman wearing uniform, her light-coloured hair tied up in a topknot, untidy tendrils escaping to frame her face. She gasped and looked carefully again but the unmistakable face of a far younger Aunty Flo stared back at her. She banged her glass down on the side table and covered her mouth with her hands. 'Oh my God,' she spluttered. 'I don't believe this.'

'Are you all right, my dear? Shall I go on?' Peggy looked at her with concern. 'Can I get you something? A glass of water?'

Paige shook her head. She felt very shaky, truth dawning that Aunty Flo was Lady Joy. And that meant Aunty Flo was her mother. She half-listened as Peggy continued to speak, wondering why on earth the truth had been hidden from her for all these years.

'That photograph was taken during the war. Lady Joy was allowed to come home for a few weeks' leave on and off during the summer of 1943. Bless her, she never could get that hair tied back neatly. Her hair was so beautifully thick, you know. I loved brushing it for her. We were quite close in age and when I came to help out at the Hall, we got on really well. Her mother was a real dragon and Lady Joy often came down to the kitchen. "I'm escaping from Mother," she'd say and I'd make her a cup of tea or coffee, when we had it. Rationing was hard during the war. Cook always had a cake or home-made biscuits in the tin she conjured from almost nothing and Joy had a good appetite. We liked the same things, you see. She wasn't lah-de-dah like her mother and friends and she taught me how to ride. She was very kind. And good fun too. She told some very saucy stories...'

That definitely sounds like Aunty Flo, Paige thought.

Mrs Ambrose turned quiet at the end of her description and wiped away a tear.

'So, what happened to her?' Paige asked. 'I want to understand...'

Mrs Ambrose blew her nose. 'Well, she was away for long stretches. Working as a secretary for the government, she told me. But I've often wondered what it was she really did. She was an intelligent girl. Anyway, she'd met somebody. It was quite obvious to me she'd fallen in love. She had that sort of glow about her.'

Mrs Ambrose turned the pages of her photo album and found another photo. In this, Lady Joy – or Aunty Flo, as she had been to Paige all her life – was dressed for the evening: a long, fitted dress in a silky material clung to her generous contours, her hair was loose, with two bouffant curls caught up on each side of her head, like in old black-and-white war films Paige had watched as a little girl.

'She looks very glamorous here,' Paige said, tracing the outline of her aunt, or her mother, with her finger, thinking she had never ever seen her dressed up like this. 'So, what happened, Mrs Ambrose? I knew nothing whatsoever about any of this.'

'Call me Peggy, my dear. Yes, Joy preferred to wear jodhpurs rather than frocks, but she scrubbed up well.' She bit her lip as she looked at Paige. 'She fell pregnant. And... the baby must have been you.'

The two women looked at each other for a long time and after a shocked silence, both started to speak at the same time.

'I can't take it in—' Paige said.

'I'm so sorry she's passed— You go first,' Peggy Ambrose said. 'It must be a big shock for you. It certainly is for me.'

'Can you tell me more?' Paige asked, her mind whirring with sadness, surprise, so many feelings about this revelation. 'Who was my father? Did you ever meet him?'

'Joy was so secretive back then. I mean, she never really told us where she had met him, but she told me she was worried about bringing him to meet her mother.'

'Who was he?'

'He was an Italian lad, apparently, but born in London. Joy always had a thing about Italy. She loved it there. Went there with her parents to their villa in Sicily most summers.'

Paige shook her head. These things Peggy was telling her – about a villa in Sicily, a handsome Italian lover – they belonged to the story of somebody completely different from Aunty Flo.

And yet, they did make a little sense too. Aunty Flo had always shown a fondness for Italy.

'What was this Italian's name?' she asked, her voice barely a whisper.

Peggy Ambrose screwed up her face in concentration. 'Savvy, or something similar. He was a looker, that much I *do* remember, from the one photograph she showed me when she came back on leave. Dark-haired, like you. And his eyes made her turn gooey when he looked at her, she said. Deep, deep brown: almost black. I could totally understand what she saw in him. He wasn't very tall apparently, a smidgen more than Joy. But she was a tall girl anyway. At any rate, when she told Lady Celia – her mother – that she wanted to invite him to stay at Somersby Hall, the old cow had a hissy fit. I was cleaning in the drawing room and I overheard everything, you see. It was so embarrassing. Her wretched mother told her that a foreigner from who knew where wasn't good enough for her daughter and that she should marry a man from the county – somebody more her class. And that if this young man turned up, she wouldn't allow him in.'

From the few minutes she'd spent in the old lady's company at the door of Somersby Hall, Paige could easily picture the scene. Poor Aunty Flo. Squirrels was a total contrast to the stately home she'd been brought up in. Presumably money had been no problem when she was growing up. But later on, Aunty Flo had basically struggled from one month to the next... oh for goodness' sake, it was impossible to imagine a better mother. Her aunt, to all intents and purposes, had been a *perfect* mother in her book, but she had never been able to call her Mother. Why, oh why had she been denied the truth? Why all these secrets?

'She came back for a while before the war ended. When she was expecting. I don't think they wanted her working anymore as a secretary. It was like that in those days. If you were with child out of wedlock, it was a scandal. I felt so sorry for her. There were rows and eventually, she left the Hall.' She fiddled with a ring on her finger. 'I believe Lady Celia was intercepting letters this Italian sent to Joy. I found part of an envelope addressed to her in the ashes one day when I was cleaning out the grate in the old cow's sitting room. I couldn't be sure but... it's the sort of thing she'd do.'

'That's dreadful... and so sad,' Paige said, hating the old lady even more for her interference.

'I think her mother set up some sort of fund for Joy. Poor girl. I tried to find out where she'd gone, but the old dragon insisted she didn't know. More likely she didn't want to tell me.'

It made sense now to Paige: the way Aunty Flo had so often used that phrase, 'We'll be fine when my next payment arrives.' She'd heard it umpteen times. It was likely referring to those cheques arriving at the bank. Paige had assumed it was some kind of return on an investment. Never had she imagined it was money from her grandmother to salve her conscience.

Mrs Ambrose looked at Paige, tears in her eyes. 'Was she happy, my dear?' she asked. 'I really do hope so. She was so lovely. She deserved to be happy.'

'She never married, if that's what you mean. And I had no idea until today of *anything* you've told me. I wish she'd told me. It's so unbelievably tragic. I'm absolutely flabbergasted.'

'Where were you both all this time?'

'The other side of Suffolk. On the Shotley Peninsula.'

Peggy Ambrose blew a huge sigh. 'If only I'd known. I did try hard to look for her, you know. Her father was a kind man, but very henpecked, bless his soul. I'm certain he wouldn't have let it happen if he'd been alive. He worshipped his little girl. He'd have let her stay on. Lady Joy would never have had a termination or given you away, although that's what her mother wanted. She was a good, kind girl.' She looked at Paige again, her eyes moist as she asked, 'I reckon you must be, what, about thirty now? Born at the tail end of the war?'

'I'm twenty-nine. And yes, my birth date is February 13th 1944.'

'Do you have a young man?'

'No. Not now.' Paige left it at that and Peggy didn't press her.

'I'd have loved to have babies but I never met Mr Right. I could have helped Lady Joy with her baby but I'd already left the Hall by then. I couldn't stomach the old so-and-so anymore. I tried nursing but I'd always dreamt of opening a tea shop and I've managed that until now. I've loved every minute. Oh, I'm so glad we've met, my dear. Will you come back and see me again?'

'I'd love to. And you won't mind my asking you heaps more questions? I feel I don't know anything about the young person my au—' she corrected herself, 'the person my mother was.'

'I won't mind at all. Now, stay and have a bite to eat with me. It's only cheese on toast, but I'd be so happy to have your company and while I'm preparing in the kitchen, you can look through the photos of my time at the big house. There are quite a few of Lady Joy in there.'

Paige shed tears as she pored over the album, trying to take in the photos of her mother as a young woman. She wondered how many women of that era had suffered the way she had. The war had brought liberty of a kind to so many, changing lives radically. Women had taken over the jobs of men in factories, offices and farms while they were away fighting and helped run the country. But it hadn't necessarily made their lives any easier. She wondered how many babies had been brought up by single mothers, cast out by families because it was considered shameful. Tomorrow she would lay fresh flowers on her mother's grave: a huge bunch of wild blooms. And she would sit for a while by her side. She smudged tears away with the backs of her hands as Peggy returned with a supper tray.

CHAPTER 29

Back at Squirrels, Paige dialled Charlie's number, armed with a glass of the last of her mother's whisky. She mixed it with a dash of almost flat dry ginger found at the back of the pantry and plonked herself on the saggy settee waiting for him to pick up. A message on his answerphone began to spiel out: 'Hi there, I'm currently engaged in bodybuilding...'

Charlie's voice cut in. He sounded breathless. 'Hello! Charles Snelling here,' he panted.

'I don't believe you're really bodybuilding.'

'Might just as well have been. Bloody lift is out of action again. Sixty-two steps ascended, including a spiral staircase. Hang on, let me get a drink and I'll be back.'

She could hear him clattering about in his kitchen, the sound of ice dropping into a glass, the fridge door banging shut.

'Gin and tonic sorted. Fire away. Any luck up there in beautiful Suffolk?'

'Yes, and I have something absolutely amazing to tell you, Charlie. My mother was Aunty Flo but my mother was also Lady Joy. And she was more or less kicked out by her awful mother, whom I actually met before I realised she was the

grandmother from hell. Horrible old lady. Her housekeeper –
God knows how she can bear working for the old hag – she put
me in touch with a lovely woman who owns a tea shop and
knew my mother thirty years back. She told me my father was
Sicilian—'

'Woah, slow down there, Paige, while I take it all in. So – to
summarise: Lady Joy and your aunt are one and the same. Your
aunt was really your mother. This is a more complicated plot
than my latest bonkbuster. And… your father was Sicilian.
Then, that pendant in the box *was* a clue. I knew it. What's his
name?'

'The woman I spoke to – Peggy, she's called – said she never
met him but remembered his name was something like Savvy.
But she never saw or heard again from my mother after she left
Somersby Hall. Apparently, just before the end of the war, she
realised she was pregnant. With me! All hell broke loose and
she was kicked out. She never got in touch with her mother
again. Just think, we were only living about twenty-five miles
down the road all the time. Families, eh?'

'Tell me about it. I had to wait until Pa died to come out.
But you know about all that. Are you going to go back and question your horrible grandmother?'

Paige sighed. 'I can try but I'm not banking on anything.
But I've made up my mind to go to Sicily.'

'Wow! I think that's *amazing*, Paige… or do I have to call
you *Lady* Paige?'

'Don't be an idiot. Oh, Charlie, I do wish Aunty Flo had
told me she was really my mother. It's so sad. How hard must it
have been for her to keep it from me all these years? And why,
for goodness' sake? We're in the seventies now. Nobody cares
about unmarried mothers nowadays.'

'Well, darling Paige, she didn't make that decision in the
1970s, did she? Life wasn't easy for single mothers back then.
There was loads of prejudice and the poor women ended up in

homes, having to give their babies away. She obviously thought it was best for both of you whatever she did. And she loved you, that's the bottom line. And, anyway, wasn't she about to tell you?'

She sighed. 'You're right, of course, Mr Sensible. But it still hurts. I'm finding it hard to think of Aunty Flo as my mother.'

'Just think of her as *her*: the extraordinarily lovely and eccentric woman she was, who adored you so much she didn't give you up for adoption or leave you in a shoebox outside a church. We don't need labels when push comes to shove.'

'We only have one mother but we can have several aunts.'

'True.'

'Would Bertha make it all the way to Sicily, do you think? Am I being bonkers wanting to drive there, Charlie? And where to start? I can't just turn up on the island of Sicily and flap around.'

'Take a deep breath, Paige. *Ommmm!* Don't have second thoughts. First of all, get Bertha serviced. She's a Morris Traveller, isn't she?'

'Yep. Aunt— Damn it... *Mother* and I did use it for a camping trip once down to Cornwall. But it was cramped. You know how tall she was.'

'The envelope you showed me was stamped SIR, if I remember. Siracusa, Syracuse as we know it. Start there. Even if you find nothing, it'll be a fab city break. When was the last time you had a holiday?'

'When you and I went to the Isle of Wight Festival.'

'Call that a holiday, woman?'

'It was fab.'

'*Muddy*. Sicily will be a whole lot warmer. You can camp. Buy awnings and stuff to attach to the car, can't you? I'll come out and join you once you get there. It'll be fab.'

'Oh! Thanks a bunch. So, you'll let me do the perilous driving part when I break down by the side of the road. And then swan over by plane.' Paige fiddled with the telephone cord, another thought making her wonder if she was being too impulsive. 'I'll have to take more time off school. It's half-term week soon, but that's not enough.'

'Plead for more compassionate leave. Get a doctor's note and take off a month. They'll most likely keep your job open. I know how hard you work. *They* must too. They can use supply teachers for part of the summer term.'

'I suppose I *could* lay it on a bit. I *have* been finding it hard to concentrate on my teaching.'

'Nothing ventured, nothing gained, Paige.'

'It all seems hasty and self-indulgent and I've hardly anything to go on, after all. And what if my father – if I ever found him – is dead? And my turning up out of the blue makes it awkward for him if he's still alive because he has a family and ten *bambini*?'

'I'm going to ring off now because you're rambling and putting up excuses when you really know you want to go. And that you *must*, honeypie. By the way, you've given me a cool idea for a new book. I shall scribble down a plotline while it's fresh in my mind. Hey! I can legitimately join you on a research trip once you're over there and put it on expenses.'

She laughed. 'You're incorrigible, Charlie. Bye for now. I do love you.'

After she'd put down the phone, she flicked through her diary. She landed on the page that Jeremy had marked with a red asterisk. He'd often done that kind of thing when organising future dates: taking over her diary, making sure she didn't arrange anything else for that day. This particular red asterisk marked the date of their wedding on the second May bank holiday. She smiled wryly. Perhaps she would see if there was a ferry crossing for that day at the exact time when she had been supposed to traipse down the aisle in her meringue dress.

The phone conversation with the headmaster left her

feeling half-worried at the ease with which he had agreed and granted her a month's leave. Was she such a terrible teacher that he wanted to replace her? That afternoon, she drove to the travel agency in Ipswich and picked up half a dozen holiday brochures for Sicily and southern Italy. Back in Squirrels, it didn't take her long to select a couple of apartments. The owner of one stated that English was spoken and Paige surprised herself by picking up the phone and dialling the long Italian number to book it. She'd made the first step. Now all she had to do was solve the small matter of her mother's mysteries. She pulled out the chocolate box again and sat with the pendant in her hands. The world as she had known it with the woman she had called aunt felt like a lie.

CHAPTER 30

1943, BLETCHLEY PARK

JOY

Everything felt unreal to Joy. It was as if she were watching events unfold on a cinema screen to somebody else. Scene one: the diagnosis of pregnancy confirmed by the kind female village doctor. She hadn't wanted to go to the clinic in BP when Mrs Perkins had suggested she might be pregnant because Joy had been convinced it was a stomach bug. And her periods were always irregular, anyway. The village doctor's words, 'About eight weeks,' as she'd handed her iron tablets and told her to look after herself, were a shock. 'Your husband will be delighted, I'm sure,' she'd said. 'We all need good cheer at this time. Is he overseas or in this country?'

Joy, dazed, had mumbled something about not being sure and the doctor had looked at her sympathetically. 'So many secrets to keep, eh? Make an appointment with Nurse on your way out so we can monitor you.'

Joy had wanted to ask her if she was absolutely sure, tell her she'd only been with a man for one night and with protection, but she'd felt shy and ignorant. Then she'd remembered how

Savio had worried when he'd withdrawn that first time, not wearing the horrid sheath. But, surely, only spending one night with a man didn't mean you could fall pregnant? *Fall*, she'd thought to herself. A word heavily loaded with judgement. She was a *fallen* woman, fallen into sin and bad ways. That's what her mother would say when she found out. Because she couldn't possibly keep this a secret forever.

When she'd returned from the village surgery, she'd told Mrs Perkins it was a stomach bug after all. 'There's a lot of it about,' she'd said and her landlady had raised her eyebrows as if to say, 'Pull the other one, girl.'

Over the next days, Joy felt as though she was continuing to watch this black-and-white film at the cinema, herself in the main role. The unfolding scenes after the village doctor's diagnosis showed her struggling on at BP. Thankfully, she'd stopped being sick but after another couple of weeks, she'd had to fasten her skirt with a safety pin. She was always tired, dog-tired and snappy. She couldn't sleep at night with the worry about her future. What should she do? How long could she keep her pregnancy a secret? How could she let Savio know? *Should* she let him know? Would he care? She'd had no contact from him whatsoever, except perhaps for those two spurious lines she'd looked over nights ago: lines purporting to be from a Dante, the connections to which were probably all in her imagination. She'd hauled herself from her bed each morning, unrested and troubled. Her sickness returned occasionally when she felt stressed and she had to dash for the toilet at work.

'I'm worried about you, Joy,' Rosie had said one evening. 'Maybe you should get advice. You don't look at all well. That stomach bug has taken it out of you. You should get a tonic from the doctor.'

Was she showing that much already? Had Rosie guessed? Joy made sure to dress and undress into her baggy nightdress and increasingly tight and uncomfortable uniform in the bathroom. She was almost twelve weeks gone. She couldn't hide it for much longer.

She'd dragged herself to work. The only way to get through the day or night shifts had been to immerse herself in what was put in front of her. The messages she'd been translating were mostly arriving from northern Sicily now. The heat streaming through the tiny windows of the hut had been almost as stifling as the southern Mediterranean summers she remembered. How she'd longed to dive into the sea to cool down. Her head had thumped and she'd made several trips to the cloakroom to pee. Every time she'd put up her hand for permission, the supervisor had frowned. 'You should drink less tea, Harrison. We can't be having these constant interruptions.' Joy had tried to hold it in but it was too uncomfortable. She'd thought she would burst.

The climax of this horror film in which she was the starring actress came when she was reading an article in the newspaper in the canteen. Censorship restrictions had been lifted; there'd been a whole spread about the progress of our lads in Italy and how they were forging ahead. Operation Husky had taken place in early July and the report told of night landings on the south-eastern coast of Sicily on a peninsula called Maddalena. She sat forward, devouring the words.

She knew this place. The landings had occurred at a point known as Murro di Porco. Her finger retraced the words. Of course! The pig's snout. The word 'porco' had been in that cryptic message nobody had properly understood that night. And the name: Lamba Doria. It hadn't been a person: it was the name of an Italian battery. That was why the name had rung a bell. She'd swum there with her Sicilian friends, picked a bunch of sea lavender for her mother, stuffed it in the handlebars of the rusty red bike they'd lent her to take back to the villa.

How stupid she'd been not to remember the names that

night. But she'd felt so nauseous and weary. It had been hard to concentrate on anything except reaching the cloakroom to avoid being sick at her desk in the hut. Joy read on, taking in tragic details of the many men lost from gliders that had missed their landings. So many drowned soldiers. Only fifty-four out of the original one hundred and thirty-two gliders had made it to their marks, she read, and many men had been lost in the waves. There was a list of the lost and she scanned the columns. Her heart went out to their loved ones. And then she let out a scream and clasped her hands to her mouth, shouting, 'No! No! No!' over and over while her eyes remained glued on one particular name: *Rizzo, Savio. Killed in action, July 10th 1943*. She felt herself falling and was aware of people rushing to pick her up before everything went black.

The Park doctor confirmed she was pregnant. She'd known that already, of course. And she'd known she would be dismissed from duties at BP and would be reminded that if she were to divulge anything whatsoever to a soul, certain imprisonment or worse would follow, no matter if she was with child. She'd known all these things, of course she had, but she'd tried to delay the day. And now, to add to the shame of being pregnant, she was consumed with guilt. She made herself ill, convincing herself that if only she had understood the strange message in time, she might have prevented the deaths of Savvy and so many other men. She'd dismissed the lines as having no relevance but there must have been a hidden meaning behind those words. The deaths were all her fault – she knew it. It was too much to bear and she went to pieces.

She poured her heart out to Rosie, who visited her in the camp infirmary. Rosie stroked the hair back from Joy's clammy face and told her it couldn't possibly be her fault. But Joy was too ill and distraught to be persuaded. She turned her face to the wall and told Rosie to go away.

'If you carry on like this, you'll lose your baby. Is that what you want?' Rosie asked.

Joy hadn't thought of the wretched thing inside her causing so much sickness and trouble as a baby. She turned round slowly to face Rosie.

'I'm sorry, Rosie. You're being very kind. Everything seems impossible at the moment. I know I'm being pathetic. What sort of a life will my baby have? Without a father?' Her tears fell as it hit her that Savio would never see the child they'd created. Created, she wanted to believe, from so much love.

'Lots of women bring up children alone,' Rosie said. 'You won't be the first and you definitely won't be the last. Or do you want to give the baby up for adoption? It's easy to arrange.'

It was that question which decided Joy. She would *never* give up this baby. It would be like losing Savio all over again. She would return to Somersby Hall and drop the bombshell to her mother and seek shelter for a few months until she could work something better out.

She swung her legs round to sit on the bed and at that moment, as if the little being inside her had heard her words, Joy was suddenly made very aware of her swollen belly. Instinctively, she moved her hands to protect her womb. 'Rosie,' she said, her eyes glistening with unshed tears, her voice trembling. 'There's life inside me, isn't there?'

Her friend bit her lip and nodded. She sat down and put her arm around Joy and the two of them stayed quiet for a few seconds until Joy wiped her eyes.

'No way shall I give up this child.'

CHAPTER 31

JULY 1943, SICILY

SAVIO

When Savio came to, the gunfire had increased, more grenades were being exchanged like balls tossed in a deadly game and his head hurt like hell. But he was alive. Savio lay near the man who would hopefully save his life. *You died to save me, mate,* Savio wanted to tell him. *You didn't die in vain.* As an afterthought, he pulled his Arab shemagh from his neck and arranged it round what remained of the dead man's neck and shoulders. It would be further proof of identification. The scarf had kept the Palestinian sun off his own neck. The temperature here was almost as hot and sticky.

There came a point when he couldn't hide any longer. Savio made his way back to the cave under cover of darkness. He'd promised Carmelo's woman he'd return and although he'd found no medicines, he would donate his own atabrine malaria pills and do what he could for his cousin. They'd learned basic first aid at Glenaig, but Carmelo would need proper medical help if gangrene set in. *One step at a time, Savvy. You can do this.* He'd have to ensure he evaded not only Tommies but Italians too, dressed as he was in his mish-mash of Tommy uniform. Near a farmhouse, luck handed out another favour when he came across washing strewn across gorse bushes. He snatched up a pair of old trousers and a patched shirt and entered the house with caution, his gun poised. A kerosene lamp burned in a downstairs room but the place was as quiet as a morgue. On a wooden table in the kitchen, half a loaf, a hunk of cheese, a dish of beans and an unfinished bottle of wine told him a meal had been interrupted. Two of the glasses contained wine. He listened for maybe five minutes to make sure there were no snipers lurking and still he couldn't hear anything, except sporadic gunfire in the distance. Every now and then, a glimmer from an explosion lit the darker corners of the simple room like flashes of lightning. He stepped quietly to the table, picked up the loaf and cheese to take to the family in the cave and knocked back the wine from both glasses. It was rough and slightly acidic – home-made like the wine his uncle had poured him, bringing back nostalgic memories. This was his place. There was no justification for killing his own kind.

A muffled sneeze alerted him that he wasn't alone. His fingers went to the trigger of his gun.

'*Chi c'è?* Who's there?' he called.

The sound of snivelling came from a cupboard at the far end of the kitchen. He moved over the rough flagstones as quietly as he could, Sten ready in one hand and, with the other, he flung open the cupboard door.

'*Ho fatto pipì addosso.* I've wet myself.' A tiny girl hunched up on the bottom shelf, her mouth puckering as huge tears rolled down her face. 'Where's Mamma? I want Mamma.'

Savio swore inwardly. The child would alert everybody in the vicinity if she kept on whining like this. Why was it he seemed to attract little children in moments of danger? He was no Pied Piper, for fuck's sake.

'*Shh!*' he said, not unkindly. 'Mamma will be back soon.'

He couldn't even give the child his chocolate ration. It was in his kit bag next to the dead Tommy. He put his gun down and played one of his party tricks and, extracting a coin from his pocket while she wasn't looking, he pretended he'd found it behind her ear before handing it to her. The child beamed up at him and watched him with huge eyes as he moved into the next room to change. The sooner he removed his uniform, the better.

A woman lay on the bed and he started at the sight of her, moving cautiously nearer, cursing himself for having left his weapon in the other room. He wasn't thinking straight. She could be armed, hiding a gun beneath the sheets. His boot crushed a shard of glass as he stepped nearer and the splintering sound was loud in the room but she didn't flinch. As he drew nearer, it was the beauty of her young face that stopped his breath: her skin smooth, her olive complexion flawless, thick dark hair framing her heart-shaped face. Her green-brown eyes were wide open, staring at the ceiling. Then he saw blood staining the sheet that covered her breasts and pieces of glass scattered around her from bullet holes that had penetrated the window above. He felt for a pulse but she was already marble-cold and he closed her eyes before pulling the sheet over her face. With his back to her, he quickly changed out of his uniform and into peasant clothing. He kept his stout boots on and at the last moment remembered the key to the cave and the promised atabrine in his trouser pocket. As an afterthought, he took the copy of Dante's book from his shirt and shoved it down the pocket of the peasant trousers, which hung three inches above his regulation boots.

He didn't have the heart to leave the child alone with her dead mother. Taking her might either hinder his escape or help, making him blend in better as an Italian civilian. In any case he had to do the decent thing and remove her from this house of misery. He pushed the bedroom door to and returned to the cupboard.

'Let's go and find Mamma,' he said, holding out his hand. *'Come ti chiami?* What's your name?'

'Loretta, but Mamma calls me Lori. What's yours?' she asked, her small warm hand nestled in his.

'What do you think my name is? Have a guess,' he said as they stepped outside into the heat.

'That's a silly question. There are trillions of names to guess and it will take me all my life.' The child stopped suddenly. 'I need to change my drawers before we go to look for Mamma. She'll be angry if she sees I wet myself.' She pulled her hand away to run inside and he grabbed her. He didn't want her to find her dead mother.

'I know somewhere we can find you a new pair,' he said. 'Come!'

'Turn your back then, while I take off my wet drawers,' she said.

He kept one eye on her to ensure she didn't make a dash to the house and he smiled as she hid her pants under a stone before slipping her hand in his again. How trusting she was; how simpler life would be if adults could hold on to innocence.

The sun glinted from his watch face as they moved off. A peasant could not afford a watch and he removed the telltale from his wrist and shoved it into the pocket of his threadbare trousers, before noting it was almost midday. Not a good time to travel under the July sun. Cicadas chanted their persistent chorus and a cat lay stretched under the shade of a fig tree, nursing a litter of kittens. Loretta scampered over to them and the mother cat yowled. Savio picked her up. 'She'll scratch you. Leave her to feed.'

They made more pace with her in his arms. She was a skinny little thing, her hair as soft as dandelion seeds beneath his chin. Soon she fell asleep. The soldiers had advanced away from this area now. For a moment he wondered if his absence had been noted and if they had found the body and his dog tag and kit. Would Moyes be annoyed or at all upset he had lost his scout? Would he be taken in by Savio's ruse? He was a clever man, meticulous with his battle plans. And then Savio pushed away all distracting thoughts and continued to the cave. He was glad the child was asleep when he came across more bodies along the way: Italians, Tommies, a baby, its tiny limp arm poking from beneath its dead mother, flies feasting on death, the stench filling his nostrils. It lingered about the place and he wondered if it would ever go away.

CHAPTER 32

SUMMER 1943, SUFFOLK

JOY

Joy had not known where to turn after she was dismissed from Bletchley. Reluctantly, she boarded a train to Suffolk and made her way to Somersby Hall.

'You are a disgrace to us all,' her mother said when Joy turned up on the doorstep. 'Shop-soiled goods.' She offered no hug, no sympathy at all as she turned on her heel, leaving Joy to stand on the mat with her suitcase. It was Peggy who came to help her up the stairs to the spare bedroom with her luggage and opened the window to fresh air.

'Is there anything I can get you, my lady?'

Joy sat down on the bed, sighing, 'Shall we drop the lady-ship business, Peggy? You and I know each other better than that. Anyway, what are you doing back here? I thought you'd joined the Land Army.'

Peggy nodded. 'I did. But I've been given leave to help at home. Ma's not well. And...' – she twisted her white pinafore in her fingers – 'fact is, money's tight and I offered to help out with your mother when I can. You happen to have picked one of the two days a week I'm here.'

'I'm sorry to hear that, Peggy. But not sorry to see your friendly face again. Mother hasn't changed her ways, I presume.'

Peggy rolled her eyes. 'I ignore it most of the time. Means to an end and all that. The money is a help, so I grin and bear it.'

'I'll freshen up and then come down to the kitchen for a chinwag. Lots to catch up on.'

When Peggy left the room, Joy lay down wearily on the top of the bedcovers, watching the summer breeze lift the net curtains. She hadn't expected warmth but neither had she expected such frost in her mother's greeting. She'd returned to Somersby Hall because, frankly, she couldn't think where else to turn. Father would have been disappointed about her condition but he wouldn't have been so cruel. He would have put his arms around her, patted her back, soothed her. 'There, there, Joy. It will be all right. You'll see. You'll get through this and be stronger as a result.'

But he'd used those words whenever she'd taken a tumble from her horse, or one of the Labs had to be put down. Not when his daughter had fallen pregnant.

Fallen, fallen, fallen. Those words drummed in her head. She was lost and had never felt so alone. But she told herself off. She must get a grip and give the baby in her womb a chance. She would love the child when it arrived and this would be her main purpose in life. It was not the baby's fault after all. No matter what, she was never going to part with it and she drifted to sleep with that thought. When she woke, she saw someone had left her a cup of tea. Peggy, no doubt. It was cold but she drank it all the same. Peggy must have left her to sleep and moved quietly about the room. Not the sort of kind gesture her mother would have made. When she made her way down to the kitchen, Peggy wasn't there.

She knocked on the sitting room door. Her mother was seated in an armchair, staring through the window.

'I hate the view from this wing. The lovely lawn dug up for potatoes; my beautiful rose bed full of beetroot and salads.'

'It'll only be until this war ends, Mother. You've done the right thing by digging for victory. When this is all over, you'll have the place back to how you want it.'

'I shall have to sell up. There will be nobody left to tend to everything. The world has changed.'

'Despite the awfulness of war, I feel the world is changing for the better. You've no idea the variety of interesting people I've met these past months – the sort of people I'd never have had occasion to spend time with.'

The look on her mother's face was venomous. 'The world is changing for the worse when girls like you jump into bed with any Tom, Dick or Harry from whatever class or country. You can't stay here with... that bastard thing growing inside you. People will talk.'

Joy felt her blood pressure rising as she struggled to remain calm. The door opened and Peggy entered carrying a bucket and mop.

'Not now, girl. Can't you see we're talking?'

'Sorry, Lady Harrison, but you asked me to finish off in here and I have to go home to Mother soon—'

'Leave it, stupid girl, leave it.'

'You can't talk to her like that, Mother.'

'I shall talk to my staff how I want to. And I don't need *you* to tell me how.'

Joy followed Peggy out of the living room before she said anything to her mother she regretted.

'I'm so sorry, Peggy. Mother is as awful as ever.'

'I'm used to her by now. But I shan't be staying a moment longer than I need. Once Ma is on her feet again, that's it. I shall find another job. Even if it means cleaning out a hundred pigsties every day. But are you going to be all right staying here?'

'I have no choice at the moment, Peggy. No choice. I have no savings to speak of. Where I worked didn't pay much and... in my condition, where would I find employment?'

'It's a rum old life at times, isn't it?'

'You can say that again.'

Over the following weeks, Joy made sure to keep out of her mother's way in the east wing as much as possible and volunteered herself to help in any way she could with the busy VAD nurses in the main part of the west wing. She made herself useful winding bandages or sweeping round beds in the main ward set up in the dining room. Occasionally she would sit and chat with patients who never received visitors.

'Can you read something for me please, Nurse? That is, if you can spare a couple of minutes,' a young man, his eyes and hands swathed in bandages, called out as she walked past on a gift of a warm October afternoon. He was the only patient in the ward at that time, the other men having taken advantage of the unexpected weather to be wheeled outside in invalid chairs or, if they were able, to move around the neglected gardens on their crutches.

'I'm not a nurse,' she told him, coming to sit on the chair next to his bed.

'I expect you can read, though,' he said. 'You sound as if you could.'

She smiled. 'I can certainly read. And I do have time.'

'There's something in the locker drawer. I...' He hesitated. 'I've been putting it off until I could read it myself. But Doc tells me that's unlikely to happen any time soon.'

Joy could not find a book but on top of folded clothes in the drawer sat an unopened package.

'Do you mean this small parcel?' she asked.

He nodded. 'That's the one. One of my chums in here, he read me the address on the back. It's from my girl in Windsor. She's the only one who writes to me.'

Joy pulled off the brown paper wrapping. Inside was a matchbox and an envelope, marked simply: *Norman*.

'There's a letter, I think. Are you sure you want me to read it?' Joy asked. It felt wrong to be reading something personal, potentially intimate.

'Go ahead,' he said. 'I prefer the idea of a woman reading to me than one of the clumsy oafs in here. And anyway, we're alone at the moment. Am I right? It's quiet in here for a change. Doc says I have to start using my other senses to the max.'

She slit open the crumpled envelope and withdrew a single sheet of expensive notepaper.

'*Dear Norman*,' she read aloud.

'*This letter is very hard to write and I've been putting it off. You don't know how many times I've made a start, only to rip it up. There's nothing for it but to come straight to the point.*'

Joy hesitated.

'Don't leave me hanging,' said the young man, whom she now knew was called Norman.

'*When we received news of you missing, it was simply awful. I waited in hope but then I met someone. I wasn't looking for anyone else, I promise. The fact is, Norman, we fell madly in love. Jeffrey and I married last month. How was I to know you would turn up alive after so long? I mean, I'm pleased you are alive but it was a shock too.*

'*I wish you well. You'll meet somebody else someday, I know it. And someone better than me.*

'*Have a happy life and thank you for all the fun.*

'*I lost one of the diamond stones in the ring, I'm afraid, but I'm returning it to you as it doesn't seem right to hang on to it.*

'*Patsy*'

There was a single x at the bottom but Joy decided not to tell Norman about that. It was like part of her signature, she told herself. An automatic flourish, rather than a genuine kiss. There was a lump in her throat as she folded the notepaper and replaced it in the envelope. She couldn't bear to open the matchbox to find the ring and she put it back in the locker drawer, under a pair of socks.

'I'm sorry,' she said, feeling inadequate at bearing such devastating news.

There was a long silence before Norman answered. 'I suspected already when she didn't visit. Just as well she never came. She might have felt duty-bound to stay engaged to me. She loved dancing, you know, and going to parties. Pretty little thing...' His voice trailed off and he bit his lip.

Joy felt useless. She couldn't even take hold of his bandaged hand to offer comfort. She sat there for a while, not knowing what to say.

Norman sighed. 'What about you? Tell me something about yourself. If you're not a nurse, what are you doing here? You have a nice voice.'

So, Joy told him she was pregnant, that her boyfriend was dead. She naturally did not mention BP, simply told him she'd been engaged in clerical duties with the services but could no longer continue in her condition. She explained how she had returned to her mother at Somersby Hall until she decided what to do next.

'I thought you sounded posh,' he said. 'An upper-class girl. So this is where you grew up. Tell me, what's this place like? Is it very grand? I suppose we're out in the sticks.'

'It might have been grand once upon a time, but Father left debts and it's been increasingly hard to maintain everything. Having you all here in the hospital has put life in the place again. We're in Suffolk, near Bury St Edmunds. Did they not tell you?'

'I've only just arrived. Been in East Grinstead for a long spell. Treated for burns and what have you. Suffolk, eh? Should have known from the air. Used to spend holidays at our country cottage here as a youngster, sailing with the family, pottering about on the estuary, camping overnight. *Boys' Own* type of holiday. Nothing like it.'

'Where in Suffolk?'

'Over towards Ipswich. *Swallows and Amazons* country. Loved those books when I was a nipper.'

'So, what happened to you to get those injuries?'

He hesitated and she apologised. 'Sorry, please don't tell me if it's too upsetting. I can be clumsy sometimes.'

He shook his head. 'Don't worry. It's actually good to talk. Tell me your name.'

'It's Joy. But...' She bit her lip. 'I'm seriously considering changing it to something else. My life is not exactly a bundle of joy at present.'

'Well, that makes two of us.'

Their quiet conversation was interrupted by the arrival of patients returning from outside.

'Pissing it down... whoops, sorry, miss,' a young lad on crutches said, as he came through the French doors. His right leg was missing below the knee but he was surprisingly agile. 'Didn't realise you had company, Norm, old chap.'

Joy rose from the chair next to Norman's bed. 'I'll come back and chat again another time, if I may,' she said, bending to speak to her new friend.

'I'm not going anywhere, Joy. That would be capital. Make a change from listening to Jimmy's filthy stories.'

As Joy made her way back to the other wing, she felt angry at the devastation the war was wreaking on so many lives. But, in comparison with poor Norman, who would never see again, her plight seemed less awful. As she walked, she brought one hand to her stomach. At least she had new life inside her. And a purpose. A new life to love.

CHAPTER 33

Sitting with Norman most afternoons developed into a pleasant routine. It wasn't simply a way of avoiding her mother, Joy told herself. Norman had a great sense of humour and she admired the courageous way he looked on the bright side despite everything life had thrown his way.

On a chilly but sunny afternoon in late October, she wheeled him to a sheltered corner of the grounds. The path to the grotto near the ornamental lake was almost overgrown but she had a pair of secateurs in her bag to clear it as they went. She was reminded fleetingly of the evening she'd done a similar thing with Savio when they'd escaped from Glenaig for the drink in the pub. But she pushed that memory away as quickly as it had popped into her head. What was the point of dwelling on sadness? And anyway, there was no time for love in war. She wished she had known that before.

The little corner that Father had nurtured with rare ferns collected over the years was neglected but over the past days she had begun to work on it whenever she had time. Pulling up weeds and cutting down brambles was soothing and satisfying work when the shape of Father's designs began to reappear. It had become a corner where she retreated when she could. Mother never ventured to this corner of the grounds and she wondered if perhaps Father had also used it as a haven.

As she pushed his wheelchair Joy described the surroundings to Norman, explaining how run-down the rose garden was, how the fishpond had silted up and the paths were full of weeds. 'It was all rather spectacular before,' she told him. By now, she knew he liked to know where he was. 'You are my navigator,' he'd told her more than once. 'A pilot needs a good navigator.'

She tucked in the rug round his knees and as she did so, he caught her fingers with his left hand. The right was still heavily bandaged, taking longer to heal. The skin on his remaining two fingers was red raw, strained over curled-up bones which would likely never straighten again.

'Thanks, Joy,' he said. 'How old I feel being wrapped up and tended to like this. But I'm only twenty-seven, for Christ's sake. I have to remind myself of that each morning, otherwise I'd give up.'

She could have said something trite like, 'You're as old as you feel,' but she didn't. If he felt old, he felt old. Instead, she asked him if he was ready to tell her how he had sustained his injuries.

'Do you really want to know?' he answered. 'You've never told me what exactly it was you did before you returned here. And that's fine. I suppose you had to sign the OSA and swear not to tell a soul and whatnot. Am I right?'

'You are right and what I was doing is for me only to know. I'm sure you understand that, Norman.'

'Fair enough. It's all over for me now. I was returning from a mission that your lot no doubt knew about. Dropping supplies over France. To partisans. Done it a dozen times or more already but unlucky thirteen finally struck.'

He paused and she waited; there was no point in dropping trite comments into conversations with Norman.

'We copped it over the sea, minutes before landing back on Blighty. The most dangerous time. When you think you're almost home: picturing the beers you're going to down in the mess, or the warm bed you're going to sink into. It gets perishing cold up there in the skies, you know. My mind was on other things.'

There was another pause. Joy waited again, watching the breeze lift the delicate fronds of a maidenhair fern by her feet. She wanted to give him all the time he needed, knowing by now how it helped patients if they could free up their nightmares.

'I haven't told you this either,' he continued, his voice low, filled with emotion, 'but I'd only recently lost my family in London. Wiped out by a doodlebug. Not a thing left of our place. My mind was full of them and I didn't see the Messerschmitt. But it certainly saw me.'

She touched his poorly hand and he tried to grasp hers in his damaged fingers. They felt like claws to her and she tried hard not to feel repulsed even as she felt guilty.

'I got picked out of the sea by fishermen. But... my crew didn't make it. I feel so bad, Joy.' His voice finally broke and his shoulders heaved.

She let him grieve until eventually his shoulders ceased shaking. *This bloody war*, she thought, *wiping out so many young people's futures*.

'Sorry about that,' he said, dabbing at his face with his bandaged hand. 'Haven't allowed myself to let go. Stiff upper lip not always so easy, you know.'

'There is absolutely no need to say sorry. None at all, Norman. Think of the partisans you helped and how in turn they will have helped others. We're all part of a chain of rescuers in our own ways,' she said. 'And there is absolutely nothing wrong with grieving. We're only human. We'd explode if we didn't let the corks pop sometimes.'

He sniffed and laughed. 'You are so right, Lady Joy.' He'd started to call her that occasionally to tease her.

For a while, both of them sat in silence, engrossed in their own thoughts until Norman spoke.

'Your talk of corks popping. I'd love to take you out to dinner. Would you let me, Joy? To thank you for all the time you've spent with boring old, useless me. You'd have to be navigator, mind. And I'd have to request permission from Doc to see if I'm up to it.'

There was no hesitation in Joy's voice. 'I'd love to. And... you're not boring or useless, Norman. Never think that. Where is it you want to go?'

'The Savoy, of course. Ideal place to wine and dine. Even if it will be wartime food and the wine not up to scratch. But there's a dance floor and I've still got my legs if you hold on to me tight.'

If he could have seen her, he would have noticed her eyebrows shoot up and her mouth open slightly in astonishment. Dancing? The Savoy? No ordinary restaurant, then. But if that was what he wanted, then she would help make it happen. They were both suffering, both propping up each other with this friendship, Joy thought. It was the least she could do. She would use Father's Bentley parked in the stables and petrol rations she had so far not used to drive them up to London. A train journey would be too complicated with Norman's disability. It would be a change for both of them and she wouldn't breathe a word to Mother. When she found out, which she probably would eventually, it would give her something else to moan about. But Joy had grown used to switching off, filling her mind with other things, while her mother moaned away.

. . .

On the evening of the outing, she walked into the makeshift ward wearing the best dress that still fitted her and was greeted by wolf whistles. She raised her hands and told Norman's friends to put a sock in it, embarrassment making her flush. Jimmy and the lads in the other beds had helped dress him in uniform. The bandages on his eyes had been replaced with two eye patches which made him look like a pirate, and she told him so.

'But pirates don't polish their buttons,' he told her. 'Tell me what *you're* wearing. You smell delicious.'

She had sprayed Mother's Four Seasons Coty on her wrists and behind her ears and Peggy had helped her arrange the sides of her long blonde hair into two fashionable rolls. She'd brushed the rest that hung loose until it shined.

'Well, I've ditched my baggy skirt and twinset for the night and dug out my pearls.'

'I hope you are wearing more than pearls, dear Joy.'

'*Cheeky!*'

He laughed along with his friends and she realised it was probably the first time she had heard him sound happy. It made her feel useful.

'My dress is blue, like the sea. Matches my eyes, according to my friend Peggy. Drop waist to cover my bump. Silky material. Will I do?' She did a twirl and the material brushed against his legs and the men around her wolf whistled again.

'Who is going to help me get Captain Hetherington into his carriage?' she asked the eavesdropping audience and the whole lot clustered around, fussing. To Joy it felt as if she should be taking a couple of them in the car with her, so involved were they in the whole project. But Norman had assured her there would be help at the other end. He knew the doorman on duty. There would be no problem on that score.

.   .   .

Norman dozed off as the car purred along the empty country roads. 'I'll have a kip to keep up my strength for later, when we dance,' he'd explained at the start and Joy was quite content to simply drive without talking. It was good to be on the road and away from the silent arrow-darting glances her mother threw her as they shared meals in the evenings. It was quite possible they might be stopped for using the car for private motoring, but Joy was hoping Norman wearing his uniform would smooth the way.

The friendly doorman, First World War medals gleaming on his jacket front, lifted Norman gently from the back of the Bentley and into his wheelchair, whereupon Joy took over. A table near the dining room entrance had been arranged for them, easier for Joy to navigate the wheels. The Art Deco surroundings were as opulent as Joy remembered from her debutante days, the cocktail bar with gold swans seeming to defy the fact there was a war going on, but blackout curtains now replaced plush thick velvet curtains. Chandeliers glistened in soft light and music played in the background, produced by a quartet of older players. A couple danced close, sequins on the woman's shoes sparkling as she moved to a foxtrot.

'Is it all right?' Norman asked. 'Everything up to speed?'

'It's wonderful,' Joy replied.

He leant in close and lowered his voice. 'Can you see Winston anywhere? They say they keep a room here specially for his post-prandial naps.'

She glanced round surreptitiously. 'Nope. Lots of important-looking people swigging champagne, but no Winston, I'm afraid. It's all wonderful. Such an adventure. I could almost switch off from the war for a couple of hours.'

The fact there were many officers, predominantly in American uniform, belied this statement but she wanted to go along with the mood, for Norman's sake.

'Good! Then I shall switch off too. I shall pretend my

injuries were sustained by falling from a tree. I was rescuing a
cat and the branch snapped. Who are you this evening?'

She laughed. 'I am Florence Caister, named after two of my
absolute favourite places. Caister where I spent a couple of holi-
days by the sea, with my beautiful horse, would you believe?
And Florence because it's a city I've always dreamt of visiting.
I've never really liked my name and I like it even less now.
Being named Joy drags an awful lot of expectation in its wake.'

She sipped at her champagne, a very pleasant change from
the watered-down shandies she'd drunk in the refreshment hut
at BP. One glass this evening would do no harm, she thought,
taking her hand to her stomach as the baby inside her kicked,
reminding her of its presence.

She topped up Norman's glass and guided his fingers to
the stem, ready to help him if needed. He spilled some down
his shirt front but as he couldn't see, she didn't dab at it. What
he didn't know didn't matter. '*Cin cin!*' she said, clinking his
glass. 'Delicious champers! Wonderful surroundings. Thank
you so much for dreaming up this evening of escape, dear
Norman.'

'Least I could do.'

He was sweating and she watched as his fingers searched in
his pocket. She moved to help him and he brushed her hand
away. '*No*, Joy,' he said, brusquely. 'I have to do it by myself.'

It was agonising watching him struggle and eventually she
handed him his serviette and he mopped at his face. As he
reached for his cutlery, he knocked over his drink. The glass
splintering onto the parquet floor had the couple on the next
table turning to stare and a young waitress rushed over to help.
Joy noticed their pitying looks before they turned away, whispering to each other as they continued their meal. Maybe this
evening had been too ambitious, Joy feared, but Norman had
really wanted it to happen and she was determined not to let it
end in failure.

As the main courses were being served to the tables, the ominous wail of air raid sirens sounded loud and clear.

There were a few gasps but no panic as waitresses sprang into action, guiding diners towards the stairs to the Savoy's opulent private shelter beneath the principal dining room. Norman was scooped up by the doorman and Joy followed the crowd down a flight of stairs to where a secondary dining room had been set out.

To her astonishment, almost immediately a stream of waitresses filed in carrying plates of food to each table so that meals could continue uninterrupted. The band tuned up their instruments and struck up music again as candles were lit and conversations continued.

'That's from Verdi's *Il Trovatore*: the "Anvil Chorus",' Joy said. 'One of Father's favourites that he used to play on his gramophone.'

'They're playing that to muffle the sounds from above,' Norman said.

It was a true demonstration of defiance and what the propaganda posters everywhere urged: *Keep Calm and Carry On*. Dull thumps could be heard occasionally from above, followed by a line of dust sifting through the ceiling, but after each dull thud, the buzz of conversation, sounds of cutlery on chinaware and bursts of laughter resumed.

Joy handed Norman his cutlery and he mumbled a thank you, but he didn't eat a thing. She considered asking him if she should cut up his beef. Hers was rather tough and she gestured to a waitress, who came over straightaway.

'Is there a choice?' Joy asked. 'Something easier for—'

'It's fine,' Norman interrupted. 'I'm fine. Please don't fuss.'

The waitress looked at Joy, compassion in her eyes, and hovered at a short distance, in case she might be needed again.

'Don't think I'll be up to dancing later after all,' Norman said, pushing his cutlery to the side of his plate.

He was sweating again, his face ash-grey and Joy was concerned. He'd asked her not to fuss, so she took the onus on herself.

'Actually, I'm feeling a little queasy,' she said. 'Shall we call it a night as soon as the all-clear sounds?'

'Are you sure?'

'Positive. I'm not up to it, really. This baby is going to be strong-minded – it's telling me it wants to go home.'

Norman called for the bill, the waiter helping him by pulling out the correct banknote from Norman's wallet and as soon as they could, they left. After the doorman had arranged Norman gently into the back of the car and shut the door, Joy discreetly put a couple of shillings into his hand and he raised his cap slightly in acknowledgement.

Norman slept for most of the journey back. At one point as she was driving through Essex in the small hours, she had to swerve to avoid a badger in the middle of the road and he cried out in pain. They'd been foolish to even contemplate an evening like this, Joy thought. She only hoped the experience hadn't set back his recovery, but Norman had assured her the doctor had encouraged the outing.

At Somersby Hall, she parked the nearest she could to the hospital wing and opened her door, about to go and wake one of his ward mates to come help lift him from the car. There were so many unforeseen things she had neglected to plan and this was one. Life for Norman was not going to be an easy ride.

'Sit with me in the back for a bit, Joy. I don't feel like going in to those snoring blighters just yet.'

She hadn't realised he was awake and she hoped he wasn't going to try anything on. They'd had a date of sorts, yes, but if he tried to touch her or kiss her, there was no way she could respond. Nevertheless, she climbed into the back of the car, making sure to keep her distance at the far end of the leather seat.

'Don't worry, Joy. Or should I say, Florence. I'm not going to molest you. I just want to talk, that's all.'

'I...' she started, without really knowing what to say. The trouble was, she felt sorry for him. This war was beastly; what it was doing to everybody too awful for words. Norman deserved happiness. He was a young man whose fiancée had ditched him, but there was no point in putting false hopes into his head. He didn't arouse the slightest twinge of romance in her and she felt bad now about agreeing to this crazy night out in London. Had she somehow led him on? She felt out of her depth.

'No need to say anything,' he said, as if reading her thoughts. 'This evening was a bit of a shambles, wasn't it, and I'm sorry for suggesting it. Look, Florence-Joy. The fact is, I've been thinking. I'm up the creek without my paddles and you're not much further behind. I know you're struggling here with your dragon of a mother. But...' He paused. 'Would you let me help you? I mean...' He stumbled over his words. 'Oh crikey, I know how to fly all kinds of crates but I'm no good at this sort of thing.'

The rest of his speech poured out in one go and Joy couldn't interrupt him.

'If you were to marry me then you'd be home and dry. My parents were rich. You wouldn't want for anything. Your baby would have a father. You wouldn't have to work and you could escape from your mother. You've told me often enough how you hate living here with her. You've made me happy these past days. You don't have to answer now. Think about it, Florence-Joy. Sleep on it.'

There was a long silence after he'd finished. Eventually Joy opened the car door. 'I... I'll go and get one of the chaps to help you inside,' she said, wanting more than anything to escape from Norman's sudden, strange marriage proposal, her instincts warning her to turn him down immediately, the practical side in her brain urging her to accept and thereby kill two birds with one stone: a solution for the future and the avoidance of hurting the poor man. In a complete tiswas, her mind spinning, she poked her head back into the car. 'I'm flattered, Norman. Truly I am.'

For the time being this was all she could offer as an answer, but her heart was screaming at her. In pain. Why, oh why couldn't it have been Savio talking to her like this?

Back in her room, she pulled open the drawer of her dressing table and found Savio's pendant beneath a pile of cotton handkerchiefs. He had apologised at the time and promised he would buy her something better as soon as he could. She hadn't quite realised it had been a kind of proposal. One which she would have accepted without question. But what was the point? He was dead. When she looked in the mirror, she saw she was crying and she shoved the pendant back and started to wipe cold cream on her face to remove her makeup. There was no point in crying, but her tears continued to fall.

CHAPTER 34

1943, SICILY

SAVIO

The little girl was awake again when Savio unlocked the door to the cave and she started to cry when she realised her mother wasn't in there. She kicked Savio's legs with her bare feet, wailing that he had lied to her. 'Where's Mamma? I want my mamma.' One of the old ladies called out, 'Loretta?' and the little girl ran over to her, shouting, 'Nonna, Nonna, I can't find Mamma.' Her grandmother pulled her onto her lap and soothed her, rocking her back and forth and Savio pictured how the child would be brought up by the old lady instead of her mother. At least she had family and would hopefully be cherished.

Carmelo had deteriorated and the young woman hurried outside to fetch more water to cool down his burning body. 'He needs a doctor,' Savio said.

'The doctor is dead,' the old man said. 'Killed by your people. You can't fool me, dressed like that. You're still an *inglese. Bastardo.*'

Now was the time to explain to the old man about his past.

This was the next danger to thwart. The old man could easily turn him over as a traitor. This fate was worse than dodging bullets: he would either face a firing squad for desertion or a lynching by locals. The next few minutes were amongst the most vital of his life if he was to have a future. He sat down next to the old man, who turned his back while Savio explained everything that had happened to him over the past years, months and days. The women listened too as he spoke and when he occasionally faltered over a word, someone prompted the Sicilian for him as his story progressed. He felt, rather than saw, the old man soften as he turned to listen, eventually looking Savio in the face as he came to the end of his explanations.

'So, you see, my heart has told me I belong here,' Savio finished. 'On this island where my parents toiled so hard. Where they planned to return to spend the rest of their days. I am not your enemy. How could I kill my own people?'

'I knew your father,' the old man said. 'We worked the fields together many years ago. We helped each other at harvest time. I liked him and I was sorry to see him go to America.'

'Not America,' Carmelo's woman interrupted, from where she kept vigil at her husband's side. 'The gentleman told you it was *Inghilterra*.'

The old man shrugged. 'It's all the same. Once you leave Sicilia, everywhere is the same to me. He left for somewhere over the sea far from here. So many of our friends leave, saying they will return. Even my son left. He packed a lump of our earth in his suitcase to take with him to plant seeds in his new country. He said he'd left his heart here. But he never came back. He was killed, working down a stinking mine. They all say they will come back, but they don't.'

'*I* have come back,' Savio told him, touching his arm. 'And I mean to stay.'

The old man stared into Savio's eyes for a long minute, before finally touching his arm. 'I believe you.'

Savio relaxed his shoulders and silently expelled air from his lungs. For the time being, he was safe. But he would need his wits about him at all times. He pulled the malaria tablets from his trouser pocket and handed them to the young woman and she thanked him.

'I will give him one when he wakes up. I hope he doesn't vomit it up. His fever is still raging.'

'Where is the doctor's house? Perhaps I can go to fetch medicine for Carmelo.'

She shook her head. 'There's nothing left. It was bombed. He was our neighbour, so we feared for our own place and that's why we fled to the bunker.'

Savio's heart sank. His cousin needed proper medical help. First aid was not enough. His only chance of survival was in a hospital. The nearest would be in Syracuse and that was under attack. What about a field hospital? If he took Carmelo there it was a possibility he might be recognised, even dressed as he was in peasants' clothes. But if he disguised himself well enough, as he'd been taught during the courses at Glenaig, he might get away with it.

'I need you to shave off my hair,' he told Carmelo's woman, 'and we need to get hold of a cart, or a donkey, anything to help us carry him to a doctor. It's the only way.'

Her eyes widened. 'Cart? Donkey? It's impossible, signore.'

The old man spoke up. 'The only animal left is the cow. But we've hidden her. She's all we have left.'

'That could work. Do you have a cart she could pull?'

'I know how to handle her and yes, we have a small cart. Easier if *you* were to pull it, though. The cow never has and she's a stubborn one. Like all females,' he added, his wheezing laughter ending in a spasm of coughing.

Savio had been about to ask the old man if he would accompany him but he was obviously not well enough.

Carmelo's woman reappeared with a long razor, shaving cream and a small, cracked mirror. Savio started to work the cream into a lather. 'I can do the front, but I need you to finish the back.'

Her fingers trembled a little as his hair fell to the ground and he tried to put her at ease.

'What's your name?'

'Graziella,' she replied. 'I remember you. You're Savio. You used to come here on your holidays. You never wanted us girls to join in with your games.' She giggled.

Savio peered at her in the mirror behind him and vaguely recalled a raggedy girl with tangled plaits, running in bare feet, always wanting to hang about with Carmelo and his gang. She was a fast runner, he remembered, but they'd constantly teased her, telling her to go away and leave them in peace. Once, they'd told her they were all meeting outside the church. Of course, it wasn't the correct venue but somehow or other she'd managed to winkle out the truth and follow them. She'd joined in their football game with the ball they'd made from a pig's bladder. And she'd scored the only two goals and played better than half their team too.

'You caught up with Carmelo in the end, then,' he said, winking.

She blushed and patted her stomach. 'We are having a baby. Please keep him alive for us, Savio.'

He finished off the job, noting with dismay in the mirror that where his hair had been removed, his skin was pale as eggshells. The young woman laughed but went to where her husband lay and returned with an old straw hat. 'This will cover you. Pull it down firmly. And, signor Savio, *I* shall come with you to the hospital. Nonno is not strong enough. You can pretend you're my brother. If we're stopped by Italians, don't open your mouth. Your Sicilian is very good, but... not good enough. And I will help you pull the cart. I'm strong.'

As a plan it was as sound as it could be but he needed to know how to find the field hospital first. 'Who could tell us where the soldiers' hospital is? Can you find it?'

She thought for a moment. 'The *parroco* will know. He always knows everything, our parish priest. I swear he can see inside people's heads and know when they are telling lies at confession.'

He smiled at that. Hadn't he been caught out several times by their own padre in London? Sunday morning Mass had been an imperative when they were growing up. His mother would accept no excuses to avoid it. He'd had to serve as an altar boy until well into his teens.

Graziella returned half an hour later, a beam on her face. 'I told him I thought I was losing my baby and needed to see a doctor and he believed me.' She made the sign of the cross rapidly over her chest. 'May God forgive me, but the lie was necessary. There is a hospital on this side of Siracusa. They are treating everybody who turns up. Padre told me there are even *tedeschi* there. We should leave later when it's not so hot.'

He congratulated her. 'You are amazing, Graziella.'

'I will do anything to save him,' she replied. '*Anything*.'

Savio felt humbled at this declaration of love. He wondered if anybody would ever feel this way about him and while they sat in the cave and he watched Graziella do what she could for her young husband – cooling him down, stroking his hair back from his burning brow, talking softly to him as she changed his soaking shirt – his thoughts turned again to Joy. He liked the idea of spending a life with a good woman like Joy. She wasn't complicated and needy like so many women he'd met. But would she adapt to a life in Sicily? She'd talked fondly of her holidays in Syracuse. But spending holidays in a grand villa would be very different from the simple way of life Savio knew here.

Earlier, they'd tried harnessing the cow to the cart but Nonno had been right and the animal refused to budge and she'd emptied her bowels over Savio's boots in protest.

'*Merda!*' he shouted and Graziella giggled.

'Yes, you are right, signor Savio. *Merda!* Shit is useful for feeding our fields, but not so good for filling your boots.'

Savio thought it strange the girl who used to be their equal in childhood games should call him signore. But he knew it would be impossible to persuade her to use just his Christian name. That was the way with country folk.

'I need you to call me something other than Savio,' he told her, 'in case there should be anybody at this hospital who recognises me. How about Nunzio?'

She raised her eyebrows. 'You do look very different now, signore. Especially with that scar you've drawn under your eye. Nunzio you shall be.'

Savio had scavenged a rag from Graziella and planned to tie it to cover his right eye before they approached the hospital. And to add to his disguise, he would stoop. He thanked the stars for the training in Glenaig, a million miles away from where he was now. If they had known they were teaching a traitor how to hide away, what would they have thought?

Carmelo was made as comfortable as possible in the cart padded out with old sacking, but he yelped each time the cart bumped over stones in the rutted track. Savio worried he would not make the journey in what effectively amounted to little more than a wheelbarrow. It was hard work pulling but Graziella didn't complain once. She was a strong young woman, although there wasn't much flesh on her. He encouraged her to rest more than once, fearing for her unborn baby, but she adamantly refused.

Every now and again, the sky lit up as mortar fire was exchanged over towards Syracuse and Savio hoped Moyes had progressed further to the port of Augusta, the next intended part of Operation Husky. If he and his men had been held up, however, and were still around this area, it would be curtains for Savio if he was recognised. He knew he couldn't conjure a story the major would believe. He was an astute man and didn't suffer fools. But Savio couldn't abandon his cousin either.

They pulled over to the side of the track as a vehicle approached and Savio hurriedly dragged the rag around his head and eye, automatically stooping as a white truck slowed down. Savio made out letters painted in English on the side of the door: *No. 2 Mobile Operating Unit.* A young man in the passenger seat, dressed in soldier's uniform with a white band round the top of his shirtsleeve, stuck his head out of the window. He spoke in Italian but his accent was unmistakably English as he asked, '*Volete un passaggio?* Want a lift?'

Graziella glanced at Savio, who nodded almost imperceptibly. '*Grazie,*' she answered.

Passenger and driver jumped from the ambulance. Both wore grey uniforms and Savio noticed an emblem resembling a star. Could they be Jews? He was puzzled. It wasn't a regular uniform but neither had Moyes expected his men to be kitted out as if for army parade. The two chaps quickly assessed Carmelo and Savio heard the passenger who'd spoken to them in Italian mutter, 'Poor blighter. Doesn't look good. Should we give him a chance?'

'He's young,' the driver said. 'I say yes. Infection hasn't progressed too far.'

They fetched a stretcher and gently and expertly lifted Carmelo into the back of the truck, before indicating that Graziella and Savio could ride with him. Savio hesitated.

Graziella would be all right: she and Carmelo were in safe hands now and he had no wish to put himself in unnecessary danger, but she pulled on his shirt and whispered, 'Don't leave me alone with them.' He clambered up beside her. A Tommy, blood oozing from a binding round his shoulder, sat hunched in pain on the floor beside him and Savio did his best to avoid any communication. The wounded soldier swore each time the ambulance swerved. 'Fuck, fuck, fuck,' he repeated. 'Bloody fucking Hitler. Bloody fucking Mussolini.'

The field hospital was well arranged with half a dozen tents, crosses on the canvas, erected in an olive grove overlooking the sea. While they waited, Graziella whispered to Savio, 'We were warned about the *inglesi*. How they rape women. I didn't want to be alone. Thank you for staying.'

He touched her arm, keeping his voice low. 'You shouldn't believe everything you hear.' How else could he reassure her? War was war. There were always going to be a couple of mosquitos buzzing about, he thought, using one of his mother's expressions.

Two nurses with white armbands and the letters FAU embroidered on their blouses handed out water and dry biscuits while Savio and Graziella waited.

'We can look at your eye too,' one of them said in slow Italian, pointing to Savio's face.

Savio shook his head vigorously, almost dislodging the dirty binding and the second nurse bent down to talk to him. She was dark-haired, attractive and as she gently touched Savio's arm, he detected the very English scent of lavender talcum powder. Her Italian was excellent. 'It won't hurt. But it might need cleaning. You don't want to lose your sight, do you? How will you work if that happens?' She turned to Graziella. 'How did he do it, signora?'

As if coached, Graziella invented a story on the spot, lowering her voice. 'There's nothing wrong with my brother, signorina. He's...' She tapped the side of her head with her finger, lowering her voice even more. 'He's a bit slow and he likes to pretend he's hurt, so he wears those bandages. But he won't let you anywhere near him. He might lash out if you do.'

The nurse nodded and straightened up after handing Savio a couple more biscuits, smiling sweetly as if he were a child.

While they waited to see how Carmelo was, another soldier was carried in, one of his legs a bleeding stump. He wore the black shirt of the Italian militia and Savio realised this was no ordinary field hospital.

After almost one hour, a doctor came out to talk to Graziella. The dark-haired nurse stood at his side, acting as interpreter.

'Doctor says he wants to keep your brother in for the night under observation, signora. Come back tomorrow and try not to worry.'

The doctor had been eyeing up Savio while the nurse spoke and Savio's heart hammered as he listened to what was said next, almost wishing he didn't understand English.

'Tell this young man that I don't know how he acquired his boots, but he must get rid of them. They might be comfortable but a local boy was severely beaten yesterday by British soldiers who caught him removing boots from their dead companion. We, in this hospital, are not fighting people; we treat everybody equally. We believe in carrying out peaceable acts and we do not take sides. But tell him to hide them.'

While the nurse translated, Savio cursed inwardly. How stupid he had been. They'd been warned during training at Glenaig about such errors when creating their disguises. One of their SOE agents had been caught in France. She'd popped her favourite lipstick into her purse at the last minute. An English lipstick. She'd been shot as a spy.

Disguise had to be meticulous and his high-quality British army boots, despite being covered with half the contents of a cow's stomach, were an immediate giveaway. He slouched lower where he sat and hung his head, avoiding the doctor's gaze, while Graziella translated. He thanked his lucky stars he had bumped into these conchies and their ambulance unit, about whom he had heard a little. Moyes hated them, called them cowards. But if they were cowards, Savio thought, why did they put themselves in danger by working in the midst of battle? Friends, they were known as. They had been real friends to him. But he couldn't wait to put distance between all this and find a corner of Sicily where battle was not raging. Did that make him a coward? And what would Joy make of his decision? Would she want nothing more to do with him? His fingers went to his pocket, where her copy of Dante's poem rested. As soon as it was possible, he would write to her to explain.

CHAPTER 35

1943, SUFFOLK

JOY

Like a coward, Joy skipped spending visiting time with Norman on the day after his surprise proposal. She'd spent a sleepless night weighing up the pros and cons of the solution he was offering her and she didn't know what to do for the best. It would solve the worry of providing for her baby if she married Norman and she wouldn't have to stay at Somersby Hall with her insufferable mother, who never missed an opportunity to drop acerbic comments about the shame Joy had brought upon her. But she didn't love him. Not like she'd loved Savio.

Could she devote her life to a man who would need help for the rest of his life, be a nurse to him, rather than a proper wife, simply to provide shelter for herself and her baby? The thought made her wither inside. Was any of this fair on Norman? He deserved a wife who truly loved him, not somebody marrying for convenience. And yet, what alternatives did she have? If she'd been married to Savio, then she would have been eligible for his army pension. But she hadn't married him. He had no doubt forgotten about her even before he'd died. If this, if that:

the hypothetical questions squirmed around her brain like greedy maggots sucking at her sanity. She told herself that 'If' served no purpose. She had to make up her own mind. Until such time, she would steer clear of Norman.

It was Peggy who came up with a solution on the following Monday when she knocked on Joy's bedroom door.

'I've come to flick the duster around in here,' she said with a cheeky grin. 'Your mother sent me. Said you'd been in here the last two days and the bedroom needed airing. Have you two rowed again?' She stood, hands on hips, staring at Joy, who was still in pyjamas.

To Joy, the thought of sharing another breakfast with her mother had been too depressing. The baby had kicked all night like a little football player and she hadn't slept a wink. There'd seemed little point in getting up that morning.

'Are you feeling sick again, Joy? Been overdoing it?' Peggy perched on the end of Joy's bed. 'This room looks perfectly tidy to me. I gave it a spring clean only last week. What's up?'

'Nothing, really.'

'That sounds like "everything, really" to me. Has she been horrid again? Must be hard for you to come back here after spending time away.'

Joy sighed. 'I'm angry with myself for getting into this state. If I weren't pregnant, I'd still be working at... still be carrying out important secretarial work,' she said, correcting herself in time. 'Instead, I'm dependent on Mother to provide a future for this baby. I think I shall go mad.' She twisted the fringe of the bedcover round her fingers. 'I had a proposal a couple of nights ago.'

Peggy's face lit up. 'Why, that's marvellous, Joy.'

'Is it?'

'Oh. It's like that, is it? You don't sound one bit excited. Still, lucky you! I've never been proposed to. Was it very romantic?'

Joy pulled a face. 'It was totally unexpected and, no, it

wasn't romantic. If I tell you who it was, you must promise not to breathe a word. I would hate him to know we've been chatting behind his back. It would hurt him enormously.'

'Do you love this chap?' Peggy asked before Joy could tell her who it was.

Joy shook her head. 'That's just it. No. In fact, I feel sorry for him.'

'The wounded officer you went out with?'

Joy nodded. 'Quite badly injured. Norman's blind and... his hands are very damaged. He's going to need oodles of patience and care for the rest of his life. I... I feel selfish. I mean he offered me and the baby a future. But—'

Peggy interrupted. 'Marriage is not a bowl of cherries, Joy. You need to be in love in the first place to go through good and bad times together. Take it from me. My sister's having a dreadful time. Her chap came back from France a different person. He has these awful mood swings. She tells us her black eyes are caused by falling down the stairs. Don't believe that, for starters. But she says she loves him, the silly cow.'

'If I stay here in this house any longer, I think I shall go round the twist, Peggy.'

'Borrow the old shepherd's hut we got.'

'What?'

'In the woods beyond our field where the ponies graze. Pa gave up on sheep farming long ago, so Ma used it when we were nippers. For holidays. Us kids slept under a canvas slung from the trees but she had the bed inside.'

Joy looked puzzled and Peggy laughed. 'I know! It's only a stone's throw from our place but she made it into a huge adventure and we felt we were miles away. We swung from the trees into the pond, cooked on open fires and Ma read and read and refused to go anywhere near our home for the whole week, in case she found jobs to do. Dad hated it, so he never joined in, but she left him plenty of prepared meals. Anyway, it's *very* basic, but you could escape there.' She stopped and pulled a face. 'Might be a stupid idea really. This house is so grand. Why would you want to go and sleep in an old hut in the woods after this? Forget I said anything.'

'Oh, Peggy,' Joy said, clambering out of bed and hugging her. Her growing tummy prevented her from pulling her friend closer. 'I think it's a splendid idea. Just for a week or so. To give me space to think.'

'While I'm at home I could pop along and keep an eye on you and ask Mum to bring you milk and what have you, between times. She's a lot better now. The walk would do her a power of good. And you could stock yourself up with tins from the larder here before you leave. Your mother has stacked a load away at the back of the pantry. She'll never notice if I pinch a few.'

Joy felt suddenly lighter in spirit. Her brain felt so scrambled at the minute; she could do with time away to get perspective. 'I'll tell Mother I'm going up to London to visit a friend. You'll keep schtum about where I am, won't you, Peggy?'

'Of course. Our secret will remain between you, me and Ma. We women got to stick together.'

That evening, she sat as usual in the small parlour next to the dining room, watching her mother sip her sweet sherry substitute: home-brewed parsnip wine available from under the counter in the village shop. Joy had gone off alcohol and her tipple these days was a glass of water.

'I've come to a decision,' Lady Harrison pronounced, placing her glass on the polished occasional table. 'You are to go away for the rest of your confinement. You're beginning to show and the news will be all over the county soon. Your aunt has offered to have you until you give birth and she knows of a young couple desperate for a child, eager to adopt. The alternative will be a home for unmarried mothers. I've set up an account in your name which will provide a small, monthly allowance. I believe your father would have approved. It will be better for all of us, don't you think?' She handed Joy an envelope.

'It seems I don't have any say in the matter,' Joy said, taking it from her mother and pulling out a cheque book bearing her name.

'As long as you're here under my roof, no, you don't actually.'

Joy stood up, her mind reeling, finding it hard to take in her mother's coldness. She'd expected to stay at Somersby Hall until she gave birth. After that, she had thought Mother would tolerate her presence until she found some other way of fending for herself. But this? Her mother's attitude was callous. She had no energy to fight and what, after all, would be the point? 'I'll leave tomorrow. I presume you will also *organise* the train ticket money to Aunt Mabel in Wales?'

'Of course.'

'I'm not hungry, Mother. I won't dine with you tonight. I'll pack instead.'

Although she sounded in total command of her emotions, Joy was shaking at her mother's cruel nature as she walked from the parlour. How could a mother treat her only daughter like this? She had never been affectionate but her father must have seen something to like in her when they'd first met. What had happened to make her like this? Had she no desire whatsoever to know her only grandchild?

It was pointless to argue and there was no way she would catch that train to Wales. She blessed Peggy for her timely interim solution. Tomorrow she would go through the motions of climbing onto the train to London and she would get off at the very next stop, pocket the rest of the rail fare and make her way back to Peggy's cottage to get directions to the shepherd's hut. The hut in the woods would be like a palace in comparison with the prison created by her mother in this big old mansion bereft of love.

Each morning, Joy woke early in the shepherd's hut to the chorus of birds in the woods and fell asleep in her cosy built-in bed as night shadows lengthened. Strangely, although Peggy and her mother were the only people she had seen over the past ten days, Joy didn't feel lonely and she slept well. A family of squirrels had built their drey in the vast beech tree that shaded the hut and she was kept entertained for hours by their antics as they scampered up and down the thick trunk, swinging from slender branches and balancing with their gossamer-grey tails. They were thieves too: it didn't do to leave anything outside. At first, she had kept milk, bread and a small pat of margarine in a string bag hanging from a branch, but she soon learned her lesson and kept all food inside. A badger sometimes lumbered into view at day's end and one evening when she sat on the wooden steps eating a bread and cheese supper, she was enchanted to see tiny cubs emerging from the sett, their furry little bodies curling about each other as they played and squeaked. The mother kept a watchful eye on her young, letting them stray a little, but always guiding them back.

That is how motherhood should be, Joy thought. *I shall protect but not smother*. She truly hoped she would be able to provide a decent life filled with love for the little being inside her. The baby kicked, as if in agreement. As soon as she was able, she would put distance between herself and her own mother and start a new life in a new place. After that, she never wanted to see her again.

After a wonderful fortnight in the hut, Joy decided she should make a start on coming down to earth. She planned to contact Norman and turn down his kind proposal. Then she would try to find some sort of part-time employment and generally stir her stumps. She was making her list when Peggy turned up.

Peggy leant her bike against the beech tree and hurried over.

'I can't stop for long, Joy. It's my lunch break and I have to hurry back. Your mother is going spare this morning. She's found out you're not in Wales and she's on the warpath. I've come to warn you. Here, take this,' she said, thrusting an airmail letter into Joy's hand. 'It was on the doormat as I left. The mood your mother is in, she might have torn it into shreds, so I rescued it. I've seen her remove letters addressed to you before. I think she suspects I know where you are but I feign innocence. Wouldn't put it past her to have me followed next time. So, be careful and lie low.' She placed a small pot and a brown paper bag on the hut steps. 'Ma sent you boiled mutton and spuds. And her famous beetroot cake.'

'I'm so sorry I'm causing all this trouble. I really think it's time to go back and face the music.' Joy placed her hands over her stomach. 'But there's no way on this earth I'm giving up my baby or being banished to Wales.'

'Well said, that girl.' Peggy hugged Joy. 'Look, I'll be back when I can, even if I have to disguise myself,' she said, laughing. 'If an old tramp turns up in the woods, it's me. Bye for now!'

Joy waved her off and when she had disappeared along the path, she looked down at the envelope in her hands. The stamp was Italian and she made out the postmark: *September 1943*. It had taken weeks to get here, but it was amazing it had even arrived with war raging. The services tried their best to keep mail coming through as it was good for the morale of troops and families. She read her name on the address: *Miss Joy Harrisson*, written with a double 's', instead of one. An easy mistake to make. The address was incomplete and incorrectly spelled:

Sumersbey Hall, Suffolk, with no town added. It really was a small miracle the letter had ever arrived.

And then her heart sank. Could it possibly be from Savio? Written before he died? She'd told him where she lived but never written down her address. It was strange to be receiving a letter now when he hadn't sent any before. Her hands began to shake so much she couldn't open the envelope and she had to sit back down on the hut steps. It was a good five minutes before she steeled herself to climb into the hut to fetch a knife to slit open the envelope. But when her eyes scanned the writing on the flimsy lined paper, she could make neither head nor tail of the contents. It amounted to a series of numbers and capital letters and a couple of strange messages, two in English and the other in Italian: *i vivi vivono con i morti*.

Her eyes lingered on the name at the end of the strange note: Dante – Savio's code name from when they had trained at Glenaig.

> *I am in paradise.*
> *VIII, 15*
> *I, 55, 4*
> *I, 88, 5*
> *XXV, 110, 8-L*
> *VIII, 38, 4, 5*
> *i vivi vivono con i morti*
> *I can't plan in a muddled place, 9 Last n=a.*
> *Dante*

Could this strange page *really* have been composed by Savio?

The spelling on the envelope was incorrect and this fitted in: he'd struggled over words. She read the lines over and over until she felt dizzy. They made little sense and she replaced the sheet inside the envelope, lifting it to her nose to breathe in any possible scent of him, before dropping it into her lap.

Joy, you are being ridiculous. Even if he had sent this to me, he is dead. She'd read it in the paper. His name was on the list. In black and white. Dead. Not missing. *Dead.* There was no point in trying to extract a significance to a jumble of numbers and letters. But neither did she want to throw it away. It might have been the last thing he had touched, before... she did not want to think of the way he might have passed. News of the Italian campaign described the invasion of the toe of Italy and the hard battles in the suffocating heat. She started to shiver and crawled to the shepherd's bed, pulling blankets around her, cradling her belly with her arms, willing herself not to let go, not to cry, to be brave. How easy it would be to give up, stay in the hut, sleep and sleep until sleep carried her away. But her baby kicked and kicked. *You have to carry on, Joy. You're not alone, you know.* So, she hauled herself from the blankets, went outside to coax the fire back to life. Then she filled the billycan from the pond to hang from its hook above the fire so she could make herself a hot drink.

She read the note again, willing her brain to make sense of the lines. Had Savio been trying to tell her where he was? Her crossword-brain told her that the line beneath the list of numbers was an anagram, the word 'muddled' leaping out at her as an instruction. The Italian phrase translated as 'the living live with the dead'. It could mean anything: catacombs, a cemetery, perhaps, even a battlefield strewn with bodies. Certainly nothing to correspond with the opening phrase: 'I am in paradise'. What had he been trying to tell her? And, anyway, what was the point? The baby kicked again as if to say, *Concentrate on me!* I'm *very much alive.* She replaced the note within the thin envelope and tried to sleep.

. . .

She woke to a thin layer of frost on the inside of the hut window. There was no way she could give birth to a baby and look after it on her own here in the woods. It was time to go back to civilisation and sort herself out. Maybe she had no choice but to accept Norman's proposal after all.

CHAPTER 36

MAY/JUNE 1973, SICILY

PAIGE

Paige parked in a lay-by on the outskirts of Syracuse and found a bar to have her breakfast. Over a tepid cappuccino and a dry slice of jam tart, she perused the strange, coded letter again, seemingly signed Dante. She knew he was a very famous poet. But that was about all. Did anybody ever christen their babies by that name in Italy? she wondered. There were lots of Williams, as in Shakespeare, so why not Dantes? But why had this Dante written to her mother? Who was he?

She would try to ask someone about the name and also get the Italian phrase translated. Maybe that would give a clue to the strange lettering. After paying, she used the café phone for directions to where she was staying.

The woman who answered the phone spoke excellent English with a faint American twang, so Paige was spared from grappling with her small dictionary. She'd learned a couple of useful phrases: *Buongiorno* and *il conto, per favore*: *Good day* and *the bill, please.*

Her landlady instructed her to park along the seafront and

gave simple directions to the apartment. 'I'll meet you there. If you get lost, ask for the *mercato*, the market. I'll wait for you on the corner.'

She was greeted by a woman of about her own age, with smiling eyes, her jet-black hair cut in a bob. A purple midi dress and boots with high, spiky heels that Paige would never have managed to teeter about on completed her look. 'Stefania,' she said, introducing herself, kissing Paige on each cheek in the Italian way. 'Welcome to Ortigia: the most beautiful part of the island.'

Paige liked her friendly manner straightaway.

'Is this your first time in Sicily?' Stefania asked, taking Paige's case from her, despite her protests. 'You're gonna love it here. I tried living in New York with my uncle and aunt for six months but I missed this place too much. We have a lot to be proud of. Trouble is, when people think of Sicily they picture the Mafia running around with machine guns.' She smiled. 'Sure, we got our problems but you gotta forget all that and prepare yourself for total immersion in beauty.' She stopped and flung out her arms, the many bangles accompanying her words like percussion. 'I mean, breathe in this sea air, lady, and open those eyes.'

Her enthusiasm was infectious. There was a definite sea tang, mixed with the aroma of fried fish wafting from the restaurant two doors down.

'Are you hungry?' Stefania asked, not waiting for an answer, as she pushed aside the fly-curtain hanging over the entrance. 'Zio Turridù,' she shouted, followed by a stream of words that Paige couldn't catch. It didn't sound anything like the Italian she'd tried to follow on the cassettes she'd packed.

A middle-aged man emerged from the kitchen at the back of the tiny restaurant, wiping his hands on an apron enveloping his generous paunch.

Always the sign of a good cook, Paige thought.

'This is my uncle Turridù,' she said, introducing the smiling man, her arm around his shoulders. 'The best cook on Ortigia. He's going to rustle us up his trademark *pasta alla siciliana*. You're never gonna forget it.'

Paige didn't mind being organised if it was going to be like this. Her journey across Europe to get here had been long and her heart had always been in her mouth with the worry that Bertha would not make the almost two thousand miles – especially the tortuous drive across the Alps. But she'd stopped regularly to open the bonnet and let the engine cool down. After five days' slow driving, she was relieved to be here. It was an achievement and she felt exhausted.

The area was a little scruffy and a dozen scrawny cats lay on the sea wall absorbing the southern sun. The temperature was far warmer than the weather she'd left behind in Suffolk. She followed Stefania into the unassuming restaurant, thinking she'd never have realised it was an eating establishment as there was no sign outside.

'Never bother with places displaying tourist menus,' Stefania said, pouring water into Paige's glass, after they'd seated themselves at a small table. 'Look for where locals go and you'll eat a hundred times better.' She opened a packet of grissini and offered one of the slender breadsticks to Paige. 'Oh my God,' she said, biting on hers. 'I noticed one of the tourist joints in the city offering burgers and French fries.' She made a disparaging click through her teeth. 'I mean to say. We're in Sicily, not Downtown New York.'

Two plates of pasta with a sauce of aubergines and mozzarella appeared almost immediately, followed by a half-litre jug of house white, and the two women got stuck in.

Paige hadn't eaten anything since early that morning, before catching the ferry from the mainland to Messina. A small crowd of curious onlookers had gathered around Bertha, asking Paige how old the car was, patting her kindly when they heard, as if in consolation. Paige had found this inquisitive friendliness all through southern Italy.

The pasta was divine. She'd never eaten anything like it. She struggled with winding the long strands around her fork and Stefania grinned. 'Learner, eh? Try this,' she said, picking up her dessert spoon and showing her how to use it to guide the spaghetti onto the fork.

That made it easier but when her plate was empty, she still had to wipe sauce from around her mouth and there were splashes of red on her cream cheesecloth top. Observing the other diners, she saw many had tucked cotton serviettes into their collars, like bibs, and she resolved to do the same next time.

'What brings you to this part of Sicily?' Stefania said, after ordering fruit for dessert. 'Do you have work here?'

'No.' Paige fiddled with the empty grissini packaging, smoothing out the creases. How much to confide in a complete stranger?

But the wine answered for her. She didn't usually drink at midday. But neither did she normally eat the most exquisite dish of pasta she'd ever tasted in her life. And on an island in the Mediterranean bathed in May sunshine.

'Somebody I loved dearly died recently,' she said, 'and left me with... a puzzle to solve.' It sounded ridiculous, Paige thought. But it was what it was. She suddenly felt tearful. She would never see Aunty Flo again, and she rummaged in her rucksack for a tissue.

Stefania leant in and took Paige's hand, concern in her eyes. 'Are you all right? Will it help to chat? I'm a real good listener. And, besides, I *do* love a mystery.' Stefania's already sparkly eyes sparkled even more as she leant in nearer to listen to Paige.

Paige drew a deep breath. She had come to Sicily to try to get to the bottom of Aunty Flo's past, so she needed to make a start and this woman seemed genuinely interested.

'My aunt died. We were extremely close. And then I found out she probably wasn't my aunt after all; she was my mother. And she'd left me a written message that she couldn't finish... because she died before she could tell me. And there's some kind of Sicilian connection. So, that's why I'm here...' Even as she talked, the whole thing sounded so bizarre and Paige shook her head, leaning back in her chair, exhausted. Not only from the journey but from sharing her story with a complete stranger. She wiped her eyes again as tears spilled.

Stefania offered her a silk handkerchief from her bag. 'I'm so, so sorry, Paige. It's like you've lost two relatives in one go: your aunt... and your mother.' Her eyes widened and she let go of Paige's hand and her bangles did that noisy thing again as she flung her arms wide. 'But... my God – it's like a Fellini film. You have to write a book about this. And with a name like Paige, you should be an author. And then you can get film rights. I have a friend who makes films. But... rather naughty ones, to be honest. Tell me, what has Sicily got to do with your mother?'

'Well... I've started by coming here because of a strange letter she left me. The envelope is postmarked Siracusa. Sent during the war. 1943. So I was thinking, I need to find out what was happening here in Siracusa in the wartime...' She stopped as a sob escaped. It all seemed so pointless. What was she thinking? Where to even begin?

'I'm only sorry I don't have more time today to help you, Paige. But... I do know someone who has studied that period. Leave it with me, *cara*. Tomorrow I'll have *plenty* of time. I'd love to help.'

'I need all the help I can get, Stefania. *Grazie.*'

The restaurant owner approached with a bottle of limoncello and two liqueur glasses but Stefania shook her head. 'Do you want a glass, Paige? I won't as I have this work appointment.' She glanced at her watch and then exclaimed, '*Dio mio.* I'll be late. Look, we need to hurry to the apartment and I'll return tomorrow to see how you're getting on.' She threw a couple of banknotes onto the tablecloth and shook her head at Paige when she pulled out her purse. 'I always treat my clients to their first meal. This is literally on the house.' She laughed as she gathered up her bag and jacket, insisting again that she was fine carrying Paige's suitcase and swept Paige from the family-run restaurant with a cheery goodbye to her uncle, who enveloped her in a hug and grabbed Paige afterwards.

'You come back, signorina.' It was most definitely a statement rather than a question.

The *monolocale*, as Stefania described it, was the equivalent of a bedsit but that term didn't do the place justice. The large room was on the top floor of an old building that from the outside did not promise much, rather like the restaurant. But when Stefania flung open the door, Paige was overwhelmed by its charm. It was even better than the photos in the brochure Paige had shown Charlie.

'I guess you'll find everything you need in here,' Stefania said, pointing, to the accompaniment of her bangles. 'Kitchen, bed. Bathroom over there behind that curtain. Use anything you find in the cupboards and you know my number. There's a call box in the bar downstairs. You need a "*gettone*": a phone token. Sorry, Paige. Gotta go! I'm late already. I'll pop by tomorrow.'

The walls were a mixture of old stone and whitewashed plaster. It felt like being inside a cave that had been given a luxurious makeover. A large double bed, curtained off from the rest of the room with pale-lilac gauze curtains, was piled high with velvet cushions in rich jewel shades. A low-hanging chandelier lit the area. A leather settee was positioned by a pair of windows artistically fitted into an ancient archway. The view overlooked a narrow street and a couple of bars and restaurants. The kitchen area was basic with a small hob and charmingly furnished with shelves of copper pans, a moka coffee pot and a set of hand-painted pottery. Paige could not imagine using the space for more than making herself a cup of tea. She'd brought a packet of tea leaves with her, in honour of Aunty Flo, or Mother, as she should be calling her. But it didn't come easily to her lips. The woman who had brought her up in her own loving way would always be Aunty Flo to her.

There was no kettle and so Paige filled a saucepan with water and set it to boil. As for meals, she would eat out as much as possible. Her culinary skills could no way match up to today's lunch. *While in Sicily*, she thought, *live like a Sicilian*.

After she'd unpacked her clothes and hung them on a rail, she sat on the sofa to drink her tea. There was no strainer and, after swallowing tea leaves, she jotted *Buy strainer* on a to-do list. On the wall next to the window were black-and-white photographs of the island arranged in a circle. She recognised a few images from her guidebook: a night view of the famous cathedral in the centre of Syracuse, lights reflected in puddles of rainwater, the iconic bikini-clad Roman women of the mosaic floors of the Piazza Armerina villa, the imposing Greek temple of Selinunte, bright poppies and spring flowers in the fore-ground, donkey carts painted with scenes of stories, like in comic books, images of peasants picking lemons, close-ups of men with wrinkled, sun-beaten faces.

But it was the china figure in the centre of the arrangement that grabbed her attention: a colourful plaque of a man's face, his hair formed of snakes and fish, three bare legs jutting anti-clockwise from his head. It was similar to the pendant she'd found in Aunty Flo's box. She fetched it from her handbag and compared the two ornaments. Not identical, but almost.

She hoped Stefania could get in touch with this war histo-rian or whoever and perhaps there was a museum in the city she could visit. Maybe coming here was pointless and she was searching for a needle in a haystack. But she was here now and she would have a jolly good try. She hadn't driven all these miles to Sicily to come to a full stop.

Paige slept well that night after a simple supper of savoury biscuits and a glass of wine from the welcome basket that Stefania had left on the table. The long journey had finally caught up with her and as soon as her head touched the pillow, that was that.

She woke to a cacophony of shouts and the rumble of wheels trundling over the cobbled road outside her window, interspersed with horns blaring and what sounded very much like insults. Groping for her watch on the bedside table, she peered at the hands and groaned. Five thirty a.m. It was barely light outside. What the hell? It was far too early to stir and she pulled a pillow over her head to drown the sounds. But it was impossible. As she passed the window to reach the toilet, she peeped through the curtain. In the gloaming, she could see stalls being set out below: fruits of all types, baskets of figs, pomegranates piled in pyramids, oranges and lemons, chilli peppers of various colours and sizes hanging from strings. A pile of crates containing wriggling fish waited to be emptied on fishmongers' slabs.

Paige swore. Stefania hadn't said anything about the flat being located slap bang in the middle of a busy market place. Maybe that was why the price was so reasonable. Still, it didn't justify being woken up every morning at this unsociable hour and she could hardly ask the market sellers to keep their noise down just for her. She sighed. There was little point in trying to sleep in with this din carrying on. She'd slept over nine hours anyway, but she was definitely not going to go to bed every night at nine p.m. to get in her eight hours' sleep. She decided to have an early morning explore and return to the flat later to catch Stefania and give her a piece of her mind. She wanted her deposit back. She wondered how easy it would be to find some-where else to stay at the last minute. It was more than annoying.

After downing another cup of twiggy tea, she pulled on jeans and a light fleece and descended the stone stairs to emerge in the centre of the market place.

'*Buongiorno*, signorina,' a ruddy-faced woman with matt-black hair called as she passed. She held out an orange. '*Per lei*. For you.' Paige took it and fumbled for her purse.

'*No! No! Regalo*. Gift.'

'*Grazie*,' Paige replied, putting it into her bag, thinking what good salesmanship it was but when she was offered a cake at another stall, she began to realise it was friendliness and not marketing. Her tea hadn't been enjoyable and the smell of fresh coffee lured her into a busy bar where huddles of men and women crowded round the counter, knocking back espressos and eating pastries wrapped in paper napkins. She ordered a cappuccino and a couple of tiny *cannoli* filled with pistachio cream and took her early breakfast to a corner table to observe the action. Although there was a lot of shouting and waving of hands from people gathered around the bar, it was not done in anger, she realised. There was backslapping and laughter accompanying the loudness and everybody seemed to know each other.

She wandered further afield into another open piazza to an area full of stones and columns ringed off from the public. A sign told her it was the Greek temple of Apollo and she marvelled at such antiquity a mere stone's throw from where she'd slept. Paige bought a postcard from outside a tobacconist's shop to send to Charlie. It showed the temple and, in the back-ground, a corner of the building where she was staying. She marked it with a cross and scribbled a note.

I'm here. You'd love it. P. xx

She made her way back to the apartment to wait for Stefania. What was Aunty Flo's connection to this place? She had never talked about being in Sicily. Why not? What had happened in her life to connect her to this island? The letter was always on her mind, those numerals, those strange lines. It had to give her answers.

CHAPTER 37

WINTER 1943 ONWARDS, SUFFOLK

JOY

Joy walked from the shepherd's hut straight to the west wing of Somersby Hall instead of going to first speak to her mother. At the entrance she stopped for a moment, setting her shoulders back and forcing a smile onto her face before stepping over the threshold. There was a whiff of disinfectant about the old house. The hall table, rather than bearing Mother's bowls of flower arrangements, held piles of newspapers, a small notice-board with details of upcoming concerts and a pile of post. As she made her way towards Norman's room, Jimmy came out, leaning to one side on one stick, minus crutches now, swinging his gammy leg straight to take cumbersome steps.

'How marvellous, Jimmy. You've made good progress since I last saw you.'

He smiled. 'Still a bit sore, but they've kitted me out with a false leg,' he said, bending to pull up his trousers to show her. 'It's hollow too.' He tapped the shin. 'Could make a useful spy now, don't you think? Carry all sorts in here: grenades and what have you.'

She smiled, thinking how brave he was, putting on an act. A bit like herself, but minus the bravery.

'Well done, you! I'll catch up with you later after I've seen Norman.'

The expression on Jimmy's face changed. 'Oh, good grief, Joy. You don't know?'

'Know what? Has he been moved back to the burns unit?'

He came over and took her arm. 'Let's go and sit in the conservatory. Nobody sits there now the cold weather's hit.'

She followed him, wondering what had happened to Norman. With each step Jimmy took, his false leg made a squeaking sound, as if it could do with an oiling. Later she would remember this noise whenever she recalled Jimmy's agonised explanation.

Mother's prized palms and aspidistras had withered in the conservatory and it was bone-biting cold, but her shivers were not from the temperature as Jimmy sat opposite her in a cane chair and started to talk.

'Norman's gone, Joy. I'm so sorry. He managed to get himself to the far end of the grounds. To a place nobody ever went, so they didn't find him until the following day.'

'Had he fallen? Was he near the grotto? It's... it's a secret corner I showed him.'

'He didn't fall, Joy. I'm afraid... he hung himself.' He reached for her hand. 'I'm so sorry to give you such dreadful news. I know you two were fond of each other.'

She crumpled, her hands at her mouth as she slumped forwards in the chair. It was her fault. Again. Everything was her fault. It had been cowardly not to respond to Norman's proposal straightaway and run away to the shepherd's hut, but she'd been so confused. Savio's death had been her fault too and now Norman had died because of her selfishness. She was poison. No good to anybody. Her sobs came out as strangled gasps for breath and Jimmy hurried away, muttering, 'I'll get someone. Wait there, Joy. What a blinking mess. I'm so, so sorry.'

Matron bustled into the conservatory and put her arm around Joy's shoulders. 'Come along, my dear. You can't stay sitting here in the cold. Come with me.'

She walked Joy along the hallway and asked a passing nurse to fetch a tray of tea straightaway to her office.

'This used to be Father's snug,' Joy said, wiping her nose and sinking into the sagging armchair where he used to read his newspaper each morning after breakfast. His desk was tidier than she'd ever seen it and the books on his shelves had been arranged by size and height like a row of orderly soldiers. There was no aroma of tobacco smoke about the room. It smelled instead of carbolic soap. Father's presence had been wiped clean. How she missed him. It seemed anybody who was dear to her was destined to die before she did.

'I'm sorry, Matron,' Joy said, as her tears started to fall again. 'It's such a shock. One thing after another, I suppose.'

'Quite so. But you'll have to pull yourself together,' the middle-aged matron said, not unkindly. She poured tea into one of Mother's china cups as she spoke and Joy noticed a chip on the saucer. Mother would be incandescent.

'You must think of your baby. Have you made arrangements? Are you going to stay here? Because if so, we can help you, my dear. I understand you and Captain Hetherington had an arrangement. You won't be the only fiancée to be left holding the baby because of this wretched war.'

Joy had the opportunity in those few moments to set Matron straight, but she didn't say anything. She and Norman hadn't been engaged; in fact, Joy had been about to accept Norman's proposal but there was no point in revealing this. What purpose did it serve?

'Do you want me to fetch your mother?'

The vehemence with which Joy shook her head was message enough. 'I shall go and find her later. Thank you. You've been so very kind.'

'We have Captain Hetherington's possessions and wondered if you wanted them. He has no family left, does he?'

'I... he told me they'd all died. Poor Norman. Yes, I'll take them.'

Matron went to a tall cupboard where Joy's father had once kept his fishing rods and pulled out a small canvas rucksack. 'There you are, my dear. Come and see me whenever you wish.' She checked on the watch face pinned above her large bosom. 'I must leave you now. Time to sort medications. Stay here for as long as you want to collect yourself, my dear.'

Joy preferred to be outside. She wanted nothing more than to escape again from Somersby Hall, back to the shepherd's hut. The air was still, the path icy, puddles of water cracking underfoot like crystals. Holly berries were rimmed with vestiges of this morning's frost as Joy walked blindly, setting one foot in front of the other, Norman's bag weighing like a symbol of guilt upon her shoulders. Normally, the sight of fluffy seed heads of old man's beard threading the hedgerows and spiralling patterns of breath in the frosty air would lift her spirits, but she felt numb. What was she going to do now? She was annoyed with herself for feeling so confused and helpless. She had once carried out important, secret work, so the authorities at BP had constantly reminded her and the other women in the hut. But now she felt redundant. In her heart she knew what she had to do: stand up to her mother, remain at the Hall, refuse to go away. She'd take advantage of Matron's offer of helping her in the last months of her pregnancy and bring her baby into this world. Her mother would make life unpleasant, yes, that she expected, but she wouldn't dare throw her out, surely? But before she confronted Mother, Joy wanted to spend one last night in the shepherd's hut to gather her courage and find strength to live another day.

There was still precious tea left in the caddy in the hut cupboard and a tin of pilchards. Her last supper in her refuge, she told herself. It didn't take long to collect dry twigs and make up a fire in the ashes of the past couple of weeks. While she waited for water to boil in the billycan, she sat inside on the bed and opened Norman's rucksack.

It was sad to think these few things were all that was left of him. Joy hadn't known him for long, knew almost nothing about his past save for snippets about flying and Patsy, his ex-girlfriend. She felt intrusive as she pulled out a thick Aran sweater and a pair of leather flying gloves. She pulled the sweater over her head. It was long enough to cover her bump and she warmed up almost immediately. The wool held a faint whiff of cigarette smoke and a spicy aftershave scent. What it was, she had no idea.

To think she had gone to Somersby Hall that morning with the intention of telling Norman she would accept his marriage proposal; that she had decided to share the rest of her life with a man who was effectively a stranger was bizarre and incredibly sad at the same time. She smudged away an annoying tear from her cheek and pulled out a small, battered volume of Rupert Brooke's poems, a watch, its clock-face cracked, the time stopped at twenty past three, a small frame containing a photo of a pretty girl, her face lifted in laughter, sprinkled with freckles, curls escaping from her patterned head scarf. *To my darling Norman, from Patsy* was scrawled across the photograph, the swirl of the 'y' at the end of her name ending in three kisscrosses. Joy wondered if Patsy knew about Norman's tragic passing but she had no idea how to contact her. At the very bottom of the rucksack was an envelope. *To Florence Caister*, it read. Her heart skipped a beat. He had remembered the name she had invented for herself. On that strange night out at The Savoy. Another tear trickled down Joy's cheek as she pulled out the letter. Another letter that had arrived too late.

CHAPTER 38

1943, SICILY

SAVIO

Savio's cousin Carmelo was kept for five days by the Friends Ambulance Unit. Although he was still weak, there were plenty of patients in a worse state who needed more attention and he was discharged with ointments, instructions and pills. When Savio and Graziella went to pick him up, Carmelo was sitting on his bed, having a conversation with a German lad who had learned Italian at music college. There was a mix of nationalities taking up the ward and Savio wondered if it was deliberate on the part of these peace-loving Quakers, or if space necessitated enemy sleeping next to enemy.

Savio's new 'family' had by now vacated the cave and returned to their own farmhouse. The bloodstained mattress where Loretta's mother had bled to death had been burnt. Savio had no idea what the little girl's grandparents had told their granddaughter about her whereabouts, but she seemed calm enough.

'Come with me to see the kittens,' she implored Savio one afternoon, tugging at his sleeve. He walked the short distance to where they'd last seen the litter. Sure enough, they were still there and he found an old wooden box lying outside a house and carried them back for Loretta. Nonna scolded at first. '*Madonna buona* and all the saints. Haven't we enough mouths to feed without you bringing me five more?' she said, shaking her head and clasping her hands together dramatically. But the family of cats kept Loretta occupied, gave her something to love, and Nonna was even seen to be playing with the kittens of an evening, dangling her apron strings above the heads of the furry bundles to tease their tiny paws.

There was little time to think of anything else as Savio did what he could to help the family. He worked alongside Settimio, the old man who had known his father, and pruned grapes, hanging dusty and dry along his vines. 'It's late to be doing this,' Settimio grumbled, 'and if it doesn't rain soon, they will shrivel to raisins.' He taught Savio to use a long scythe to cut the hay. Savio was clumsy at first but once he got used to the rhythm, it was satisfying work in which he could lose himself for a while.

In the middle of the small vineyard, the stench of putrefying flesh led them to the rotting corpse of an English soldier, one of the airborne glider division. Savio removed his boots to put by for when it was safe to wear them. The clogs Settimio had found him were too small and dug into his heels. It was easier to walk barefoot but each night he had to check between his toes for ticks. They buried the Englishman at the edge of the hayfield. Settimio fashioned a cross from pieces of wood scavenged from a damaged bed head in a bombed house and Savio nailed the dead man's dog tag to it as he mumbled a short prayer. His family would need to know about his death. The tag would identify him.

He felt a twinge of guilt as it made him think of the dead man whose identity he had stolen before going AWOL. That man would be forever missing. His family might wait in hope for years that he would turn up eventually. Savio still had his tag, hidden near where he slept. Perhaps one day he would try to make good his deception. But not yet.

He enjoyed lazy, cooler evenings at the end of the still hot days with the family after their simple suppers and this was when he thought of Joy. He had resumed his sketching, using stubs of charcoal from the ashes and drawing on the backs of paper bags and he tried to bring her image to life. Soon he was besieged with requests for portraits and he obliged. Somebody produced paper and pencils found in the ruins of the school and he was away. The simple act of moving his hand over paper and reproducing pictures calmed him. One evening as he lay on his rustic bed, he tried to capture an image of Joy, the look on her face after they'd made love, her arms stretched above her head, her full breasts half covered by her long, blonde hair. He didn't show this to anybody but folded it up to keep for himself. He'd lost his photograph of her and he didn't want to forget her beautiful face.

Ten days later, he was raking up hay when two men shouted, 'Hey, you, we need food.'

Savio decided to act dumb, continuing to rake without acknowledging them, his senses on high alert. From the corner of his eye, he noted they were not in uniform and they weren't local either: their accents were not Sicilian. Graziella and the others had talked about when the *inglesi* soldiers had turned up, how a good few of the militia had run away, realising the fight was hopeless: they'd removed their black uniforms and found civilian clothing, even demanding trousers and shirts at gunpoint from locals.

They approached Savio and he tightened his grip on the rake. His Sten submachine gun was hidden beneath a floorboard in the farmhouse. He'd grown complacent and, anyhow, to carry it about or conceal the gun on his person had seemed unnecessary by now. He would put on a good act at playing thick.

'We asked you a question,' one of the duo shouted, pulling Savio round to face him and Savio feigned fear, dropping his rake and started to shake and gibber rubbish. The fear wasn't all fake: he was on his own, unarmed and the men were young and fit.

'Food,' one of them insisted, bringing a hand back and forth to his mouth, miming eating.

Savio continued to stare with round, startled eyes at the two men and pretended to sob.

One of the men laughed. 'Leave him be, Franco. He's soft in the head.'

A stream of curses interrupted the discussion and both men turned to see Graziella striding across the stubbly grass. '*Bastardi!* Leave my cousin alone, you louts. Haven't you anything better to do than taunt a defenceless idiot? Shame on you. *Vergognatevi!*'

She brandished the knife she'd been using to clean wild salad plants from the ditches and one of the men laughed at her.

'What have we here? A woman, eh? A woman with spirit.' It took only a second to snatch the knife from her hand and pinch her jaw with his other hand. 'And what a pretty mouth. It should be used for kissing, rather than shouting filth.'

Graziella dug her teeth into the man's hand and he yelped. '*Puttana.* Whore.' He slapped her round the face and then tore at her thin blouse, revealing a plump breast. He bent to bite on her nipple as she wriggled and screamed in agony.

Savio didn't have to think twice. He swung his rake at the onlooker, flooring him and, with a howl, he tore the other man off Graziella, swinging him round and punching him hard in the face, smashing his nose to a pulp, before kicking him repeatedly in the groin. The other man lay still on the ground, blood oozing from his nose, the second ran off and Graziella pulled at Savio. 'Leave them, come away. Come now.'

He took off his shirt and handed it to her, turning away as she buttoned it to cover her breasts, the blood from her torn nipple seeping into the thin material.

Back at the farmhouse, she wanted to bathe his bleeding knuckles but he called for Nonna instead to see to her daughter. Afterwards, they sat in the kitchen, nursing glasses of country wine.

'I can't stay here,' Savio said. 'And you should move on too. What if they come back to seek revenge?'

'Until Carmelo heals, we're not going anywhere,' Graziella replied. 'I'm not worried about them. We'll be fine.'

'Brave words are not enough,' Savio said. He rose and moved outside to the semi-derelict farm building they had cleaned up for him. He slept there on a simple mattress stuffed with the husks of dried corn cobs. At first the rustling each time he turned over had woken him, as well as the mice that shared it, but it was comfortable enough. He removed his revolver he'd hidden in a niche in the wall and made sure it was loaded. His other gun, the Sten, was too cumbersome for Graziella and difficult to conceal on her person. But the revolver would fit in her skirt pocket.

Graziella was tending to Carmelo upstairs in the farmhouse and he climbed the rickety ladder to find them. He was sitting up today, looking brighter. He smiled at Savio and beckoned him over to sit on the chair next to the double bed.

'Thank you, *cugino caro*. Not only do I thank you for saving my life, but also protecting Graziella from those men.' He held out his hand to his young wife and she sat down next to him on the bed.

'Savio,' he continued. 'You have to go. Graziella heard women in the village talking at the village fountain. They know you're not *siciliano*. And they don't believe you're Italian either.

Sooner or later, somebody will report you. Not everybody hates the *fascisti* as we do.'

Savio produced the revolver. 'I'm worried too. Those men this morning. They might return... I want you to take this. I'll show Graziella how to use it.'

'Those men are cowards. *Vigliacchi*. I doubt they will return.'

'I will rest easier if I know you have this. I have another weapon for myself.'

'Show me now,' Graziella interrupted.

Carmelo laughed. 'Always impulsive. If you start shooting now, the whole village will be alerted. Listen, Savio. There is a place we know where nobody will find you. Graziella will take you early tomorrow at first daylight. You will be safe there. And once you arrive, you can show her how to use the weapon. Nobody, save wolves and eagles, will hear you.'

Carmelo took the revolver and spun the barrel before nodding his head and handing it back to Savio. 'Graziella, prepare a sack with foodstuffs to last my cousin for a while. You know the paths well enough to that place but I will explain a faster route that bypasses homesteads.'

He fell back against his pillow. 'I'm tired now. Make sure you sleep well tonight. It's a long difficult walk you both have to face tomorrow.' Before he shut his eyes, he looked at Savio. 'I shall never forget what you have done for us. Never.'

Savio left man and wife alone and descended the ladder. It took him no time to pack up the few belongings he owned: a spare pair of trousers donated by his cousin and Settimio's old straw hat as well as Joy's book: it might while away the hours. Now was the time to use the boots from the dead Tommy and he arranged them next to where he slept. Finally, his Sten gun, which he hoped he would not have to use. At the last minute, he shoved the dead soldier's dog tag into the sack with the rest of his things. Best not to leave any telltale details behind. His knuckles smarted and he winced as he flexed his hands. Punching the living daylights out of thugs probably didn't match up to the Quaker philosophy, but what else could he have done? Turned the other cheek and let them do what they wanted to Graziella? No! That did not sit right with him at all. As he lay on his corn mattress waiting for sleep, he wondered where Graziella was taking him in the morning. He needed somewhere for the future, where he could invite Joy to come and be with him. It might be a pipe dream, but it was good to have dreams, he thought, as sleep finally claimed him.

CHAPTER 39

1973, SICILY

PAIGE

'*So, so* sorry, I'm late,' Stefania said.

It was after midday. Paige had fallen asleep reading, tired after her early morning start, and Stefania woke her when she appeared at the door in a blaze of flowers. Today's flowing maxi dress was patterned with huge poppies and she carried a basket brimming with sea lavender. She'd tied back her hair with a bandana in the same dress material and her large hoop earrings swung to and fro as she gesticulated. Very few Italians didn't wave their arms about as they spoke, Paige was beginning to realise. As if discussions were music to be conducted.

Stefania pulled a colourful pottery vase shaped like a Moor's head from a cupboard and arranged the lavender as she spoke. 'I hope you're hungry, Paige. I arranged a table at Lo Splendore – a real treat as I managed to get a last-minute booking. We'll be eating on the terrace, so bring a shawl or something. It's breezy today. Oh!' She stopped talking and held Paige's arm. 'And bring anything you have about your intriguing enigma. There are people I want you to meet and I'm sure together we shall help you solve your clues. Just like Sherlock Holmes and Watson. I *so* love a mystery.'

Is that what her family was? A silly mystery to be solved? Paige couldn't get a word in edgeways and, bleary-eyed, she went to splash water over her face and drag a brush through her hair. She grimaced at her reflection. There was a mark down her right cheek where she'd fallen asleep on her book but it would disappear. She grabbed her box of clues, as she'd started to call the oddments left by Aunty Flo, and pushed it into her rucksack.

'Did you not sleep well?' Stefania asked as she clattered down the stairs to outside. She was not the type of person who would ever make a quiet entrance, Paige thought, bangles and stiletto-heeled boots her trademark.

'You never said anything about a market being right beneath my nose,' Paige said.

'It's a *wonderful* market, isn't it? Nothing like it anywhere else. I love to wander about taking photographs. I never appreciated it before I travelled to the States. All of life can be found in a market, don't you think?'

'But the noise. It woke me so early. I don't think—'

Before Paige could launch into her planned rant about how unfair it was not to have warned her about a market beneath the windows of the apartment, how she'd found it impossible to sleep in and that it was unreasonable to expect guests to retire to bed at nine p.m. every night to cope with the early morning cacophony; how she wanted her money back and help with finding another apartment at the same price, because that was all she had budgeted for and if not, Stefania would have to make up the difference, Stefania put her arm around her shoulder.

'*Carissima*, my darling girl, the market is only on Wednesday and Saturday and my guests *always* grow to love it. You honestly cannot come to Sicily without participating in these spectacles. I will provide you with special ear plugs and furthermore I shall introduce you to friends who have fish and fruit stalls and they will give you special prices for your snacks. If you were staying in some lousy hotel, you would never have this immersive treatment. Now, before we meet my friends – who I think will be of tremendous help to you – I'm treating you to an *aperitivo*. Come...'

So later, when Paige was seated at the little bar overlooking the harbour, a sea breeze gently lifting the edges of tablecloths and fronds of sun umbrellas as she sipped her delicious Aperol Spritz, her prepared diatribe about the unsuitability of the apartment had already disappeared to the edges of the sun-speckled ocean.

They ambled further down the sea wall to a restaurant where Stefania was warmly greeted by a handsome waiter. He murmured something in her ear and Stefania responded with a low laugh. '*Dopo, dopo,*' she said. It was one of the few words that Paige knew. It meant 'later' and Paige had little doubt that something deliciously intimate was planned.

They were ushered by the owner to a table at the very edge of a wooden terrace that jutted over the sea lapping beneath. Stefania was greeted warmly by him. *Popular woman*, Paige assessed. It was not surprising. She herself had quickly fallen under the spell of Stefania's vivacious personality.

'Meet my dear friends Domenico and Pietro,' Stefania said, pulling Paige forward. 'I think they are going to be such a great help. Each, in their own way, is an expert on Siracusa's culture and history.'

Paige's hand was grasped firmly by the shorter of the two men and she was pulled towards him to receive a kiss on each cheek. It seemed standard to Paige, very unlike the stuffy English way of shaking hands.

'I am Pietro. Delighted to meet you, signorina,' he said with a little bow, sitting down again. The sun glinted off the gold watch on his bronzed arms beneath his rolled-up shirtsleeves.

'Pietro is our prince. *Literally*. He is *Principe* Benevento of *Siracusa*. If you want *anything*,' Stefania said, adding with a chuckle, 'anything at all, you go to *him*, Paige.'

'You always exaggerate, dear Stefania,' Pietro said, adding something in Italian that sounded half-chastisement, half-flirtation.

Stefania turned towards the other guest, who had remained seated at the table.

'And this is Domenico.'

A younger man, black hair curling onto the collar of his denim shirt, nodded his head with a smile. But he remained seated. 'Call me Dom, please,' he said with absolutely no trace of an Italian accent.

Before she could comment, a dog moved from under the table and jumped up at her.

'*Giù, Sporca, a cuccia!*' Dom ordered sternly, pointing under the table. 'Down! To your bed.'

He smiled at Paige. 'Sorry about that. She's rather inquisitive. I'm still training her. She was a stray.'

'Please don't worry. I love dogs,' Paige said, bending down to tickle Sporca behind her ears.

'Good!' Dom said as they all settled at the table.

'Domenico, when are you going to change that dog's name? You can't go round shouting "Come here, Sporca". It sounds like an insult,' Stefania said.

'Don't the English customarily call dogs Fido or Bonzo?' the prince asked, in less perfect English.

Paige wondered if the question was addressed to her but, it was addressed to Dom, or Domenico, whatever he was called. His accent was perfect. Maybe he had lived in England for a while.

Domenico grinned and turned to explain to Paige. 'I call her Sporca, which means dirty, because when I found her that's what she was. Filthy and covered in sores. God knows how long she'd been tied up, poor wretch. She was living on a farm in the hills. Abandoned.'

Paige instantly liked this dog-loving, kind-hearted guy who spoke perfect English. She looked forward to finding out more about him as well as learning how he could help her.

'You *inglesi* are crazy about animals,' Pietro said, as he raised his hand to attract the attention of the waitress. 'There's an *inglesina* in the city who has opened a cat sanctuary for stray cats. The money she collects is better for orphans, not animals.'

'The cats should be sterilised to keep down their numbers,' Dom said.

Pietro's eyes shot up and he threw up his hands in horror. 'This is a Catholic country, *amico mio*. You'll be talking about *la pillola* for cats next.'

'Not such a bad idea,' was Dom's response.

'*Ragazzi!* Chaps,' Stefania said. 'I haven't brought Paige here so we could talk about castrating our cats and dishing out contraceptives for animals. There's more to Sicily than this. You're giving her the wrong impression.'

'More's to the point, what shall we eat?' Pietro asked as he tucked a large white serviette into the top of his white shirt. He also removed a silk paisley cravat and hung it on the back of his chair. 'Eating here is serious, is it not, *cara* Stefania?'

It certainly was and the next hour surpassed the first meal she'd enjoyed at lunch the previous day with Stefania. That had been a mere snack compared to the feast presented before them. Starters of delicious prawns on skewers, a salad made from breadcrumbs, cucumbers, fresh tuna and basil leaves, tiny, succulent morsels of squid and huge platters of cockles and mussels kept coming as soon as their plates were empty.

Just as Paige thought the meal was over, a huge platter of fried fish appeared, carried aloft by yet another handsome waiter who could easily have been on a Milan catwalk. He walked with pride and he was beautiful: jet-black hair, a gold medallion on a chain resting on his sun-bronzed chest where his top two buttons were undone. Why was everybody here so attractive? Was it the diet? Sunshine and wine? The way Italian mothers brought up their children? Whatever it was, it worked, Paige thought. When she could tear her eyes from the waiter, she saw her plate had been served with slices of breadcrumbed sole and at the side a sea urchin, cut in half to reveal a buttery inside.

'Lemon,' urged the prince. 'You must squeeze on lemon to bring out the flavour of the *riccio*.' He did it for her and showed her how to tip back her head and swallow the inside of the sea creature.

Observing her look of surrender afterwards, Dom laughed. 'Ideally you should starve yourself the day before coming here. If you can't manage it, Paige, we'll help you out.'

'Ask for a doggy bag,' Paige said. 'I hate waste. Won't Sporca eat it?'

'She doesn't like fish for some reason.'

'She's very good,' Paige said, lifting the tablecloth to look down at the boxer.

'Wasn't always so. It's taken time for her to trust people.'

Paige picked up a chip to feed to the dog but Dom grabbed her hand.

'Please don't. She'll become a pest if we start on that.'

He is right, Paige thought. Aunty Flo had been very strict about not feeding Bonnie from the table and she hadn't been allowed on the settee either.

After finishing off the meal with tiny cups of espresso, Pietro pulled out a silver cigarette case and offered it round. Paige held up her hands and Dom declined too. Stefania took a cigarette and Pietro lit it for her, cupping her hands with his until the tip smouldered.

'*Grazie, caro.*' She leant back and exhaled into the salty air. 'And now that we have eaten and fed our stomachs and brains, let us see what we can do to help dear Paige. She has an interesting quest. The stage is all yours, Paige,' she said, gesturing to the table with her heavily bangled arm. 'Show these two lovely men your box of secrets.'

Pulling out the vintage chocolate box from her rucksack, Paige was momentarily nonplussed.

'It's all a muddle, really. I came to Sicily because I desperately want to discover more about my...' She faltered. 'My mother's past.'

'Why Sicily?' the prince asked, leaning back in his chair.

'Because my... mother received a letter from here. Postmarked Siracusa and because of this...' she said, scrabbling in the box to produce the pendant. 'I have found out this is—'

'The *trinacria*,' Prince Pietro said. 'A symbol of Sicily. That seems quite old. May I?' He took it from Paige to examine more closely. 'Little value except maybe of sentimentality. Mass-produced in the last century.'

'But my aunty Flo— Oh, for goodness' sake, I keep calling her that, but she wasn't my aunt.'

Dom looked at her quizzically.

'Paige's aunt was really her mamma,' Stefania explained. 'But when she found out, it was too late to ask because her mamma died. It's just like a *romanzo*, don't you think?'

'This sort of thing happened all the time during and after the war,' Dom said.

'That's why I invited you here today, *caro* Domenico,' Stefania explained. 'Because Paige told me the letter has the date 1943 and we all know you are a student of war.'

'Specifically of the last two Great Wars. It's my work,' he said.

'Are you a historian?' Paige asked.

'I studied history at university and it helped me find my job.'

'He looks after graves,' Stefania said.

Paige was puzzled. She hadn't had him down as a gravedigger.

'What Stefania means is that I work for the Commonwealth War Graves Commission,' Dom explained with a grin. 'It's a bit of a mouthful, but I'm in charge of war cemeteries here in Sicily and southern Italy. Our regional headquarters are in Rome and I'm mostly to be found up there.'

'They are magnificent places,' the prince said, stubbing out his cigarette. 'You should take signorina Paige to visit, Domenico. They are, how would you say in English... *luoghi di dignità.*'

'That's the aim, Pietro. Fitting final resting places of dignity to honour our brave dead. These cemeteries are located on plots of land generously donated by nations where battles took place. Have you never visited any war graves cemeteries, Paige?'

'No, I haven't,' she said, thinking such places were not on her usual list of holiday sights.

'Then, I'll take you on my next site visit.'

'Show them the rest of the things in your mystery box,' Stefania said, 'before we all leave for our siestas.' She gestured over to the waiter to bring the bill and Paige noticed the lingering touch of the hand as she took it. Perhaps Stefania's siesta would not be spent alone. *Good luck to her*, Paige thought.

Paige placed the coded letter carefully on the table, weighing it down with the oil and vinegar cruet. The last thing she wanted was to lose it. A warm breeze stirred the fronds of the sun umbrella and lifted the edges of the white tablecloth, now spattered with stains.

'I'm puzzled by the name Dante,' Paige said, pointing to the bottom of the letter. 'Do Italians ever christen their children with that name?'

'But of course,' the prince replied. 'Dante Alighieri is part of our culture.'

Dom bent over, scrutinising the figures on the page.

'It's obviously in code,' he said. 'Fascinating. We have a group of detectives at the Commission who work out the puzzles of the dead so they can properly identify them and track down relatives. There are still bodies turning up on the land even now, when farmers plough their fields, and that kind of thing. I don't usually get to help in working out such details, but I love a challenge. Would you trust me with this?' he asked Paige.

Paige hesitated. She had only just met Dom. He might be the nicest man alive – he had certainly given her a great first impression – but he might not. She was reluctant to part with something that had obviously been so precious to her mother. 'I'd prefer not to let it out of my sight, to be honest.'

Dom nodded. 'I understand. Tell you what. How about we check it through together? I know the perfect place.'

She smiled her thanks. 'You're on. Two heads are better than one. *Grazie*, Dom.'

'You're welcome.'

The prince settled the bill, despite protests from everybody. 'Next time, next time,' he said, pulling out a smart leather wallet. 'But today is my treat.' He took Paige's hands and bestowed a kiss on the back of each.

'It's not every day that I treat a beautiful *signorina inglese*. Welcome to our island, Paige. As Goethe said, "To have seen Italy without having seen Sicily is not to have seen Italy at all, for Sicily is the clue to everything." Maybe you too will find your missing clues here.'

Despite the prince's corny manners, Paige was delighted with her welcome. Apart from the exquisite meal and surroundings, she had enjoyed the interesting company and more to the point, felt she might get somewhere with their help. They were the last group to leave the restaurant; the staff had already removed most of the tablecloths and lifted up the chairs. There were kisses all round as they said goodbye under the hot afternoon sun.

Dom turned to Paige. 'Let's go and find some shade and talk this through. Your story has intrigued me. *Andiamo.*' She walked with him to the car park. 'Hope you don't mind simple transport,' he asked as he led her towards a shady spot beneath scented lime trees. 'This is my old run-around Topolino, ideal for me and Sporca. It's a bit cramped but it's perfect for the crazy traffic in Siracusa. I drive a new Ford Consul for work but I prefer this,' he said, opening the door. Sporca jumped in and settled down on the tiny back seat, more of a ledge. 'And we have air conditioning too,' he said with a laugh, rolling back a canvas flap from the roof of the old Fiat. 'Climb in.'

He took a road out of town, driving along roads lined with drystone, sun-bleached walls, past squat houses set back behind olive trees and hedges of vivid pink oleander. 'I'm taking you to a place that's special to me,' he said.

Paige was enjoying herself. The ride might not be as smooth as in Jeremy's Aston Martin, but she felt very much at ease with her new friend. She settled back to enjoy the stunning scenery, wondering where Dom was taking her, and hoping above all that together they might find a key to the coded letter.

CHAPTER 40

1943, SUFFOLK

JOY

Joy sat on the steps of the shepherd's hut to read Norman's letter, her hand to her mouth as she read the contents.

Dear Florence,

Thank you for putting up with me these past weeks. Thank you for taking time to care.

For a while, I felt life was bearable again. But life will never be easy for me and living with me, even less so. Believe me, what I'm about to do is not your fault. Not at all. Forgive me.

We both toyed with the idea, didn't we? But toying with a future built on flimsy foundations was bound to fail. In both our hearts I think we knew that.

I've instructed my solicitors about the Suffolk cottage I told you about. Such happy childhood times there. It's yours, Florence. I have no family left to whom I want to leave it.

*Squirrels will be good for you, like it was for me in the inno-
cent days. If only the clock could be turned back.*

*Go to Cunningham and Durrants, my solicitors in
Ipswich. They will hand over the keys once you present this
letter. It's all been arranged. Make it into a home for yourself
and the baby. Do it for me, but most of all do it for yourself.*

*Be happy, Florence. Be happy and good luck in this funny
old life.*

Fondly,

Norman Hetherington

She read it more than once, deep sorrow at the waste of yet
another young man's life flooding her heart. She cursed the
damned war. If only she had talked honestly and openly with
poor Norman earlier, she might have saved his life. They could
have come to some sort of an arrangement. Would he have been
able to accept her as a live-in housekeeper? Might love have
come later, like in the romantic library books she used to read as
a youngster? She remained on the steps until darkness loomed
and night chill seeped into her sad bones. A fox shrieked clear
and cold from within the woods and an owl answered mourn-
fully as she pulled the door to and curled up on the bed. Baby
was quieter tonight and she cradled her stomach in case the
child inside her was cold and sad. '*We'll be fine,*' she whispered
aloud – as much to convince herself as the child waiting to be
born. '*We'll be fine. You'll see.*'

Tomorrow she would catch a bus to Ipswich and find the
solicitors. Norman had been clever. He'd deliberately not
addressed her as Joy anywhere. There was not a single mention
of her old name. She supposed the papers for the cottage would
similarly be addressed to Miss Florence Caister. What if the
solicitors asked her for proof of identity? Norman had said the

letter would be sufficient. But would it be? Would she have to invent something? Like, she'd lost all her papers when her house was bombed, maybe. There would be no official records of a Florence Caister anywhere. Did that matter? Would the solicitors require authentication?

War was raging, events hotting up in Italy. Stray bombs still randomly fell on British cities: Reading back in February, Hastings in March, over Hampshire in August... folk must be losing their papers all the time with homes destroyed, leaving the displaced and orphaned without photographs or mementoes from the past. Norman had said everything had been arranged. So, she must trust in him and not concern herself with detail. How very lovely he had been to give her this chance. He had gifted her an opportunity to write a new page in her life. 'Page,' she said aloud, caressing her swollen belly. *If you are a girl, I shall call you Paige. You are a little girl, aren't you? I can sense it, despite all your kicking. A little tomboy, I think. A little girl with spirit.*

She didn't want this baby to be classed as illegitimate. She would tell people she was her aunt and hide her pregnancy for as long as possible – tell anybody who needed to know that the child's parents had passed in a house fire. Her brain buzzed with possibilities while she lay snuggled in the hut. There was too much prejudice and stigma surrounding unmarried mothers and Joy would eliminate that disadvantage in this way for her child. Life would be hard; there wouldn't be much money but she would manage. She had to. *'Florence Caister, everything will be fine,'* she whispered. The name sounded good on her lips. Joy was banished forever. There'd been little joy in her life so far anyhow.

She fell asleep eventually to the outside sounds, the wind occasionally brushing the branches of the beech tree in soothing motions against the roof, like a hand gently wiping hair from a lover's face. That night her dreams were of Savio and Norman.

They were sitting by the sea, knotted handkerchiefs on their heads, waves lapping at their bare feet, chatting to each other like friends who had known each other for years and years.

'We were so very sorry to hear about Norman. Tragic. Absolutely tragic. Such a fine young man,' the elderly solicitor told Joy as she signed the documents placed before her.

A stuffed owl sat in a case on the mantelpiece behind the solicitor's polished desk. A small fire was lit in his office and flames glinted from his spectacles as he shuffled papers together and tidied them into a folder.

'These originals are for you to keep and we shall hold copies in our files. Now that's the business done, so would you like a cup of tea, Miss Caister?'

This was the part Joy had been dreading. The time when she might be questioned and let down her guard – when she might give the game away that Norman had cleverly set up.

'That's very kind,' she told him, 'but I have a bus to catch to Holwood. There's only one a day.'

He smiled at her kindly. 'Well, if you need us, you know where we are.' He rummaged in the drawer of his mahogany desk and produced a bunch of keys with a brown label bearing the name: *Squirrels Cottage*, written in neat italic script. 'Good luck, Miss Caister. Norman was a good man, like his father before him. A great loss. We are losing so many young men and women to this war. He won't be the last, I fear.'

As she hurried to the bus station, she caught a sideways glimpse of herself in a shop window. Norman's thick Aran sweater worn over her baggy slacks convincingly hid her bump. Her new persona, her new story, had to be correct from the outset. Nobody must realise she was pregnant.

The bus was almost full and Florence, as she now was, found a seat at the back, trying to make herself inconspicuous amongst the other passengers. A woman seated in front of her was knitting a shawl and for the first time Florence thought about her baby's layette. She had no idea how to knit and was hopeless at sewing. She imagined the baby would need umpteen items of clothing and she needed to make a start on informing herself about these things. By her calculations, she had three months left of her pregnancy. For a moment, she panicked. How on earth did she think she could cope alone? And then she told herself that mothers had been having babies since the year dot. Surely it was not that difficult? *Brace up, Florence*, she told herself. *You've made your choice. Now get on with it.*

The bus stopped at a crossroads and the young woman driving the bus called out, 'This is Holwood.' With road and village signs having been removed in case of invasion, Florence would have had no idea otherwise that this was the correct stop at which to alight. She shuffled to the entrance behind an elderly couple and climbed down the step. Behind the bus stop was a church, a huge yew leaning its dark-green leaves over the entrance, higgledy-piggledy gravestones lining the path. At the far end of a street lined with crooked cottages in pale-washed colours, she made out a huddle of shops and a pub, its sign swinging in the breeze. Smoke spiralled from the chimneys of a few cottages and as she walked towards what she guessed was the centre of the village, she admired tiny pockets of neat front gardens, a couple of them planted with cabbages, turnips and other winter vegetables.

She had no map of the village and neither had the solicitor explained where Squirrels was. He'd no doubt assumed she had visited it before as the future wife of young Norman, as he had described him, so she hadn't wanted to ask.

As Florence pushed open the door to a grocer's shop, a bell

chimed her arrival. The store smelled of a mix of soap powder, polish, spices and the appetising aroma of baking. She realised she was very hungry. A woman who could have stepped from a children's book illustration appeared from a back room. She wore a clean white apron over a floral-patterned dress reaching almost to her ankles. Her hair was pepper-and-salt grey and tied back in an untidy bun from which wisps escaped to frame a plump face. Her cheeks were apple-red and she wore wired spectacles. 'Good afternoon, my dear. What can I get you today?'

Her question made Florence feel instantly at home: as if she was a local who came in regularly.

'Some of what you're baking for starters. It smells divine,' she said. 'And then, I was wondering if you could direct me to Squirrels Cottage.'

The woman bustled into the back of the store and reappeared with a cottage loaf and a wire tray holding a dozen or more cakes. 'How many would you like? They're my beetroot cakes. Sugar being rationed, I've started baking with all sorts. They're not half bad, though I say so myself. Try one, my dear.'

Florence bit into the still warm cake. The flavours melted on her tongue: rich, spicy and sweet enough.

The woman was peering up at her anxiously. 'I added a dash of cocoa powder. What do you think? You're my guinea pig. I found the recipe in this week's *Woman and Home*.'

'I'll take half a dozen. They'll sell like hot cakes.'

Both women laughed at the pun.

Florence bought a tin of Spam and half a cottage loaf.

'May I use my coupons in here?' she asked, eyeing the cheese behind the counter.

'Strictly speaking, you have to register with me, my dear, but the farmer has brought me plenty this week.' She cut a couple of ounces of cheddar for Florence.

'Thank you so much.' Feeling welcomed already in this

village, she gazed around the store whilst the shopkeeper wrapped up her purchases. A sack of russet apples leant against the counter, a note saying *Help Yourself* perched on top, and she picked out three.

'They're from the vicarage gardens. Their trees are laden this year. We all try to share here in Holwood. Points and coupons never go far enough,' the shopkeeper said, taking them from Florence and adding a couple of pears from behind the counter, placing them all in a brown paper bag. 'And these are from my Bert's allotment.'

Florence smiled and looked at the noticeboard leaning against the counter, filled with useful information: second-hand items for sale – a wardrobe and a fur coat – offers of help with gardening in exchange for vegetables or eggs, a Lost and Found section and an advert for an upcoming whist drive with prizes for the home, to be held the following week.

'Not seen you round here before,' the woman said, taking Florence's money and counting out the change in coppers and threepenny bits. 'Are you on holiday?'

'I'm moving into Squirrels Cottage,' she said. 'So I'll definitely want to register with you...' She hesitated in explaining too much, but she might as well set the chins wagging. 'Mr Hetherington left it to me...' she started. 'We... we were good friends.' She left it at that.

The woman came around from the counter and clasped hold of Florence's hands. 'Oh, my dear. How very sad for you. We were shocked when we heard of his passing.'

'I... I'm afraid he never got round to showing me the cottage. With his flying missions and everything.' The lies weren't tripping easily off her tongue. But this was to be the rest of her life: living a lie as a different persona and she had to get used to it. 'I will be coming and going for work,' she said enigmatically, thinking ahead for when she would disappear to have the baby. If she could hide her pregnancy until then.

'But I shall be basing myself here, so you'll be seeing me again.'

'Well, I hope you'll be very happy. I'm always saying to customers that we are very lucky to live in a place like this. The Germans aren't interested in dropping bombs on us but...' She lowered her voice. 'You never know, do you? They dropped a bomb on Newmarket recently. But I'm glad we're not living in a big city. When those little evacuees arrived, it broke my heart to see them with their brown labels pinned to their coats. Poor little mites. I thought about taking a couple, but with the shop I wouldn't have the time to look after them properly.' She wiped her hands down her pinafore and led Florence to the door, stepping outside.

'Squirrels Cottage is half a mile down that track opposite the village pond. A stream runs alongside. It's the only place down there so you won't be pestered by noisy neighbours. The track turns into a narrow footpath after Squirrels and takes you to the creek.'

'Thank you, Mrs...?'

'Mrs Brown,' she answered, pointing to the sign above the shop: BROWN'S FOR ALL YOUR NEEDS. 'I expect we'll see you soon, but we deliver too if you order a few days beforehand.'

Florence stopped a couple of times along the track to catch her breath. Her suitcase was heavy, containing everything she'd been able to cram in for her new life. Anything else would have to be collected when her time came, because at the moment, the only place she could think of giving birth was back at Somersby Hall in the hospital wing. Matron had offered her that lifeline and for the time being that was her only solution.

She stopped the second time to watch a muntjac half-hidden by tall reeds, sipping at the edge of the stream. In the same moment, a flash of emerald-blue feathers caught her eye as a kingfisher flew up from its perch close to the water. Nature would be her companion, she decided. She wouldn't be lonely and once the child was born, she'd have her hands full and no time to dwell on gloomy thoughts. Maybe there was a library in Holwood where she could borrow a field guide to delve deeper into the flora and fauna.

Florence rounded a bend and stopped in her tracks. The cottage facing her was a biscuit-tin picture. The paintwork needed touching up round the window frames and front door and the garden was a ramble-tangle of flowers. Tall, scarlet hollyhocks had flopped over the front path and she had to step over them to reach the door. A brass fox-head acted as a knocker and she was about to use it when she smiled. Of course! She didn't need to knock. She had keys at the bottom of her handbag. She *owned* this cottage.

CHAPTER 41

AUGUST 1943 ONWARDS, SICILY

SAVIO

Savio wondered where on earth Graziella was taking him. She was light of foot, like a mountain goat, Savio thought, as he trailed after her along the narrow path that wound its way in and out of a gorge. He'd offered to carry her heavy sack. She was pregnant and surely should not be doing this trip. She'd made a disparaging sound through her teeth when he'd mentioned this.

'This is nothing, Savio. And I'm only having a baby. I'm not ill.' They'd stopped for a quick break, dipping their fingers into the waters of a clear, cool stream, cupping their hands to their mouths. The sun was already high in the sky and Savio gazed up at two birds of prey circling in the azure sky.

'They'll pick our bones when we drop,' he said.

'You are such a city boy,' she jeered. 'They are not interested in us; they're looking for snakes and small birds. Let's get going again. We still have a long way to go.'

And she was off again, scrambling up a steep rise, the scent of herbs and aromatic plants wafting to him as she brushed past scrubby bushes. At one point a snake slithered across his path and he froze, watching its tail disappear into a hole.

After another couple of hours, it felt to Savio that she was taking him to the end of the world. They had not seen a soul since they had skirted round a small town, its squat, flat-roofed houses clinging to the hillside. 'That's Sortino,' she told him. 'Useful for topping up your provisions at the market. You'll think the locals are not interested in you, but make no mistake, they will be. Give nothing away of your whereabouts. Otherwise, those *fascisti* who you beat up might come looking. Best you stay away until you look more weathered, Savio. I'll come to find you whenever I can. And Carmelo too, once he's better.'

Towards the end of the afternoon, after they'd stopped for a snack of hard bread and cheese, they walked along the narrowest part of the valley that snuck its way through the gorge, through which a river gushed. Graziella pointed up to craggy, limestone rocks where hundreds of square openings had been cut from the cliffsides. 'They say this valley is the most northern tip of Africa. It's thousands of years old,' she said. 'Some say these man-made caves are haunted by the spirits of the first *siciliani*. They were burial places but they've been used as dwellings by all kinds of people over the years.'

Savio stopped, placing his burden down on the path, shielding his eyes with both hands. The sight was like nothing he'd ever seen. Colourful succulents clung to the side of tufa rocks; butterflies danced their way from plant to plant. The openings invited exploration. The place was primeval, menacing and alluring at the same time. He itched to draw the sights on which his eyes were feasting but he was sure he could never do it justice.

'Where are we?' he asked.

'They call it Pantalica.' She shrugged. 'There's nothing here save wild animals and one or two abandoned huts. You might see an occasional shepherd, but you'll be safe here. Don't worry, we won't abandon you, Savio.' She giggled. 'Are you worried? Come, we're nearly there.'

She branched off from the main track and descended towards the sound of running water. Here and there were signs of recent civilisation, a simple symbiosis between man and nature. They walked through a small olive grove, past a handful of fruit trees, then a small meadow of overgrown rye until a couple of hundred metres before the banks of a river, he followed her into a clearing. A small stone hut, built into the base of a cliff, stood in the shade of a carob tree. An almond tree framed a low wooden door secured by a thick chain padlocked through a crude metal door handle. The hut was almost camouflaged and he took in the rock cave above it, possibly providing space for additional accommodation or storage.

'*Eccoci!* Here we are. Carmelo's great-grandfather's place.'

She dumped her sack on a low stone bench built into the front of the hut and took a large key from her pocket.

'*Benvenuto alla Casa del Mandorlo,*' she said. 'Welcome!'

Welcome to the Almond House, Savio translated in his head, taking in details of this protected corner, thinking how ideal the situation was with its supply of water in the full river only a stone's throw away. The cliff face offered protection too from severe weather for crops as well as being a suntrap.

'His *bisnonno* even built a well,' Graziella said, pointing to the far end of the stone bench where a wooden lid sat on top of a section of circular stonework. 'You won't even have to carry up buckets of water.'

'It's ingenious.'

'Inside is very simple, but it's dry. Cool in summer with its thick walls and cosy when the temperature drops.' She added, her voice sounding shy, 'It's where Carmelo and I spent our first weeks together. You could call it our holiday house. There are plenty of trout in the river. We even find crayfish sometimes. In the morning before I go, I'll show you around. For now, let's get the fire started and we'll eat.'

While she busied herself snapping dry twigs and setting him to chop a small pile of logs piled by the hut, she talked.

'Bisnonno was a strong man. His wife died in childbirth, giving birth to their sixth child,' Graziella said, making the sign of the cross hastily across her chest. 'He never took another wife and he brought up his children alone here, cooking for them, rearing them to help with the land and animals. He had a flock of sheep and a couple of cows.'

She began to stir soup in a battered pan on a rudimentary stove built into the cliff which acted as one of the walls inside the hut. A hole in the ceiling went straight into the open air but until the fire caught, smoke percolated round the room, causing Savio's eyes to smart. If he was to stay here for any length of time, he would make his fires outside, he decided. There were plenty of rocks lying around. He would build a stove next to the well.

'Animals slept inside here too,' she said, pointing with a crude wooden spoon to the back of the room where the ceiling sloped down to the mud floor. 'It kept everybody warm,' she said. 'But the smell...' She waved her free hand across her nose. 'After a while, you get used to it.'

The place was basic indeed, but Savio had slept in far worse places in the past months. He thought back to the stable in Kempton Park, his isolation cell on the Isle of Man and more recently the desert in Palestine with Moyes and the others. And then there'd been the trench in Sicily, death all around. In comparison, this place was a palace and it would do for a while. He tried to picture Joy here; she was the type of woman who would make a go of anything. It would be grand to be together again. Properly.

'I'm really grateful for this, Graziella.'

She laughed. 'I imagine you are used to far better in

Inghilterra. What is it like? Is everybody rich? Do they live in big villas and drive cars?'

He took a while to answer. '*Inghilterra* is not my home anymore. My family are all gone. Home is where the heart is and... the way I was treated... my heart is no longer in that country.'

'So, you are searching for your heart?'

He nodded slowly. It was a good way of putting it. She was a perceptive young woman. 'Yes, Graziella. I think I am.'

'So, you do not have a woman to share your heart?'

Again, her words shot straight to the essence.

'I am not sure. But... there might be someone.'

'And is she beautiful, this someone?'

'She has the face of a madonna.'

'Maybe you should try to write to this madonna. Next time I come, shall I bring paper?'

He smiled at her. 'I've already written to her a few times and I hope she's received my cards and letters. There's no way of knowing – I couldn't send a return address. Yes, I'd like to write again now. I have some paper... but I shall need an envelope and a stamp.' He turned to chop another log, the idea of sending her a letter from this place suddenly seeming a hare-brained idea. 'Forget it, Graziella. I have no money for a stamp and there's a war going on. It's pointless. Best forget.'

'You should at least try, Savio.'

She'd gone in the morning before he woke. He rummaged for his watch but it had stopped. When the sun was high in the sky later, he would set it to noon and he would try to keep track of the days by marking them off on the door. It felt strange to be totally alone in this primitive place but he felt safe. He set off to explore his new neighbourhood.

.   .   .

Ten days later, he pushed his way into the undergrowth near the small olive grove upon hearing the bleating of a goat and a voice. He hadn't seen a soul in all this time. He was half curious to make contact with whoever it might be, whilst his head warned him to be wary. So, when Graziella appeared, a basket on her head, flicking the animal onward with a slender length of willow, he hurried over to embrace her. He felt her immediately stiffen and he dropped his arms and stepped back.

'I'm *sposata*,' she reminded him, a blush spreading over her olive complexion. 'I'm a married woman.'

'*Certo*. Of course. But... it's good to see another human.'

'You will have to learn to talk to yourself. Like Carmelo's great-grandfather. When his children left him to go to work in the city, he refused to come away from here. He died in his bed.'

Savio couldn't help thinking his spirit probably lingered in this place along with thousands of other lost souls. When the wind blew, funnelling up the river valley, several times he had thought he'd heard whispers carried in the air.

Graziella looked tired and for the first time the slight bulge of her stomach was evident through the threadbare skirt on her slender frame. 'I'm very thirsty. Can you draw me fresh water from the well?' She placed the basket on the stone bench and leant back in the shade, the leaves of the almond tree playing patterns on her glistening cheeks. 'This September weather will break soon,' she said, mopping her face with the hem of her skirt.

After she had quenched her thirst, she opened the basket to reveal a hen sitting quietly on a little mound of straw. The bird was broody, she told him, and there were half a dozen eggs beneath her.

'This is a gift from Carmelo. He sends his best wishes. You should put her in a quiet corner of the hut, give her water, pick greens each day and she might hatch her chicks.'

Then she produced a few provisions from within a small

sack: a small *salame*, flour, and a round of cheese. 'I have seeds for you to plant too. You have to be self-sufficient now, Savio. I can't make this journey once the baby is born and... Carmelo, he's not well. I can't leave him again.'

'I should come back to help.'

She touched his arm. 'You cannot come back. Those thugs, the *fascisti*, they're still snooping. They've been looking for you. It's not safe.'

He looked down at her strong fingers browned from the sun, the nails stubby and lined with earth. It was not right she was doing all this for him.

'I could return at night to help you.'

'It's too dangerous. And if they catch you with us, we will also be in trouble.'

She was right.

'I cannot come again for a while, Savio.' Her hand went to her head. '*Che stupida che sono.* I am so stupid, I nearly forgot.' She pulled out a brown envelope and a notepad from the bottom of the sack. 'I could not get you a stamp for *Inghilterra*. The man in the post office would have thought it strange. But will this do for you to write your letter?'

'It is more than enough,' he said. 'I'll see about a stamp myself.'

Graziella left that same night and the place was lonelier for her not being there. He occupied his mind with thinking how best to write his letter to Joy, gazing up at the pin-pricked sky, wondering how she was and if she ever had time these days to simply sit and watch the stars like he was doing.

CHAPTER 42

1973, SYRACUSE

PAIGE

On the drive out of town, Paige attempted to read her mother's letter again but the roads were winding and she felt carsick so she put it away, concentrating on the views from Dom's car. He was quiet on the journey too and apologised for the noisiness of the old engine. 'I won't shout at you, Paige. Plenty of time to talk when we get there.'

There was no time to even make a start on interpreting her mother's letter because they didn't stop talking once they were out of the car. They walked and walked along the sea that washed up at a resort called Fontane Bianche, a popular holiday village where many villas were still closed for winter.

Paige was surprised that despite the lazy lunch she had enjoyed with her new friends, she began to feel peckish. Dom led her to a homely pizzeria where half the tables were occupied.

'Eating pizza is usually a typical Sunday evening event,' he told her as they scrutinised the long list on offer. 'In August, we'd struggle to find a table here. But it's very early season, and we're lucky they're even open on a Saturday.'

'I didn't think I could eat ever again after that huge fish lunch,' she said, patting her stomach. In the end she opted for a Quattro Stagioni and Dom shared some of his Marinara.

After the pizza, they walked further along the shore's edge and sat down to watch the sun slip behind the sea in an explosion of jewel shades. A fishing boat passed in front of the fiery ball and she reached for her camera to capture the image: the boat silhouetted against gold melting like liquid onto the horizon. The moment was over and gone in a few seconds. It was a pity, she thought, that the camera couldn't capture the mood of this evening. She felt at ease in Dom's company despite having only met him earlier in the day.

They remained on the beach talking into the small hours, finishing off a bottle of Nero d'Avola they'd started in the pizzeria. Domenico removed his jacket and arranged it over her shoulders as the temperature fell and she learned more about him and his upbringing. His father had taken part in the 1943 Allied landings on the island, he told her, and fallen in love with a beautiful Sicilian girl hiding in a semi-ruined house where he and his troops had been sheltering.

'It was quite a shock for my mother to leave for a new life in England once they'd married. But every year, they returned to her home village near Noto. Dad had promised her parents he would do this,' Dom told her as he poured more wine into a plastic beaker. 'It was one of the conditions of their acceptance when he asked for her hand in marriage. And so, that's why I speak Italian and eventually found my job here. We used to come every summer holiday and the island is part of me. I love it.'

'That's such a romantic story. What's your mother's name?'

'Silvia.' He paused. 'She passed away earlier this year. She had ovarian cancer.'

She reached to cover his hand with hers. 'I'm sorry. I know how hard it is.'

He laid his other hand on top of hers and they stayed like that for a few moments.

'I feel like my mother is a stranger to me now. I mean... my aunt brought me up with so much love, but I feel kind of cheated that she kept her real identity from me. I need to understand what she wanted to tell me and the letter is really nagging at me, Dom,' she said as they disentangled hands.

'Do you have it in your bag?'

'Yes. I carry it with me all the time now. As well as the pendant,' she said, pulling it from beneath her cheesecloth smock.

'Let's go and look at this letter under the street light.' She watched as he stepped towards where he had parked earlier. He was athletic, at ease with himself and attractive as hell. *Whoops*, she thought, *you've drunk too much, Paige Caister*. She was in need of water to dampen down these strange new feelings Dom was stirring. Feelings she could do without at the moment. She'd only just finished with Jeremy. It was far too early and getting involved with a new man was... well? What was it? It was something she could do without.

They perched on a low wall and he leant over her shoulder as she pointed to the name, Dante.

'Is this a reference to a real person or to the famous Dante, do you think?' she asked.

He took it from her, his hand brushing hers and sending an annoying tingle down her body. She watched his mouth as he spoke the phrases to himself, noticing a tiny scar at the corner of his top lip.

'I am in paradise. *Of course!*' he said, turning to her, a look of triumph on his face. '*Paradiso* is the title of the third volume of *La Divina Commedia*, arguably Dante's most famous work. So, it's highly possible these references are lines in his poem.'

'I've never had a reason to come across Dante's work, Dom. I was stuck on the idea that someone called Dante had written the letter. But... now I think of it, my mother had a couple of volumes of his work. I was going to give them to a charity shop, but they're leather-bound and attractive.' She realised she'd used 'mother', without thinking twice.

'I had to study his works on my uni course. I majored in history with Italian as subsidiary. Felt I had to – out of respect for my roots.'

'So, now we need to get hold of a copy of *Paradiso*, don't we?'

'Shouldn't be too difficult. Mine's back in Rome, though.'

'Can't we break into a bookshop this evening? I need to know now.'

He laughed. '*Pazienza*, Paige! Steady on! The *libreria* will be open on Monday and if you can wait a day, I'll help you decipher.'

She was relieved when he turned the key in the ignition and pulled away from the pizzeria. She wouldn't have trusted her actions if he'd remained close to her for much longer, his scent and body heat offering more than a small distraction.

Outside her tiny apartment in Ortigia, he kept the engine idling while he said goodnight. 'It's been great getting to know you, Paige. I have meetings Monday morning, but I'll bring you a copy of *Paradiso* later on and we'll see where that gets us.'

It had been too soon to invite him in for a nightcap, but when he'd driven off with a tinny hoot on his little car and she'd opened the door to her *monolocale*, as Stefania had described her bedsit, she regretted it. For a while she sat on the wide bed, wishing she had at least offered him a coffee... or something.

'Really, signorina Paige,' she said aloud, 'what are you like?'

·   ·   ·

Sleep wouldn't come. She was too high-wired. The meaning of the letter was almost within her grasp and she couldn't wait to unlock the words. But her mind also kept creeping back to the time she'd spent in Dom's company. Was he too good to be true? He was kind, fun, intelligent, good-looking. She tried to distract herself from thoughts of him and eventually switched on the bedside lamp and pulled the letter from the envelope. The line references would have to wait until later but the English phrase at the end puzzled her: *I can't plan in a muddled place, 9 Last n=a.*

She stared at it for ages and just when she was about to give up and settle down to sleep, she gave a squeal. *Of course! It is an anagram.* How many crosswords had she done with Aunty Flo – damn it, with her mother? The word 'muddled' meant she had to unscramble the letters to find a new word. *A place* was what she was looking for. She jumped out of bed to fetch her notebook and Biro and, on second thoughts, grabbed her tourist map. The letter had been sent from Syracuse, so the place hopefully was not too far away – or maybe it was within the city itself.

She wrote: I CAN'T PLAN in capital letters at the top of a fresh page, substituting the final N for an A, and then pored over the map, until, with another squeal, followed by 'Eureka,' she punched the air. She had found what she had been looking for: in very tiny print her finger stopped on a place along the River Anapo called Pantalica. It fitted all the anagram pointers. It was about thirty kilometres due south of Syracuse. Perfectly doable in a day. Pulling out her guidebook, she flicked to the index, her heart thumping. There were only a few lines devoted to Pantalica. She read that it was the site of an acropolis and later a necropolis, dating back centuries before Christ.

She couldn't wait to tell Dom what she had come up with. But her watch told her it was three twenty in the morning. A phone call would have to wait. It was two twenty in England, but she reckoned even Charlie would not appreciate being woken in the middle of the night. Pulling the sheets over her head, she willed sleep to come. Otherwise, she would be a wreck in the morning and she needed all her wits about her.

CHAPTER 43

SEPTEMBER 1943, SICILY

SAVIO

In the gorge, Savio worked hard to keep himself and his animals fed and watered as long as the sun was in the sky. Each evening he fell onto his rudimentary mattress as tired as he could ever remember having been in his life. It was a struggle for survival. There was no mirror to see how brown his skin had turned or how long his hair had grown and there was no time to brood either. His father would no doubt have taken a sharp razor to his beard and locks, but it really didn't matter to Savio. He was alive and although lonely he was free, occasionally breaking into a one-way conversation with the goat and hens.

He yearned for rain or a break in the dry autumn heat, so that he would no longer have to water the plants growing in the patch of land he'd dug as a vegetable garden. After burgeoning shoots had been uprooted once too often by some marauding animal, he laboured to build a fence and stayed up that night guarding his patch, his gun at the ready. He'd dozed off when he heard snuffling noises and opened his eyes to see a wild boar pawing at his stockade. A single shot to the eye and the animal

slumped to the ground. Savio ate well for a few days before the
meat turned bad. If only he had known how to cure the meat,
he thought, he could have provided himself with a few months'
respite from fish and eggs.

His battered copy of Dante's *Paradiso* was the only printed
matter he possessed and he read one page each evening as a
form of discipline and entertainment. It was hard going, written
in language from long ago, and he had to decipher scholastic
notes at the bottom of the page to understand. He felt proud of
himself: for the first time in his life he was being studious. It was
on one of these evenings when he finally hit upon a way of
getting a message through to Joy. It would have to be in code in
case it was intercepted for censorship. If some clever boffin
managed to trace his whereabouts, he would be up for court
martial for going AWOL.

He calculated by the marks he'd made on the door that he
had been in Sicily over two months. It might be too late by now.
Joy had probably given up on him and met somebody else. He
bristled at that thought but he knew he was being illogical and
had no right to think this way. Albeit for the briefest of times,
they'd had something special. Something special that he longed
to have again.

He took pains to work out a code, using her book, and felt
sure she would unlock it. She was a brainy woman, had been to
university, she'd told him. As long as the letter arrived, there
was a good chance she could eventually find her way to Sicily
and come to him. Was it such a mad idea? He realised it
wouldn't happen any time soon: the war was most probably still
raging but it could surely not last forever. He decided to make
his way to Sortino, find the post office to buy a stamp and disappear sharp once he had posted his letter. It was all very well
living in the back of beyond, but he would be far happier
sharing it with a loving woman like Joy.

There was only one clean sheet left in his sketchpad and he wrote:

I am in paradise.

It was the kind of message people jotted on holiday post-cards. But surely, she would know where he was really driving her to look. It took him two more evenings to work out the rest of his message. He painstakingly transcribed numbers and words from the text, being extra careful with his writing, remembering to use the tips Joy had shown him, double-checking before he formed any of the letters. Finally, he worked out an anagram to give her a clue as to where he was. Map coordinates would have been simpler, but too obvious.

VIII, 15
I, 55, 4
I, 88, 5
XXV, 110, 8-L
VIII, 38, 4, 5

Underneath the figures he added the words:

i vivi vivono con i morti
I can't plan in a muddled place, 9 Last n=a.

He signed off with *Dante*, hoping she would remember his code name from their training days and that it would be obvious she needed to consult Dante's great work.

He hoped the message was neither too obscure nor obvious, doubt starting to creep in. Joy had told him she enjoyed working out crossword puzzles. He'd often seen her bent over a newspaper, fathoming clues in the common room at Glenaig. She had even set him a simple one to complete himself during a reading session, explaining a little about cryptic clues. If he made the message any clearer and the letter fell into the wrong hands, he'd be discovered. It was a risk he was taking, but a risk well worth taking if it meant they could be reunited. And the War Office had more important things to pursue at the moment than deserters, he reckoned.

He wrote her address as he remembered it on the envelope and sat back, pleased with his efforts. Tomorrow he would venture into Sortino to the post office.

When he woke two days later, he had to think hard about what had happened. His mouth tasted foul, his head smarted and when he sat up, the cliff walls of the hut closed in on him. He staggered outside and vomited several times onto the grass. Had it been a good idea to venture into the village? Had he blown his cover? He vaguely remembered stealing away from the *osteria* in the piazza in Sortino late in the night and lurching down the path to the river, hoping nobody would follow him. After buying a stamp much earlier in the day, the woman behind the counter of the tobacconist's had commented that nobody had ever asked for a stamp for *Inghilterra* before. America, yes. Plenty of people from Sortino had emigrated there, she said, trying to engage him in conversation, he imagined.

'I need to check the amount,' she'd said, disappearing into the back of the shop, pushing through a fly screen. He'd almost turned tail and fled right then. Was she calling the *carabinieri*? Did she suspect he might be a soldier on the run? He stood firm while he waited, eyeing up a wooden stool to use as a weapon if any funny business started. She returned with a ledger and proudly presented him with the correct stamps. 'Let's hope it gets there with this war,' she said. '*Speriamo bene*. But at least we are now allies with the *inglesi* and *americani*.'

He had no idea what she was talking about. He thanked the

woman and left. A board leaning outside the shop proclaimed the latest news from the front page of *Corriere della Sera*: *Le ostilità cessate tra l'Italia, l'Inghilterra e gli Stati Uniti*. Well, well, well, so Mussolini had capitulated. Hostilities had ceased between Italy and the allies. The Germans wouldn't like that one bit. But it meant Italy was no longer an enemy. Small mercies, he thought, hoping it might make life easier for him from now on.

He should have returned immediately to the hut in Pantalica but it had been so long since he'd seen people and he'd felt the need to celebrate news of this armistice. Women washing clothes at the font in the middle of the piazza looked up at him, covering their mouths as they talked. A group of men slapped cards down on the table in the shade of the Osteria Iblea. In the corner a stall selling cheeses was doing a brisk trade. It was good to see fellow human beings. One drink in the *osteria* would do no harm, would it? How long had it been since he'd talked to anything other than the goat and hens?

Of course the men were curious about this strange-looking newcomer with bird-nest hair and scraggy whiskers. They wanted to know where he had sprung from but he was elusive in his answers. 'My name is Nunzio. I was discharged from the army. Injured. I'm from Rome and I'm on my way home.'

He'd relished the attention and he'd drunk it up like he'd swallowed the many tumblers of rough, blood-red wine they'd pressed on him. He was unable to reciprocate; he had no money but they'd slapped him on the back, saying, 'Next time, *amico* Nunzio. Next time... it's enough you help us celebrate today. The war will soon be over now we've joined the *inglesi*.'

They'd encouraged him to join in with *bocce*, a game similar to carpet bowls but more entertaining, as old and young men remonstrated and gesticulated as if they were waging war and not playing a simple country sport. By the time he had shown them how to play a game of cricket, using three full wine bottles as stumps, he had been more than well away.

Once back in his stone hut by the River Anapo, he fully expected *carabinieri* to turn up to arrest him. Somebody in the *osteria* was bound to talk. So, he carried his gun about with him each day and kept his ears cocked for the sounds of approaching strangers. But two months went by and he'd grown more relaxed when one afternoon in November he heard the sound of crying. At first he thought it was a wounded animal and he'd fetched his gun at the thought of a potential meal. His gun at the ready, he was flat on the ground in a thicket of gorse when he saw a woman approach, a crying baby strapped to her front.

He stood up, relaxing his grip on his gun when he saw who it was.

'I've come to help you,' Graziella said, putting down the large sack she'd carried over her shoulders and immediately bursting into noisy sobs.

CHAPTER 44

AUTUMN 1943, SUFFOLK

FLORENCE

Florence pushed against the door to Squirrels Cottage, the wood swollen with damp and as it suddenly gave way, she fell straight into a living room. It smelt musty and as she moved forwards, a cobweb brushed her face. Through a window where curtains didn't quite reach, light fought to enter and she yanked it open to let in fresh air.

If the outside had looked like a biscuit tin picture, the inside was a detailed illustration from a child's storybook. A wide inglenook, flanked by two large armchairs covered in faded floral chintz, took up most of the far end of a heavily oak-beamed living room. Shelves bulging with books occupied the rest of the wall. The floor was paved with large flagstones and a tatted rug sat beneath the chairs. On the walls were oil paintings of landscapes and the sea. A wireless set and an old gramophone player stood on top of a painted cupboard. She saw possibilities. It was a room where she might be content.

A small kitchen was reached via a door on the left-hand side. Daylight strained through flimsy check curtains that had seen better days. An old range, meat safe, copper pots and pans hanging from a dresser, a round pine table and three chairs provided all the necessities.

Another door led to a short winding staircase of oak steps. At the top she had to duck beneath a low door to enter a bedroom, the floorboards wide and crooked, listing a little to the left where the oak had warped with age. Two tiny casement windows on either side of the bed gave out onto fields and woods. A set of shelves and hooks behind a curtain patterned with sailing boats took up the rest of the bedroom space. Another low door led to a small single room with a bed built into the end wall, like a ship's cabin. Perfect for baby eventually, but she would need to get hold of a cot for the early days.

She spent the rest of the day airing the place and tidying up her new kingdom, making up the double bed with linen and blankets found in a trunk at the end of the bed. At first, she hadn't noticed the lean-to bathroom downstairs attached to the kitchen, with its old-fashioned boiler system requiring a fire at its base to heat the water. But at least she wouldn't have to use an outside privy or haul a tin bath to wash herself beside the inglenook fire. The cupboard in the kitchen had revealed a plentiful stock of tins: corned beef, pilchards, ham, peaches, prunes and a variety of jams. At the back of the overgrown garden she found an orchard, its trees laden with apples and pears. Next time she visited the shop, she would take in some windfalls to share. After the baby was born, she would dig a vegetable garden and buy hens. She wouldn't starve in this place.

Later, with the fire lit, a cottage book in her lap, she leant back tired but happy in one of the capacious armchairs. 'Thank you, dear Norman,' she murmured, as she opened *The Guide to Butterflies* to see his signature scrawled on the cover. 'Thank you.' She glanced towards the stack of books and saw boxes of games and cards on a lower shelf. The ghost of Norman's past lingered in this cottage but somehow it didn't scare her. Rather, she was comforted, her soul brimming from his generosity.

There would be lonely times ahead, she sensed this. And when the baby was born, she would miss Savio not being with her. But he was dead. She had never questioned that. At Bletchley she'd talked to a girl who had been sent a telegram: her fiancé was missing, presumed dead and she'd been eaten up with the possibility he would turn up any day. But Florence wanted no such prolonging of agony. The newspaper had stated plainly that Savio Rizzo was dead. Not missing. The peculiar letter was unfortunate in its timing. Written before he was killed, but sent afterwards. A cruel twist of fate. In the meantime, she had plenty to occupy her mind. She would be fine. Just fine.

She forced herself to settle down and turn the pages of the book, the flickering and crackling of the fire keeping her company as the shadows outside lengthened.

CHAPTER 45

FEBRUARY 1944

FLORENCE

She is so beautiful. I cannot stop gazing at my sleeping daughter, her tiny arms stretched above her head, fists curled, fingernails like the tiniest of delicate shells washed up on the estuary shore.

Her mouth is pursed with milk blisters from her night feed. We've developed a pattern in these early days. I reach down for my baby as she stirs in the bottom drawer of the chest lined with soft blankets and I cradle her to my breast. It's a special time together. I pull open the curtains on the casement windows – each pane framing a portion of the countryside: a black sky spangled with stars, shapes of trees like coral cut-outs, the moon as it waxes and wanes, changing the sky over the weeks. It's a time for the two of us and it would be perfection if only there were three of us in Squirrels. *Daddy is looking down on his family, little Paige. He knows we're doing well. But we miss him, don't we, darling little one?*

If only I could believe this were true. How comforting it would be to be convinced of a heaven somewhere in the clouds where we would be reunited with Savio when the time comes. But I concluded long ago it's a fantasy I cannot follow. If God exists, why does He allow such misery? The war has split up families, maimed children, made widows of young women... So many fighting men and women have endured awful traumas. I keep abreast of the news in the papers; I've read about the poor soldiers in Italy holed up all winter in trenches on the Apennines, pored over details of the battle of Monte Cassino. Why I do it, I have no idea. Because Savio is dead and never coming back from Italy.

Dorothy was my absolute salvation, not God. Matron Dorothy from Somersby Hall. I joke and call her Goddess to myself. She's been so kind to me, warning of the depression I would likely suffer. And I did. It hit me like a trolley bus. For all her prickly demeanour, she's been a diamond. When I turned up at the hospital wing at the Hall, my labour pains were already well established. Baby was a little early but her birth was easy enough. Afterwards I sank to somewhere deep. Dorothy nursed me in a room next to her own and even attempted a reconciliation with Mother but she showed herself yet again to be an uncaring, cold and vindictive woman, expressing no interest whatsoever in seeing her granddaughter: 'the spawn of a soldier's pick up', as she so indelicately put it. And Dorothy saw sense not to pursue it.

Dorothy keeps my secret. She drives over on her free days to visit, bringing baby clothes, food and plenty of wise counsel. We've become firm friends.

'Why do you come to visit, Dorothy?' I ask after the third week of her driving over in her rattling Austin 7. I am still undressed in my soiled nightgown, in need of a bath and hair wash, dirty dishes piled up in the butler's sink. Dorothy rolls up her sleeves and helps me wash my hair and then bustles about the kitchen tidying up. She is gentle but firm as she encourages me from my black hole.

'I was never lucky enough to have a family of my own, my dear,' she tells me. 'I was brought up in an orphanage. When I met Sidney, I thought heaven had fallen down to earth, that we would have our own family to love. But he died in the trenches.'

She produces a dozen new towelling nappies and a couple of nightdresses made by the WVS, folding them neatly away as she speaks but I see the emotion in her eyes.

'I went into nursing to offer what I have to others. So, allow me to treat you as my little family. Your secret will remain with me, but I can't see you struggle like this on your own. If you struggle, baby will struggle too. We can't have you falling about like a piece of old wrapping in a breeze, can we?'

With the help and encouragement of this dear woman I understand the special responsibility I have towards my daughter. That is what drags me from the claws of the black dog. If ever I feel down, I think of Dorothy and her kind but no-nonsense approach to life. She has become my role model. All the protection and care my own mother never showed me will now be poured instead into Paige's upbringing. It isn't hard to love my daughter. Not at all. And I shall turn Squirrels into a home for us and teach Paige to be upright and honest. One day, when the right time comes, I will be honest with my daughter too and tell her the truth about her father.

One day, before it is too late.

CHAPTER 46

1973, SICILY

PAIGE

On Monday morning, after two double espressos to wake her up, Paige was outside the door to Feltrinelli's Bookshop minutes before it opened. She was the first customer and the helpful manager provided her with all three volumes of Dante's *Divine Comedy*.

'It is pointless to have one without the other two,' he said, handing the books over with reverence, his English slow and correct.

'Do you have English translations?' she asked.

'I can order. For next week.'

'Don't worry. I can't wait that long. I'll manage,' she told him, thinking instantly of Dom and his fluent Italian.

She tried to phone both Charlie and Dom but neither answered. Despite telling herself she should put the *Paradiso* volume aside and wait for Dom's help, Paige tortured herself by returning to the shop to buy a dictionary and, outside a café, while her tepid cappuccino grew colder, she had no difficulty finding the line references indicated in the letter. Trying to translate the mysterious message herself was more difficult, however. Half the words weren't in the dictionary. She managed to interpret part of the first line: *la donna mia* – meaning 'my woman', and in the second line: *qui*, meaning 'here', but the combination of a sleep-deprived night, lack of Italian and a non-linguistic brain forced her to admit defeat and she returned to her *monolocale* in the market street to stretch out on the bed for a nap.

Paige woke an hour and a half later with an urgent need to find this place called Pantalica. She grabbed a bottle of water, map and car keys and hurried to the car park to be reunited with Bertha.

It took some time to get out of the city but within forty minutes and just after midday, Paige parked her car in the small central piazza of Sortino, the village nearest Pantalica, and wandered into a bar. The counter was covered in gaudy red tiles and the shelves behind the bar were laden with silver cups. Photos of footballers took up one wall, together with a couple of black-and-white photographs of fishermen by a river, proudly holding up their catches. A gang of four elderly men were playing cards and sipping at glasses of wine. They looked up at her for an instant as she entered: a *straniera* in town. But almost immediately they went back to slapping their cards on the table, voices raised as if in anger as they played. But their interspersed laughter and jeering at each other told her otherwise. It was the usual friendly banter.

A scrawny cat wandered over hopefully but she was only ordering a cappuccino and panino and it soon slunk away when it realised there were no scraps on offer. The island was crawling with strays. She'd seen foil trays of pasta placed outside the big doors of apartment blocks in Syracuse. Most of the cats looked as if they were wild, covered in sores, their fur dirty and matted.

'*Caldo, caldo,*' she exhorted the barman after her order, as Dom had recommended at their pizza evening.

'Italians like to knock back their morning coffees on the go,' he'd told her. 'So, lukewarm is best for them. You have to stress you want it hot: *caldo, caldo.* And if you order a cappuccino after a meal, that's an immediate giveaway you're a foreigner,' he'd added.

As she sat in the piazza, enjoying her cappuccino *caldo, caldo* and a ham *panino*, she gazed about her. But Sortino was a small world and the streets were dead. From the houses came the sounds and smells of midday meals being prepared.

Paige looked at her tourist map again and after double-checking directions with the barman, pleased he understood her questions and, more to the point, that she roughly understood his answers, she set off down a footpath towards Pantalica.

She walked slowly, placing one foot in front of the other in the narrow furrow of a path running alongside the river. Holm oak, thick brambles and spiky wild rosemary grew alongside, the sharp scent of the herb mixing with the odour of stagnant mud. Here and there were holes and animal prints in the cloggy ground. The place smelled of wildlife and antiquity.

Paige thought fleetingly of Jeremy; how he would have absolutely hated to be here walking, his smart shoes dirtied with mud. He would likely complain and ask how much further they had to go. It felt good to be free of him and she stopped to lift her face to the sky.

Above her in the cliffs were hundreds of square holes hacked out like tiny doorways and she remembered what she had read about Pantalica being an acropolis – a citadel or fortified part of an ancient Greek city. The guidebook mentioned it had been founded most likely in the thirteenth century before Christ. It was hard to conceive of the age of this isolated corner of the country-side. Once upon a time it might have been bustling: market places thronged with customers haggling for goods, oxen or goats and scratching hens littering the place. Now, there was a deep sense of calm and silence, save for the ripple of water flowing in the river beside her. Dark pink oleander shrubs waved slender branches in the gentle breeze. Birdsong punctuated the quiet and a couple of raptors circled high above in the thermals, their calls high-pitched and mewling. Her steps were lighter as the path widened out. But there was nobody around and no houses. The place was empty and she wondered why on earth Pantalica had been mentioned and clouded with such secrecy in the letter to her mother.

Aunty Flo would have adored it here: stopping every few minutes to use her binoculars or to look up the name of a plant in her little pocket guide. Her death had left Paige with huge questions and Paige wondered if she would ever be able to work out the answers. Had Dom managed to make a start on the code? Yesterday she'd spied a similar pendant charm in an antiques shop in Ortigia. It had some worth as a curiosity, the shopkeeper had told her and collectors would be interested. He'd wanted to buy it from her there and then. But Paige would never sell it. Her aunt had wanted her to have it. She corrected herself again: *her mother* had wanted her to have it and she would respect her gift. She had taken to wearing it under her clothes, against her skin, and she pulled it out. It hung from her neck like a compass, as if guiding her to solutions, she hoped.

Paige walked on, the path leading her through a disused railway tunnel and out into the light again. She emerged to the spectacle of hundreds more – no thousands more – tiny door-ways in the cliffside. She stood for a moment holding her breath at the sight. Pantalica seemed like the end of the earth: beautiful and wild. But what on earth had it got to do with her mother?

The scene before her held such a unique sense of history and was almost indescribable. The guidebook had told her that besieged Siculi had adapted homes from tombs in ancient times. They were the original inhabitants of Sicily, and she shivered as she imagined how many dead might be buried in these little dwellings. Maybe there were still bones in some.

The sky turned a menacing grey. Fat raindrops began to fall, splashing in polka dots onto rocks, and she ran for shelter. She hadn't thought to bring a waterproof in her knapsack and she was going to be drenched in seconds if she remained in the open. She bent down to squeeze into one of the lower cave holes and sat hunched, her arms round her knees, while curtains of rain temporarily obliterated her view of outside. Gradually her eyes grew accustomed to the gloomy interior. She looked with trepidation about her, checking there were no skeletons. A farmer or somebody working on the land must be using the space for storage because a hoe and a spade with a pointed edge leant against a rough wall hacked from the hillside. A channel ran along the back and when she moved over to examine it, she saw how it extended through holes into the neighbouring tombs – a kind of pipe-system for carrying water, maybe. Onions hung from a couple of strings woven from plaited raffia and a pile of straw heaped in the far corner looked as if it had been used recently as a simple bed.

The rain stopped and she stepped outside to check the sky. It was paintbox-blue again, a sudden contrast from the stormy grey. Next to her shelter was another wooden door, this one ajar, and curiosity made her pull it wide to peer inside. Canvases of all shapes adorned the walls and pots of paints, brushes and turps were stored on a table made from an old door resting on makeshift trestle supports. Somebody had been using this place as a studio. And yet, moments earlier, she had thought she was the only person alive in this strange valley. Maybe whoever it was had heard her approaching and was watching her from a hiding place. Suddenly, Pantalica turned from stunning to spooky and she couldn't wait to get away.

A tuneless whistling pierced the air and then she heard footsteps. A man was approaching. His clothes were patched and his long grey hair was tied back from his face. He raised a hand in greeting but Paige, feeling suddenly vulnerable in these isolated surroundings, turned to hurry back the way she had come.

CHAPTER 47

The way back up the track was steep but she quickened her pace. She couldn't explain why she'd suddenly felt so spooked at seeing the man appear from nowhere. But nobody except the barman knew where she was if anything were to happen. *What exactly you expect to happen is only in your stupid imagination,* she chided herself. *Stop being so suspicious.* But the feeling she had was the stuff of Friday-night horror movies that her mother used to laugh all the way through, much to Paige's annoyance.

When she arrived back at Bertha, she locked herself in the car. She was perspiring like mad and it took some time to calm down before she turned the ignition. By the time she arrived back in Syracuse and had parked, she felt annoyed with herself. She had achieved very little in her visit to Pantalica. Daylight was fading from the pearly sky. Lights reflected from restaurants on the harbour wall twinkled in the water. It felt good to be amongst people again and she walked slowly, absorbing the sounds of the city as it prepared for the evening. At a small *alimentari* shop tucked down an alleyway she bought, bread, fennel, slices of salami and a plate of ready-roasted stuffed peppers for her supper. Her last hope was with Dom helping her make the lines from *Paradiso* come alive to provide a decent clue. That time couldn't come soon enough, as far as she was concerned.

Paige giggled at the note pinned to the door of her flat:

In bar on corner near where sexy fishmonger was working.

There could only be one person to have written that.

The market stalls had been replaced with dining tables along the street and she wove her way past diners until she reached Mario's Bar halfway down. Charlie, flanked by two attractive girls, was sitting at a table and he stood to beckon when he spied her, sweeping her up in his arms as she arrived. '*Buona sera, carissima,*' he said and the two girls clapped their hands in approval.

'I've been having an Italian lesson from Clara and Lodovica,' he told her. '*Vuoi ballare con me?* Do you want to dance with me?'

The girls laughed and then stood up to leave, but not before he bent to extravagantly kiss their hands. As they made their way down the street, they turned once to wave and he blew them kisses.

'You are incorrigible, Charlie,' Paige said, 'raising their hopes.'

'But weren't they *gorgeous*? Anyway, where have YOU been? I arrived early this afternoon and was forced to find alternative entertainment.'

'If I'd known you were coming, I'd have been here to welcome you. How on earth did you find me anyway? I only sent a postcard very recently.'

'You showed me the place in your brochure before you left, remember? And I made a spur of the moment decision: got a last-minute flight and wanted to surprise you. I'd reached a sticky point in my manuscript. Thought a trip south would boost creativity. *Where* have you been all afternoon? Have you met a gorgeous Sicilian? Does he have a friend for me?'

She smiled. 'It's a long story.' She looked at his half-finished glass of white wine. 'Drink up and I'll take you back to my flat and explain everything.'

On the way, Charlie stopped at a store still open, insisting he needed to try local produce, despite Paige telling him she'd already bought supper. He bagged a selection of olives, *cacio ragusano* cheese, spicy *capocollo piccante* sausage, a bag of almonds and a bottle of Nero d'Avola that Paige selected.

'I'm being seduced by these names,' Charlie said. 'Lord knows what the stuff tastes like, but the words are luscious. I feel a Sicilian-themed book coming on.' His enthusiasm as usual brightened Paige's spirits as she helped carry one of his brown paper bags brimming with goodies.

'Well, this is far nicer than the *pensione* round the corner,' he said as Paige unlocked the door to her bedsit. He went over to test the bed, kicking off his shoes and flopping back against the velvet cushions. 'Open that bottle and tell me what's been going on since you arrived. Don't spare me any detail.'

While they shared supper in the kitchen area, she told him about solving the anagram and driving to Pantalica, omitting to own up about her hasty retreat. 'It's a beautiful place but... eerie. Can't quite put my finger on it and I still don't understand the connection it has with Aunty... my mother.'

'Any progress on the rest of that cryptic letter?'

'A friend is helping me.'

He raised his eyebrows. '*And?*'

'My landlady introduced me to him. Dom works for the Commonwealth War Graves Commission.'

'*And?*'

'Stop saying "and" like that.'

'What's this Dom like?'

'Half Italian.'

'You're killing me. What aren't you telling me, honeypie?'

'There's absolutely nothing to tell, dearest Charlie. I don't need a man in my life at the moment.'

'Do you think he'd like *me*?'

'Not your type,' she said swiftly.

'Do I detect a bit of "hands-off, Charlie"?'

'Now, you're beginning to be annoying,' she said.

When she turned back from the sink, his eyes had closed and she removed the empty glass from his hand and left him to doze. *Honestly, he is like a child sometimes*, she thought. She scribbled him a note to say she'd gone for a walk and gently pulled the door to.

She needed to think over today's trip and walk away from Charlie and his teasing. Was it so obvious that Dom had woken something in her? She really didn't need that complication in her life right. She made her way down the narrow streets to the Arethusa pool and gazed at the fish swimming in and out of the reeds. She read the sign that explained the complicated story of Arethusa, a girl who had strayed to the banks of the River Alpheus and swum naked in its refreshing water. The River Alpheus had fallen in love with her and transformed itself into a handsome blond spirit with human features. Paige smiled at the way love could be conjured into so many different stories.

It was a secluded area and a young couple were kissing on one of the benches. Feeling like an intruder, she left them, and stepped down to where dozens of yachts were moored, the sounds of their stays clanking rhythmically in the darkness. It was peaceful but she didn't fancy walking further on her own. It was most likely safe but this afternoon's encounter with the man looming from nowhere still caused shivers to run down her spine when she thought of it. It was time to return to Charlie.

As she turned the key in the door, she heard Charlie talking to somebody inside and she hoped she wasn't about to walk into anything embarrassing.

Charlie was sitting close to a man on her bed and, their backs to her, they were examining a map spread out on the quilt.

'I let your lovely friend in, honeypie,' Charlie said, getting up to hug her. 'Hope that was all right.'

'Dom!' Paige stuttered when he turned round and she recognised him.

'Paige, I think I've worked out your letter,' Dom said excitedly, gesturing to her to come over to the bed. He held up a book, tapping its cover. 'My hunch was right and in the end it was simple to decipher the figures. Look!'

He held up a piece of paper with letters and numbers and words scribbled next to them. 'The message *is* composed of words within Dante's *Paradiso* and the numbers and letters reference lines within the poem.' He read out in Italian:

'*La donna mia ch'i vidi far più bella, qui ti l'aspetto pien d'amor.* The penultimate line doesn't quite work, so the writer has written this,' he said, pointing to *XXV, 110, 8-L.* 'If you minus the "L", then the sentence does make sense: *qui ti aspetto...*'

Paige beamed at him. 'And I have worked out the anagram at the bottom after giving up on trying to fathom the Italian. Translate what you just read out to me.'

Dom shook his head. 'Yes, how stupid of me, I forget you don't speak Italian. And it's written in old Italian too – almost another language.' He held up his notes again. 'The message roughly reads: The woman that I see as the most beautiful, here I wait for you, full of love.'

'That's lovely,' Paige said. 'But it still foxes me. I actually went to Pantalica this afternoon after I eventually worked out the anagram. But I think I made a mistake because there's absolutely nothing there. Maybe it might have made sense to my mother. But... it means nothing to me,' she said, feeling like they had come to the end of this crazy goose chase. 'Maybe there's another place in Sicily with the same letters but in a different order?'

Dom tapped his fingers on the final lines. 'No, no! I'm *sure* you went to the right place. Now I understand the meaning behind those last lines. I'm not a crossword buff and I didn't realise Pantalica was an anagram. "*I vivi vivono con i morti.*" The living live with the dead. It makes sense now.'

'So, where the living live with the dead is referring to the acropolis and necropolis. I read about that in the guidebook and saw the tombs-cum-dwelling places for myself today. But *why*? There's nothing there. Why invite her *there*?'

'The writer of this love letter – because that's what I believe it to be – asks your mother to come to Pantalica. So, we need to go there again.'

'And do what?' Paige asked. 'I repeat, there's *nothing* there.'

'We'll go to Sortino and speak to people.'

Charlie interrupted. 'I haven't got a clue what you're both yapping on about. Can somebody kindly explain?'

'I told you about the special place I went to this afternoon,' Paige explained. 'An isolated valley crammed with cave dwellings thousands of years old. *That's* Pantalica and the writer of the letter must have been inviting my mother there for some unfathomable reason.'

'Presumably your father?' Charlie offered.

'I think so,' Dom chipped in.

'But so long ago,' Paige said, scrabbling for the original letter in its envelope. She peered at the stamp. 'And it could have been sent by anyone. It's blurred but the postmark is September 1943.' She sighed and replaced the letter in the box. 'It's too late to get to the bottom of all this now, guys. Thirty years have passed and there's *nothing* in Pantalica. I really think we've come to the end of the trail.'

'Personally, I haven't come all this way to see you give up,

Paige Caister. No way,' Charlie said, hands on hips. 'Where's your chutzpah gone?'

'I agree you shouldn't stop now, Paige,' Dom said. 'If this was sent by your father, as Charlie said, someone might remember him. We should go to Sortino and ask in the bar – ask one of the older residents who hang out there. In villages like that, everybody knows everything about everyone.'

'*If* he's still alive!' Paige said with a sigh.

'Who's being negative again?' Charlie asked.

'I'm sorry but, you have to admit, it's all stabs in the dark.' She looked from one to the other of her friends, reading the disappointment on their faces. She was disappointed in herself, if she was honest – tired and upset over the way she'd had to discover her real mother in such a roundabout way. She huffed and turned to Dom. 'I don't suppose you're free any time soon, are you, Dom? It would be so much easier for you to talk to locals in Italian.'

He smiled. 'I can do next Sunday. Tied up until then. I have to see a farmer on the Isola peninsula who's found what he believes to be the remains of two soldiers. There are British helmets amongst the bones. Even after thirty years, the war continues to unearth its secrets. So, don't you give up, Paige. It will bug you if you stop now.' He handed Paige his scribbled notes and stood up from the bed. 'See you Sunday? Nine?'

'Well, he's a find and a half,' Charlie said after Dom had gone. He picked at the dishes of food Paige had prepared before going for her walk. 'Very different from Jeremy.'

'I told you, I'm not interested,' Paige said, popping an olive in her mouth.

She ignored the look Charlie gave her.

'Right, I have to leave on Sunday afternoon,' Charlie said, 'so I can't join you on your trip but maybe you can help me explore Syracuse in the meantime and eat lunch in the cathedral square. Your guidebook tells me it's a must,' he said, slicing himself more cheese.

Dom was dressed casually in flared denims and a tight T-shirt when he arrived on Charlie's last morning and Paige glared at Charlie when he widened his eyes and pretended to fan himself. Fortunately, Dom hadn't seemed to notice and Paige pushed her way in front of Charlie, treading on his foot in warning. She really didn't want him embarrassing her.

'It's really kind of you to drop Charlie off at the station, Dom.'

'You're welcome. Have you got the letter and pendant on you?' Dom asked. 'You never know whom we might come across.'

Paige patted her shoulder bag. 'The letter's safe and I'm wearing the pendant.'

'I've brought the Consul today,' Dom continued. 'Not enough room in the Topolino for three of us, and Sporca is staying home too. I thought it would be easier.'

Paige chose to sit in the back seat behind Charlie, ready to pinch him if he misbehaved. She listened as Dom pointed out landmarks as they drove through the outskirts, marvelling at how he navigated the crazy traffic.

'You have to give as good as you get, otherwise you'd never arrive anywhere,' Dom said, laughing as Charlie covered his eyes as he manoeuvred through an impossibly small gap between a bus and a Lancia.

As Charlie hugged Paige goodbye at the station to catch his connection to Catania Airport, he murmured, 'Phone me and let me know what happens. Don't keep me hanging on.' Before he let her go, he whispered, because Dom was within earshot, 'Hang on to this one, honeypie. He's a hunk.'

. . .

On the way to Pantalica, they stopped at a fishing village for a meal. The restaurant was busy with families enjoying Sunday lunch. But the proprietor magicked them a table for two over-looking the sea. The sky was a palette of blues that merged with the calm azure sea, the sun glittering like spangles off the surface. Paige was transfixed.

'This island keeps on giving,' she said. 'It's so beautiful, with so much history. It's hard to take it all in in. And from what I've seen so far, the architecture is very varied.'

'Reflecting various invasions,' he replied. 'The island has been besieged and occupied by many different cultures.' He counted off on his fingers: 'Phoenicians, Carthaginians, Greeks, Romans, Vandals, Normans, French, Spanish, Ostrogoths and more... in no particular order.'

'I haven't even heard of some of those peoples.' She was finding it increasingly difficult to concentrate on what he was saying. Not because it wasn't interesting, but on account of the way his eyes danced enthusiastically as he spoke, full of a passion that she wanted a piece of.

He'd shrugged at her comment. 'I studied ancient history at university, remember. I suppose I'm infatuated. Indulge me!' He smiled at her before continuing. 'Sicily is the largest island in the Mediterranean. A hugely important trading stop with its own distinct culture.'

She watched his hands as he fiddled with his cutlery setting, his long, tapered fingers with a few dark hairs on the knuckles. Her eyes strayed to the open collar of his shirt where more hairs showed. She imagined herself in his arms, his hands caressing her body and then she shook her head free and tried to concentrate on what he was saying.

Dom clinked his glass against Paige's and they tucked into a first course of *spaghetti alle vongole*; the tomato, shellfish and garlic sauce had a hint of the sea and he recommended she mop every last bit up with a *scarpetta* – a corner of bread.

'Good things always happen to me on a Sunday,' Dom said as they waited for portions of stuffed roasted aubergines and peppers to accompany another course of fish. 'You know my name comes from the word for Sunday? I was born on a Sunday.'

'I didn't! But I do now and... I'm enjoying my Sunday.'

He put his glass down and stared intently at her. 'Perhaps we can have more Sundays together?'

Her heart fluttered a little, but what was the point? 'My time here is nearly up, Dom. I...'

He took hold of her hand. 'But you could come and visit again. Come to Rome. It's the most amazing city. I know an agency that offers cheap flights; I... would love it if we could get to know each other better.'

She was quiet, her head full of questions. It was too soon. But why not? What was stopping her? Dom was looking at her with those deep-brown eyes. She realised she was going to miss him.

'I can't fully explain it but... I *do* feel a strong connection with this place, so I'd like to come back again to visit – and see if I can get to the bottom of this mystery.' She took a deep breath. 'And... I'd love to see you too.'

There, she'd said it. And he looked delighted at her answer. In fact, he had taken both her hands in his and pulled them to his mouth and he was staring at her with those eyes she was sure she could drown in. There was no harm in seeing how things went, was there? People fell in love in mysterious ways. Apparently, it was something you couldn't plan. Suddenly, she didn't feel hungry any longer. It was enough to feast her eyes on Dom.

After he'd paid, he held out his hand as they walked to the car and the fit of her hand in his felt right.

. . .

The barista in the small bar in Sortino recognised Paige and greeted her with a friendly smile. 'Did you find Pantalica?' he asked, wiping clean a glass.

She nodded and asked Dom to take over.

'Do you know anybody who was here in Sortino during the war, signore? A stranger to the area, maybe? Somebody who might have had connections to *Inghilterra*?'

The barman pointed to the men playing cards in the corner. 'All that lot were here, I reckon. And a few more besides. Not many people leave this place, except in their boxes. I suggest you chat to them. They know everything.'

Paige ordered two espressos and they took their drinks over to the table next to the card players, waiting for them to finish their game. There was lively exchange between two of them and Paige smiled at what must be the post-mortem. Nobody liked to lose.

She let Dom do the talking, guessing he was enquiring about September 1943, recognising the word Pantalica in his questions. There was much conferring and hand waving until they seemed to nod their heads and agree. Dom thanked them and she watched as he went to the bar, returning with four full tumblers of red wine. There were handshakes and waves as they left and one of the old men grabbed Paige's hand to kiss it. '*Bella, bella*,' he said, a twinkle in his rheumy eyes.

'How much do I owe you?' Paige asked outside. 'You paid for lunch too.'

'I'll send you a bill,' he replied with a cheeky grin.

'What did they say?'

'They all agreed on one name: Nunzio. Apparently, he wasn't local and turned up out of the blue in '43 and lived down by the river for years. But now he lives in a house on the way to Pantalica. Bit of a loner but pleasant enough. Keeps himself to himself. His daughter is more sociable, apparently.'

'Shall we drive there?'

'It looks like rain. I say yes.'

Three quarters of the way before reaching Pantalica, Dom parked his car at the side of the road next to a metal gate and a path leading to a small house set back on its own. She hadn't noticed it on her first visit as it was almost concealed in a garden packed with almond, fig and peach trees. She'd noticed a straggle of similar flat-roofed houses perched below the old town. But this place was isolated. Dom ushered Paige up the stony path lined with cacti and she knocked on the door.

A man opened and she stepped back in surprise. He was dressed like a hippie, albeit a little older than the usual flower-power type. His shirt was collarless and patched with an assortment of colourful materials. A dog sat patiently behind him: a huge off-white mongrel, half Alsatian, half something that could have been wolf.

It was the same man she had seen in the gorge.

CHAPTER 48

'Can I help you?' the man asked.

'Signor Nunzio?' Dom asked.

'Sì. But if you're selling something, we're not interested. We have everything we need, thank you.'

He started to close the door on them but a young woman suddenly appeared, her voice raised as she stepped in front of him. Paige understood the word, *scusate*, sorry, thrown at her and Dom before the pair started to argue.

'I've seen this man before,' Paige muttered, as the argument continued.

'What do you mean? Where?' Dom asked, one ear on the heated discussion. 'She's telling him off for being anti-social. I think she's his daughter.'

Paige noticed his appreciative look and she experienced a puzzling sense of jealousy. The girl was stunning, dressed in skin-tight jeans and a white top that left little to the imagination.

'He was down by the river.'

The girl turned from her father with a smile that lit up her face and said something to Dom, whereupon he laughed. Paige felt quite left out as they continued to talk before the girl ushered them in, the older man known as Nunzio glaring as he turned to follow.

The door led immediately into a kitchen-cum-living room, simply furnished: a table made from an old door, polished but with the hinges still showing, deer antlers used as hooks above a sink, from which tea towels hung, chairs carved from tree trunks and padded with animal hides. But most spectacular were the paintings of all sizes on every space on the walls, showing views of cave dwellings, the river, some in charcoal, some brightly coloured. Large abstract canvases completed the quirky interior.

The girl gestured to the seats and Dom and Paige sat down whilst the hippie man remained standing, looking suspicious, wary.

Dom said something and the girl immediately answered in English. 'Don't worry. We both speak English. Don't we, Papà?'

Her English was good but heavily accented. Her father nodded and folded his arms. The girl followed Paige's gaze and commented, 'Papà loves to paint. Sometimes he manages to sell his pictures.'

'I think I must have found his studio down near the river,' Paige said.

Finally, the man called Nunzio spoke. His English was word perfect, with the slightest trace of a cockney accent.

'I work best outdoors. I lived for a few years in a cottage down by the River Anapo, but my wife, Graziella, she found it lonely. And it was best for Stellina to live up here. Why have you come to see me? What do you want?'

'Your accent is so interesting. Did you learn English in London?' Paige asked, not answering his question right away.

There was a pause and a look passed between father and daughter. When he spoke again, brusqueness had returned to his voice.

'I lived in London a long time ago and I've never forgotten my English,' he replied. 'You said you had some questions.'

Suddenly Paige didn't know where to start. Her insides had turned to jelly and she asked if she could use the bathroom.

'Sure,' the girl said. 'Follow me.'

The bathroom was spartan but on the wall above the old-fashioned bath tub, two large canvases of women painted in simple brush strokes were prominently displayed. In one, the woman was naked, her blonde hair spread behind her on a pillow, one arm raised above her head. Her eyes were closed and she had a lazy smile on her lips. It was sensual and Paige felt almost embarrassed to be sharing its intimacy. The other was maybe of the same woman, dressed, leaning against a wall, one long booted leg crossed over the other, her long hair curtaining her face. In the background a horse leant its head over a fence and fields stretched to the horizon. The mood was totally different from the paintings of the gorge and the ancient dwellings in the rock faces in the kitchen. It could almost have been an English country scene.

When Paige emerged, the girl was still waiting. As they returned to the kitchen, Paige asked, 'Is that your mother? In those paintings?'

'No. Mamma was not blonde. Papà painted these after she died. I don't know who the woman is. Maybe she is only, how you say, *una fantasia...* He paints many strange things. It helps him. He was ill for a time. To paint is a *terapia* for him.'

'He's very talented.'

'Do you feel better? You're very pale.'

Paige nodded, although her stomach was still churning. She sat down again at the table, Dom looking anxiously at her, and she decided it was now or never. One of her mother's expressions came to mind: *In for a penny, in for a pound.*

'Right!' she started. 'What I have to tell you is going to sound very strange. I'm trying to solve a mystery.'

Father and daughter looked at each other again, their expressions puzzled. Nunzio fumbled to light a cigarette and before her nerve completely failed, Paige outlined a brief explanation and finished by producing the box with her mother's letter and removed the pendant from around her neck. 'So, I'm looking for anybody who can help me solve what my mother wanted to tell me.'

Nunzio lifted the pendant and held it close to his eyes and then took the letter, his hands trembling as he drew in a sharp breath. Then he shuddered and clutched at his chest, his face draining of blood.

Paige rose quickly to touch him on the arm, looking anxiously at Dom for help. 'Nunzio. Are you all right? Put your head down, right down,' she said, convinced he was about to faint.

He brushed off her help, muttering something she couldn't catch, clutching at the table, the pendant and letter still in his hands. 'I need... air. I...' he said, wrenching open the door to leave Paige staring after him, wide-eyed, anxious.

'Papà?' His daughter made to run after him but he told her to stay with the guests. She looked at Dom and Paige. 'What is going on? Who are you?'

Dom spoke rapidly to her and she listened, her hand over her mouth, shaking her head, as she stared intently at Paige.

'I think you must talk to him,' she said. 'I will wait here with your friend. But, be gentle with him, please.'

CHAPTER 49

Paige found him slumped on a stone bench at the far end of the neat lines of olive trees, almost hidden by their thick, gnarly trunks, a curtain of green-white leaves shading him. He looked up as she approached, his face still as pale as the sun-bleached walls surrounding his land.

'Where did you get those things?' he asked, his voice thin, old.

'I told you, it was my mother who left them to me,' she replied.

'Was she called Joy?'

Paige hesitated for a moment, hardly daring to believe what was happening. 'I knew her as Aunty Flo. But she changed her name, apparently. I've only started to piece things together recently. She didn't tell me anything about her past.'

'How is she?'

Paige paused, the conversation tearing at her heart. It was absurd. He couldn't be... *he* couldn't be her father, could he? This kind of thing only happened in films: when soppy music started playing and you had a painful lump in your throat and you had to bite back tears, hoping nobody in the cinema would notice you were blubbing your eyes out. Paige wasn't crying, but her heart was going berserk.

He repeated his question. 'How is she? How is Joy?'

It felt instinctive to take hold of his hand then and gently break the news of her death. She explained how the woman he'd known as Joy had left the letter, pendant and the start of an explanation about what had happened in her previous life, but how she had been knocked down by a lorry before she was able to. All the time Paige spoke gently, as someone talks to a child, and he stroked the back of her hand with a work-rough thumb.

The breeze rustled the olive leaves when she stopped and there was silence between them for a few moments before he began to speak.

'For months, even years, I hoped she would suddenly turn up but it was foolish of me to believe she would ever receive my letters.' He lifted the pendant, the sun's rays dancing from the tarnished metal as he spoke. 'This belonged to my mother. I gave it to Joy. It was the only precious item I could give her at the time to show how I felt.' He turned to Paige. 'I truly cared for her, you know. I sent her several letters and cards, but I never heard anything back. So, after a while, I gave up – believing she had found somebody else.' He paused. 'I cared for Stellina's mother too. But in a different way. She'd lost her husband, had a tiny baby. They both needed looking after. And she wanted to look after me.'

'That baby is the girl in the house?'

He nodded. 'Stellina. My step-daughter.'

She wondered if he had already worked out what she was about to tell him. She was still holding his hand, keeping the link between them. 'Joy was pregnant, Nunzio.' Her voice trembled as she spoke and tears ran down her face as he turned to her, his expression bewildered.

'You?'

He pulled his hand away to cup her face and wipe her tears

with his rough thumbs, gazing at her, questions in his eyes. 'You?' he said again, shaking his head over and over in wonder. 'I had no idea.'

His eyes were brown like her own, she noticed. With the same flecks of hazel. Her mother's eyes had been blue, her hair blonde. 'There are so many gaps to fill in, Nunzio. Where should we begin?'

He squared his shoulders. 'My real name is Savio. Only Stellina's mother knew that. And, yes, I have a lot of explaining to do.'

She could hear Dom and Stellina calling, asking where they were and if everything was all right. Savio, not Savvy, as Peggy Ambrose had remembered, pulled at her arm.

'Come back tomorrow, Paige. On your own. And I'll tell you more. Today has been such a big shock. I need to gather my thoughts.' Again, he cupped her face in his hands. 'My daughter, I can't believe it.'

Paige spent the whole of the following day in the company of her father. They walked down towards the river and he filled her in with his story, relating details of how he and Joy, as he continued to call her, had met and trained during the war.

Aunty Flo had never given a hint of any of this. For Paige it was like listening to a stranger's story. She remembered how Charlie had suggested being a single mother back in the 1940s would have been considered shocking. Nevertheless, Paige would have preferred to have known the truth from the mouth of the woman she had loved but never been able to call Mother. But who was she to criticise? They had indeed been different times back then. How was she to know how she would have reacted in her mother's shoes?

When they reached the House of the Almond Tree, they sat on a stone bench outside and Savio described how he had lived there alone at first and then with Stellina and Graziella, struggling to be self-sufficient.

'It was hard – a huge learning curve. I was a hairdresser in my youth, would you believe?' he said with a self-deprecating smile, holding up one of his long grey strands of hair. 'We have so much to catch up on, Paige. And I want to learn how your mother managed in all those years since we parted. But, first of all, there's something that's been weighing on my conscience for years. One more link in the chain of events from the past.' He went inside the hut and returned with an old tin, prising open the lid before taking out a metal chain holding a small metal disc.

'Now is the time to come clean, seeing as we've found each other and you've got me to open up,' he said. 'I'm not proud of what I'm going to tell you, but... you might understand how bitter I was all those years ago when I fill you in on how we Italians in Britain were treated by Churchill. I've thought a lot about what I did and... oh hell!' He held out the dog tag for Paige to take.

'What's this?'

'My escape route. I removed it from a dead soldier and replaced it with my own ID tag. That way I feigned my own death.'

She tried to make out the name, puzzled at this new twist in her parents' complicated past. 'So, if you were reported dead, my mother would have accepted you *were* dead, surely? No wonder she didn't come to find you or even bother to work out your message. I wondered about that. She was so clever at crosswords and puzzles in general.'

His expression was grim. 'I know. I shot myself in my own foot, I suppose you'd say. I'd hoped she would receive my letter and understand the hidden message but... the timing was obviously all wrong. My idea wasn't well thought out – one of my many failings. I'm impulsive, Paige. Once she believed I was dead, what would have been the point of coming out here to me? I hadn't thought through everything.'

'Exactly. Plus, with a war going on how could she travel over to you? What a mess!'

She couldn't bring herself to address Savio as Dad. Not yet, anyhow. And maybe she never would. She didn't know him well enough. Maybe her mother hadn't known him that well either. Paige had read about wartime romances: the way relationships flared and fizzled when people were desperate to find comfort.

'I've thought about that dead soldier's family so often,' Savio said, taking the tag from Paige. 'On nights when I couldn't sleep. It's time to give them resolution.'

'If you want to do the right thing, Dom could help you. He works for an organisation that deals with these matters. Do you want me to ask him?'

He looked at her. 'I feel ashamed. Much of my life has been a lie. And, effectively, I was a deserter. I'll be treated as a coward.'

'Don't be hard on yourself. The way you stepped in and brought up Stellina, that's no lie. She worships you. You've done well.'

He smiled. 'You're kind. Like your mother.'

'I miss her so much. She gave me a fabulous childhood. She did the best she could and I'm sure the same applies to you, Savio.'

On the following Sunday afternoon, her stay drawing to a close, Dom drove her to the Commonwealth War Graves Cemetery on the outskirts of Syracuse. The road outside was noisy with traffic but once she stepped inside, a feeling of deep peace enveloped her as she gazed on the neat lines of white stones. The grass was cut trim like an English lawn, each grave adorned with beautiful plants: lilies, amaryllis, succulents, roses or plumbago. Trees all around the periphery offered seclusion. Dom pointed out the information board and she read there were over one thousand dead lying at rest here, including six entirely unidentified. Paige thought how easy it had been for her father to get away with his disappearance.

'The majority of these graves belong to men of the airborne force that attempted landings west of Syracuse on the night of 9th to 10th July 1943,' Dom read aloud from a metal sign by the gate.

'That's what Savio told me,' Paige said. 'He talked to me a lot about that night. How the winds were gale force and many of the gliders didn't hit their mark. He said how awful it was that they couldn't stop to help the men in the sea, but they were bent on their own mission of landing on the coast by craft.'

'The fighting went on in Sicily until mid-August but they couldn't stop the Germans from moving on to the mainland,' Dom said, gazing over the cemetery, hands by his side.

'I can't imagine how awful it must have been,' Paige said. 'And Savio wasn't committed to the cause in the first place. He used the invasion to get back to his parents' homeland. I think I can forgive what he did. What about you?'

Dom shrugged. 'Not for me to judge but I think he's courageous in wanting to set the record straight. Let's go and find the grave,' he said, consulting the cemetery register. 'By my reckoning, it's up at the back near the trees.'

Paige stopped occasionally to read the writing chiselled into the pristine stones, immensely moved in this place of respect where the dead were honoured with such dignity. She had to wipe tears away upon reading some of the lines: *Known unto God, A British soldier of the 1939-1945 War, 12th July 1943; Through the mud and the blood, the green fields beyond, until we meet.*

One particularly poignant stone made her think of Savio

and her mother, waiting in vain for one another: *Blithe spirit waiting. Over the bridge, darling*. She let out a strangled sob and Dom came over to put his arm around her shoulder.

'I know. The very personal messages really get to me too,' he said.

'There's only so much Savio can tell me about my mother's past. The war led them to lose each other, despite their being alive. It's too sad. They lost each other before they even began, really.'

She felt the lightest of kisses drop on the top of her head and, comforted, she walked on, Dom staying by her side.

The stone was third along the back row, next to a grave marked, *Known unto God*. She read the words aloud. 'Savio Rizzo, 10th July 1943. Age 29 Special Raiding Squadron.' There were no poignant messages as on other graves and Paige stood for a few moments staring at the lie. 'What will happen, Dom?'

'The soldier buried here won't be exhumed. We don't like to disturb the dead. But the headstone will be changed. We have enough evidence from Savio to prove that this is not his name on the stone. But everything will be done with the utmost dignity and the soldier's family will be informed.'

'Will Savio have to be involved?'

'The family might ask about the circumstances. But we can find a way of keeping him out of it as much as possible. Don't worry.'

'I think he's already suffered enough.'

A light rain began to fall as they walked back to Dom's Fiat Topolino and she shivered.

'If it stops raining, I'd like to show you where your father most likely landed on Isola.'

'Thank you, Dom. At the moment, I feel like my parents are both strangers. Maybe if I can understand a little more about what happened, it might help.'

She was quiet throughout the drive. A sea mist had rolled in over the fields, scrubby grass and drystone walls lined the road, the drabness broken by an occasional patch of wild pink flowers. The sullen sky matched her wistful mood. Dom turned off the road down a narrow track and after about a kilometre, where the road stopped at an abandoned house, he parked. The wind had blown up and they had to hold the doors firm to stop them slamming.

Paige followed Dom along a sandy path leading towards the cliff's edge. The wind was furious now, snatching their words, whipping Paige's hair against her cheeks, the sea a churned-up foam of white breakers.

'This is one of the first places the allies attacked on the night of July 9th to 10th 1943,' Dom said, forced to raise his voice against the wind. 'Your father would have been amongst the men. My own father too. There were gale-force winds worse than this that night. Imagine trying to land and scale this coastline.' He pointed to a group of abandoned buildings across the surf on a spur of land. 'Those were the positions of a World War Two battery... the big guns of Emanuele Russo,' he said, when Paige looked puzzled. 'We're not supposed to, but I can show you inside the ruins, if you like. There's untouched graffiti on the walls and you really get a feeling for the battle that waged there.'

Paige clambered over the sharp tufa rock, thankful she was wearing sturdy boots and jeans. They descended steps into the bunker and Dom pointed out pits in the concrete where grenades had exploded. He flicked on a torch and read out some of the writing on the walls, untouched for thirty years, simultaneously translating into English: 'The fate of your comrades at sea and on the ground is entrusted to your wise silence. Be quiet! Enemy ears can be anywhere.'

Outside in the wind, he pointed to mounds where pieces of

metalwork protruded and he told her where big guns had once been positioned.

'It must have been difficult for Savio,' Paige said. 'Although he was brought up in London, his parents were Sicilian. How torn must he have been. War is...'

'... Complicated and fascinating.'

'Hmm! I was going to say, pointless and cruel,' Paige said.

'Not if it rids the world of evil dictators.'

'Do the solutions outweigh the tragedy war brings in its wake? The effects on the many ordinary people, innocent children?'

'It's never easy,' Dom said. 'But in our line of work, we try to honour those victims and in so doing, attempt to bring comfort to those left behind.'

Paige was quiet, staring at the ruins of battle, thinking that her mother had done the best she could. Her father, too, although some might disagree. She leant her back against Dom, gazing out over the waves, and he put his arms around her, pulling her against his chest. For a while they stood, buffeted by the sea wind.

'Hey, Paige. Don't go gloomy on me. It's Sunday. How about we do the traditional thing and go and find our pizzeria again this evening? Are you hungry?'

Paige dragged herself away from her thoughts and turned to smile up at Dom, his hair tousled from the wind. He looked, if anything, even more handsome in this dishevelled state.

'I'd love that, Dom. It's on me this time. Let's start as we mean to go on.'

'I like that you say, "go on".' He pulled her into a long kiss.

For the first time since Paige had lost her mother, happiness crept into where loss and sadness had coiled itself around her heart. She stayed in Dom's arms, enjoying the feeling of being loved but also happy she was back to being herself again after far too long. She no longer felt lost.

A LETTER FROM ANGELA

Dear reader,

A huge thank you (*mille grazie* as the Italians say) for choosing to read *The Sicilian Secret*. If you enjoyed it, and want to keep up to date with all my latest releases, simply sign up at the following link. Your email address will never be shared and you can unsubscribe at any time.

www.bookouture.com/angela-petch

One of the joys of writing these books is when I'm able to reveal lesser-known aspects of Italy's past through my characters' stories. I spent formative years of my childhood living in this fascinating country and now that I have the opportunity to spend six months every year there, I have time and opportunity to winkle out more stories. I hope my writing makes you want to visit and discover Italy for yourself. Did you know anything about the way Italian immigrants were treated in Britain during World War Two? Have you visited Sicily? What did you feel about Joy's story? Did you approve of Savio's actions? And was it fair on Paige to keep secrets from her?

If you enjoyed *The Sicilian Secret*, it would be wonderful if you could write a review. It only need be a couple of lines but I'd love to hear what you think, and it makes such a difference helping new readers to discover one of my books for the first time.

I enjoy hearing from my readers – you can get in touch through social media, or my website.

Thanks,

Angela Petch

www.angelapetchsblogsite.wordpress.com

 facebook.com/AngelaJaneClarePetch

 x.com/Angela_Petch

 instagram.com/angela_maurice

ACKNOWLEDGEMENTS

'Write what you know', Mark Twain said. When I write my books I do invest a lot of my own experiences and emotions in the story.

Sicily features strongly in *The Sicilian Secret*. In the 70s I worked there and fell in love not only with the island but with a young man who became my husband. I lived outside Syracuse along the coast in a holiday village in Fontane Bianche. *Little did I know* at that time that this part of the coastline was where the first Allied invasion by an elite group of Special Raiding Squadron SAS commandos had landed in 1943. They were an important part of Operation Husky, planned to pierce the 'soft underbelly of Europe' in the early hours of July 10th. Along this very spot I used to swim, waterski and sunbathe in my early twenties, ignorant of its historical importance. Fifty years later I revisited with a different outlook in order to write my new story. The background to Savio's story is true but I have teased a few facts around the events. *The Sicilian Secret* is not a history book but I am always keen to show the ripple effects of war on ordinary people and have researched extensively.

I'm always worried when the time comes to make sure to acknowledge everyone who helps me give birth to my stories. James Holland's wonderfully detailed *Sicily' 43* was indispensable for reference, but special thanks must go to Giovanni Abela and our serendipitous meeting. In May 2023 my husband and I revisited Sicily specifically to research Operation Husky. A security guard turned us and Giovanni away from the landing sites. I speak fluent Italian and I was moaning to Giovanni, who turned out to be a keen, amateur historian of that very period. He showed me books he had in his car boot and then, when the guard had disappeared, sneaked us down a footpath to explore the ruined barracks and battery positions. To be able to see the inscriptions on the walls, still intact and relatively unspoiled after eighty years, to stand on those cliffs battered by the wind and waves and imagine what happened on that night, was gold dust. He took us to other battle sites too – including the Lamba Doria battery near where his grandfather had been positioned, which is what had given rise to his interest in this period. A makeshift shrine of tatty plastic flowers showed that somebody still remembered the fallen and fresh ideas were born in my mind. I could picture Savio's escape into another identity so vividly. Giovanni has become a friend and he introduced me to a Facebook group dealing solely with these battles, but seen from the Italian point of view. Anything that can help an author step into a scene also helps the reader. *Grazie*, Giovanni.

Still in Sicily, the necropolis of Pantalica was a favourite haunt for me and my husband back in the 1970s and I wanted to capture the unique atmosphere of this haunting place as it was then. We used to take a two-man tent and camp by the river with our dogs at weekends. We saw nobody, except on one occasion when a shepherd passed through with his sheep. It made perfect sense to me that Savio would hide away in such an isolated location. Now, it is a UNESCO site, which is good because the area is properly protected. In those early days we clambered in and out of the caves, exploring wherever we wanted. I wanted Savio to live in a rock dwelling built into the caves and we came across a ruined stone house that fitted the bill. I christened it the Almond House – we writers are allowed to embroider the truth. If you get the chance to visit Sicily, do add amazing Pantalica to your itinerary.

I know about the Commonwealth War Graves cemeteries

because my father was a Regional Director of the Commission in Rome and I lived in the Eternal City for six formative years. He took his children to visit cemeteries around Italy and France and I am always moved to tears when I gaze over the masses of white gravestones, thinking of the huge sacrifices made by so many for our freedom. I would like to thank Jennifer Kossak and Patricia Keppie of the CWGC for their help in answering my queries. If only I had asked my father more details when he was alive... but they stepped in for me. It only features in a tiny section of *The Sicilian Secret* but the Commonwealth War Graves Commission is hugely important for the dignity the organisation provides for our war dead in such manicured, peaceful locations. #lestweforget

I stumbled across a radio programme while studying the BBC Archives, narrated by actor Tom Conti. He explored the shocking story of Italian internment in Britain during the Second World War from a personal perspective. This treatment of 'alien enemies' plays an important part of Savio's story, so my thanks go to Tom Conti and the BBC for revealing this dark period of our history, when Churchill ordered the authorities to 'collar the lot'. Conti's father ended up on the Isle of Man for a while and I have borrowed some of these details and also referred to Connery Chappell's *Island of Barbed Wire* and *The Island of Extraordinary Captives* by Simon Parkin. I also referred to the Isle of Man Museum archives for the background to this part of *The Sicilian Secret*. Any mistakes are my own.

I devoured *The Bletchley Girls* by Tessa Dunlop, awestruck at the amazing contribution of a whole army of staff who were sworn to secrecy in their incredible codebreaking work. The female staff alone amounted to 7,500. Churchill described these people as the 'geese who laid the golden egg and never cackled'. Many were still reluctant to talk about their roles long past 1974 when the public was given more access to the Park's secrets. Sadly, most of the clever Bletchley crew are lost to us now. Secrecy and discretion were drummed into them all and many historians credit Bletchley's codebreaking to shortening the war by at least two years. I visited BP, X or the Park, as it was variously called, in September 2023 and consulted with Doctor Thomas Cheetham, research officer at Bletchley, who helped with specific queries about Italian intelligence. I may have tweaked a few facts to shoehorn Joy into this environment and I hope I haven't strayed too far.

I lived in Suffolk for more than twenty-seven years, near the Stour and Orwell Estuaries, so I'm pleased this special part of the county has crept into Joy and Paige's stories. I wonder if anybody might recognise where my fictitious Holwood might be?

Thank you to my lovely writing friends. I hope you know who you all are. A fairly new group, The Tuscan Scribes, helped keep me sane over a difficult summer. Rosanna Ley and the participants of her brilliant course at Finca El Cerrillo in Andalucia helped me at the 'What If?' stage. My Facebook Motivation group, run by the inspirational Carla Kovach, the Ladies who Launch, The Nook Writers, Apricot Plots and all my other Twitter, Facebook and Instagram friends – thanks so much to all. Who says social media is a waste of time? The writing community is supportive and I hope I haven't left any of you out.

Ellen Gleeson from the fabulous Bookouture team... without you, where would I be on my writing journey? Ellen is the editor who keeps me focused (or tries to!) and has helped spread my words far wider than I ever could. Thank you for your patience and encouragement.

Last but not least, special thanks to you, the reader. I still have to pinch myself that you want to read my books and I hope to uncover more stories to keep you entertained.

PUBLISHING TEAM

Turning a manuscript into a book requires the efforts of many people. The publishing team at Bookouture would like to acknowledge everyone who contributed to this publication.

Audio
Alba Proko
Sinead O'Connor
Melissa Tran

Commercial
Lauren Morrissette
Hannah Richmond
Imogen Allport

Cover design
Nikki Dupin

Data and analysis
Mark Alder
Mohamed Bussuri

Editorial
Ellen Gleeson
Nadia Michael